Two

Love

Two Risky to Love

Lisa Jane Lordan

Two Risky to Love published in Great Britain in 2020 by:
ENIGMA PRESS
An imprint of PARTNERSHIP PUBLISHING

Written by Lisa Jane Lordan
Copyright © Lisa Jane Lordan

A CIP catalogue record for this book is available from the British Library.

ISBN 978-1-9162251-0-7

Book Cover Design by: Partnership Publishing
Book Cover Images ©Shutterstock 51784129

Book typeset by:
PARTNERSHIP PUBLISHING
Barton upon Humber
North Lincolnshire
United Kingdom
DN18 5RG
www.partnershippublishing.com

Printed in England
Partnership Publishing is committed to a sustainable future for our business, our readers and our planet.

This book is made from paper certified by the Forestry Stewardship Council (FSC), an organisation dedicated to promoting responsible management of forest resources.

Book One

IN THE

'Two Series'

One

"Kara are you up yet?" I can hear my flatmate Jodie calling me from down the hallway of our two-bedroom modern ground floor flat.

"Yes I'm just getting up," I shout stretching in my double bed whilst turning off the alarm clock to see it's 6.00am. Pulling the red and white polka dot duvet off my legs I reluctantly drag myself out of bed and peek through a gap in the red curtains to look outside. I can see blue skies on this July Monday morning and feeling the warmth of the sun shining on my face it tells me it's going to be a lovely day.

I take a quick shower and get dressed in a short blue denim skirt and a white t-shirt with a pair of pink lips imprinted on the front and go to find Jodie in the kitchen.

"Morning Jode," I smile seeing her sat at the table drinking a cup of tea whilst applying her make-up.

"Morning sleepyhead, the kettle just needs re-boiling and I've put a teabag in your favourite love heart mug for you."

"Thanks Jode, have you had your breakfast yet?" I ask flicking the kettle on yawning and pouring myself a cup of tea.

"Yeah I have, I've put some bread in the toaster for you."

"Thanks babe." I pop the bread down in the toaster and then join Jodie at the table with my tea.

Jodie is not only my flatmate but she's also my best friend. She's an early riser because she loves to take her time to get ready in a morning. Me on the other hand, I love sleep too much and I try and leave it as late as possible before getting out of bed. I guess if it isn't for Jodie calling me and my alarm clock, I would most definitely be late for work.

Before I moved in with Jodie I lived with my mum and dad, Graham and Jules Davis, they are devoted parents and I have a great relationship with them. Being an only-child, I never felt like I missed out on having siblings because the close friendship I have with Jodie certainly fills that void. I live in a town an hour outside of London and I have lived here all my life. I've known Jodie Black since secondary school, we always used to walk to school together because Jodie lived the next street down with her mum and dad,

Alan and Carol Black, and older brother Michael otherwise known as 'Mikey'.

After leaving school and getting jobs Jodie and I were given the opportunity to get a flat together. Jodie's Uncle Rick is a Bar Manager and worked at a popular club in town. He has since moved to Spain and was in need for somebody to rent the flat, so it worked perfectly for Jodie and I. Plus the added benefit with renting off family is great. As far as landlords go, he is easy going, he isn't around to do regular inspections and the rent is cheap so it was an ideal solution for everyone.

Jodie and I are complete opposites when it comes to looks and personality. I'm 5 foot 10 inches tall with an hourglass figure, long blonde hair, blue eyes like the purest ocean and an impressive chest. Jodie is smaller in height at 5 foot 5 inches, slim and has brown hair with dark brown eyes to match. Jodie is the more sensible type, she likes to be organised and plan everything, so in looks and personality we couldn't be any more different.

But as friends we just work and match perfectly.

Jodie is 25 and works at the local primary school as a teacher, she loves her job and looks forward to going into work every day.

Me on the other hand, I never knew what I wanted to do when I left school. At the age of 24 I am still working at 'Walt's Coffee Shop' where I initially started working part-time and haven't left since.

"So, what have you got on today then babe?" Jodie asks.

"You know, the usual, making cups of coffee and tea for anyone who wants them, oh and a sandwich or cake if they want that too, the exciting life of a coffee shop assistant." I sigh.

"Well like I keep telling you why don't you stop the moaning and do something about it instead of drifting along in a job you don't want to do as a career, you can do anything Kara but it means putting the work in."

"I know you're right, I do need to do something," taking a slurp of my tea as my toast pops up.

"You know only you can make exciting things happen in your life Kara, you need to start thinking about what you want to do instead of complaining all the time about your job. Anyway, enough of the lecture, you haven't forgotten that Matt will be coming around later have you so can you make yourself scarce for a bit?"

I glance over to her while I'm buttering my toast and she's grinning at me with a pleading look on her face. I shake my head and smile as I re-join her at the table.

Jodie has been seeing Matt for almost a year now and they are still in that 'honeymoon stage' of a relationship where they can't keep their hands off each other. Matt is 28 and 6ft tall with blonde hair; he is a builder and loves Jodie to bits. They met the old-fashioned way, a 'right place right time' moment and they are besotted with each other which is all I have ever wanted when it comes to relationships. I've not had many boyfriends since I started dating at the age of 18 and have only had one serious relationship which lasted a year and then after that some which have only lasted a few months.

I lost faith in men when my most serious boyfriend, Rob, did the dirty on me with a friend.

"No, I haven't forgotten Matt's coming around, don't worry I'll leave you two lovebirds to have some alone time together and I will come home about 10.00pm, will that be enough time to do whatever?" I grin biting into a piece of toast.

"Yes, and I'm only thinking of you as you don't want to walk in on us again do you?" Jodie laughs as I pull a face at her remembering something I would prefer not to.

"No definitely not especially after the last time… I still have nightmares about that… I'll go to the cinema or something it's no problem."

"Great, thanks Kar," Jodie giggles, "yes probably best if we don't talk about that, I thought I might cook him a nice meal and then watch a film, anyway I'm going to get off to work now babes so I'll see you later about 10pm."

"Yeah have a good day and enjoy your alone time with Matt," I call.

Jodie picks up her black tote bag and car keys hanging by the fridge and heads out the door.

Hearing the front door shut and having finished my breakfast I look at my watch thinking 'shit I need to finish getting ready for work because I still have to put my make up on'.

Sitting and staring for a few moments out the kitchen window at the trees as they gently sway in the breeze, I think about what Jodie said and she's right I do need to sort my life out and sooner rather than later.

Two

"Morning Kara," my boss Sally shouts as I unlock the door of Walt's Coffee Shop using my Yale key, giving it the classic nudge with my foot as I enter the building.

The coffee shop is a 15-minute walk from my flat and it has been in the town a long time, almost 20 years and is owned by Walter Shaw and his Wife Nancy. Each table has a menu on detailing the sandwiches which can be made to order with a choice of filling, a selection of home-made cakes and the different types of coffee served. The floor is covered with beige quarry tiles, it has a long counter at the back of the shop with a glass cabinet next to the till displaying a selection of cakes.

Sally Jeffreys is the Manager and has been working in the coffee shop for the last six years, the same amount of time as me. Sally is eight years older than me at aged 32 and is very mature and old for her years.

She is slim with brown wavy shoulder length hair and hazel eyes. She has a heart of gold and a really kind face.

Sally is not only my boss but she's also a good friend and a good listener if I ever have a problem.

I do talk to Jodie about stuff but having a good natter with Sally at work about life's ups and downs always passes the time.

Sally is married to Tim Jeffreys, they don't have any children yet because they have been enjoying their time as man and wife, but I think it could be on the cards soon because every time there is a baby in the coffee shop Sally goes all broody and starts cooing over them.

We both work Monday to Friday and Walter and Nancy always cover the Saturdays so they can keep involved in the running of the place. It works well as this means Sally and I always have weekends off.

"What a lovely sunny day, are you ready for a fun and exciting day at work?" Sally says in a chirpy voice.

"Morning Sal, yes I can hardly wait to see what today brings," I smile walking past her to put my bag in the back office and grabbing my navy apron emblazoning Walt's Coffee Shop logo off the peg.

I put it on and wander over to where Sally is stood at the counter. She is carefully placing the mouth-watering cakes in the glass cabinet that have been delivered earlier by Joe the local baker.

"How are you then Sal? Did you have a good weekend?" I ask turning on the coffee machine to heat up and leaning on the counter.

"Yes, I did thanks, didn't really do much apart from washing and cleaning but it was nice, how about you?"

"Yeah the same, washing and cleaning."

"I'm looking forward to this weekend though because Tim is taking me out Friday night for our wedding anniversary; I can't believe we've been married two years already."

Another loved up friend.

I smile. "Oh yeah that's gone quick; I remember your wedding like it was yesterday. Where are you going anywhere nice?"

"We're going to that new place on Bridge Street I've heard they do great steak, gammon, sausages … I do love a good sausage you know." Sally giggles.

"Don't we all," I wink at her.

Sally laughs, "Anyway how's your love life, how did your date go with what's-his-name from the Newsagents the other night?"

"Oh, you mean Greg? It was pretty awful actually he took me to the cinema and not that I mind paying for myself but when he went to pay, he paid for himself and then walked off to the sweet section. After I had paid, I walked over to him and while he was picking some sweets he mumbled to me that the sweets from the Newsagents are much cheaper and that their selection was better than the cinema. To top it off, the film was as boring as he is, so you could say I won't be seeing him again in a hurry, yes my love life is pretty great." I snigger sarcastically. "Jodie on the other hand, she's still all loved up with Matt and I have to make myself scarce later because he's going to see her at ours and I imagine they will be entertaining each other and I don't want a repeat of last time."

"Oh yeah, I bet they were embarrassed when you walked in on them like that and you for that matter."

"You could say that it definitely put me off chocolate for a while and you know how much I love chocolate."

"Yeah!" Sally laughs.

I continue to prepare things for the day at the back of the counter. Sally looks at the clock above the door and seeing it's almost 9.00am it's time to open up.

Just as she has turned the sign to 'Open', unlocked the door and is heading back over to the counter the front door chimes and I see a gentleman walk in out the corner of my eye.

Sally greets him. "Good morning sir, it's a lovely day today."

The sun is shining through the large glass windows lighting up the shop.

"Good morning, yes it's lovely and warm isn't it?" the man replies walking over to the counter where Sally is stood.

I take a quick look at him.

He is obviously a businessman because he is dressed in a designer dark grey suit, white shirt and dark grey tie with expensive looking shoes, he smells divine as the scent of his aftershave fills the shop. He is 6ft tall, slightly tanned, looks to be in his late twenties and has short, dark wavy brown hair, which is short at the sides, slightly long on top and swept back. He has piercing dark brown eyes which are like a rich dark chocolate, morning stubble and a sexy smile showing white teeth that would make any girl go weak at the knees. He looks very masculine in his tailored suit and there is obvious muscle underneath the expensive material. 'What on earth is he doing in Walt's Coffee Shop surely there are more upmarket places he would rather go to get a cup of coffee?'

"What can I get you?" Sally asks giving him one of her friendly smiles.

"I actually just came in for some directions as I'm a bit lost, I'm looking for a property on Danes Avenue and my Satnav doesn't seem to be working, it must have the Monday morning blues or something because it's not woken up yet this morning. My phone is also flat so I can't use that. As you can see, I'm not having a very good day," he laughs. "I was wondering if you can help me by giving me some directions please, do you know of Danes Avenue?"

"Not a great start for you then?" Sally chuckles, "yes I can help you with that I know Danes Avenue."

"Oh great, thank you I really appreciate it."

The man notices me looking at him over my shoulder. I turn away with my back to him but curiosity gets the better of me, so I take a quick look again and notice that he's looking me up and down.

He obviously likes what he sees by the look on his face, our eyes lock I blush and look away.

"Danes Avenue is lovely it's on the outskirts of town almost into the countryside, there are some big houses around there it's not far though it would probably be easier if I draw you a little map rather than trying to explain." Sally says grabbing a piece of paper and a pen from under the counter. "Is that all I can help you with or would you a like a cup of coffee while you wait for me to draw the map?"

"Yes please, I will have a cappuccino with no sugar thanks."

"Would you like to drink it here or would you like it as a take-out?"

"Take-out would be great thanks."

"Certainly sir."

Hearing the conversation and the man's alluring sexy voice I turn around to face them stood at the counter. Now I'm able to take a proper look at him I'm given the most striking view of a man so gorgeous I feel like I've died and gone to heaven, I can feel my jaw dropping as I look at him in awe.

"Good morning," he says giving me a knockout smile.

'It's certainly a good morning now'.

All I can do is stand and gawp at the beautiful man stood before me, I'm in a trance and as much as I want to get my mouth moving to say good morning back, two simple words is all that is needed I can't seem to say anything I have lost my voice and the ability to speak. I can feel my cheeks becoming flushed as I continue to stare at his handsome face. The man stares back, his eyes captivating and he seems equally taken by me.

"Are you okay?" he smiles.

"Kara…Kara…" I can hear someone calling my name but all I can do is look at this gorgeous man who has taken my breath away. I hear a cough and "Kara." Sally's voice snaps me out of my trance and I suddenly feel embarrassed. The man is still looking at me as he has not taken his eyes off me for a second. "Err sorry…yes, sorry Sally yes." I look at her and see her grinning at me.

"Would you mind getting this gentleman a cappuccino no sugar to go while I draw him a map of directions please?"

Taking a deep breath and feeling stupid at the way this man is affecting me I clear my throat and smile "Sorry yes of course, good morning sir, I will get on him … um on it right away."

I turn around red-faced feeling awkward sensing the man's stare burning into my back and begin to prepare his cappuccino with no sugar to go. Sally walks over to one of the tables to sit down to draw the map explaining where Danes Avenue is. I'm hoping that the man follows her, I see that he hasn't, and he's still stood at the counter watching me. Having a quick glance over my shoulder and seeing the man mesmerized by me I turn back.

'Please be kind to me dear coffee machine, I feel flustered already without you playing up and making it worse for me'.

Thankfully, the coffee machine is playing ball today unlike the gentleman's Satnav. I try to look professional as I make one perfect cappuccino for my awaiting customer I turn around and place it on the counter in front of him. I can't help noticing his perfectly chiselled features as he smiles at me and accepts the drink. The man is simply breath-taking, and I'm so drawn to his mouth as I bite my lip imagining what it would be like to kiss those soft perfectly formed lips of his.

My eyes travel upwards to his gorgeous face and I can feel the warm flush on my cheeks becoming hotter.

"Thank you Kara that's great," he says taking a sip of the hot liquid.

'I wonder how he knows my name? Oh yes Sally said it earlier when she was calling me out of my daydream, I'm such an idiot.'

Licking his lips the man looks across the counter at me with a straight face his eyes roaming up and down my body lingering on my breasts not hiding the fact that he is looking over every inch of me.

'I wonder what he's thinking?'

I know what I'm thinking and it's making me aroused, the tingling sensation between my legs a sign of a sexual need that has been buried for some time and it's definitely starting to surface.

This man is affecting me and I have never experienced anything like it before especially not by just looking at a man.

The sexual attraction is very apparent and he seems to be undressing me with his eyes as I imagine what delights are underneath his suit too.

'Oh my god, what is wrong with me?'

I fan my face with my hands feeling hot all of a sudden and snapping out of the sexual thoughts I'm having I finally find my voice, "Its hot today isn't it? That will be £2.25 please."

"Yes you do look hot," he replies in his sexy voice smiling and it's obvious he isn't talking about the weather. Putting his hand into his suit trouser pocket for some change and not breaking our eye contact he takes out some money and places the coins into my outstretched hand. Our hands touch as I accept the coins and I feel the magnetism as our skin comes into contact, making me gasp and drop the coins all over the counter.

"Oh, I'm so sorry!" I blush. I'm so embarrassed, he must think I'm such an idiot. I try to stop the coins from rolling onto the floor. I catch a coin under my hand and the man places his hand over the top of mine and smiles, "Don't be," he says making me blush some more. The gorgeous man scoops up the rest of the coins from the counter and passes them to me.

Sally walks over interrupting us, our eyes glued to one another and feeling breathless I deposit the coins into the till then go to serve an old gentleman who is stood waiting; he's a regular and has come in for a pot of tea. Sally takes the businessman to one side and explains the map she's just drawn on the paper while I can't help glancing over to look at them as I go to make the pot of tea.

'What a great first impression he has of me and what on earth just happened I'm never normally like that around guys?'

After serving the old gentleman I busy myself wiping the counter that doesn't really need wiping while I keep an eye on the stranger who has his back to me while reading Sally's map. It's my turn to take in his fine physique and check out his cute bum and I am completely taken aback at how perfect he is. As the man thanks Sally for her help he turns around to look at me stood at the counter staring at him and in his sexy voice he says, "It was lovely to meet you Kara and thank you for the delicious cup of coffee."

"Your very love... um your very welcome sir," I smile then watch him walk out the coffee shop door into the sunshine. He turns to look at me one last time and then he's gone.

As soon as the door closes and he is no longer in sight I can't contain the squeal I have been holding in as Sally comes over to me.

"Oh my god … who on earth was that? He's not from around here, men who look like that are definitely not from this town." I shriek as Sally stands looking at me giggling.

"That my girl, is a man you would call 'drop dead gorgeous' and obviously has eyes for you."

"Don't be daft Sally; he was only being polite because I made him a nice cup of coffee."

"I've seen that look he was giving you Kara and that was not being polite, that was pure lust."

I laugh nervously.

"I don't think so, you're just feeling the love because it's your anniversary, besides he is probably a womanizer. He might even be married or has a girlfriend or something, you don't look like that if you are single. Oh well, it's certainly made this day at work a hell of a lot better anyway."

"I wonder if he has family in the area and that's why he was looking for Danes Avenue." Sally says looking lost in thought.

"Maybe … but I doubt we will see him again, I have never seen anyone so hot in all my life," I sigh.

"You never know what's around the corner Kara, love can strike when you least expect it. He could be the one you've been waiting for."

"Oh Sally you do make me laugh!" I chuckle.

As I stand daydreaming about the striking man who came through the door this morning, the door swings open and we both look up desperately to see if he has returned. But I'm disappointed when I recognise the student regulars looking for their early morning caffeine fix.

I smile and think even if I don't get to see the gorgeous guy again it was worth it just to see him the once because I will always have the image of him in my mind and what an image it is.

Three

Closing up for the day, Sally turns out the light and locks the door of Walt's Coffee Shop and we both step out into the warm early evening sun as we say our goodbyes.

I spot Tim, Sally's husband, parked across the road in their blue BMW waiting for her, you can't miss his bright ginger hair as he waves at us through the car window.

"See you tomorrow Kara, I know who you will be dreaming about tonight." Sally shouts as she crosses the road to get into Tim's car.

"I certainly will, see you tomorrow Sal."

Sally and her husband both wave as they drive past and I start walking down the street towards home feeling the warm sunshine across my face as I walk. As I pass the pub on the corner I suddenly remember that I can't go home because I promised Jodie that I would make myself scarce tonight.

Turning around and walking back towards the town centre I begin to feel hungry realising it is dinner time after all, so I decide to walk down to the local chip shop.

'That will pass a bit of time but what to do after? Go visit mum? No, she's busy tonight at one of her clubs. Go to the cinema? No, fed up of looking sad and lonely going on my own when everyone else is either with friends or partners hmm … what to do? I know I'll have some chips then find a quiet spot at the late-night internet café and look through the job ads.'

On my way to the chip shop I notice an Aston Martin DB9 black coupe pull up beside me.

I glance over at the car glumly knowing it will take a hell of a lot of coffee shop tips to be able to afford a car like that.

"Hello again."

Startled and confused because I don't know anyone who drives a car like that I suddenly recognise the familiar sexy voice from earlier today.

Bending down slightly so I can see his face I gasp when I see him for the second time because he looks even more breathtakingly handsome from what I remembered him to look like.

"Um, hi are you lost again?" I ask nervously.

"Hello, yes I am I don't suppose you could direct me to The Kingsman Hotel on King's Road could you? I checked in there this morning and I now can't seem to find my way back. I don't know this area very well and so yes you could say I am very lost," he grins.

"Oh The Kingsman? Yes I know it, is your Satnav still not working?"

"No, but it seems like it's done me a favour though."

"What do you mean?" I ask looking confused.

"Well if my Satnav was working then I wouldn't have bumped into you at the coffee shop this morning when I was asking for directions and somehow fate has brought us together again."

"I can draw you a map but I don't have a pen or any paper, have you got any I could use?" I respond shyly.

The man looks at me smiling, "I haven't no, so how about you come with me and direct me to the hotel then I can buy you dinner as a thank you, I take it you haven't eaten yet?"

'Strange not having a pen and paper being a businessman?'

"You really don't need to do that, I was just going to buy some chips." I smile.

'Really? Of all the stupid things to say.'

"I really do Kara because I'm quite lost, I don't know anyone from here apart from you, I'm hungry and I'm sure they serve excellent chips in the hotel if that's the deal breaker and well to be honest it would be nice to have some company."

"You don't know me and I don't know you, I don't even know your name, for all I know you could be a murderer trying to entice me into your car, have your wicked way with me and then dump me in a forest somewhere."

The man laughs, "I can assure you I am no murderer. As for my wicked way with you, although that sounds very appealing I would rather just start off with dinner first because I'm starving. I don't do forests because I'm a city boy and besides you do know me because we met this morning and my name is Evan Hamilton, so what's it to be?"

I stand there silent.

'Don't be stupid Kara, this man could be anyone and remember what you were taught when you were a child about getting into stranger's cars. Who would know if you went missing because you're not due home until 10pm.

But how many invitations do I get like this, a gorgeous, sexy man in an expensive car asking me to dinner?'

Evan notices me looking uneasy, "I'm sorry, are you okay?

I apologise I didn't mean to make you feel uncomfortable. Whatever you decide is fine, I'm sure I can find my way or ask someone else. It's just not that great eating on your own and you seem really nice and I would like to get to know you better, sorry if that sounds like a cheesy line it's not meant to but I really would appreciate having some company," he smiles.

Snapping out of my thoughts and making a decision I decide to take a risk, "Yes sorry I'm fine, it doesn't matter if I don't have chips. I'm on my own tonight anyway so I suppose it would be nice to have some company too. I don't have much money on me, I wasn't expecting to go for dinner in a posh hotel also I'm not really dressed for the occasion either. I said to my flatmate that I would be home by 10pm so if I'm not home by then she will worry and probably start doing a ring around or call the police or something and well ... yes I guess what I'm trying to say is I would love to have dinner with you, thank you that would be very nice."

Evan laughs, "Great, then hop in and don't worry about money, dinner is my treat as a thank you for helping me out and showing me the way to the hotel. I would like you to feel comfortable and at ease so if you are feeling underdressed to sit in the hotel's restaurant we can always order room service. I promise I will be the perfect gentleman it's your choice. I think you look lovely by the way, I love your lips."

'He loves my lips, oh my god.'

I remember that I'm wearing my white t-shirt with the pink lips on the front and that's what he is referring to.
I feel silly, my mind is getting carried away with sexual thoughts and I really need to calm down.

"Okay thanks." I smile heading around to the other side of the car to get into the passenger seat.

As I get into the car I can't help thinking any normal person who has just been asked to have dinner with a complete stranger and offering to order room service would have run a mile, but there's something about Evan apart from the fact that he is drop dead gorgeous I find him intriguing and I want to know more about him.

'Where is he from? Why is here in my hometown? Does he have a girlfriend?'

I can't wait to have a nosy around The Kingsman Hotel, I've only ever seen it from the outside when I've driven past in my mum's car and it looks quite impressive.

I feel like I'm in a scene from 'Pretty Woman' as I direct Evan to the hotel, it's one of my favourite films although

I'm certainly no prostitute; I don't even kiss on a first date never mind anything else.

I'm hoping for my own fairy tale when it comes to love and who knows this may just be the start of something.

Four

On arriving at the hotel, I feel like a movie star as the valet steps up to park Evan's car, then I look down remembering what I'm wearing bringing me back to reality.

I'm feeling out of my comfort zone and extremely nervous. I take my hair out of the ponytail and try to make myself feel and look more presentable by smoothing down my hair and applying some lip gloss from my bag before stepping out of the car and into the hotel. I think Evan can sense I'm nervous from my body language, "Hey relax you look lovely and don't worry I've stayed in plenty of hotels like this before and the chips were excellent," he says making me laugh and feel more relaxed as we get out the car and walk to the front entrance of the hotel.

On entering the impressive reception area with high ceilings and patterned tiled floor I take in my surroundings and I'm amazed at how grand the hotel looks inside.

The female receptionist immediately notices us and looks up from behind the grand oak desk and seeing Evan walking towards her she says with a flirtatious look on her face, "Good evening Mr Hamilton, have you had a good day sir?" with pouting lips.

"Yes I have thanks." Evan replies not really looking that interested as she gawps at him.

"Would you like a reservation for dinner sir?" she asks looking me up and down with a snooty look on her face.

Evan looks at me and I shake my head to say no because if the receptionist is looking at me like that at what I'm wearing then I would definitely feel uncomfortable walking into the high-profile restaurant where everyone else is dressed up. I think Evan seems more than happy to have room service from the big smile on his face.

"No we're fine thank you. I would appreciate it if you could organise for someone to look at my Satnav in my car as it doesn't appear to be working."

"Yes of course sir, I'll organise it for you right away," she smiles batting her eyelashes at him as I roll my eyes.

'Can you be any more obvious.'

"Thanks, I'm free tomorrow morning if someone can look then."

"Certainly sir, I will call the garage now and will let you know, is there anything else I can help you with?" her eyes roaming all over his body.

"No, thank you that is all." Evan places his hand on the small of my back and ushers me towards the lifts. Walking through the hotel lobby I can't contain how impressed I am of the place.

"Wow, this hotel is so posh," I grin looking around making Evan laugh as we enter the lift and he presses a button on the control panel.

"It's alright," he smiles.

The doors of the lift close and Evan stands watching me as the lift starts to ascend, I lean against the lift wall wishing my nerves would go away. Wanting to break the awkward silence I say the first thing that comes into my head. "I think the receptionist lady wanted to assist you with a lot more than your car, did you notice the way she was looking at you?"

'What did I say that for? Yes, I am in a lift with a gorgeous man who is looking at me like he wants to rip my clothes off but I need to play it cool and now he is going to think I'm jealous of that woman. I am jealous of that woman.'

"Really I didn't notice, why, are you jealous?"

"No." I protest.

I instantly blush and bite my lip, of course I'm jealous.

I look away from him hoping that the lift will soon arrive at its destination. Being in a confined space with such a gorgeous man, I'm struggling to keep my cool and my hands to myself. I think Evan can see that I'm struggling with my feelings, I'm sure he knows that I want him from my body language as I feel myself blush whenever he looks at me which is definitely a tell-tale sign of how he is affecting me and from the way he is acting I know he wants me too.

The lift pings and stops signalling we have arrived on the top floor.

"Oh my god, are we really at the Penthouse Suite?" I squeal eagerly walking out of the lift.

"Welcome to my home for a little while," he grins.

'A while, how long is a while?'

I'm excited that he's staying here for some time and not just a night. I've never been in a Penthouse Suite before and I'm eager to have a look around the place. Evan slides his hotel card into the door slot and the door clicks open and then he opens the door for me.

Walking into the suite on the highly polished wooden floor I gaze around at the plush surroundings.

"Wow." The floor to ceiling windows are dressed with long draping gold curtains that touch the floor and the fixture and fittings give it a luxurious but homely feel making my face light up as I walk around the room.

"I'll give you a tour in a minute if you like but first I could really do with a drink, what would you like Kara, a glass of wine, beer, water?" Evan walks over to the mini bar which is in a small kitchen area within the room.

"A glass of wine would be lovely thanks." I put my bag down on the floor next to a black leather couch and look around the room.

"Would you like, white, rosé or red? The hotels mini bar has a great selection," he smiles.

"I'll have white, thank you." I feel like I'm in a dream, I would never in a million years have thought a man like Evan would ask me to have dinner with him, I mean things like this don't happen to me every day and I can't help the permanent smile on my face.

Evan pours us both a glass of white wine and then walks over to me and passes me one.

"Here you go."

"Thanks." I take it from him, his hands briefly touching mine again sending sparks throughout my body making me draw breath and Evan notices.

"Did you feel that too?" he smiles wanting to state the obvious.

"What?" I reply feeling nervous, embarrassed and excited all at the same time.

"Come on Kara, I know you felt it, I felt it the first time I laid eyes on you at the coffee shop and I know you felt it too."

"I don't know what you mean?" I feel shy talking like this to a man I hardly know but he's right I did feel the connection straight away but I'm not going to tell him that, not right now anyway. I remember what Jodie always tells me 'don't make it easy for them, play hard to get and if they really like you then they will try that bit harder and let it be on your terms not theirs.'

"I think you do," he smiles. "Anyway let me give you that tour." We put our half empty glasses of wine down onto the glass coffee table next to one of the two large black leather couches which dominate the living area and then Evan shows me around.

The suite is open plan which gives it a spacious feel and the polished wooden floor guides you to different areas of the room.

In one area there is a small kitchen with a refrigerator and mini bar, in another corner of the room is a study area with an impressive oak desk. There is a dining area with a large dining table that would easily seat eight people for entertaining and all of it wraps around the central living area in the middle of the room.

Just off the study area is a corridor which leads to a luxurious bathroom with its freestanding roll top bath with marble sink and marble floor and beyond the bathroom are the bedrooms.

All the rooms are decorated exquisitely, "And these are the bedrooms down here," he says pointing down the corridor with doors either side.

"There are two bedrooms, the door on the left is a bedroom with a king-sized bed and en-suite bathroom and then this door on the right leads to the master bedroom with a dressing room and en-suite bathroom," opening the door for me to walk through and take a look.

I nervously step inside the master bedroom and my eyes are immediately drawn to the magnificent bed that dominates the room. It looks so inviting with its luxurious fabrics of white and gold complimented with scatter cushions.

Evan sees me gawping at the size of the bed, "I can assure you that it's very comfortable, care to try it out?" he asks moving closer to me. I can feel him stood behind me, his warm breath on my neck, my heart beating fast, and as much as I want him to kiss my neck and take me in his strong arms my sensible side kicks in so I turn around and smile, "I thought you were hungry?"

He looks me up and down, staring at my chest with greedy eyes then finding piercing blue eyes looking back at him he smiles, "I'm so hungry right now."

He moves closer towards me, I place my hands on his firm chest to stop him coming any closer I can feel the solid muscle beneath my hands, tingling sensations radiate throughout my body and I'm beginning to feel hungry myself but not for food but for the gorgeous specimen of a man stood in front of me. He definitely works out because you don't get a body like that without going to the gym.

I can feel myself becoming wet, I could quite easily push him onto the bed and devour him here and now but wanting to find out more about Evan Hamilton before I let myself be absorbed by the lust and sexual need that could so easily take over I look at him and smile. "Well you had better get some food ordered then because you did promise me dinner."

I walk around him with a smile on my face and make my way back to the lounge area hearing Evan taking a deep breath and letting it out slowly before he follows me, I can feel his eyes on me the whole time.

I take a seat on one of the big black leather couches, feeling the creaks and coldness of the leather on my bare legs as I sit on it. I pick up my glass of wine then down the whole lot to calm my nerves.

Evan grabs the room service menu off the table and then comes to sit down next to me. "What would you like to eat?" he asks licking his lips, his eyes travelling down to my chest as he looks at my cleavage that is peeking above the round necked t-shirt I'm wearing.

I can't help noticing that Evan seems distracted by my assets and so teasing him I arch my back and push out my chest pretending to stretch, "Anything with chips would be great thanks." I smile as he draws in a breath clearly affected by me.

I can smell his alluring aftershave and I am finding it hard to resist him. Raising his eyes to mine he gives me a cheeky smile, "How about me with your chips?"

"Hmm … I do enjoy eating my chips with a nice piece of meat," I tease licking my lips, "so I'll have a medium steak with them please."

"As you wish but I can assure you Kara that I'm better than any meat you may have had before, once you've had a piece of me you will want more and more."

He gives me one of his sexy smiles making me blush and then I watch him get up and walk over to a table at the side of the room with a hotel phone on it.

He picks up the phone and dials room service.

'Yes I imagine you will be better than any meat I've had before and I will definitely want more.'

Evan orders two medium fillet steaks, chips, onion rings and a side salad and noticing my empty glass on the coffee table he tops up my wine and then comes to sit down next to me again.

Feeling more and more flushed by the minute and it's not because of the wine I'm drinking and more to do with thoughts of skipping the main course and going straight to dessert … I decide I need to get to know him better.

Trying to control my urges and thoughts running through my mind, I turn to him and ask, "So what brings you to my hometown, business or pleasure?"

"Both I hope," he replies cheekily.

"No seriously what do you do?"

"Anything you want baby."

I roll my eyes, "Really … I'm trying to get to know you and you're not making it easy for me," I smile.

"Okay, okay, I'm sorry." He laughs, "I own and run my own hotel business."

"Oh wow."

"Yes, I buy large houses that are suitable for turning into hotels and then reap the rewards once they are up and running."

"So how many hotels do you own?"

"I have just bought my sixth hotel, have you heard of Hamilton's Hotels?"

"No, sorry I haven't, I don't get out of town much and I haven't really done any travelling either so I've never heard of them; it sounds like you are doing quite well though."

"It pays the bills and gives me a great life," he says shrugging his shoulders smiling at me.

"So I take it you don't have a girlfriend back home? Oh my god you're not married are you?"

Evan looks uneasy at this question, "No, I'm definitely not married and I don't have a girlfriend, in fact I don't do relationships full stop, I'm too busy working I don't have time for all that."

"So you just pick up random girls from wherever you are buying your next hotel, seduce them into having dinner with you and then leave for your next purchase and encounter?"

"You make me seem so shallow, but yes something like that, at least I'm honest," he smiles.

"Anyway, how come you don't have a boyfriend?"

"How do you know I don't have one?" I frown turning to look at him.

"Because if you had I would question why you are sat here and having dinner with me in my hotel room, also from the way you looked at me in the coffee shop this morning I would say it has been a while."

"What's that's supposed to mean?"

"Just by the look on your face when you turned around and saw me you looked like you were really pleased to see me in more ways than one if you know what I mean."

I blush.

"No I wasn't, besides you're the one who asked me out for dinner and just openly admitted that you are out for a bit of fun so what do you say to that?"

There is a knock at the door and Evan gives the most breath-taking smile, "I'd say dinner's arrived."

He gets up to open the door and ushers the hotel attendant into the room, the short, stocky, balding man dressed in a black suit, white shirt with a black tie places the dinner cart next to the dining table and nods at me.

"Evening madam," the man then turns to Evan and asks "would you like me to serve dinner for you sir?"

"No we're fine thank you." Evan slips him a note into the top pocket of his jacket for his kind service.

"Thank you that's very kind of you sir, enjoy your meals." He closes the door as he leaves the room.

Evan takes the hot meals off the trolley and places them on the dining table and asks me to join him.

Taking my wine glass with me I take a seat at the table on one of the red plush velvet covered chairs while Evan grabs his wine and takes a seat opposite me. Evan tops up both our glasses while I watch him, raising his glass in the air he says, "Cheers to a lovely meal, good company and getting to know each other."

I pick up my glass and we chink glasses, "Cheers and thank you for inviting me to dinner it looks lovely."

Cutting into the tender fillet steak on the plate I put a small piece into my mouth. Evan salts his chips as I taste the steak, "Hmm … oh wow this steak is so tender, it's delicious," I moan savouring the flavour and chewing it slowly in my mouth while Evan watches me. I can't help noticing his tongue as it comes out of his mouth to lick the salt off his lips making me wonder what it would feel like to have his tongue and lips on me.

Feeling turned on I pop another piece of steak into my mouth and moan with pleasure at the thought and the taste. Evan shifts in his seat, "Kara those noises you are making are extremely pleasurable but very distracting and whilst I love hearing them I would rather it was me making you make those noises and not the steak you are eating."

'Oh my god did he really just say that?'

I almost choke on the food at the comment he just casually makes, "I'm sorry I can't help it I'm enjoying it." I reply feeling embarrassed and picking up my glass of wine taking a huge gulp as I think how on earth am I going to play hard to get with comments like that when he turns me on with his forwardness.

I can feel tingles between my legs, I squeeze them together trying to block out any sexual thoughts and concentrate on eating the food.

"I can assure you that you would enjoy me a lot more, in fact I guarantee it," he says licking his lips staring at me.

'Oh god this man is so hot, all I want to do is rip his clothes off and feel him inside me.'

I clear my throat feeling the warm flush in my cheeks and the dampness in my knickers.

Deciding the best tactic to keep my sexual need under control is to change the subject, so I ask, "How long are you in town for?" popping another piece of the steak into my mouth and being careful not to moan with appreciation of the flavour.

Evan smiles and loosens his tie then takes it off obviously feeling hot himself, I watch him waiting for an answer.

"A few days, weeks maybe, I've purchased the Manor on Danes Avenue and it's a huge renovation project, that's where I've been today when I was asking for directions, I was having a look around to see what needs doing to bring it up to my hotel's superior standards. I'm meeting my site manager and architect there tomorrow afternoon but I'm here for as long as it takes."

"What made you decide to go into the hotel business then?"

"Well I used to travel around a lot as a child as my father worked all over the world, he would buy companies in distress and either fix them or sell their assets to make money from them. He was really good at his job and made lots of money. My mother didn't work so home schooled me, we followed my father everywhere staying in some of the best hotels so I found it quite exciting as a child. I was able to see the world and stay in lots of different places.

I guess it gave me my introduction to hotel life and I always said when I was little that one day I would own my own hotel. When my father unexpectedly suffered a heart attack and passed away he left me a good sum of money in his will so I bought my first hotel. After a lot of hard work my business took off and here I am buying another property to turn into another hotel."

"I'm really sorry about your father." Now I feel awkward.

"It's fine, it's a while ago now since he died and well he would have loved what I've done with the money he left me. He always had a good head for business and I think I've inherited some of that from him or I've just been lucky," he says smiling at me.

"What about your mum, where is she?"

"Oh my mother is living the high life on the millions he left her; she has a new toy boy nearly every month and spends most of her time on her yacht in Monaco."

I sense he was closer to his father than his mother from the way he speaks about them.

"Do you have any brothers or sisters?"

The smile on Evan's face drops and he looks extremely uncomfortable like I'm asking too many personal questions.

I suppose we have only just met and noticing my wine glass is empty he changes the subject.

"Would you like some more wine?"

"Yes please."

Wanting to know as much as possible about this intriguing man sat in front of me and thinking if I don't ask I don't get to know, I decide to remind him of the question, "So have you any brothers and sisters?"

"No, I'm an only child."

"Oh right I'm an only child too."

"Oh that's something we have in common then!"

"How old are you?" I ask. He must be a similar age from the look of him.

"I'm 30 I know I look young for my age don't I," he grins, "how old are you?"

"It's not polite to ask a woman's age but seeing as you told me your age I'll tell you, I'm 24 nearly 25, it's my birthday in a couple of weeks actually."

"Well thank you for telling me I feel honoured."

I blush.

"You look cute when you blush," he smiles.

"I do?"

"Yes you do, anyway that's enough about me, tell me about you."

"Oh there is not much to tell really, I've lived here all my life, my mum works at the local library and my dad is a long distance lorry driver. I've been working at the coffee shop since I left school and as you know I'm still there but I'm hoping that will change because I don't want to work there all my life. My best friend and flat mate, Jodie is entertaining her boyfriend Matt at home tonight so I said I would keep out their way until 10pm which is why I was grabbing food out tonight. That I would say is pretty much my life, it's not as exciting as yours is it?"

"Your life is just different to mine that's all, you have to enjoy life and things will happen when you least expect it. I mean who would have thought we would be sat here having dinner together this evening? My father used to say, 'be fearless in the pursuit of what sets your soul on fire,' life is what you make it Kara so just enjoy it and see where it takes you. Anyway if you have finished your meal shall we go and sit somewhere more comfortable and then you can tell me some more about yourself? I don't even know your last name."

"Yes I have thank you, it was delicious and it's Davis, Kara Davis."

I stand up and sway a little, I grab the edge of the table to get my balance before walking over to the lounge area feeling tipsy after all the wine I have consumed.

Sitting down on the couch Evan comes over to sit next to me and I suddenly panic, I don't know what time it is.

I anxiously look at my watch.

"Sorry am I boring you?" he says raising his eyebrows noticing me checking the time.

"No, not at all I was just wondering what time it is."

"Relax it's only 7.30pm you've ages yet before they send out the search party."

I smile feeling pleased that I don't have to leave yet because I'm having such a nice time getting to know Evan.

"Would you like dessert?" he asks with a lustful look on his face.

"I'm fine thanks." I blush knowing what he is thinking.

"Are you sure, can I not tempt you?"

Feeling that the wine has most definitely gone to my head and sitting looking into the gorgeous brown eyes of the man who has been making me feel horny all night I think, 'oh what the hell.'

I lunge myself at him knocking him backwards and end up laying on top of him. Evan laughs. "Well that was unexpected but I'm not complaining," he smiles pushing my hair out of my face on one side and tucking it behind my ear as he looks into my eyes.

I suddenly feel awkward and embarrassed.

"I just want to make something perfectly clear, I don't normally kiss on a first date, not that this is a date, and I certainly don't sleep with anyone until after at least three dates but seeing as you bought me a nice dinner and I've had a few glasses of wine I thought a little kiss wouldn't hurt unless you don't want to that is, I'm sorry I didn't mean to...?"

Evan stops me from rambling by placing a finger on my mouth and then moving his hand he strokes my cheek with his index finger.

"You are so beautiful," he says bringing his hand around the back of my neck. I look into his eyes and feel myself relax.

He smiles then slowly brings his soft, wet kissable lips to mine. For a moment I think the earth stands still for both of us, the sexual chemistry between us is like a lightning bolt passing through our joined mouths as we share the most passionate first kiss.

The feel of his lips on mine, his tongue grazing my bottom lip then asking to be invited into my mouth which I gladly accept. Our tongues exploring each other's mouths is mind blowing and our first slow passionate kiss is a kiss I think we will both never forget.

After a few moments we come up for air and I can feel Evan's growing erection beneath me becoming harder as it presses into my front as I lay on top of him. Gently moving me off him Evan stands up and holds out his hand, "I don't suppose you fancy trying out that bed now do you?" looking at me with his gorgeous face and pleading eyes.

I don't hesitate for a second and take hold of his hand and stand up. "Well you did say it was comfortable and it would be rude not to try it out I suppose." He grins and scoops me up in his arms, both of us feeling excited of what is to come.

'God we're really doing this; we're really doing this.'

I've never been with a man as gorgeous as Evan before and I feel like all my Christmases have come at once.

"Do you have any protection?" I whisper kissing his neck smelling the seductive scent of his aftershave.

"Yes don't worry, but the only protection you are going to need is from me right now because since the first moment I laid eyes on you I wanted you. I know I said I would be the perfect gentleman but that all went out the window when you were making noises enjoying the steak and turning me on."

"But it was good." I giggle, "and I do love a good piece of meat," teasing him.

"Well like I said earlier this is going to be better than any meat you have ever had before," he growls as he pushes the door open to the master suite with his foot carrying me into the bedroom and placing me on my feet next to the bed.

I have never wanted anyone so badly in all my life.

Staring at each other intensely, Evan unbuttons his short-sleeved white shirt and takes it off letting it fall to the floor revealing his muscly toned, tanned abs and hairy chest to me for the first time. 'Oh wow!'

My eyes are glued to his perfect body as I bite my lip at the sight of him, desperate to touch him but feeling nervous I wait for him to take the lead. Still fully clothed I can feel myself becoming more wet in anticipation of what he is going to do to me as he looks me up and down with greedy eyes.

"We had better get rid of these clothes because I want to see what beautiful delights are underneath," he says moving towards me. I nervously grab the hem of my t-shirt to take it off but Evan stops me with his strong hand. "No, let me, I want to unwrap you bit by bit so I can enjoy you a little bit at a time," looking at me affectionately.

'Where have you been all my life?'

Goose bumps are prickling all over my body in readiness for his hands on me. Before starting with the first layer of my clothing he pulls me into his arms and holds my face in his hands.

"You are so beautiful, I'm going to savour every inch of you," he whispers before giving me another mind-blowing kiss making me breathless.

Pulling away Evan takes hold of my t-shirt and slowly lifts it upwards, I raise my arms to help him so he can pull it off over my head before throwing it onto the floor. The first sight of my large breasts and protruding nipples through the white lace bra I'm wearing makes Evan draw breath, his eyes fix on my chest and he licks his lips, "Wow."

He places his hands on my breasts for the first time feeling how plump they are and begins rubbing my nipples with his thumbs through the delicate material making me moan, "Oh god."

"You are amazing, I'm one happy boy," he says feeling the fullness of my breasts whilst cupping them. I can see how happy he is by the look on his face and his prominent erection jutting from his suit trousers. Evan continues to circle my nipples with his thumbs as I relish in the feel of his hands on me. Reaching out to touch his straining erection through his trousers I can feel the hardness and size of his impressive cock and he groans with pleasure as I rub him.

Trying to undo his belt Evan places his hand over mine to stop me. "I want to devour you first before you have this," he says gently pulling my hand away so he can concentrate on my needs. Moving my long blonde hair away from my neck slowly with his fingers sending tingles all over my body he kisses me gently behind my ear, down my slender neck to my shoulder arousing me some more and making me feel hot with desire.

"Hmm …" while Evan kisses me I think how lucky I am to have such a gorgeous man wanting me in this way.

Reaching around my back he runs his hands up and down my delicate soft skin and stopping to unclasp my bra he frees my large breasts from the lace material and lets my bra drop to the floor leaving my top half exposed.

"You have the most perfect tits Kara," he says standing back to admire my huge assets. I give him a shy smile but I'm feeling massively turned on and sexy from the way he is so complimentary about me. He encourages me to lay back onto the bed so he can devour me properly.

Evan climbs onto the bed at the side of me licking his lips he takes hold of one of my breasts in his hand and brings his mouth to my erect nipple.

I moan as he sucks and nibbles it gently, teasing it with his mouth and tongue sometimes softly and sometimes sucking hard then giving the other breast the same attention. The feeling is incredible going straight to my core.

"Oh god your mouth feels so good." I moan throwing my head back and grabbing hold of the duvet.

I have never felt pleasure like it. I think how lovely and attentive he is to actually concentrate on my needs before his own, he is such a refreshing change.

Evan revels in making me moan by sucking my nipples and cupping my breasts feeling every part of them as I arch my back pushing them outwards giving him full access.

Trailing his tongue down my body he reaches the top of my denim blue skirt, "I think it's time to peel off another layer," he says undoing the button and zip at the front of my skirt, I lift my bum and he pulls it down my legs.

Looking up at me he smiles. "Your legs are so silky and soft," trailing his fingers lightly up and down them.

He trails his tongue up the inside of my inner thigh towards my knickers hoping that he will touch me there in that special place. I arch my back moaning at the sensations I am feeling in my groin, my inner muscles clenching and pulsating as I become more and more turned on.

"These definitely need to go," he says looking at my white lace knickers and pulling at the sides of them as I lift my bum again so he can roll them down my legs.

"Just beautiful," he says looking up and down my naked body making me feel shy and exposed as he sits at the side of me trailing light fingers from my ankle up my legs.

"I want you." I pant parting my legs giving him a sign that I'm ready for him to take me.

Evan pushes two fingers inside my wetness. "You're soaked and so ready for me aren't you," he says easing his fingers in and out of me while I continue to moan.

"Please I want you," I cry as he moves his fingers in and out watching the emotions showing on my face.

"Oh that's so good." I pant as his thumb rubs against my clit in slow circular motions with the pulsating throb between my legs pure ecstasy bringing me closer and closer to an orgasm.

"Do you like that baby?"

"Yes ... oh god." I've not experienced anything so good in such a long time and I know if he carries on doing that any longer it's not going to be long before I come and I want this incredible feeling to last for as long as possible. "Evan stop or I'm going to finish," I plead.

Sensations are rippling through my body in waves with every touch and it's getting stronger and stronger by the second.

"It's okay I want you to, let it go babe," he says continuing to caress me between my legs watching my face as it shows every feeling of enjoyment.

Grabbing hold of the duvet my head thrashing from side to side I moan over and over again and not being able to hold back any longer I cry out "I'm coming... oh god I'm coming... OHHHHH..." and my whole body tenses and shakes as my orgasm surges through my body like a thunderbolt as Evan takes delight in watching me enjoy the ultimate pleasure.

"Bloody hell," I smile panting as Evan moves up my body and snuggles into my neck kissing it as I try to catch my breath. "Wow that was just ... oh my god ... I never knew it could be that good." Evan sits up and strokes my face with the back of his hand.

"Watching you orgasm, the noises you were making was incredible," he says in his sexy voice leaning forward and kissing me, delving his tongue into my mouth as I hold his face in my hands. Suddenly I feel embarrassed at the fact that a gorgeous stranger I have only known for a few hours has just given me the most powerful orgasm I have ever experienced in my life and has just watched me have it.

I start to blush and I can feel my cheeks becoming hotter and redder.

"There's that cute blush again," he says continuing to stroke my face.

"I'm sorry."

"What for?"

"I'm sorry that I was quick it was so good and I've not felt feelings like that for a long time if ever," looking at him with a shy smile.

"Hey don't be sorry and I'm not finished with you yet, are you ready for round two?" he asks grinning at me.

"Yes please," I smile having got my breath back and still feeling turned on.

Evan stands up at the side of the bed and removes his trousers and black boxers giving me my first sight of his naked form and his impressive cock.

'God he's big, I hope it fits.' I lick my lips feeling more than ready for him to take me fully as he bends down to pick up his suit trousers to find his wallet. His toned muscles on his legs, his solid ass, his taut abs and manly physique, this man is simply breath-taking.

Opening his wallet to find a condom, Evan sheaths himself with it and I giggle nervously. "A man who is prepared for any eventuality."

"Well it's better to be safe than sorry," he grins.

I can't seem to take my eyes off his solid, hard impressive cock as he climbs onto the bed and on top of me.

"Ready baby?" he asks positioning at my wet entrance.

"Yes I'm ready," I reply looking into his eyes.

He gently pushes inside me slowly filling me completely.

"Oh my god … shit."

"Are you okay?" he asks concerned he's hurting me.

"Oh, yes I'm more than okay." I pant as my body adjusts to the size of him filling me deep and making me moan loudly.

"You feel so tight."

"You feel so big." I moan making Evan laugh as he starts to move slowly circling his hips and grinding into me.

"Hmm you feel so good." He gradually picks up the pace and I pull my legs up around his waist. "Aargh you feel amazing," he groans as he pounds his cock into my warm insides forcefully making us both moan loudly from the pleasure it's giving us.

"Oh yes," I cry feeling every gorgeous inch of him as he thrusts into me over and over again, in and out, in and out. I hold onto him as Evan takes over my body pleasuring me with every stroke.

I have never had sex like this before, the strong physical connection between us both and how our bodies harmonise together is unbelievable and the pressure building inside me is nearly at the point of no return again.

"Oh Jesus, are you nearly there baby?" Evan says through gritted teeth trying to hold back on his own release.

"Yes I'm close ... oh god ..."

I'm so pleased he's nearly there too because I don't think I can stop myself from finishing even if I tried because he is just too good. A few more strokes and I cry out, "OHHH ..." and digging my nails into Evan's muscly back clawing at his flesh as the sensations soaring throughout my body fill my brain I orgasm and Evan joins me too his body stilling and he lets out a guttural moan as he finds his own release.

His cock jerking inside of me as he pants breathlessly and our sweaty bodies clinging to each other as we experience mind blowing orgasms, both of us enjoying the moment of having sex together for the first time.

"That was incredible," he says trying to get his breath back. "Are you okay did I hurt you?" he asks looking at my satisfied face.

"No I feel fantastic, I can't remember the last time I had one orgasm like that never mind two," grinning at him.

"Well I can give you plenty more where they came from," he grins as he climbs off me removes the condom then pulls me to him for a cuddle and a slow, lingering kiss. After pulling away he laughs, "so what do you think to the bed then?"

"Honestly I would definitely recommend it I haven't been so satisfied from a good lay in a bed for a long time."

"I take it we are still talking about the bed?"

"Of course what else?" I say with a cheeky smile.

With Evan's arm wrapped around me I snuggle into his side and we both feel happy and contented as we lay holding each other in silence.

After a while Evan stretches out his arm and looks at his watch discreetly. "As much as I could lay here all night with you and I don't want to spoil the fun it's 9.30pm and you said your friend would be worried if you were home late."

"Yes she would be. I suppose I'd better get my ass out of this bed and get going then," not really wanting to leave.

"Hmm … and what a fine ass it is Miss Davis," he says grabbing my bum cheeks in his hands and giving them a squeeze. I don't want to leave I'm quite content in this huge bed with Evan but Jodie will be worried if I'm late so I begrudgingly get up in search of my clothes that are strewn around the bedroom floor. While I'm picking them up the hotel room phone rings at the side of the bed.

"Evan Hamilton." Evan answers all official, "okay, yes that's great, can you organise for a taxi to be here in 15 minutes out the front please and charge it to my account, thank you," and hangs up. "I would have taken you home myself but I've been drinking so I can't."

"No it's fine, thank you for arranging one and anyway you might have got lost again so it's probably for the best I get a taxi."

"Yeah you're probably right," he grins watching me gathering up my clothes. "That was reception telling me my car is booked in tomorrow morning to have the Satnav looked at so it seems I won't need you to give me directions anymore Miss Davis, I will have to think of another excuse now to come and see you."

"Well you don't need an excuse Mr Hamilton, just come and see me I would like that" I smile. I bend over to pick up my white panties giving him a good look at my peachy bum.

"If you keep doing that, you will be late for your taxi," he says still laid on the bed naked, liking what he sees.

"As much as I would love to stay and sort that out again …" I say pointing to his semi-erect cock with my eyes "I now have a taxi coming so I need to get dressed," I say jumping around putting my underwear back on.

"You look hot in your underwear, but even hotter without it," he says clearly excited stroking his cock in front of me his eyes fixed on mine.

"Stop it you are making this harder for me to leave." I giggle.

"And you are making this hard for me," he says continuing to stroke himself.

I laugh, loving how relaxed we seem to be in each other's company, it doesn't feel like we have only just met today, it feels like we have known each other for a long time.

Quickly pulling on my skirt and t-shirt I sit down on the edge of the bed to put my shoes on.

Evan crawls up behind me, "You make me so horny just by looking at you, this is new to me I can't get enough of you," he says cupping my breasts through my t-shirt and pushing his now fully erect cock into my back.

"Well the feeling is mutual, but I really need to go because the taxi will be here soon." But before I leave, I turn around to face him, smile then bend down and take him into my mouth taking all of him and sucking hard, tasting him.

"Oh fuck …" he cries grabbing my head with his hands.

"Hmm …" I moan as he hits the back of my throat and fills my mouth.

After sucking his cock a few times and teasing the tip with my tongue I pull away. "Yes you are right that is better than any meat I have ever had before," licking my lips and then getting up and walking out of the bedroom with a smile on my face.

"What are you doing to me? Wait a minute," he calls and I can hear him running around the bedroom looking for something to wear. He walks into the lounge area wearing a pair of jeans and a t-shirt to find me grinning at him as I pick up my bag.

Stalking over to me he grins. "You little minx," grabbing hold of me for a deep kiss plunging his tongue into my mouth and holding my bum, pushing and grinding into my front. Pulling away breathless he looks into my eyes and then strokes the side of my face with the back of his hand. "I'll give you my number in case you feel like finishing what you started a minute ago."

"Hmm … I would love to," I smile rubbing him through his jeans.

"Please can I have your number? I would really like to see you again while I'm staying here if you want to?"

I smile, "Definitely and I would love to meet up again too."

I take my hand away from his crotch and reach into my bag and take out my phone. I type in Evan's mobile number as he reads it out to me and then I ring the number so he has my number saved in his contacts before putting it back into my bag. Evan then takes me into his arms again and gives me another sensual, slow kiss, neither one of us wanting to break the contact because I have to leave.

"I really need to go the taxi will be here Evan," reluctantly pulling away.

"Come on then, I'll walk down with you," showing me to the door to the awaiting lift. We both travel down in the lift just staring at each other wanting a repeat of what just happened but both of us knowing that if we start something again we wouldn't be able to stop.

On arriving in the reception area, Evan takes hold of my hand and we walk hand in hand to the front door and then kiss each other briefly.

"I'll be in touch," he says then watches me walk out of the hotel through the revolving door. I wave goodbye to him before getting into the awaiting taxi.

Evan

I feel strange, I'm experiencing feelings that I've not felt in a long time. I feel different to how I normally would after entertaining a girl in my hotel room, I'm usually pleased when they've gone after having some fun and I certainly never swap phone numbers.

All I want is no strings, no dramas, just sex for a bit of fun, I've only just met this woman and I'm already having relationship thoughts.

'What is wrong with me? 'Why am I feeling like this?'

I don't do relationships my life is busy enough already and I don't have time for anything other than work. Plus relationships are bad news but meeting Kara today for the first time in a long time she has affected me like I've never known before.

I really like this girl; she's beautiful, sexy, funny, she's down to earth and such a refreshing change from the girls I normally meet on my travels. There is just something about her and these feelings I'm having is scaring the hell out of me. I don't know what to make of them but one thing I do know for sure is that I have to see her again and the sooner the better.

Five

I arrive home at five minutes past 10 and walk through the front door, all is quiet in the flat, Matt must have gone. I lock the door behind me and walk into the kitchen to put the kettle on. I can't help the big smile on my face when I think about Evan.

'Did that really just happen?' As I take a coffee mug from the top cupboard Jodie walks in grinning from ear to ear in her dressing gown.

"Hi Kar, you making coffee I'll join you," she says sitting down at the kitchen table. I get another mug out of the cupboard and fill them both with coffee and one sugar in each mug.

"It was a good night then?" I smile.

"The best, thanks for making yourself scarce, I really appreciate it, so how did your night go? What did you end up doing?"

Pouring the hot water from the kettle into the mugs and putting a dash of milk in each one I place the steaming mugs of coffee onto the kitchen table then sit down opposite Jodie.

"Oh, I had a good night too. I ended up having dinner in the Penthouse Suite at The Kingsman Hotel with this really hot, rich guy I met today and then we ended up having the most amazing sex I have ever had in my life," grinning at her.

"Yeah so what did you really get up to?" Jodie laughs.

"Seriously that's what I did," still grinning at her.

Jodie looks at me seriously for a moment to work out if I'm joking or not and when I don't say anymore she gasps, "No way seriously, I need to know everything and I mean everything," looking at me excitedly. I have a smug look on my face ready to tell her all about my exciting night.

After finishing our coffees and filling Jodie in on all the juicy gossip, it's late and she is feeling tired after her night of entertaining Matt so she takes herself off to bed.

"Night Jode, see you in the morning." I grab my bag from the kitchen floor, turn off the light and head to my bedroom. Taking my mobile out of my bag I check to see how much power it has and it says 86% so I put it onto the bedside table and go take a quick shower.

After putting on my favourite pink pyjamas my mobile phone signals a new text message. Climbing into my bed making myself comfortable I grab my phone and open the message.

Good Evening Miss Davis, I'm lost again can you help me? I'm lost in this huge bed wishing your sexy ass was here too. Just wanted to say I had a lovely evening, hope you did too? Evan xx

I squeal. 'Oh my god, he actually messaged me!' I'm shocked because I thought it might have been just a one-night thing.

Despite swapping numbers, I doubted that he was actually going to contact me. The amount of times a guy has taken my number but not actually phoned or messaged has made me think they never will, so I've stopped getting my hopes up. The fact that he has sent a text the same night I feel beyond happy.

I contemplate my reply and then type out a message feeling giddy with happiness and press send.

Mr Hamilton, how lovely to hear from you, as for you being lost in your huge bed I would gladly keep you company anytime. I have just got into bed after taking a cold shower because I was feeling extremely hot thinking about our dinner date. I had a wonderful evening thank you. Off to sleep now, sweet dreams. Kara xx

I wait expectantly and then moments later another message comes through …

I really enjoyed your company tonight and I might just take you up on your offer to keep me company in bed again. I keep thinking of our dinner date too and my dreams will certainly not be sweet Kara. Sleep well. E xx

I feel so happy, I have had the best night and feeling exhausted I turn off the bedside light and lay in my bed thinking over the whole day's events. I can't believe I've met a gorgeous man who is unbelievable in bed and wants to see me again.

With thoughts of Evan I drift off to sleep with a big smile on my face wondering what tomorrow will bring.

Six

"Morning Sal!" I feel exceptionally happy today as I walk through the door of the coffee shop wearing a black t-shirt and white denim skirt. Sally looks bewildered as to why I'm so happy to come to work.

"Good morning Kara, what's put you in such a good mood? Did you picture a gorgeous stranger in your dreams last night by any chance?" Sally says with a quizzical look on her face.

I give her a cheeky smile as I walk past her and go into the back office to put my bag away and to fetch my apron. Walking back into the coffee shop I look at her with a smirk on my face, "Well you could say that, but it was more than a dream."

"What do you mean, have you seen him again?" Sally asks excitedly as she comes over to me for more details.

"Well after Tim had picked you up last night, I bumped into him again," smiling at her as I tie my hair back into a pony tail and turn on the coffee machine to warm up ready for the day ahead.

"What really? This is so exciting tell me everything," she grins.

I'm just about to tell her what happened when there is a knock at the door and the delivery of cakes has arrived from the bakers.

"His timing is unbelievable, hold on I'll be right back," she says unlocking and opening the door. "Thanks Joe, see you tomorrow," she says taking the cakes off him, shutting the door quickly not wanting to engage in a conversation and scurrying back to the counter to where I'm stood.

I excitedly tell Sally all the details of my evening with Evan and she revels in all the juicy gossip I am feeding her!

"Oh god I told you, didn't I tell you yesterday he was interested and not just being nice," Sally smiles.

"Yes you did but with my track record of men I didn't think he would be interested not in the slightest."

"Confidence is key honey." Sally pats me on the back with a big grin on her face and heads towards the door to open up the café.

"What's his name?" she asks.

"Oh, it's Evan Hamilton."

"That's a good name, Kara Hamilton, it has a nice ring don't you think?"

"Hold your horses I've only just met the guy." I laugh.

Sally laughs, "So do you know when you will be seeing him again?"

"I'm not sure, I guess I'll just wait and see if he contacts me today."

"Well I know when you'll be seeing him again," Sally says clapping her hands with excitement.

I look at her puzzled, "What do you mean you know?"

"Well as I unlocked the door just now I saw a flash car parked across the road and I could see him walking this way so I would say you are going to see him again in the next few minutes."

Suddenly I feel flustered and don't know what to do with myself, "Sal, do I look alright?"

"You look great," Sally shouts as I quickly run out the back just as Evan opens the door and comes inside.

I apply some lip gloss and take my hair out of the ponytail letting it fall around my shoulders.

I peek through the gap in the door from the office and listen to find out what he wants before I go back into the shop.

I can see Evan is wearing a navy suit today with a white shirt, slightly unbuttoned at the top. He looks just as handsome today as he did yesterday.

His hair is a little windswept and he's running his fingers through his hair to make himself look more presentable.

He smiles at Sally and walks over to the counter to where she's stood.

"Good morning sir, are you lost again or did our coffee taste so good you just had to come back for another cup?" Sally says giving him a friendly greeting.

Evan smiles and looks around the coffee shop noticing that I'm not there and his face drops, "Actually I was wondering if it was possible to have a quick word with Kara, but I see she's not here?"

"Oh she's here she's just out the back, Kara you have a visitor!" Sally calls.

I walk into the shop feeling shy.

We were so intimate with each other last night and now he's standing here in front of me looking gorgeous but serious and I don't really know what to say or think.

"Hi."

"Hello, do you think I could have a word in private somewhere for a moment, would you mind?" Evan says looking towards Sally for approval.

'Oh no this is where he tells me he's been thinking and that last night was a big mistake and he doesn't want to see me again.'

"Yeah sure." I look at Sally feeling nervous, "is it ok to have a quick word out the back Sal?"

"Yeah of course, just take him in the office, I'll be fine for a little while." Sally winks at me because she can get away with it, Evan isn't looking at her, his eyes are transfixed on me.

"Okay thanks Sal, I won't be long."

Evan looks like he has something on his mind, he follows me through the door of the office and I can feel my heart thumping fast in my chest, my mouth has gone dry and I feel sick. 'I wonder what he wants?'

After our encounter yesterday I had hoped that we would be having a repeat of last night when I saw him again but seeing his serious face I knew it was too good to be true, a gorgeous man like Evan wanting me again.

'Why do I always meet the wrong guys?' Taking a deep breath and bracing myself for the bad news I close the office door and turn around to face him.

No sooner have I turned around Evan is on me so fast pushing me up against the back of the wooden door and crashing his mouth onto mine.

The kiss is a hungry kiss and so passionate, the type of kiss when two lovers have not seen each other for a while and Evan seems desperate to touch me, his hands are everywhere.

I'm so relieved he still wants me and not to mention turned on as his hands cup my breasts through my t-shirt and apron.

Totally consumed by Evan I forget where we are for a moment and begin to fumble with the belt on his trousers, his touch making me wet and needy for him.

"Wait not here," he says breathless.

'Oh my god what am I doing?' He puts his forehead on mine and stares into my blue eyes.

"Hi," Evan says giving me one of his sexy smiles.

"Hi," I smile, happy to see him again.

"I'm sorry, I shouldn't have interrupted you at work but after last night I couldn't wait to see you again."

Looking into his eyes I feel the same, "I'm so pleased to see you. And I can tell you are more than pleased to see me," I smile cupping his erection through his trousers then kissing him softly.

"I can't help it, you make me hard just by looking at you, thinking about you and…," groaning as I rub him.

"I wish I could take you right now on that desk but we

can't, not here, will you meet me later beautiful?"

"Yes I'd love to. I thought you were coming to tell me that last night was a mistake and that you didn't want to hook up again you looked so serious."

"Sorry I was nervous." Evan cups my face.

"I wouldn't have thought a confident man like you would get nervous." I smile nuzzling into his hand.

"I'm not normally, but after last night I can't seem to get you out of my head, I woke up this morning and all I could think about was you. But I wasn't sure how you would feel, you might have decided that you didn't want to see me again."

"I do want to see you again."

"Listen, cards on the table I would love to carry on hooking up while I'm staying in town, but you need to understand Kara that this is only for fun so don't go developing feelings for me. I don't do relationships and I don't want you to get hurt okay."

"Okay, it's just for fun I understand. I do want to keep seeing you but on one condition," I smile.

"What's that?" Evan replies looking puzzled.

"You keep giving me mind blowing orgasms."

Evan laughs, "Okay I promise to give you plenty while I'm here so we both know where we stand then so it's a deal?" Evan reiterates and I nod in agreement.

"It's a deal. Do we need to shake on it or something?"

"I can do better than that," he says giving me another passionate kiss. "How long do you get for your lunch break?"

"I only take half an hour, why?" I'm desperate to have Evan again as I stand encased in his arms.

"Damn it, that's nowhere near enough time for what I want to do to you, what time do you finish work?" Evan asks with need in his voice.

"I finish at 5:00pm which is my usual time."

"Okay, I'll pick you up at 5.00pm and then we can spend some more time getting to know each other," grinding his hips into my front making me laugh. "I have to meet my building contractor and architect this afternoon but I'll make sure I'm done by then, is that okay with you?"

"Yes that's great, I can't wait." I reply.

Evan gives me another slow kiss and then pulls away, "I'd better go because I have a guy coming to collect my car from the hotel at 10am to look at the Satnav."

"Okay I'll see you later then, I hope they can fix it" I reply with a grin.

"Yes I'm sure it's nothing major. I'll look forward to seeing you later beautiful."

Evan gives me a quick kiss followed by one of his knockout sexy smiles before opening the door of the office and walking back into the shop. He thanks Sally for allowing him some time with me and then he bids her goodbye and walks out the door.

Sally is serving some customers when I reappear in the coffee shop. She knows from the huge grin on my face that Evan's visit was obviously a good one. I tie my hair up again while Sally serves two regulars a pot of tea and two pieces of carrot cake and then makes her way over to me.

"All okay?" she smiles.

"Yeah fine Sal he wants to pick me up after work and do something," I giggle knowing full well what Evan wants to do.

"Oh this is so exciting," she grins.

I want the day to have finished already so I can be in Evan's arms again and thoughts of what we will be doing later keep creeping into my mind and it's making me more and more impatient.

The weather has turned even windier and it has been raining on and off all afternoon, people have been sheltering by enjoying a nice hot cup of coffee in Walt's Coffee Shop so the afternoon has gone quickly which I'm pleased about.

It's nearly 5:00pm and I've started to get butterflies in my stomach, Evan will be picking me up soon and nerves are starting to kick in.

"It's time to go and meet lover boy." Sally grins.

We hang up our aprons on the coat peg and collect our bags from the office. I take my hair out of the ponytail give my hair a quick brush and put on some lip gloss before walking through the coffee shop to the front door with Sally ready to leave.

"See you tomorrow Sal." I walk outside feeling the wind hit my face causing my neatly brushed hair to get all messy again. 'Damn it!'

Turning off the lights Sally locks the door, "See you tomorrow love, can't wait to hear all about it," she says and runs off down the street waving goodbye before getting into Tim's awaiting car.

Thankfully the rain has stopped, I stand and wait for Evan to arrive in his flashy car as I lean against the red brick wall of the coffee shop. Looking at my watch seeing the time is now 5.20pm, he is running late.

'I hope he's going to turn up. How long should I wait? Where is he?'

I hear the roar of a V12 engine and the distinct sound of the twin exhausts coming down the road towards me.

I look up and see Evan's car, I smile as I think no one else drives a car like that around here.

"Hey you, sorry I'm a bit late, my architect kept me talking and I was struggling to get away but I'm here now, get in."

I smile feeling relieved that I've not been stood up and walk around the front of the car to open the passenger door to get into the black leather seat smoothing down my wild hair from the wind.

"Hi," he leans his gorgeous face towards me and gives me a long, lingering kiss followed by a cheeky smile.

"I was beginning to think you weren't coming."

"Sorry beautiful, I didn't mean to keep you waiting."

"That's okay. You smell divine by the way," I smile.

"Thanks. I take it your flatmate knows where you are tonight so there will be no calling the police if you are home late?"

"Yes I text Jodie in my lunch break so she knows where I am, but I didn't give her a time when I will be back because I wasn't sure what we would be doing," I smile.

"I think you have a good idea," he grins, "are you nervous?"

"Yes a little." I reply, noticing that Evan sees me fidgeting in my seat.

"Well don't be, I'll soon have you feeling relaxed, I thought we could head back to the suite and have dinner again. It's strange how I only met you yesterday but I feel like I've known you for ages, are you sure we haven't met before? I feel so relaxed with you you're like an old pair of slippers."

I smack his arm playfully, "Are you joking? Like an old pair of slippers ..."

"You're right, you are too beautiful to be an old pair of slippers, but you know what I mean," he says grinning at me.

"I know what you mean because I feel the same; we just seem to click don't we. Anyway are we going for dinner or are you just going to sit there dishing out insults all night?"

"Hey it was definitely meant as a compliment."

"I know I'm only messing with you."

"Okay, well we'd better go then if the lady is ready," he says putting the car into gear and driving off down the road.

"Yes I'm ready," I reply giving him a cheeky smile and feeling less nervous now and more excited about what is to come.

I can't help but stare at him, he is so captivating. I find myself watching him while he drives, he is so powerful.

I love how confident and sexy he looks in his navy designer suit as people's heads turn as we drive past. His masculine aftershave awakens my senses, I take in his scent and it's causing me to feel hot and flustered as sexual thoughts fill my brain.

These thoughts are becoming more regular whenever I'm around him, this gorgeous man makes me feel sexy and alive like no one else has before and I don't think I can stop these feelings and thoughts even if I tried.

"What are you thinking about?"

"Nothing much." I blush.

"I think I can guess."

"I like your car it's really nice … did you get your Satnav fixed?" I say, trying my best to divert the conversation away from myself.

"Thanks, yes I had it fixed this morning it was a loose connection apparently so I can find my way around now and there will be no more getting lost again" he smiles.

I'm so pleased that he got lost and walked into Walt's Coffee Shop yesterday.

I'm looking forward to finding out more about Evan Hamilton on our second dinner date although from the vibe I'm getting it sounds like we are not going to be doing much talking later but more entertaining and I can't wait.

Arriving back at The Kingsman Hotel the valet parks Evan's car while he leads me into the hotel reception. The same woman who was on the reception desk last night looks up to see us both walking through the revolving door.

"Mr Hamilton," she calls beckoning him over to the desk.

"Good evening," Evan replies and the lady blushes.

"Was everything okay with your car; I hope they fixed the problem for you?" pushing out her chest whilst running her fingers lightly on the oak reception desk looking gooey eyed at him.

"Yes everything is working fine now, thanks for organising someone to fix it," giving her one of his knock out smiles.

"Oh it's no trouble at all, anything I can help you with at any time please do let me know," she says playing with her hair and pouting her inflated red lips at him.

I stand listening to their conversation, rolling my eyes.

'Can you be any more obvious, he's with me or am I invisible? She needs to back off.'

"Are you ready babe, I really need to get out of these clothes?" grabbing hold of his hand and squeezing it.

"Yeah sure." Evan smiles.

The lady gives me a scowl and I smile at her as we walk

off to the lifts hand in hand.

"She definitely fancies you, surely you noticed it this time?" I whisper.

"What can I say, I have this effect on women I mean you practically wet your knickers when you saw me for the first time yesterday, I could tell you were turned on."

I hit him playfully on the arm, "Alright yes I was but I bet you were too you were practically undressing me with your eyes, I saw the way you were looking at my tits."

"I was and what gorgeous tits they are," he grins as we both get into the lift and the doors close.

Within seconds Evan has me pinned against the wall kissing me fiercely pulling up my black t-shirt so he can feel and see my breasts properly that are dressed in a black silky bra.

"Evan stop, what if people want to get in the lift?" I whisper feeling breathless before recommencing our wild kiss.

"Don't worry babe this is an exclusive lift providing private access only to the Penthouse Suite," pulling my bra cups down to reveal my pert nipples and taking one in his mouth sucking and flicking it with his tongue.

"Oh thank god." I pant and press my head back against the lift wall as he teases the sensitive nub in his mouth.

Pulling my skirt up around my waist he growls when he sees my black silky thong knickers.

"You are so sexy," he says pulling the thin strap of silky material to one side and plunging two fingers inside my wetness pushing them in and out slowly while I moan softly into his mouth while he kisses me. I feel naughty as Evan pleasures me in the lift, I've never done things outside the bedroom before and this is a whole new world to me which I'm enjoying every minute of.

Dropping to his knees he pulls my knickers down my legs and opens my legs wider before plunging his tongue into my opening and then dragging it slowly up my core to my throbbing clit. "OHHH …" I cry out placing my hands on the back of his head for support. His tongue performs soft light circles giving me just what I need, what I've been craving all day since he came to see me at work this morning.

"Oh, that's so good." I cry. Evan smiles and looks up at me then continues doing what he's doing with his tongue.

The lift arrives on the top floor and Evan stops, gets up off his knees and scoops me up in his arms striding out of the lift with purpose to open the door of the suite.

Placing me down to find his key card in his pocket he swipes it through the slot on the door, opens it and then carries me through the door, my knickers still around my ankles. I kiss his neck driving him wild with desire. Shutting the door behind him, he puts me down and looks at me with serious, 'I want to fuck you eyes.'

"Take your clothes off," he says staring at me with serious intent. Taking off his jacket, he then begins to unbutton his shirt, his eyes fixed on me the whole time. I start to undress when his mobile phone starts ringing in his jacket pocket. "Shit," he says taking it out and seeing who is calling. "Don't stop what you are doing I just need to take this, it's the hotel manager at my hotel in Spain, I'll be as quick as I can," he says annoyed at the timing of the phone call.

'Wow he has a hotel in Spain.' I kick off my knickers and then take off my skirt, t-shirt, and bra until I'm stood fully naked in front of him staring at him on the phone. From what I can gather there seems to be a problem with a member of staff, Evan tries to advise him what to do while keeping his eyes firmly fixed on my naked body.

While Evan is trying to discuss important matters on staff issues with the hotel's manager he's struggling with his words, he is aroused and he wants to attend to another important matter that is standing naked right in front of him ... ME.

Placing my hands on his hairy chest as we look into each other's eyes I finish undoing the buttons on his shirt and then pushing it back I place my warm hands on his chest feeling the firmness as I stroke my hands up and down his torso. Helping me to remove his shirt he chats away and feeling brave I undo the belt on his trousers followed by the button and the zip.

He doesn't stop me so I carry on and pull his trousers down to his ankles so he can step out of them.

His erection is tenting his tight white boxers and as I pull them down his legs he clears his throat and takes a deep breath struggling to talk for being so turned on.

Pulling his boxers off his feet and throwing them to one side I look up at him knelt on the floor, his huge erection now free and ready for action.

I remember the comment he made last night about finishing what I started before I left him to get my taxi home and as his eyes lower to me I lick my lips and he watches me as I take hold of his hard length and guide his cock straight into my mouth.

"Oh Jesus ... err yeah sorry mate I'm fine I just stubbed my toe on the chair," he says struggling to continue the conversation as I grin and laugh around the end of his cock then continue to suck and lick his hard length like it's the most delicious treat.

Evan screws his eyes shut and holds his breath and then with a shaky voice he says to the person on the other end of the phone, "Sorry mate, I really need to go something's come up that I need to deal with urgently, I'll call you tomorrow." He then ends the call.

'Yes, it's definitely come up and it's not going down anytime soon.' I suck whilst cupping his balls in my hand and he groans throwing his phone onto the nearby couch and grabbing hold of my head gently as I glide my wet mouth over him, pleasuring him.

"Hmm I love your cock." I circle the tip with my tongue tasting him before taking all of him in my mouth again. I can tell he's enjoying it by the noises he's making and this pleases me more than anything.

"You look so hot," he pants as he watches me take it in my mouth fully sucking him hard over and over again teasing and tasting him bringing him closer to orgasm.

"Hmm … it's so big and hard," I moan.

"Jesus Kara, I'm going to finish soon."

His breathing is fast and his legs are shaking slightly as he holds onto me.

I don't stop and I carry on and on, sucking and licking, swirling my tongue and cupping his balls enjoying hearing the noises he's making until I've taken him to the point of no return.

"FUUCCKK," he cries and he spills into my mouth, jerking and twitching as he cradles my head, the overwhelming feeling filling his brain. "That was fucking incredible," he grins pulling me up off the floor taking my naked body in his arms and kissing me, tasting himself on my lips as he kisses me passionately.

"Well you did say if I wanted to finish what I started last night I could," I smile.

"Anytime you fancy doing that it's fine by me preferably not when I'm on the phone though," he laughs.

Picking me up he carries me over to one of the couches lays me down gently then kneels in front of me.

"My turn," he grins, I smile as he lowers his mouth onto one of my nipples and sucks it sending pleasure straight to my core.

"Hmm … I love you doing that," I moan as he concentrates on one nipple then the other.

"Hmm … your breasts are so perfect and I love doing it," he replies giving them his full attention as he slowly moves down my body.

He moves down until he is nestled between my legs, he carries on what he started in the lift finding my clit with his tongue and circling and pleasuring me.

I'm soaked and turned on to the max as he devours me with his mouth with expertise.

I moan in appreciation arching my back pushing out my breasts loving the sensations it is giving me.

"Does that feel good baby?"

"Yes so good you are unreal," I pant holding the sides of the couch.

Evan knows just how to bring me to orgasm with his skilled mouth and tongue and it's driving me crazy, my insides are pulsing and each flick of his tongue followed by a slow circling motion brings me closer and closer to orgasm.

"Oh god Evan, I'm going to come," I'm breathless and needy for my release.

"OHHHH god ... yes ... yes ... I'm coming" I cry and after a few more strokes of his tongue I scream his name as my orgasm rushes through my body making me see stars. "Evan ... oh stop ... stop." I moan, Evan moves his mouth away as the intense feeling is becoming too much to bear and I can't cope with his tongue there anymore.

"You okay baby?" Evan grins looking at my satisfied face.

"Yes I'm more than okay," I smile, feeling exhausted.

The next thing I feel is Evan's lips on mine and he gives me the sweetest kiss.

"You're amazing," he smiles.

"You're amazing giving me orgasms like that." I whisper.

"I aim to please," he grins. "Do you fancy having some dinner now and then we can have a bath together afterwards if you like?"

"Yes please that sounds lovely," I reply thinking a bath together we only just met yesterday? But liking the suggestion as Evan helps me up off the couch so we can find our clothes.

We get dressed, then Evan orders dinner, both of us choosing to order a chicken salad.

We sit in the same seats at the dining table as the previous night and Evan pours us each a glass of white wine to accompany our meal.

"So you had a meeting with your architect and building contractor this afternoon, what happens next?"

"You really want to know?"

"Yes I'm interested," I reply popping some chicken into my mouth.

"Okay, well I've finalised the plans for the extension and agreed any changes and I have full planning permission to go ahead on the renovations so we are all systems go and ready to start."

"So you have been in this area before then?"

"Yes but it's a while ago now, I was only here briefly to view the property and to sort out the plans. I met up with my architect and building contractor today to discuss starting the works so everyone knows what is happening, timescales etc. I still need to oversee everything as it's my business and reputation on the line and it has to be perfect."

"So when will you be starting the work then?"

"Hopefully within the next 2 weeks, less about boring work anyway, I'd rather talk about you, so how come you are single?"

"I guess I haven't really met anyone I wanted to spend all my time with."

"How about you, oh sorry you don't do relationships do you?"

"No I don't, anyway if you are finished eating we can take our wine and go and chill in the tub if you like?" he suggests clearing the plates from the dining table.

Nice conversation divert…

'He really doesn't like talking about relationships does he, I wonder why?' I pick up our glasses of wine and join him in the bathroom.

The luxurious bathroom is full of marble and gold and the roll top bath in the centre of the room is large enough for two people.

"It won't be long," he says swishing the water in the bath.

"Okay, I'll get undressed then."

Any nerves that I had previously felt getting naked in front of him are now well and truly gone. Finishing my wine, I remove my clothes ready to get in the bath and Evan watches me as well as keeping an eye on the running water pouring into the huge tub.

"You have an incredible body," he says grinning and liking what he sees.

"Thanks, I take after my mum big boobs, tiny waist and big hips."

"Well I'd like to thank your parents for creating such a beautiful woman who I am having the pleasure of spending time with," he grins.

I blush. The bath now ready and full of warm water Evan turns off the taps and stalks over to me taking me in his arms for a tongue mingling kiss which turns me on. Bringing his hand down to between my legs he plunges two fingers inside me and pulls them upwards over my clit.

"You're wet already and that's before you are even in the water" he smiles.

"Hmm … I can't help it when I'm around you; hurry up and take your clothes off, I want you naked," enjoying his fingers massaging me as I caress the back of his neck. Dropping his hand, he smiles and starts to remove his clothes while I get into the bath and lay down looking at him.

I rest my head back on the bath, my blonde hair flowing around my shoulders as the water laps gently over my breasts.

"You look like a goddess laid there surrounded by marble and gold."

"I feel like one." I smile watching him undress until he's standing naked at the side of the bath with an erection. Finishing off his wine he then steps into the bath sitting at one end.

"Come here," he says so I move towards him and position myself in between his legs laying with my back to him.

"I feel like I have a permanent hard on when you're around," he laughs pushing it into my back.

"I've noticed, you're very virile, I like it and I like that I turn you on, it turns me on."

Massaging my breasts under the warm water as it splashes over them he asks, "What do you like to do for fun then apart from having sex with me?" I glance at him and smile.

"Well yes that has to be at the top of my list of fun activities at the moment, but I love to go to the cinema, bowling and sometimes I will make it to the gym. Normally it is to shift post-Christmas weight but the routine doesn't last very long. I also like the theatre, going to see a West End show is on my bucket list. What about you, what do you like to do for fun as if I didn't already know?"

"Well apart from the obvious I love to ski, I love to go the races and I also love the theatre. My mother used to take me to a show when I was little when my father was working late and I used to hate it at first but then I really got to love going."

"Your social activities are beyond mine, it must be so nice to do what you want when you want, without having to worry about money all the time. I suppose you have worked really hard to get to where you are though so you totally deserve it."

'Our lives are worlds apart.'

"Yes I do work hard and that's why I can spend money doing things I enjoy, what would you do if money was no object then?"

"I would probably go on holiday, somewhere abroad because I don't really go anywhere, I've not seen much of the world and there are so many interesting places to visit that I've seen in magazines, I'd probably do that."

"Yes you're right and it's not just the places, it's the different cultures, the cuisine, it's a big world out there."

"Yeah one day I will go travelling, but at the moment I can dream."

We chat for what seems like hours, the bath water is turning cold so we get out and wrap ourselves in white fluffy hotel towels.

"Fancy watching some TV?" Evan asks.

'I would rather he take me into the bedroom for some more action.'

"Err okay," I reply trying not to sound disappointed.

Evan laughs, "I'm kidding, do you seriously think I would prefer to watch TV than amuse myself with this gorgeous body?" picking me up in my towel and carrying me into the bedroom.

I squeal as he lifts me in the air and giggle, "I wasn't sure if you were kidding or not but I was hoping for another type of entertainment." He places me on the bed as my towel falls open and he rolls me off the wet towel in one swift movement.

His towel drops to the floor revealing his solid form. He sheathes himself with a condom and then climbs onto the bed on top of me and settles between my thighs.

"I want to take you nice and slow," he whispers into my ear making me tingle all over as I feel him at my entrance.

Opening my legs wider for him he pushes into me, slowly filling me deep and we both moan on feeling the connection.

Grinding his hips slowly I straighten my legs so his body is rubbing me up and down in the right place as he plunges into me.

In and out, in and out, he drives circling his hips all the time, "You are so beautiful, I can't stop looking at you, your eyes are so blue," he pants as the pressure builds for both of us.

"You're not so bad yourself," I moan. "Oh god you feel amazing, that's so good."

"It fits you perfectly doesn't it," Evan replies grinding his hips some more hitting the spot every time.

Picking up the pace a little but still at a slow tempo, I can feel my insides gripping his cock as he slides into me.

Kissing me softly, plunging his tongue into my mouth he kisses me while I run my fingers through his hair on the back of his head.

The pressure in our groins is building with every stroke and I'm struggling to stop the incredible feeling that wants to be released.

"Evan I'm getting close," falling to pieces beneath him.

"Not yet baby, try and hold it, just a little longer."

"Oh god Evan, I don't think I can" I cry.

"I'm almost there," he moans.

"I can't hold it much longer," I pant desperate to let go.

"Okay baby let it go," and with one last thrust I let go on a scream "OHHH …"

"Aargh, fuck yes," he cries his cock throbbing, my insides pulsing as we orgasm together.

"I'm sorry, you make me come so easily," letting out a big sigh of relief after my explosive orgasm.

"Hey don't apologise, I love the fact my cock gives you pleasure and I can give you good orgasms," he says stroking my face grinning at me.

"I've never felt this good in all my life. You turn me on so much I can't help it, I'm not going to be able to walk by the time you leave as I can't get enough of you and the orgasms you give me," I laugh squeezing his bum making him jerk inside me.

"Like I said anytime baby," smiling as he pulls out of me.

"What time is it?" I suddenly panic.

Evan looks at his watch, "It's almost 10.00pm."

"I really should be going it's getting late and I have work tomorrow."

"Why don't you stay tonight?"

"Err … another time maybe."

'Why the hell did I just say that?'

Evan climbs off the bed to dispose of the condom and I get up to use the bathroom whilst finding my clothes to get dressed.

'Why didn't I just say I'd stay … it seems like he wants me to?'

I'm regretting my decision as I gaze at Evan looking delectable in a pair of blue jeans and a green t-shirt he's just put on.

"I'll give you a lift home."

"It's okay, you've had some wine I'll just get a taxi again it's no problem," I reply feeling a little awkward after saying that I don't want to stay.

"Okay you're right I'd better not risk it, I'll call you a taxi then."

"Thank you."

Evan picks up the hotel phone and orders a taxi to arrive in 10 minutes while I find my bag and then I sit down on the couch to wait.

Feeling slightly awkward and not knowing what to say about when we will see each other again I'm pleased when Evan says, "I'll give you a call tomorrow."

"Great." I smile, "I'd better go and wait for my taxi I don't want to keep them waiting; you don't have to come down with me."

I get up off the couch and walk towards the door.

"It's no problem I want to," he says catching up with me and taking hold of my hand. He walks through the reception area with me and I notice the receptionist from earlier is looking over at us.

Seeing her watching Evan, I don't like it and I suddenly feel like I need to stake a claim on him. Wanting to give her something to really look at I kiss him passionately in front of her, my hands stroking the back of his neck as I plunge my tongue fiercely into his mouth moaning as I do it.

We pull away breathless and I look at the woman who is clearly wishing it was her and give her a smile.

'1 – 0 to me, he is with me so back off and don't even think about it.'

I then look at Evan and he's grinning at me.

"Wow are you sure you have to go?" he says resting his forehead on mine looking at me with his big brown eyes.

"The taxi will be here now," we look outside and it's sat at the curb waiting for me.

"Okay I'll speak to you tomorrow then," Evan says.

I walk out of the hotel get into the awaiting taxi and watch Evan as we drive off and he waves to me goodbye.

Seven

It is the following day and despite the rain waking me up, I am feeling fresh from a good night's sleep. After having a chat with Jodie over breakfast she leaves for school and I finish getting ready. I'm just trying to find an umbrella so I don't get wet walking to work when Evan messages me.

Morning beautiful, you are going to be wet today and not just from the rain outside. Fancy meeting up later after work? I need to be inside you before the day is out; it's been too long already. E xx

I put on my navy converse and then send a quick reply.

I would love too and I like the sound of that. Just heading off to work, do you fancy doing something later like going to the cinema maybe? K xx

Evan sends a reply.

Sounds good, be in touch to arrange a time. E xx

Finding an umbrella in the bottom of my wardrobe I pick up my bag and head out the front door.

The rain is heavy and big puddles are forming on the ground.

"It's bloody July for god's sake, why is it pissing down?" I mutter shielding from the rain under the umbrella as I set off walking to work.

After walking for ten minutes and not far from work I notice a big puddle has formed in the road against the kerb and just as I get up to it a car comes around the corner and drives through it causing a huge gush of water to soak me from head to foot.

"That's just great, thanks a lot you dickhead." I shout feeling cold and shivering from the dirty rain water standing there shocked and annoyed.

Moving out the way of the puddle I get my phone out of my bag to call Sally because I can't arrive at work looking like I do.

"Hi Kara, are you alright love?"

"Hi Sal, no I'm bloody not, some dickhead has just driven through a big puddle in the road while I was walking to work and has completely soaked me from head to foot, I'm really sorry but I'm going to have to go home and get changed, I'll be as quick as I can."

"Oh no, its awful weather today isn't it." Sally laughs "don't worry that's fine, take as long as you need. I shouldn't think we will be that busy today anyway the rain will be keeping people indoors so don't rush."

"Thanks Sally I appreciate it," I shiver. "I'll see you in a bit."

I'm walking home and I recognise the purring sound of Evan's car.

I peer under my umbrella at him and he pulls up alongside me. The car window opens slightly.

"Hey babe, what on earth happened to you?" he laughs "when I said you were going to get wet today this isn't quite what I meant."

"I had an argument with a huge puddle; some idiot drove through it and splashed me, I'm just heading home to get changed."

"I was just on my way to the Manor but it can wait jump in I'll give you a lift."

"But I'm wet."

"No change there then," he grins.

I grin too. "Yes but I'll make your nice car wet though."

"It's fine, it'll dry, get in."

I shake off the umbrella the best I can, shivering before getting into Evan's car.

"Are you cold babe?" he grins.

"Freezing." I notice his eyes are looking at my chest because my nipples are poking out through the wet t-shirt I'm wearing, my hair dripping down my face.

"You would definitely win a wet t-shirt competition with those tits, you look so fucking sexy, I like it," he grins. I look down at my breasts and then to Evan's face, his eyes are nearly popping out of his head which makes me smile.

"You like this look do you?" I ask pushing out my breasts and arching my back.

"Jeez I do," he says shaking his head and adjusting his groin, "I need to get you home." He pulls away from the kerb into traffic, I can see he is aroused by the growing bulge in his trousers and I can't help smiling.

We arrive at my flat.

"Thanks for the lift, I'll see you later then," I smile grabbing hold of the car door handle getting ready to get out.

"Hey you're not getting rid of me that easily, I'm coming to help you get changed, you can't torment me with your breasts in that wet t-shirt and expect me to leave."

He knows I wouldn't say no …

"Well seeing as you're here I suppose I could do with some help and it would be rude not to invite you in and show you where I live I suppose."

"I can guarantee you it IS going to be rude when you invite me in," he grins.

We get out of the car and no sooner have I unlocked the door and shut it behind us, Evan is kissing me passionately and feeling my breasts through my wet t-shirt. He then scoops me up in his strong arms and asks impatiently, "Nice flat, where's your bedroom?"

I giggle. "Down the hallway last door on the left." He more or less runs to my bedroom with me in his arms. Pushing the door open with his foot and kicking it shut behind him he places me on the floor next to my bed.

"I like your room," he says looking around and then looking at me with hungry eyes.

"Thanks, oh I've made you all wet," looking at Evan's suit that is damp from carrying me.

"Hmm and I'm going to make you even more wet than you are already," he smiles dropping to his knees and looking up at me.

"Now let's get you out of these clothes," he says turning me on from the way he's looking at me as he begins to undo my jeans. Pulling them down over my hips and down my wet legs Evan is struggling to remove them because they are so wet from the rain that they are stuck to my legs like glue. I sit on the floor to make it easier and Evan prises them off me and as soon as they are off he says, "Stand up, I want to look at you."

He leans back on his feet and looks at me stood before him in a pair of white lace thong knickers, my wet white t-shirt is accentuating my breasts and my nipples are protruding through the material.

"Wow you look so sexy," he says standing up and taking me in his arms holding my bum in his hands and grinding his erection into my front kissing me passionately, his smooth wet tongue finding mine.

"Evan. I can't be long I have to go to work," feeling breathless and not cold anymore but hot with desire cupping his erection through his trousers.

"Don't worry this won't take long," he says.

Removing my wet t-shirt, then my bra and knickers he lowers his mouth to one of my cold nipples and sucks hard.

"OHHHHH," I cry out loving the feeling as he sucks my nipple a few times warming it up and then moving over to the other.

"Lay on the bed," he says his eyes fixed on mine as he kicks off his shoes, unbuckles the belt on his trousers and then undoes the button and zip. Swiftly removing his trousers followed by his boxers he then removes his jacket, just leaving his shirt on.

"This is going to be quick and hard," he growls as he fumbles for a condom from his wallet.

I lay on the bed watching and waiting for him, my heart is thumping fast in my chest at the sight of this gorgeous man coming closer to me with a look of intent on his face as I draw him in like a magnet. Climbing on top of me I help position him at my entrance and pulling my legs up around his waist with one quick thrust his cock is filling me deep.

"OHHH ..." I hang onto his shirt scrunching it up in my hands while he finds his rhythm and pounds into me.

He pants as he grinds his hips plunging into my wetness hard and fast. In and out, in and out, I'm desperately trying to hold onto him with every powerful thrust. He fucks me hard over and over again, the intensity building with every stroke, our orgasms wanting to explode giving our bodies the ultimate waves of pleasure.

"Oh god Evan…"

"Is that good baby?" he asks breathless powering his hard length into my warm insides.

"Yes …" I cry.

"I love fucking you and your incredible body."

"Give it to me, yes … harder!" I moan.

The expertise of his drives is forcing me quickly to my release and after a few more powerful thrusts I can't help the scream out of my mouth.

"Yes … yes … OHH …" and I orgasm a rush of pleasure filling my brain giving me the best feeling.

Evan gives one last powerful thrust and finds his own release. His body stilling then jerking inside me moaning loudly as he comes, we both cling to each other breathless and satisfied.

"Wow." I laugh feeling on a high.

"Whoever that guy was that splashed you with the puddle, I would like to buy him a drink," Evan laughs.

"Me too," I giggle in agreement.

"Well that was unexpected," Evan says burying his face into my neck, his cock twitching inside me.

"Yes it was," I smile as we try to get our breath back.

"I wish we could just stay here all day," I sigh.

"Same here but no can do I'm afraid."

"You didn't have to come here if you have things you need to do I could have walked."

"I did because I needed to come in here." he says thrusting his cock that's still inside me. "And how could I resist these beauties when they were all wet and you were looking sexy in your wet t-shirt," he says kissing me affectionately.

"I suppose I'd better get changed because Sally will be wondering where I am and why I'm taking so long," looking at him laid on top of me not wanting to move.

"Come on then beautiful," he smiles pulling out of me and disposing of the condom in my bin then getting dressed.

"Okay." I sigh wishing we could stay here instead of having to go to work. While I get dressed Evan goes to the bathroom to use the toilet. I can't help the big, satisfied smile on my face.

"You ready?" Evan asks walking back into the room a few minutes later.

"Yes let's go," I follow Evan to the front door lock up the flat and then Evan gives me a lift back to work. "Thanks for giving me a lift and you know," I smile as he pulls up outside Walt's Coffee Shop.

"No problem and thanks for making my morning a whole lot better," he grins.

"Do you still fancy the cinema later?" I ask.

"Yes, sounds good, we can make out on the back row," he winks.

Eight

Arriving home after a quiet day at work I walk into the kitchen to find Jodie preparing some vegetables for dinner.

"Hi Kara, did you have a good day?" Jodie asks looking up and seeing me.

"Yes thanks did you?"

"Yes. Oh did you have a man in the house this morning?" she asks looking at me with a questioning look on her face.

"Err … why do you ask that?" I smile.

"Well when I got home I went to use the toilet and the toilet seat was left up and Matt doesn't do that."

"Really …"

"Yes really, Kara what have you been up to?"

I smile. "Okay you caught me I was soaked this morning walking to work in the rain, some guy splashed me driving through a big puddle at the side of the road.

110

Evan happened to be driving past so he gave me a lift home to get changed then waited to give me a lift to work. He used the toilet while he was here."

"And did he enjoy helping you to get changed?" she smirks.

"Yes he was very helpful." We both laugh.

"When am I going to meet this mysterious man of yours? I keep hearing all about him but I don't know what he looks like."

"I'm going to the cinema with him tonight; he's picking me up from here at 7.00pm so …"

"Oh does that mean I get to meet him then."

"I'm sure you can say hello."

After a shower and some food I sit in the kitchen waiting for Evan to arrive while Jodie washes up.

"Are you nervous?" Jodie asks.

"A bit, I wish he'd hurry up and get here I hate waiting."

Five minutes later there's a knock at the door, "Oh god he's here."

"Yep he's here." Jodie says looking out of the kitchen window, "he drives a posh car doesn't he."

Opening the front door his eyes light up when he sees me.

"Hi." I feel nervous but I'm also excited to see him again.

"Hi." he smiles giving me a passionate kiss.

"Jodie would like to meet you, would you like to come in for a moment and I'll just get my bag and phone."

"Yeah sure." Evan replies.

I show him into the kitchen to where Jodie is stood washing up at the sink.

"Hi, you must be Jodie." Evan says holding out his hand to shake hers.

"Hi and you're Evan, I've heard a lot about you." Jodie smiles holding out her hand with a pink rubber glove on it then realising making Evan laugh.

"Oh sorry," she says removing the pink glove laughing "it's nice to meet you."

"Likewise." he smiles shaking hands with her.

"I'll just get my bag," I leave them talking in the kitchen.

When I return Evan is waiting for me and he looks anxious. 'Oh god what has Jodie been saying to him?'

"Are you ready?" I ask.

"Yes I am, bye Jodie it was nice talking to you."

"Yeah you too, bye Evan."

Jodie gives me a big grin and a thumbs up making me smile before I follow Evan out of the front door.

We get in the car and I turn to look at him. "Are you okay, you looked a bit anxious when I came back from getting my bag, Jodie didn't say anything to make you feel awkward did she?"

"No not at all, she's really nice I was just conscious that I had a hard on after seeing you when you opened the door and that kiss, I was worried that Jodie would notice," he laughs.

I laugh "Oh I see, I'm sure she wouldn't have."

"Hope not, not a great first impression, Hi I'm Evan and this is my dick we're pleased to meet you. Anyway, what film are we watching tonight?" Evan asks.

"It's a porno film is that alright?"

Evan laughs out loud. "Excuse me?"

"Just kidding, it's an action film; it's supposed to be really good."

"Cool I like getting some good action," he winks.

Evan and I arrive at the car hand in hand after our cinema date. He pushes me up against the passenger door and kisses me fiercely.

"Come on we need to go."

"Yes I think we do," I smile.

Evan opens the car door for me to get in then runs around to the driver's side. He couldn't have started the engine up any quicker.

He pulls out of the parking space and speeds off down the road towards The Kingsman Hotel.

"Someone's in a hurry," I laugh looking at him with a sultry look on my face biting my bottom lip.

"I am, I can't wait to rip your clothes off," he growls.

"Don't be getting a speeding ticket will you," I giggle.

"Shit." Evan notices he's doing 40mph in a 30pmh zone and eases up on the accelerator, we soon arrive at the hotel.

Literally dragging me out of the car after giving the valet his keys to park it he guides me inside the hotel and almost runs with me to the lift. As soon as we are in the lift, he is on me kissing me fiercely against the wall, his hands are everywhere on the outside of my clothes.

The lift door opens and Evan picks me up and flings me over his shoulder making me squeal, "Evan!"

He fumbles with his card to open the suite door. Kicking it shut behind us he walks with me straight to the bedroom.

Putting me on the bed he kisses me fiercely, pulls my top over my head and then pulls my trousers down my legs and stands back to look at me dressed in sexy black underwear that looks like it was painted on my body.

"Wow, I'm such a lucky man," he says running his warm hands all over my curves, over my breasts and dragging his fingers upwards over my knickers brushing against my clit.

"Evan," he kisses me and unclasps my bra letting my large breasts become free and lets it drop on the floor and then drags my knickers down my legs.

"Think about how good my cock is going to feel when it's inside you while I get undressed. Think about it sliding in and out of you and how I'm going to make you scream when I fuck you."

"Oh god Evan, please hurry."

I lay on the bed squeezing my thighs together the pressure building in my groin is immense.

Evan starts to undress, our eyes are glued to one another and our expressions show an all-consuming passion for each other.

"Touch yourself, feel what I feel, feel how wet you are. Touch your gorgeous breasts and your pert nipples; think about how it feels when I suck them."

"Evan please ... I need you." I moan desperate for him.

I do what he says and look at him while I'm doing it. Evan is rock hard, he watches me touching myself laid on the huge bed making him wild with desire.

"Evan oh god, I want you now ..."

I squirm the feelings between my legs intensifying craving for it to be his touch, wanting his cock so badly to fill me completely.

"I'm right here babe," he says sheathing himself with a condom then climbing onto the bed on top of me.

"Come here," I pant feeling so turned on and desperate to have him beckoning him to me.

"With pleasure," he says positioning at my entrance and thrusting into me with force causing me to scream in pleasure.

"Kara, your body was made for me, we fit together perfectly," he says powering his cock into me.

"Yes we do, oh god that's so good," I cry hanging onto the bed sheets as he fucks me hard over and over again.

Thrust after thrust after thrust, in and out, in and out, our breathless sweaty bodies riding the waves of pleasure, it's like each time we have sex it just gets better and better.

"You love the orgasms I give you don't you?"

"Yes … YES …" I scream.

"Come for me baby," Evan says through gritted teeth and then one last thrust and we're both moaning loudly as we come together in unison, our brains fuzzy from the orgasmic drug tearing through our minds and bodies.

"I love you … fucking me."

I can feel Evan tense when he hears the 'love' word.

"And I love fucking you." He replies breathlessly.

He rolls off me collapsing onto the bed, feeling shattered.

"Every time is just incredible," I'm so out of breath as I come down from a mind-blowing orgasm.

"We're having lots of fun together aren't we?" Evan says reminding me that this is just sex for fun and nothing more.

"Yes we are," I smile. I can't help but feel disappointed because I really like him. I would love for this thing between us to develop into something more. Every moment we share together and the connection we have is blossoming every day. I want to tell him how much I like him but I stop myself because I don't want to ruin what we have and the last thing I want to do is scare him away.

"What are you doing this weekend?" I ask shutting down those thoughts and hoping that his answer is something involving me.

"I'm driving home for the weekend, I have some stuff I need to do." He replies.

"Oh right," I'm trying not to sound disappointed but failing miserably thinking we were going to be spending the weekend together.

"What's wrong?" Evan asks.

"Nothing I was just thinking about all the things I need to do this weekend."

"Why what have you got planned?"

"Oh I have loads of washing and cleaning to do, then I'll probably pop and see my parents on Sunday."

"Don't work too hard will you, I want you energised and ready for Monday because I will be back then for more sexy time," he grins pushing my hair out of my face and giving me a kiss.

"Don't worry I won't." I gaze into his eyes thinking how gorgeous he is wishing I can keep him forever and wishing I could have him to myself all weekend.

"Do you fancy a cup of tea?" I ask looking at my watch seeing it's nearly 9 o'clock and feeling thirsty.

Evan smiles "I fancy you, but yes now you mention it I do."

"I'll make it," I get up off the bed and walk out of the bedroom to the kitchen area with Evan following.

"Nice bum," he grins and I turn to see he's looking at my naked bum swaying as I walk.

"Thanks," I give it a little wiggle to tease him. "How do you like your tea?"

"White with no sugar thanks."

"Okay," I fill the kettle and put it on to boil then get two mugs from a cupboard. "Have you got any biscuits?" I ask turning around to look at him to see him staring at my naked body. "Like what you see?" I smile.

"I certainly do," he says pushing me up against the kitchen worktop and kissing me.

"Evan I need to make the tea," I giggle batting him away because his hands are roaming. "Have you got any biscuits?" I ask again.

"Yes there are some courtesy ones in that tray over there."

"Oh yes." I select a packet and turn to look at him over my shoulder.

"You want some?" I ask referring to the biscuits.

"Oh I always want some," he smiles coming up behind me and rubbing his cock against my backside.

"Hmm...and what do you want?" I ask playfully.

"I want you and your gorgeous body back in my bed," he says spinning me around and kissing me again against the small kitchen worktop.

"I mean what biscuits you would like?" laughing and loving that Evan always wants me so badly.

"Umm... ginger nut biscuits?"

"You're in luck, here you go." I take a small packet of biscuits off the tray and pass them to him as the kettle finishes boiling. Evan lets go of me and I pour the hot water into the mugs and make the tea. Evan then carries the mugs while I take the biscuits back to the bedroom and we sit up in bed drinking and eating feeling happy.

"Are you a dunker then?" I ask.

"Excuse me?" Evan says looking at me confused.

"Your biscuits, do you dunk them in your tea?"

"No I don't yuk, why do you?"

"No I don't, it's disgusting when bits of the biscuit drop off in your tea and float around."

"Something else we have in common then," he smiles.

"Yes along with many other things. Have you always lived in London?"

"Yes I have, have you always lived here?"

"Yes," I reply taking a sip of tea. "Where do you do your food shopping?"

Evan laughs. "That's a bit of a random question isn't it, I don't I have someone do it for me."

"Really why?"

"Because I don't have time to walk around supermarkets."

"So you actually employ someone to do your shopping?"

"Yes and they clean my house and do my laundry."

"Do they live with you?"

"No they just work regular hours, why?"

"I just wondered that's all. Do you work out because you're pretty ripped?" looking at his toned abs.

"I try to work out a few times a week, I have a gym at home." He smiles cheekily.

"Do you have a treadmill?"

"Yes and weights, a rowing machine, quite a few pieces of equipment really."

"I always go on the treadmill when I go to the gym, I have to wear a really good sports bra though or these babies are bouncing all over the place," I laugh pushing my breasts together making Evan laugh and his eyes light up.

"We should go together; there's a gym here at The Kingsman, how about we go on Monday night after work when I'm back, we could go for a swim as well?"

"Err okay." I agree wishing I'd not mentioned the gym now because I'm getting enough exercise at the moment having sex with Evan never mind doing a session in the hotel gym as well.

"Great, it's a date then," he says grabbing my empty mug and putting it on the bedside table.

Pulling me onto his lap he looks serious at me, "Will you stay tonight, I'll drop you off at home to get changed before work in the morning?" he asks with a pleading look on his face.

"Evan doesn't that go beyond a bit of fun, surely a sleepover is breaking the rules of love them and leave them?"

"Hey, don't say that, look don't read too much into it I just thought it would be nice for you to stay the night that's all," tickling me making me laugh.

"Okay, okay I suppose as it's late I could stay," giggling and trying to pull his hand away from my side.

"Good because I'm not letting you go," he says rolling me onto my back with his body on top of mine.

'I hope you don't let me go.'

Evan continues to tickle me making me squeal.

"Stop, wait," I shout, "I need to text Jodie to let her know I'm not coming home tonight or she will be really worried if I'm not there in the morning."

"Okay," Evan lets go of me "but don't be too long because my urges are getting stronger by the minute." I climb off the bed in search of my mobile looking back at him and get an eyeful of his erect cock.

"Someone looks happy that I'm staying the night," I giggle looking at it and then to Evan.

"Oh yes he is, he is looking forward to sleeping with you all night," he smiles. 'All night, oh my god.'

I find my bag to retrieve my phone and after typing out a quick message to Jodie I join Evan back in bed where I discover his erect cock already has a condom in place he's definitely eager to begin our night of passion.

"That's presumptuous isn't it?" I smile referring to the condom.

"So you don't want me to bury myself inside you all night then?" he grins.

"Well…" and before I can say anymore Evan grabs me and is on top of me kissing me hard and his cock is buried deep inside me.

Nine

Evan

Kara is in the shower so I grab some jeans and a t-shirt to put on temporarily to meet the doorman bringing our breakfast.

While I'm waiting for it to arrive I sit on the bed for a few minutes deep in thought, Kara has overwhelmed me since I met her. We match so perfectly in the bedroom but it's so much more than just the sex. I've connected with her in so many other ways, I love spending time with her and when we're not together I'm constantly thinking about her, she's just always with me.

I don't know how to handle these feelings I'm having, I've always kept women at arm's length since my past relationship.

It's been that way for some time now because that's just how I like it, it's easier that way, no drama, no-one gets hurt. As each day passes I can feel myself getting closer and closer to her and this is not how it's meant to be. My head is telling me one thing but my heart is telling me something else, I'm so confused.

Lost in thought a loud knock at the door makes me jump. Leaving my thoughts locked away for another time I go to answer the door, breakfast has arrived.

Evan isn't long before he's showered, dressed and walking into the lounge area wearing a pair of black trousers, a white shirt and a purple coloured tie, he looks and smells divine. He walks over to me and the lovely scent of shower gel mixed with his aftershave fills my nostrils as I take in the manly smell of him.

"Hmm…you smell gorgeous," I smile.

"Thanks we had better start eating because time is getting on," he says giving me a quick peck on the lips.

"Okay," I put my mobile phone away in my bag and take a seat at the dining table while Evan gets the two breakfasts out of the server trolley.

"What were you doing with your mobile?" he asks.

"Oh I was just texting Jodie a quick hello while I was waiting for you."

I watch him dish out the breakfast, "So, what have you got on today?" I ask picking up the napkin and placing it on my lap.

"Well, I have black trousers, a white shirt and a purple tie," he grins sitting down to eat.

"Haha very funny I mean what are your plans for today?" picking up the knife and fork cutting into a piece of bacon and popping into my mouth.

"Well I'm heading over to the Manor when I've dropped you off at work and then once I've been there I'll be popping back here to get my stuff then driving back home this afternoon."

"Oh I thought you were driving home tomorrow tonight."

"No, I thought I would head off back to London because I'm not needed at the Manor tomorrow. How's your breakfast?" he smiles.

"It's yummy thank you, I'm so hungry I think all the sex we've been having has increased my appetite loads."

After finishing our breakfast Evan takes me home for a quick change into some fresh clothes and then drops me off at work.

"I'll see you Monday night then, have a good weekend and behave yourself." Evan says giving me a kiss before I get out of the car.

"Yes I will, you too," I smile.

"No going out and chatting up other men."

"Don't worry I'll be staying in catching up on some sleep after all these late nights I've been having," I grin "anyway I don't need to chat up any other men because I'm quite happy with the man I have regularly at the moment thanks."

Evan laughs then gives me a long lingering kiss to last us both over the weekend.

"See you Monday beautiful and don't forget we're going to the gym."

"No I haven't forgotten see you Monday," and I get out of the car and wave to Evan as he drives off.

I missed seeing Evan on Friday but I was glad it was the weekend after having such a busy week. I also was able to spend time with Jodie and paid my parents a visit.

As I lay on my bed Sunday evening flicking through a magazine my mobile phone rings, finding it in my bag I pick it up and see Evan's name on the screen.

Feeling excited I answer the call.

"Hello."

"Hi beautiful, missing me?"

"Yes I am actually, there's no fun when you're not here."

"Don't worry baby, I'll be back tomorrow and then I can give you all the fun you need."

"Good, what have you been up to?" I smirk.

"Working mostly I've just been in the gym for an hour, I'm all sweaty."

I imagine him wearing a pair of shorts and a sports t-shirt dripping with sweat, his hair all messed up looking sexy, oh my god I bet he looks so fit. "What are you wearing?" I ask in a sexy voice.

"I have some white shorts and a black sports t-shirt on, why what are you wearing?" I can tell he is smiling, he knows I'm picturing him.

"I have a short white skirt on and a red crop top."

"Hmm I can picture you wearing that," he replies in a husky voice.

"Hmm and I can picture you all sweaty."

"I've got a hard on thinking about you now."

"Have you really?"

"Yes I have. I always get a hard on when I think about you, you've seen how you affect me."

"Yes I have and I like it. I'm really missing our fun."

"Yes I am too. I miss being able to touch your naked body and to feel how wet and ready you are for me."

"Evan … you're making me horny."

"I bet you're wet now aren't you, touch yourself tell me what it feels like," he says taking a deep breath and blowing it out slowly.

"Oh god … okay … I'm putting my hand in my white silky knickers and I'm wet because just the sound of your voice does things to me and I'm dragging some of the wetness with my fingers to my clit and I'm rubbing myself, I'm rubbing light circles around and around and hmm it feels so good, I wish it was your fingers doing this to me."

"I wish it was too, I wish I was there with you now."

"So do I, touch yourself and imagine it's my hands on you, tell me what you are doing and how hard you are."

"God I'm so hard for you baby, I've pulled my shorts down over my cock and I'm stroking it up and down slowly and imagining how it feels when I slide inside you."

"Oh god Evan, you turn me on so much, why do you have to be at home?" I pant.

"I know, we'll be together again soon, touch your breasts tell me how they feel."

"Okay … I'm pushing my top up and I'm pulling the cups down on my white silky bra. My nipples are erect and

I'm rubbing one between my fingers making it harder with my touch. It feels so good, I love it when you suck my nipples it turns me on so much," I moan.

"Hmm … I love sucking your nipples … I'm imagining swirling my tongue around the sweet nub and sucking it making it harder and making you moan."

"God Evan this is so hard not being able to touch you, to feel you."

"I know baby, my cock is aching for you … tomorrow baby, tomorrow we get to have fun again, touch yourself Kara, imagine it's me doing it and how I make you feel."

"OHHH … I'm so wet…"

'How can someone turn me on so much?'

"I want you to carry on touching yourself and tell me what you're doing and then I want you to finish so I can hear you down the phone."

Luckily Jodie isn't in so I can make as much noise as I want and knowing she won't be back until gone 10pm I'm more than happy to do what Evan says.

"Oh yes … oh god … I'm rubbing myself circling my clit with my fingers, I'm soaked, it's giving me tingles all over and it feels so good."

"That's it baby, keep doing it, tell me how it feels, I'm with you baby."

"Oh god my breasts are aching for your touch and I've got a throbbing ache in between my legs, I can feel my insides tightening, I wish your cock was inside me filling me deep," I pant.

"I wish it was too. I'm rubbing myself imagining how it feels when it's inside you and I'm thinking about what you are doing, keep going baby," he says sounding really turned on.

"I can feel tingles, I'm rubbing my clit and the pressure is building. I'm closing my eyes and imagining it's your fingers. Oh god … it feels good … Oh … I'm so turned on, I'm imagining your tongue tasting me …" I'm breathless and I can hear Evan at the end of the phone also breathless.

"That's it baby; keep going, I'm with you baby," he says struggling with his own feelings.

"Oh god I'm almost there … oh yes … oh god that's so good."

"Kara you're turning me on so much."

"Oh god, yes, oh god oh god, Evan I'm going to come … YEEEESSSSSS …" I scream and my orgasm rips through me and I'm moaning down the phone over and over again, breathless and panting while Evan listens to me.

I can hear Evan down the line and he sounds like he's getting close.

"OHH, those noises you are making is tipping me over the edge, shit," his breathing is erratic and I can tell he's almost there. He finds his own release moaning loudly while I listen to him. The sounds Evan makes when he finishes is the most beautiful sound, I love listening to him it makes me feel elated knowing that I've done that to him.

"Holy shit …" Evan pants.

"I've never had phone sex before that was awesome," I laugh and he laughs with me.

"I'll let you into a secret, neither have I."

'I didn't think there would be any 'firsts' left for Evan, but I am glad this one was with me.'

"I can't wait to bury myself in you tomorrow, you'd better be ready for me."

"I can't wait either and don't worry I'll be ready."

Ten

"Morning Sal, it's a lovely day," I smile walking into work.

"Morning Kara, it certainly is for a Monday morning, did you have a nice weekend?"

"It was okay it would have been better if I had spent it with Evan though, he went home because he had stuff to do. Oh, how was your anniversary meal on Friday night?"

"We didn't end up going unfortunately because I had a bloody migraine."

"Oh no and you were really looking forward to it as well."

"I know, anyway Tim said we will go out this Friday instead for a meal to celebrate."

"That's good then. I'm going to the gym tonight with Evan which I'm really looking forward to ... NOT ... followed by a swim, Evan's idea, not mine."

"Oh I don't know … it might be nice watching him working up a sweat and then seeing him in a pair of speedos."

'I'd rather he was working up a sweat on top of me.'

"Yeah, he's got a great body Sal."

"Hmm I can imagine," she grins.

I pick a sexy multi-coloured striped bikini rather than an all in one swim suit and stuff it into a gym bag along with a towel and go into the hall to put my trainers on.

It's 6.30pm on Monday evening and Evan text during the day to say he will be picking me up on his way back from the Manor and it will hopefully be around 6.30pm to 7.00pm.

Jodie has gone out with Matt and I'm sat in the kitchen tapping my fingers lightly on the kitchen table waiting for Evan to arrive. I check my watch impatiently every five minutes to see what the time is.

'Hurry up.' I think just as there is a loud knock on the door. Taking a quick look through the kitchen window and seeing Evan's Aston Martin parked out front I squeal with delight and run to the door. No sooner have I opened the door he's walking in picking me up so I'm straddling his waist and he is kissing me fiercely against the wall.

Our tongues mingle wildly like they are having a dual and my hands are clasping his head as we enjoy reuniting with a passionate kiss. Pulling away he puts his forehead on mine and looks into my eyes, "Hi beautiful."

"Hi." I've missed him. He places me down on the floor and stands back to look at my attire. "Wow you look hot in gym gear," he smiles looking me up and down. "God knows how I'm going to work out without getting a hard on with you looking like that, I'm hard now."

"Well we can always skip going to the gym and go to bed instead?" looking at him with a sultry look on my face moving closer towards him and cupping his erection.

"No we said we'd go to the gym so we'll do some warm up exercises before we hit the bedroom and then we'll really have a workout, besides you're dressed for the occasion now," he grins moving my hand away.

"I can soon undress for the occasion in your bedroom," I pout with pleading eyes.

"Kara as much as I can't wait to have you, we did say we would go to the gym and after we've had a swim you can have me as much as you like in the bedroom and that's a promise," he says smacking my bum as I bend down to get my gym bag from the hallway floor.

"Ouch, okay deal," I reply grinning at him.

Arriving at The Kingsman Evan gets changed quickly into his gym clothes constantly trying to fight off my advances because I want him to change his mind and have some sexy time but he's not giving into me so we both walk into the gym full of men and women working out.

"What do you want to go on first?" he asks.

'First, I only want to have a go on one thing and then leave.'

"I'll just go on the treadmill."

"Okay I'll join you."

Programming the machine for 10 minutes I start running at a steady pace and Evan takes the machine next to mine and starts running. I notice Evan keeps glancing my way and it's not because he wants to look at my face but he's checking out that the sports bra I'm wearing is doing a good job of keeping my boobs in place.

"Hey I can see you looking at my boobs."

"I was just checking they're not escaping."

"No they are firmly in place thank you," I smile.

After 10 minutes of running Evan has barely broken into a sweat and I'm the complete opposite red faced and slightly out of breath.

"What do you want to go on now?" Evan asks.

"I want to go on you," I puff.

"But we've hardly done anything," he laughs.

"Please can we just go I've missed you," I pout trying to persuade him.

"I tell you what I'll just lift some weights for a while, you can watch if you like, then we'll go for a quick swim and then we'll go back to my room."

"Yes please, I'm just going to get some water from the water fountain, do you want some?"

"Yes please, I'll be over there at the bench press."

I walk over to the water fountain and just as I'm filling a cup with water a tall muscly guy comes over to me.

"Hi I haven't seen you in here before," he smiles taking a cup and filling it with water after me.

"Hi, I've not been here before."

"That's why I haven't seen you then, I would definitely remember your face," he smiles "I work here, are you staying at the hotel?"

"No I'm just visiting a friend who is staying at the hotel."

"Oh right, I'm Jason and your name is?"

"Kara."

"You look like you work out, you're in great shape," he says looking up and down my body and focusing his eyes on my chest.

"Err thanks, I should get back to my friend."

I begin to feel awkward, I finish my drink quickly and fill another cup with water to take to Evan.

"Hey I'll come with you I can show you and your friend some of the equipment."

"No it's fine really."

'Oh great, Evan is not going to like that.'

"It's no problem, where is she?" he asks.

'Oh he's assumed I'm here with a girl.' I ignore him and walk off towards Evan but the man follows and places his hand on the small of my back making me feel really uncomfortable. Thankfully Evan is too busy lifting weights to notice. 'I wish this guy would just go away.'

"Thanks for the offer but I'm fine really I'm going soon anyway," I smile hoping he will take the hint and go away but he doesn't.

"Oh that's a shame, listen I know this is forward but I think you're really nice can I take you out for dinner sometime, maybe tonight?"

"Err... no sorry but thanks for asking," I reply nervously looking across to Evan and seeing him getting up off the bench press with a face of thunder.

"Are you single?"

"Yes I am but..."

"Come on let me take you out?" he insists.

"Sorry, but you're not my type I'm not interested thanks."

"If you're single I don't see what the problem is?" he asks clearly not listening to what I'm saying and not liking being rejected and crowding my personal space.

"I'm the problem," Evan says stalking over to us and standing in front of me sandwiching himself between us both.

"Excuse me and you are?"

"The lady is telling you she is not interested."

"Listen it's between her and I, so jog on mate it's none of your business."

"You jog on, she's with me and she is telling you that she is not interested so do everyone a favour and go find someone else to annoy."

Evan is squaring up to the guy who is much bigger than he is but he doesn't seem to care. I'm stood behind him wishing there was a hole in the ground I could jump in to escape.

"So you must be the friend, listen mate she told me she is single."

"Well that may be so, but it still doesn't change the fact she is not interested."

"Oh whatever I don't need this. There are plenty of other women better than her that wouldn't pass up a chance to go out with me," the man says turning his back to us and walking off. Evan moves towards him looking ready to knock him out for being so rude.

Shit, I grab his arm spilling some of the water in the cup I'm holding "Evan leave it, the man is an idiot, please can we just go I really want to go."

"Dickhead…" Evan mutters under his breath taking some deep breaths to calm down. "Come on let's get out of here."

I put the cup of water down on a nearby shelf and Evan takes hold of my hand and leads me towards the exit of the gym.

"I'm sorry he just started talking to me and then he followed me I couldn't get rid of him."

"No, I'm sorry for bringing you here with all these men gawping at you, I didn't like him coming on to you, it made me mad."

"I told him I wasn't interested but he was clearly not listening."

"No he was too busy staring at your tits," he snaps sounding jealous, "I didn't like seeing you two together."

"We weren't together."

"I didn't like…"

"What? You didn't like what?"

"It doesn't matter, come on."

"Are we still going for a swim?" I ask as Evan pulls me along behind him wanting to leave the gym as soon as possible.

"No we're going back to my hotel room because if that guy was acting like that seeing you in your gym outfit I can only imagine I will be fighting men off you if they see you half naked in your swimsuit," he says pulling me through the gym door and back to reception to take the lift to the Penthouse Suite.

I can't help smiling, I love the fact that Evan is obviously jealous and squaring up to the beefcake in the gym it seems like he will do anything to protect me, maybe he is starting to develop feelings for me.

Arriving back at Evan's hotel suite his mobile phone rings from his gym bag and looking to see who it is he rejects the call and throws it back into his bag.

"Who was that?" I ask.

"It was my mother; I'll call her back some other time. Do you want a drink?" he replies glumly.

"I'm fine thanks."

"Do you want anything to eat?"

"I'm fine thank you, I know what I do want though."

"And what's that?" he says grumpily.

"This," I smile cupping him through his shorts.

Evan smiles, takes hold of me and kisses me deeply then scoops me up in his arms and carries me to the bedroom while I kiss his neck smelling his aftershave mixed with sweat feeling intoxicated by his pheromones.

"I'm sorry for getting mad," Evan says seeming more relaxed now.

"It's okay and thank you for rescuing me."

"Would you have said yes to going on a date with him if I wasn't there?"

"No I wouldn't have, he wasn't my type anyway, why?"

"I was just wondering and what is your type?"

"You."

Evan grins and falls onto the bed with me in his arms then kisses me slowly and gently, I love kissing him. He then starts to peel off the layers of my clothing which doesn't take long considering I'm not wearing much.

"Hmm, this is sexy!" he laughs holding up my sports bra and throwing it to one side.

"It's not supposed to be sexy; it has a very important job to do of keeping these babies under control." I reply pushing my breasts together making Evan stare at them with hungry eyes.

My desire for him is getting stronger.

I help him to undress until we're both naked and desperate for one another, Evan quickly grabs a condom.

"Are you ready for me baby we need to make up for lost time?" he grins climbing onto the bed and hovering over me. I reach for his cock and help him position it at my wet entrance.

"Always," as he pushes into me slowly we both moan and cling to each other revelling in the fact we are together again, both of us happy to be in each other's arms again.

The intense feeling has us both breathless and Evan picks up the pace, both of us having missed the closeness and the contact of our bodies grinding together harmoniously.

Evan doesn't say anything but keeps powering on bringing us closer and closer to our release. Feeling turned on to the max because we haven't had sex with each other for two days we are soon reaching our climax clinging to each other's naked bodies and enjoying an orgasm together. Pushing my hair out of my face Evan kisses me passionately like he's missed me just as much as I've missed him but he just can't bring himself to say the words. Rolling off me he disposes of the condom then takes me into his arms cuddling me close and stroking my arm with his fingers.

"Hey do you want to stay tonight?" he asks.

"Yes I would love to, I haven't brought any spare clothes with me though because I didn't want to assume I was staying."

"I've told you before, you don't need any clothes when you're with me," he grins as I look at him thinking he's just perfect.

I smile stretching my neck upwards so he kisses me.

"Let's get a shower and then snuggle in bed," he suggests.

We take a shower together both of us helping to wash each other's bodies and then after getting dried we wrap ourselves up in the fluffy white hotel robes courtesy of the Kingsman and go back into the bedroom. Sitting at the dressing table blow drying my hair Evan stands watching me.

"You really are beautiful," he says admiring me in the reflection of the dressing table mirror.

"Thank you," Evan looks at me like I'm the most beautiful flower that was ever created, he's always complimenting me and he makes me feel so special.

"Shall we sit in bed, watch some TV and order some snacks?" I ask turning off the hairdryer feeling hungry.

"Sounds good after that workout I am a bit peckish."

"Are you referring to the gym workout or the bedroom workout?" I grin.

"Both, here you have a look what food you would like while I dry my hair," he says passing me a room service menu looking gorgeous, his hair wet and mussed up.

Choosing to order some fries with seasoning salt, Evan rings through the order on the hotel phone then joins me on the bed while we wait for the food to be delivered.

After 15 minutes of watching a film there's a knock at the door and the fries have arrived. Evan collects them from the door dressed in his robe and then joins me back in bed to sit and eat them.

"Hmm … these are yummy," I moan tasting one and putting another one in my mouth.

Eating the fries and watching the film snuggled together on top of the bed it feels like we are meant to be.

I wish he would say how he feels about me, because he is definitely acting like we are more than just a casual thing and I know for sure I'm not imagining it.

I'm desperate to hear words like 'I really like you' and 'will you be my girlfriend?' but after the conversations we've had previously I know that Evan saying those words to me is probably never going to happen so I have to remind myself not to get my hopes up and to just enjoy the moment.

Eleven

During lunch the next day I'm sat in the office eating a ham and pickle sandwich and playing a game on my phone when I receive a text.

Hi beautiful hope you are having a good day, fancy meeting up later, I could pick you up from your flat at 6.00pm on my way back from the Manor? Don't eat anything we'll have dinner together. E xx

I can't help the big smile on my face as I text him back.

Hi 6.00pm is perfect and I look forward to another dinner date, see you later. K xx

I press send and continue to eat my lunch. Thinking I won't hear anymore from him I go to put my phone in my bag and it beeps again.

Great and bring your toothbrush and a change of clothes for work because you are staying at mine tonight I've decided. See you later. E xx

Oh you have decided have you well I would have gladly accepted your invitation anyway. K xx

Finishing off my lunch I'm feeling excited because in just a few hours I will be seeing Evan again. Starting back to work with a big smile on my face I look forward to the end of the day.

At 6.00pm Evan is on time and pulls up outside my flat. Not giving him the chance to get out of the car because I'm eager to see him I say goodbye to Jodie and then run down the path with my bag of overnight clothes to Evan's car.

Getting in the car I'm greeted with his handsome face smiling at me.

"Aww couldn't you wait to see me, you were literally running out of the house when I pulled up, not that I minded, I enjoyed watching your tits jumping up and down in that top," he grins.

I roll my eyes and smile at him. I'm wearing a low-cut black top and a short white mini skirt showing off my smooth legs.

Evan looks at my cleavage, then finds my eyes "I like your top," he whispers then leans over to me and gives me a slow hello kiss.

I smile. "Thank you. Actually I was looking out of the window and saw you pull up so I thought I would save you from getting out of the car seeing as you are getting on a bit."

"Hey cheeky, I'm only five years older than you and I have the stamina of any 20-year old," he grins.

"Yes I know," I blush.

"I thought I could show you around the Manor before we head back to the apartment for dinner, if you fancy it?"

'I definitely fancy it.'

Evan is wearing some dark grey trousers and a white short sleeved shirt today with no tie and he looks gorgeous as always.

"I would love to have the grand tour of your new hotel."

Evan pulls into the tree lined road off Danes Avenue and then drives down a private road for approximately half a mile until reaching the Manor where it's stood in all its glory. It's an impressive building from the outside with stone pillars either side of the large oak front door. It's a Victorian Manor house with huge sash windows and there are lots of them.

"Wow, I can see why you wanted to buy it, what a gorgeous house; I've lived here all my life and never knew this was even here," admiring its grandeur.

"Thanks, wait until you see inside I think you are going to be impressed," he says excitedly pulling up outside the front door and cutting the car engine.

"Are the building contractors still here?"

"No, they've gone, it's just us babe," looking at me with a glint in his eye. He jumps out of the car and moves around to the passenger door to open it for me.

I step out of the car and I'm immediately taken into his arms for a mind-blowing kiss. I've been counting the hours all day until I can feel his mouth on mine again and as our tongues mingle with each other I start to feel sensations that I can't help whenever Evan is around.

"Ready to have a look around my new hotel?" Evan says excitedly sounding like a kid at Christmas after opening a much-wanted present.

"Yes I can't wait," I reply breathless as Evan takes my hand and leads me to the impressive large oak front-door.

He unlocks it and opens it for me to step inside.

The first thing I notice is the size of the hallway, I look up to see a huge chandelier hanging from the expansive ceiling. "Wow."

"You haven't seen anything yet Kara, I'll show you upstairs first." He takes hold of my hand and guides me through the sizeable hallway and up a grand oak staircase that takes us to a galleried landing.

"There are currently 12 bedrooms here at the moment but I'm having a huge extension out to the side and at the back to increase the accommodation to 120 luxury bedrooms," he says as I look out one of the huge windows to look at the view of the extensive grounds at the rear of the property. Evan continues, "there will be 10 suites with uninterrupted views of the stunning grounds once the landscapers have completed their work. It's also going to have spa facilities, a swimming pool, a gymnasium, a wedding ceremony and function room, a restaurant and bar and in the grounds a Heli-pad will be available too."

"Wow it sounds amazing Evan it will be stunning once it's finished." His passion for his career is a real turn on.

"Don't other hoteliers get a bit annoyed when you start building your new hotel in the area because they might lose business?"

"Well my hotel is tailored towards people looking for a touch of luxury and class and they will need to have a bit of money to afford the nightly rate I charge. The smaller hotels won't suffer because they are on a different price range altogether and places like The Kingsman will only benefit because we can help each other out with referrals at busy times. Plus the Kingsman is on a much smaller scale to what my hotel will be once it's finished and a bit of healthy competition doesn't hurt any business."

Evan stands watching me with his hands in his pockets smiling at my reaction as I look around commenting how much I like the place, then he takes me to the last room that he has to show me on the tour.

"And finally this is the games room which I am planning to keep as it is for guests. Can you play?" he asks gesturing towards the full-sized snooker table occupying the centre of the room.

"Not really," looking at the snooker table in front of me.

"Here let me teach you," he grabs a snooker cue from the rack on the side wall and then demonstrates what you do.

He pots a ball into one of the pockets then says "Here you have a go." Passing me the cue to hold.

I place my fingers on the green baize cloth of the table like he's shown, bending over the table. My short white mini skirt rides up slightly giving Evan a great view of my upper thighs. While Evan stands behind me I slide the cue slowly in and out of my fingers eyeing up a ball to take the shot. Just as I'm about to hit the ball Evan comes closer, our bodies press together and I can feel his cock twitch in his trousers against my bum. I take the shot and pot the ball.

"Yes," I squeal.

"Well done," he whispers in my ear giving me goose bumps. "It's your turn," I go to stand up but Evan holds my hips and the next thing I can feel is Evan gyrating his arousal against my bum. "I've changed my mind there are other things I want to play that are far more interesting than a game of snooker."

I stand up leaving the snooker cue on the table and Evan places his hands on the tops of my bare arms and rubs them up and down before turning me around slowly. I look up into brown eyes which are dark with lust and the expression on his face is that of a man who wants a woman so badly, it's like a craving that he just has to have. Evan keeping his eyes fixed on mine trails a finger over the tops of my breasts that are visible from my low cut top and then moving his hands over my breasts he feels my erect nipples through my top and begins circling them gently with his thumbs sending tingles down to my core.

"Hmm I love that," he moves towards me and gives me a slow sensual kiss his tongue finding mine. Reaching for the hem of my top he gently pulls it off over my head and throws it to one side onto the snooker table. He stares at my breasts covered in a silky bra and places his hands over them again massaging them through the silky material kissing me passionately while doing so.

While we are kissing he reaches around my svelte back stroking up and down my soft skin feeling for the clasp on my bra and finding it he unclasps the hook releasing my large breasts which are begging for his attention. Throwing the bra on the table alongside my top he sucks in a breath at the sight of them and licking his lips he begins cupping them gently with his hands looking straight into my eyes.

"I've missed these," he smiles rubbing my nipples with his thumbs increasing the tingling sensation I'm feeling between my legs.

Lowering his mouth to one of my nipples and sucking it hard I can't help the loud moan that escapes, "Oh god."

I lean against the snooker table throwing my head back and arching my back enjoying the feeling as he teases it with his mouth. Circling his tongue around the tip of my nipple and massaging the fullness of my breast with his hand he carries on sucking and nibbling turning me on.

"Oh that's feels so good," I moan and he moves to the other nipple and performs the same routine.

"I love your tits," he breathes devouring and playing with them. Letting go of my nipple from his mouth he picks me up in his strong arms and lifts me onto the green cloth of the snooker table and encourages me to lay back. Naked from the waist up I feel the soft green baize material against my bare back as I lay there staring at him while he continues to caress my breasts with his warm hands. I moan feeling tingles making me wet and hungry for Evan to be inside me.

"Evan I want you, I need you inside me please," I pant.

He grins moving the delicate lace material of my knickers to one side, then pushes two fingers inside me making me cry out. "Evan please," I moan and he rubs my clit with his thumb causing me to thrash my head from side to side from the intense feeling.

"Soon baby," he says pushing his fingers in and out teasing me, I'm panting becoming more and more turned on to the point that I'm needy and desperate.

"Oh god Evan, I need you now," I cry as he pleasures me with his fingers, my insides grabbing them and I'm wishing it's his cock instead.

Moving his hands to the sides of my knickers he takes hold of the lace thong and tears them, ripping them off me and throwing them to the floor making me gasp.

Evan is eager now to be inside me and he is painfully hard, he's becoming impatient, he gently pulls me closer to the edge of the snooker table in readiness for filling me completely.

Reaching around to his back pocket of his suit trousers he quickly takes a condom out his wallet and pulling his trousers and boxers further down his legs, his cock is now ready and hovering at my entrance.

"Jeez you look hot laid there waiting for me to fuck you," he grabs hold of my hips and pushes inside slowly at first then pulls out and with one fast move he thrusts into my opening with force.

"OHHH ... "

He claims my body with his, the connection of his cock inside me and the explosion of feelings raging throughout my body while he moves in and out is incredible.

Evan is overcome with wild urges as he pounds into me hard over and over again while I try desperately to cling onto the edge of the snooker table, every thrust hits the spot sending me wild.

"Oh god Evan, yes that's so good," I pant and he drives into me more and more.

"Jesus," he groans as my body grabs his length over and over again.

"Yes, oh yes keep going," in and out, in and out, once, twice a few more times and then I cry out "I'm so close," and seconds later my body shakes and I'm moaning loudly as my orgasm takes over.

Evan thrusts in and out a few more times and then he stills finding his own release whilst jerking inside me while he leans over my body exhausted and breathless. Looking at the post orgasmic expression on my face he strokes my cheek with the back of his hand, "Do you realise how beautiful you are Kara Davis, your body is amazing, your tits are amazing, you are amazing and I can't get enough of you," he smiles.

We stare into each other's eyes intensely while we come down from our ecstasy.

"I think I like this game of snooker better than the real version," I giggle making Evan laugh as he pulls out of me.

"Me too." He disposes of the condom in one of the waste bins in the room then puts his cock back in his trousers.

"Are you okay?" he asks smiling and returning to the table where I'm still laid half naked with a contented grin on my face.

"Perfect," I reply. Evan helps me down from the snooker table and then I pull down my skirt which is bunched up around my waist.

"I think I owe you some more knickers," he laughs picking up my ripped thong off the floor and tossing them into the bin alongside the used condom.

"Yes I think you do," I smile.

Evan takes me in his arms and kisses me.

"Are you ready for some food now because you need to build your strength up for later, that was just for starters?" he smiles pushing my blonde hair back away from my face.

"Yes I'm starving and I'll look forward to having you again later," I smile picking up my bra and top that Evan had put on the snooker table earlier.

Not only am I enjoying the best sex I've ever had in my entire life with an amazing man but I have had so many unbelievable orgasms. I am just the luckiest girl in the world.

Twelve

The sun is still shining when we leave the Manor but there's a chill in the air. Evan locks the front door and notices me shivering, so offers me his jacket.

"Here you look cold baby," he smiles wrapping it around my shoulders. I can smell Evan's manly scent as I hold the jacket close to me.

"Thank you." I smile as he opens the car door for me to get in. I sink down into the soft leather of the passenger seat and Evan gets into the driver's side and starts up the engine. "Thank you for showing me the Manor, I love it and I would love to come back and have a look when it's finished and officially open," I say taking one last look at the place before Evan pulls away from the house driving down the lane to the main road.

"Yes you must, I'll send you an invite to the official opening when I have a date and I might even give you a private viewing of one of the suites," Evan winks.

"Oh okay, but that's ages from now and you never know I might have a boyfriend by the time the hotel opens because you won't be around here to keep me entertained will you?" I joke trying to get a reaction from him about how he feels about me.

Evan's facial expression turns serious, "Look I know we have only known each other a short while and it's crazy because I feel like I've known you my whole life. Yes I will leave and go back to London, but I will come back at some point and I would like to see you again for more fun so no boyfriend okay?"

His comment annoys me. 'What the hell, so he expects me to be at his beck and call?'

"So you expect me to wait around for you until you come back? I can't just put my life on hold Evan, I mean you may not want a relationship but I might at some point in the future and if I meet someone nice I'm not going to turn them down because you want me to wait around for you so you can have more fun with me."

The happy atmosphere in the car turns sour. We both should have known this was going to get complicated.

Evan's annoyed, "I know we agreed we are just having fun, so I have no right in saying this but I would appreciate it if you didn't get with other people. It won't be that long before I'm back and I would really like to carry on seeing you. Also I don't like hearing about you being with other guys, just the thought of you with another man makes my blood boil."

'Where has all this come from? Was it the guy at the gym last night that's triggered this?' I was only joking and now he's gone all serious dictating that I can't see anyone else.

He's acting like a jealous boyfriend and he's the one who wants to keep things casual, he can't expect me to keep myself locked away when he leaves and wait around for him to return. I feel more frustrated and angrier by the minute.

"Hang on, am I misunderstanding something here? You can carry on coming to and from London to see me as and when it suits you, yet I am supposed to wait for you and not so much as look at another guy?" I scowl, "and I am just supposed to be okay with that? You never get to make that decision, boyfriend or not, which you are not."

Evan lets out a big sigh and looks angry. "Yes I know I am not your boyfriend, but I feel very strongly about faithfulness. If you want to sleep around then we may as well stop this now because being unfaithful to someone is the worst kind of sin in my book."

"I don't believe this, can you stop the car please," I seethe.

Evan pulls over at the side of the road. I'm so mad I get out and slam the car door and pace up and down the footpath.

'Who the hell does he think he is dictating to me like that? And accusing me of being unfaithful?'

Evan gets out of the car and watches me pacing up and down like a mad woman.

I glare at him with angry eyes, "I do not appreciate you saying I want to sleep around, I have never done that and I am offended by you insinuating that I would. I have always been faithful to my past boyfriends and you clearly don't know me if that is what you believe."

"I'm sorry I shouldn't have said that," he says his hands in his pockets clearly regretting his comment.

"I'm trying to work out what your problem is Evan. I have never given you a reason to not trust me. All I can assume is someone has hurt you in the past?" Evan looks at me with an agitated look on his face. "Someone has been unfaithful to you in the past haven't they? That's why you don't do relationships isn't it and you don't let yourself get close to people?"

He looks at me with a blank expression.

"Yes and I don't want to talk about it," he snaps taking

his hands out of his pockets and walking over to a nearby wall and sitting down on it.

Feeling awkward but till annoyed I take some deep breaths to calm down then go and sit down next to him. We sit in silence for a few minutes.

"Listen, I'm sorry that someone has been cruel to you in the past but you can't punish me for their mistakes. I have had the same done to me too, I was cheated on by my ex. I'm sorry if my comment about other men annoyed you but I was merely saying I don't just want to be someone's bit of fun all the time. I do want to keep seeing you but I am not waiting around just to be someone to have sex with as and when it suits you. You can't organise your life like your business Evan."

Evan is in a dark mood now and is lost in thought and I wonder if I've ruined things between us. But why should I put this guilt on myself, when it is on him?

"I understand and I'm sorry for the things I said and upsetting you," he says with a serious face getting up off the wall and walking back over to his car. He turns to look at me. "Are you coming?" he asks.

"Yes." I hastily reply.

I'm not sure whether I want to but it's a long walk back to my flat and I don't want to leave things like this between us.

We travel back to the hotel in silence neither one of us knowing what to say. The atmosphere in the car is unbearable. Evan's mobile phone rings in his trouser pocket breaking the silence.

I look over to Evan, "Do you need to get that?"

"No it's fine I'll see who it is when we get back to the hotel."

Arriving back at the hotel Evan pulls up for the valet to park the car, as his mobile phone starts to ring again. Evan looks at his phone and rolls his eyes, "Damn it, I'll just check you in and you head on up, I need to make a call I'll be there in a minute," he says sternly.

I'm not even sure if I want to go up to his hotel suite now, I want to go home but I hate falling out with people so I walk into the hotel with Evan hoping that after his call he will have calmed down and things can go back to normal.

Luckily the usual receptionist isn't at the desk tonight, I'm pleased as I don't want to give her the satisfaction of knowing we've had an argument.

I enter the lift and we both stare at each other until the doors close. While I'm travelling up to his suite Evan goes back outside to make his phone call. Travelling in the lift alone tears fill my eyes, we were having such a good time and now I feel like everything is ruined between us.

Wiping a stray tear away from my cheek I think to myself I must be strong, the last thing I want is Evan seeing me as weak, so I pull myself together, walk into the Penthouse Suite, take off Evan's jacket and sit and wait for him.

Evan

"Fuck," I pace the floor outside the hotel feeling stressed and agitated, I could do without this phone call.

"Hello, what can I do for you?"

"That's a nice way to greet your Mother isn't it?"

"Sorry you just caught me at a bad time that's all."

"I phoned you yesterday and you didn't answer?"

"Yeah sorry I didn't call you back, I was busy."

"Too busy to talk to your Mother."

"I do have five hotels to run soon to be six, but I don't suppose you know what it's like to be busy, living the life of luxury on your yacht? How is life in Monaco?"

"Life is great thank you."

"Are you still with your toy boy what's his name?"

"Rory? No, I have a new young man now."

I laugh. "Why am I not surprised, what's the new one called?"

"His name is Ace and he is a true gentleman."

"Ace, what sort of a name is that and how old is this one?"

"He's just turned 32 and he's adorable; we had an amazing champagne party for his birthday last week on the yacht."

"Oh wow Mother, since Father you do like them young don't you, he's only two years older than me, god I don't even want to think about it."

"Well the young ones are more virile."

"I really don't want to know. As much as I love to chat what do you want, why were you trying to call me?"

"Well I wanted to know how you are and also to ask if you have spoken to Sebastian?"

I sigh. "Not this again. I'm fine and I've told you before Mother I don't want to talk about him; I don't even want to hear his name, why won't you accept this?"

"You can't keep ignoring him; things are not going to be resolved unless you talk to him."

I can feel my shoulders beginning to tense up as I pace the pavement outside the hotel rubbing a hand through my hair.

We have had this conversation time and time again and it is always the same outcome.

"How many times, I am not interested in making up with him, why don't you ever listen for fuck's sake?" I yell.

"Calm down if your Father was here he wouldn't hear of you speaking to me like that."

"Yes, but he's not here is he and if he was things would be different wouldn't they."

"I know but you can't blame your Father, he was only doing what he thought was best. You need to fix things Evan, stop being so stubborn and just sort things out with him."

"I know," I sigh. "but you can't always fix things that are beyond repair anyway if that's all you wanted I will say goodbye."

I remain quiet for a few moments and I can hear my Mother crying at the other end of the phone. "Look don't cry, I apologise for upsetting you but you need to understand he is no longer and never will be a part of my life."

"I'm sorry I just wish things were better that's all, you used to be such good friends," she cries.

"I know, look take some deep breaths and go and get a brandy or something and I'll speak to you soon okay?"

"Okay Son, take care, speak to you soon."

I end the call and feel even more agitated than I did before, why can't my Mother just leave things alone. I take some deep breaths to try and calm down then walk back into the hotel and board the lift to my suite mulling over our conversation in my head and it's making me more unsettled by the minute.

Evan walks into the room and I can sense his mood hasn't improved from when I left him downstairs in the hotel lobby.

"Is everything okay?" I ask trying to be nice but also curious to know who he called.

"Yes fine," he snaps walking over to the hotel mini bar and getting a bottle of whisky and pouring himself a glass. He then downs the drink in one go while I watch him, slamming the glass down on the kitchen counter making me jump and inhale sharply. I can hear him swearing under his breath then he walks over to where I'm sat looking confrontational.

"Well you don't look fine to me and I was only asking you don't have to bite my head off."

"I'm sorry," he says looking at me regretful.

"No I'm sorry, I don't think this arrangement we have going on is working between us, I'm leaving."

I grab my bag from the floor and stride past him towards the door but I don't get very far because he stops me by grabbing me by the arm. I spin around to look at him and give him a filthy look.

"Do you mind, let go of my arm please," Evan takes a deep breath and lets go.

"Look I apologise I shouldn't have snapped, please don't go can we just forget the last half hour and start again, I really don't want you to leave."

I don't look at him because I'm so mad I just stand there thinking for a moment. I really don't want to leave either because if I do then things will be over between us and it's not what I want.

"Okay I'll stay, but please don't take your shitty mood out on me." I walk past him and take a seat on the couch again putting my bag back down on the floor.

There is an awkward silence between us and Evan is pacing up and down looking like he's trying to find the right words to say to make me feel better while I scowl watching him.

Evan is the first to speak "I'm sorry, I don't want to fight with you, please forgive me. Let me get you a drink to relax and then we can enjoy the rest of the night," he says giving me one of his sexy smiles which makes me melt every time.

"I'll have a glass of white wine please and make it a large one," I answer looking at him with a serious face.

"Your wish is my command," he smiles walking over to the mini bar.

After pouring a large glass of wine he pours himself another whisky and then joins me on the couch.

"Kara, I'm sorry the phone call I received it was my Mother and we've just had an awkward conversation and what with our conversation in the car earlier I just got a bit wound up. My Mother she is quite controlling and I don't agree with her at the best of times, something we have always struggled with. Our conversation just then was one of those times when she is trying to control me and because I don't agree with her she doesn't like it. I am a grown man with my own decisions to make. My childhood best friend… well we don't speak anymore and my Mother keeps trying to intervene, she is trying to get us to resolve our differences but I'm not being forced to do something I don't want to do."

"I understand," I grab hold of his hand. "Thank you for apologising and I appreciate you telling me." I smile.

'How can I stay mad at him when he is opening up to me and looking at me the way he is?'

"Let's forget about it now and have some dinner because I don't know about you but I'm starving." I smile.

"Okay and thank you for being understanding."

Evan orders us some dinner which we eat sat at the dining table and once we have finished he heads to the fridge in the kitchen area and emerges with strawberries and cream that he ordered for dessert.

"Would you care to join me in the lounge?" he asks cheekily.

"Okay." I take a seat on the sofa.

"I thought we could make desert a bit more interesting. I thought I could feed you your strawberries first and then I will have mine after you," Evan says picking up one of the bowls of strawberries and pouring some cream over the top of them.

'Oh that's not what I thought he was going to say.'

I smile liking the idea. Evan plunges the silver spoon into the strawberries and cream and then looks at me. "Open wide," he smiles popping a big, juicy, red strawberry smothered in cream into my mouth.

"Hmm …" I start to chew it and some of the juice from the strawberry and cream dribbles down my chin.

Evan leans forward and licks around my chin mopping up the sweet stickiness. "Hmm delicious," I moan swallowing the fruit. Evan brings his mouth to mine and we kiss.

"More?" he teases. I'm so aroused as we taste each other.

Evan continues to feed the strawberries to me in this way until all the strawberries and cream are finished, licking up the stray droplets of juice and cream from around my mouth and kissing me after I've swallowed the fruit.

I want Evan so badly my hands are starting to wander.

"Oh no, not yet I haven't had my strawberries and cream," looking at me cheekily but with lust and desire in his eyes.

"But I'm so turned on now and I need you, can't you have yours later?" I plead trying to grab hold of him for a kiss.

Fighting me off, Evan stands up from the couch leaving me sexually frustrated, he has worked me up into such a frenzy I'm desperate for him.

I look at him pouting.

Wanting to hurry things along I'm just about to pour some cream over Evan's bowl of strawberries when he stops me.

"Wait!" I look at him confused and he takes the jug off me and puts it back onto the coffee table.

Without saying another word he takes the bowl of strawberries off me and walks over to the kitchen area, cheekily grinning back at me.

'What's he doing?' I see him pick up a knife and he starts cutting the strawberries into halves.

He looks at my confused face and grins. "These are too big I need them smaller," he says and continues to cut them up into small halves. 'I don't know why he needs them smaller, surely he can fit them into his mouth? I mean I've managed to fit bigger things than that in my mouth and never complained.'

Evan places the knife onto the kitchen worktop and comes back over to where I'm sat. "Now I'm ready for my dessert, but first I need to lay the table," he grins.

I frown continuing to look at him with a puzzled look on my face.

Evan walks over to the dining table with the bowl of strawberries and jug of cream and places them on the table. He then comes over to me and holds his hand out for me to take.

"Take your clothes off and lay down on the table," he says with a glint in his eye. Just hearing those words spoken in Evan's sexy voice has me feeling tingling sensations between my legs.

I smile at him as I pull my black t-shirt up over my head and then remove the rest of my clothes and footwear while Evan watches my every move.

Once naked he helps me onto the large oak dining table where I lay down in readiness for what's to come next.

"Oh the table's cold," I squirm.

Evan's eyes are roaming all over my naked body looking at me laying there feeling exposed.

"You look sexy laid there naked waiting for me" he says leaning down to kiss me.

I fling my arms around his neck bringing him closer as our tongues explore our joined mouths. Evan peels my arms off the back of his neck eager to start his dessert.

I wriggle on the table from the coldness of the soft polished wood on my back, it's giving me goose bumps all over my body, the cold feeling making my nipples protrude prominently which doesn't go unnoticed by Evan.

He licks his lips looking at how erect my nipples are and he can't resist running his tongue over the peak of them in small circles making me moan in appreciation.

"Hmm …" Evan leaves me turned on and panting to pick up the bowl of juicy cold strawberry halves then carefully places them onto my torso making me wince.

"Oh god that's so cold," I shiver and he grins at me while he continues placing all the delicate pieces of fruit onto my body.

"This is going to feel even colder," he says when all the pieces of fruit are in place.

I tense as Evan slowly pours some of the cold fresh cream all over my body and it trickles down my sides.

The sensation of the cold cream is almost impossible to bear but it looks and feels so erotic seeing the cream trickling all over my breasts, stomach and in between my legs making me a tasty treat for him to devour.

"Oh, wow Evan," I shift slightly as some of the cold cream trickles down onto the table.

"I know baby, try and lay still," he says putting the jug of cream down away from me then moving closer.

"Hmm... you look delicious," he smiles his eyes roaming up and down my smothered naked body, my breathing escalating as I try to lay still which is proving to be difficult because the anticipation of Evan's mouth on me is turning me on to the extreme.

"You look amazing Kara," he takes a strawberry from my body and sucks it into his mouth getting cream all over his face.

He then kisses me and lets me lick the cream off his mouth and face before devouring another strawberry. After he's eaten all the halves of the strawberries, he then concentrates on my breasts licking the cream off each one sliding his tongue over my erect nipples licking and sucking until all the cream has gone.

"Oh my god you turn me on so much," I moan squeezing my thighs together, the pressure building in my groin.

Moving lower onto my stomach he licks around my navel lapping up the cream like a cat enjoying a delicious treat until I'm all licked clean. Then trailing his tongue downwards onto one of my legs he runs his tongue up and down my inner thigh "Please Evan… please," I open my legs wider, I'm throbbing and aching, desperate for him to trail his tongue there. He licks up my other leg and then slides his tongue in between my legs licking the cream that trickled into my creases earlier. "OHHH … shit."

He traces feather light circles on my pulsating clit, licking and sucking as I writhe and moan loudly on the table.

"Does that feel good baby,?" he asks, my breathing rapid.

"Oh yes, so good." I pant.

"Hmm you taste delicious," giving me a few more strokes of his tongue.

Evan carries on pleasuring me with his mouth and tongue and I can't hold back any longer his expert strokes have brought me quickly to my release. I cry out and my body stills then jerks as the most powerful orgasm rips through my body like a wild tornado. I push Evan's mouth away not being able to take any more, I'm moaning over and over again feeling the ripples of ecstasy travel through the whole of my body.

"Shit." I swear not being able to help it due to the intensity of the feelings I'm experiencing, "that was out of this world."

"You enjoyed it then?" Evan laughs.

"That was phenomenal," I giggle with contentment and happiness. "If we ever fall out again you can make it up to me by doing that," I laugh.

Evan gives me a moment to come down from my powerful orgasm, he strokes my hair and smiles seeing the fixed grin on my face, my breathing now having returned to normal.

"Are you okay?" Evan asks.

"I'm perfect."

"That was honestly the best strawberries and cream I have ever tasted and now, because we are both sticky we're going to have a shower and then I'm going to fuck you," he smiles and picks me up in his arms.

I giggle, "Let's make it a quick shower then," clinging to his neck kissing him as he walks with me in his arms.

Arriving in the bathroom Evan puts me down on the marble floor of the shower and quickly strips off until he's naked giving me a good look at his impressive manhood.

He then joins me in the shower under the warm water.

"As much as I can't wait to be inside you I need to wash all this stickiness off you first," he says grabbing some shower gel. He washes my breasts and in between my legs to rid me of the remnants of the cream and strawberry juice. The tingling feeling has returned as he brushes over my clit. Panting softly he touches me there, the steam from the shower making everything so erotic and I've never felt so good. When Evan has finished rinsing me off I grab the shower gel off the shelf and look Evan in the eyes with a sultry look. "My turn." I squeeze some into my hand then put it back on the shelf.

I massage the soap into the fine hairs on his chest while kissing him passionately pushing him back against the shower wall. I plunge my tongue into his mouth while he holds my face in his hands.

"We need to hurry up with the washing," he says and moans when I grip his hard cock sliding my soapy hands up and down his erection.

Evan closes his eyes feeling my hands on him and continually moans from the pleasure I'm giving him. The warm water is splashing over our naked bodies while we kiss passionately in the double shower, the body wash trickling down over my breasts as Evan cups them.

While I continue to stroke his cock we kiss each other deeply, the sexual chemistry between us is immense and we are aroused to such a level that we are both getting needy and impatient.

"I need to feel you inside me," I plead.

Evan breaks the kiss. "I need to get some protection hold on."

I grab his arm and stop him, Evan looks at me. "Have you always used protection?" I ask feeling brave.

With a serious face and looking super sexy as water trickles down his face, his hairy chest moving up and down from how turned on he is he answers, "Always, the only exception was with my girlfriend and that was a while ago now."

'What?' I let go of his arm and frown. "I thought you said you don't do relationships?"

Evan takes a deep breath, "I don't now, my one and only serious relationship turned out to be a complete sham and I was burnt so badly I have trust issues so I choose not to get involved with anyone because it's easier that way."

"So you like to keep things casual because of a bad relationship. Not all relationships are bad Evan, you've just had a bad experience that's all. We have all been there. I don't know what else I can say to make you trust me."

"Look I don't really want to talk about it my cock is aching for you so let me just grab a condom and then we can carry on doing what we were doing a minute ago." He turns to walk away from me and I grab his arm again to stop him.

"Wait you can't spend the rest of your life just flitting from one woman to the next. What about love and marriage and having kids one day maybe?"

"Why can't I? I'm quite happy with my life Kara and falling in love is not all it's cracked up to be someone always ends up getting hurt somewhere along the line. I can't go through … look you don't understand it's complicated and I don't think having kids would be a good idea either trust me it's best for everyone if I just stay detached."

"I might understand if you talk to me about it? You are so lovely and deserve to be loved I think you have a lot of love in here to give if you just let yourself." I smile placing my hand over Evan's heart.

"You're probably right Kara but I can't take the risk so it's not going to happen, anyway please can we stop talking and start fucking?" he says caressing my face.

His eyes are glowing saying 'I want to fuck you'.

"Okay but this conversation is not over Evan."

I lunge pushing him against the shower wall and kiss him with so much passion. I need to break down these walls that he's built up and show him that love can conquer all and it is worth taking the risk. Evan picks me up so I'm straddling his waist and we kiss each other fiercely. Our tongues are fighting with each other and I want him more than anything so I reach down between our wet naked turned on bodies take hold of Evan's hard cock and guide it to my entrance.

"Kara wait what are you doing?" he pants, "I need to get a condom."

"I want you to fuck me Evan, I want this now, I'm on the pill, I'm clean and I'm assuming you are too if you've always used condoms …"

"Yes I am but …"

"I want you Evan, no condom, just you and me skin to skin." I say assertively waiting for his acceptance.

"What are you doing to me Kara?" he says looking at me tormented, "you make me want to do things with you that I haven't done in a very long time and this is not how it should be." Evan is obviously struggling with his feelings and having trouble deciding what the right thing to do is, I think his head is saying no but his heart and his cock hovering at my entrance is telling him to go for it.

I want to feel closer to him. I decide the best course of action is to take the initiative so I take hold of his cock and gently guide him a small way inside of me then I rotate my hips slowly and move around on his tip showing him how good it feels and he draws breath.

"Kara no, we can't … we shouldn't."

"Do you want all of me Evan because I want all of you?" I breathe looking him straight in the eyes. He blows out the breath he's been holding.

"More than anything but I can't do this Kara, it's not fair to you I will fuck this up and hurt you and it's not what I want to do. Once I am inside you there is no going back and …"

'He wants to more than anything but he's scared.'

I push down, forcing all of him inside me.

"Fuck, Kara no … shit." Evan doesn't move but he doesn't pull out of me either.

I think he wants to and what was supposed to be a bit of fun is now so much more than that even if he can't admit it and face the truth.

Moving my hips around I give him just what is needed "Fucking hell you feel so good," he screws his eyes shut like he's in pain but he's clearly enjoying the closeness of being buried deep inside me skin to skin.

"Feel us Evan, feel how good we are," I pant. I know he wants this too.

"Fuck it," he can't resist me any longer he holds my hips and pounds into me over and over again. "Oh Jesus … you feel so good," he pants the feeling of his bare cock being squeezed by my insides egging him on more and more.

He kisses me fiercely, our tongues and mouths are thrashing together and we can't get enough of each other.

We're both breathless and overcome with desire, our bodies are entwined and so in tune with each other and Evan inside me feels amazing.

The physical and emotional connection is so strong I'm in a place that I never knew existed until I met Evan, we have a connection beyond anything I have ever known before.

As I move up and down on his cock again and again it's not long before the most powerful, mind tingling orgasm rips through my shaking body making me scream.

"OHHH …" Evan joins me groaning loudly filling my insides with his seed as he spills into me.

I've never felt such an amazing feeling of togetherness.

"Wow, you are so perfect Kara," he says holding me close, his heart thumping in his chest.

"You are too and I think I'm …"

I stop myself before I say something I will regret because he's not ready to hear it yet.

I must be crazy falling in love with a man I've only known for a short while but I have, I can't explain it, I've never felt like this before. I so desperately want to tell him but I don't, he isn't ready to hear it and it is not the right time.

Things have moved at lightning speed since we first met and normally I would only just be at first base in a relationship never mind declaring my love for the man.

The more time I spend with him the more I don't want to give him up.

I have to show him that he can't live without me and I have to use every power of persuasion I have to change his mind about us before he leaves town.

"What, you think you're what?" Evan asks wondering what I was going to say.

"I was going to say I think I'm ready to get out of this shower and go to bed and snuggle," kissing him softly then lowering my legs from around his waist to the floor because they have become stiff from holding on to him for so long.

"You really didn't need to do that you know," he smiles turning off the spray and walking hand in hand with me out of the double shower.

"I know but I wanted to and I'm glad we did," I smile.

"You do realise we can never use a condom again now? When you orgasmed around me I felt every spasm it was awesome that I don't want to use them with you ever again," he smiles pulling me to him giving me a slow, sensual kiss.

"Then we won't," I smile.

"You cold?" he asks looking at my breasts.

"Yes, how can you tell?" I grin wrapping the nice warm towel around my naked body. Our hair is dripping wet so Evan grabs another two hand towels from a shelf unit at the side of the towel rail and we both dry each other's hair tenderly.

"I'll just get my bag I need my hair brush," leaving the bathroom to find my bag of overnight clothes I had left in the lounge earlier.

"Okay babe don't be long," he says wandering into the bedroom to find his comb. I return with my bag and I'm greeted with the magnificent sight of Evan's perfectly toned muscular body in just a towel combing and styling his hair. 'God I'm so lucky.'

"What are you thinking about?" Evan smiles noticing I'm deep in thought.

"Nothing much just that I'm pleased I'm here and I'm having a lovely time," walking over to him and placing my palms on his chest looking up into his eyes and then reaching up for a kiss.

"Let me brush and dry your hair beautiful."

"Oh no it's okay you don't have to do that," reaching into my bag and getting my hair brush out.

"I want to," he smiles.

Evan takes the hair brush off me and gestures for me to sit down in front of the mirror at the white distressed dressing table. I sit on the gold covered seat of the chair and he begins brushing my long, wet blonde hair.

Evan

Kara is so beautiful, I can't stop looking at her, the curve of her nose, the outline of her lips and her high cheek bones. What is wrong with me?

How can she make me feel like I never want to look at another woman again?

I can't believe we just fucked without a condom, it felt amazing. Being so close to her skin to skin felt incredible.

I don't know what the hell am I doing?

I don't want a relationship and I definitely don't want to fall in love not after what happened last time.

I keep telling myself I must keep this casual, it's for the best but it's so hard because she is just impossible to resist.

I can't help myself when I'm around her and when I'm not with her I can't stop thinking about her. 'God I'm in trouble!'

Why does my life have to be so complicated?

I think about how much I adore him, the way he looks at me, the way he makes me feel, the way he has taught me that sex isn't just a quick fumble he's definitely not a selfish lover. I love how attentive he is and how he treats me like I'm the most important thing in the world even though he tells me that I'm just a bit of fun.

I love the fact that we've had sex without a condom, surely that means something, surely if he really didn't want to be that intimate and close to me he would have stopped it? Does he have feelings for me?

Tears spring in my eyes. I want more than anything to have the happy ending that I've always dreamed of and Evan is certainly the type of man I can see myself with. There is no doubt in my mind, I'm falling in love with him.

Evan notices the tears in my eyes looking at me in the reflection of the mirror.

"Hey, what's wrong?" he asks concerned seeing me wipe away the tear falling down my cheek.

"Sorry I'm just being silly no man has ever treated me as nice as you do and it's such a refreshing change."

He looks at me with a serious face. "Unfortunately, there are some bad people in this world Kara, you just have to try and steer clear of them and surround yourself with people who are good for you."

'I wonder if he's referring to his childhood best friend he's fallen out with as one of those bad people? I go to ask him but stop myself, that's a conversation for another day.'

Thirteen

"Good Morning, hmm you smell nice," Evan says coming up behind me and kissing me on the side of the cheek as I put my make up on looking in the bathroom mirror.

"Thanks so do you." I smile getting a waft of his aftershave.

"I've just ordered a full English breakfast for us both, it will be here in 10 minutes."

"Lovely thank you, oh god what about the dining table and the strawberries and cream?" I panic remembering the mess.

"Don't worry it's all taken care of," he smiles.

I finish applying my make up then join Evan in the lounge area, sitting on one of the black leather couches.

"So what have you got on today?" I ask.

"Well I've loads of business calls to make so I'm here this morning, then I have an interview with a newspaper this afternoon.

They want to take photos of the Manor before and after the renovations are completed for a feature.

They are going to print its progress in the paper starting next week which will be great for business."

"That's brilliant," I eagerly respond.

"Oh and I have a business dinner with an interior designer tonight so I'm sorry baby, but I won't be able to see you later."

"Oh okay, I have stuff I need to do anyway. Sounds like you have a busy day planned."

'Damn I really wanted to see him later, I hate it when I don't see him.'

"Yes I do I'm afraid," he sighs.

There's a knock at the door and breakfast has arrived. Sitting down to breakfast I don't feel hungry anymore looking down at my full English.

'What is wrong with me? It's one night that he can't see me and I'm acting like I've just received the worst news ever. If I feel like this now how am I going to feel when he goes back to London? After not seeing him at the weekend and staying with him for the past two nights and getting closer I desperately want to spend time with him.'

I stare at my bacon and eggs feeling fed up and Evan notices I'm not eating.

"Hey, are you okay?" he asks looking at me playing with my food.

"Yeah, I'm fine I'm just not that hungry that's all."

He gives me a sideways glance, I think he knows I am off about something, but I don't want him to know why, so I excuse myself from the table leaving a half-eaten plate of food and walk off leaving Evan alone to finish getting ready for work.

I brush my teeth then apply some lip gloss and just as I finish sweeping the pink lip gloss over my lips, I feel Evan's presence, he's standing in the bathroom doorway watching me.

"Are you okay?" he asks looking concerned.

"Yes I'm fine" I smile.

Once Evan has finished getting ready he grabs his car keys and mobile phone off the bedside table and then we head out the door to the lift.

We step outside and it's a lovely sunny day, there is no breeze today and as we drive in the sunshine to my place of work Evan notices I'm quiet.

"Okay what's going on, you're quiet, it's not like you?" he asks. "Have I upset you because if I have it wasn't intentional?"

"No I'm fine really, I just feel a bit tired today that's all,"

I smile hoping that he bought my excuse.

"Okay, well here we are the delightful Walt's Coffee Shop," pulling over outside the shop. "I'll call you later after my business dinner okay? Have a good day." He leans towards me and gives me a lovely lingering kiss.

"Okay and you have a good day too," I reply grabbing hold of the car door to open it.

"I hope she's not one of those boring types that just goes on and on about wallpapers and paint colours all night or I might be texting you to come and rescue me." He smiles, "she sounded quite young on the phone though so I don't think she will be."

"Oh right well its sounds like you might have fun tonight then, bye," and before Evan can say another word I jump out of the car and walk through the door of the coffee shop not looking back. Hearing Evan pip the car horn as he speeds off down the road I walk up to Sally who is stood behind the counter filling up the cakes in the glass cabinet.

"Morning love how are you?" she asks looking up giving me a friendly smile and then noticing my face. "Oh Kara, whatever's the matter?"

I burst into tears and walk through to the back office. Sally comes to find me.

I'm sat at the desk with my head in my hands sobbing, I must look like such a sad case.

"What's going on in that pretty head of yours?" she asks putting her arm around me.

"I … I'm just being silly."

"Kara love," I look at her and she smiles handing me a tissue from the box on the desk so I can wipe my eyes then Sally takes a seat opposite me.

"Thanks Sally," I sniffle trying to pull myself together.

"What's wrong, I take it this has something to do with a certain gorgeous businessman, am I right?"

Sally is such a good friend to me she always makes things seem better whenever I have a problem.

"Yes, you're right, I just feel so stupid."

"Why, what's happened?"

I take some deep breaths and stop myself from crying so I can speak, "Nothing really apart from meeting a drop dead gorgeous man who is just so amazing, I feel so happy whenever I'm with him and I know it probably sounds silly seeing as I've only known him a short time but I'm developing feelings for him. I honestly feel like I've known him all my life, we get on so well and the chemistry between us is just electric. The problem is he's just not available."

"What he's married? Oh my god Kara."

"No Sally, he's not married! He doesn't have a girlfriend it's nothing like that he's not available emotionally because he doesn't do relationships, he's a love them and leave them type."

"I see," Sally raises her eyebrow looking concerned.

"He was clear to me in the beginning it was just a bit of fun and I must not develop feelings for him but how can I not when he is just so wonderful. He says the nicest things to me Sal and he makes me feel so special. I'm confused because one minute I feel like he likes me more than just a bit of fun but then he says something to make me think that's all I am to him. I have spent the last two nights with him and it was amazing. I'm falling for him and I just can't help feeling I'm going to get really hurt. It's my own fault because I knew the deal from the beginning it's all just such a mess," I sniffle. "I either keep seeing him but the more I see him my feelings are getting stronger or the other option is to finish it but then I may end up regretting it and making the worst decision of my life."

"Oh sweetheart this is a tough one."

"I think I would rather be with him for a short while and enjoy every moment we have together than not have him in my life at all but I just don't know. What shall I do Sal?"

I ask putting my head in my hands.

Sally is just about to speak when my phone signals a message from my bag.

"Do you think that's him?" Sally asks looking at my tear stained face.

"Maybe, I'll have a look," I fish my phone out of my bag "Yes it's him."

"What does it say?"

Hi beautiful thanks for another amazing night, I love waking up with you, I hope you are okay and I haven't done or said anything to upset you? I'll be in touch. E xx

"He knows you are upset then?"

"I was quiet this morning and he noticed after he told me he couldn't see me later. He's has a business dinner tonight with some young interior designer woman. When he said he couldn't see me I felt really disappointed and knowing he is meeting another woman I just felt jealous but I've no right to be because we are not even together. I don't know what's wrong with me, maybe I'm just hormonal or something."

Sally smiles at me. "I think you already know what's wrong, you're in love and from what you have told me about him it sounds to me like he is just as much into you as you are him. The thing is you are acknowledging your feelings and he isn't."

"Sally you are always the voice of reason." I nudge her.

"Love works in mysterious ways darling. Stop beating yourself up about how you feel, of course you will have feelings for him when you are being intimate with each other and he is treating you nice. He is kidding himself, it seems to me he is choosing to ignore what is really going on here." Sally looks me in the eye, "You need to do what makes you happy and what's best for you."

"I just don't know Sal." I shrug my shoulders.

"You often have to take a risk in life Kara and sometimes it pays off but you will never know unless you do. Also you said it sounds silly because it's only been a short time knowing him but you've heard the saying 'love at first sight' it is possible to have that connection with someone straight away I mean I should know because as soon as I saw Tim at the newsagents when we were both grabbing for the last banana on the shelf for our lunch I just knew he was the one."

"What you've never told me how you two met?" I smirk wiping my eyes and feeling a bit less tearful.

"Haven't I? Well I went into the newsagents on my lunch break when I was working at the flower shop and Tim was in there too. We were both hovering around the fruit section and as Tim went to grab the last banana on the shelf so did I. He took hold of the banana on one end and I held the other and our eyes met. He looked into my eyes and said, 'Sorry, you take the banana' and I giggled and said 'I can't take your banana?' He laughed and I looked at him for a moment, noticing he had lovely ginger hair and you know how much I love ginger hair, anyway he smiled and said 'Okay then why don't we share it?' so we sat outside on the newsagents wall and the rest is history. Look at us now we have been happily married for two years and been together for eight years. I knew at that moment he was the man I wanted to marry." Sally talks about Tim like a school-girl crush, she is still so dreamy eyed about him, I long for a love like that.

"You knew you wanted to marry him because he gave you his banana," I smirk then let out a big belly laugh.

"Well if you put it like that Kara, it just takes all the romance out of it," Sally smirks.

I can't help laughing as tears are no longer falling down my cheeks from being upset but from the story of Sally's first meeting with Tim.

"Well at least that's made you laugh and feel a bit better even if it was the story of Tim's banana."

"Oh don't, you are making it worse, I'm never going to look at bananas the same way again now."

"Kara, it was a piece of fruit that he was offering nothing else, I thought it was sweet."

"Hmm … I bet you did I bet when you were eating the banana you were thinking it was something else." I giggle.

"Behave, I was not thinking anything of the sort," she says with a cheeky grin.

"No seriously thanks for the chat and the advice Sal, love ya."

"No worries my love, I'm always here for you if you need me. Now go and wash that pretty face of yours because you don't want to scare the customers with your tear stained face and I'll go and open up," she smiles.

"Thanks Sal, will do, see you in a minute."

I turn on the cold water tap, scoop some of the cold water into my hands and wash my face.

I look in the mirror above the sink and Evan pops into my mind in fact I can't stop thinking about him full stop. I wonder what he's doing, who is he with and then remembering his business dinner this evening I wonder who this woman is he's meeting. I hope she's not attractive, the jealous feeling coming over me again, I hope she's really boring and he finishes the meeting early and wants to see me.

Turning off the cold water tap I dry my hands on the hand towel take one last look in the mirror to check my hair then walk back into the shop feeling better than I did earlier and with a smile on my face I'm ready for another day at Walt's Coffee Shop.

I arrive home at the end of the day to find Jodie and Matt sat in the kitchen drinking a cup of coffee. I am slightly jealous of how settled they both are I wish Evan and I were like that.

I don't fancy much for dinner so I make myself a sandwich and head to my bedroom leaving them to have some alone time. It's not long before I hear giggling and noises coming from Jodie's room which makes me even more jealous, because that is what I could be doing right now if Evan wasn't having dinner with another woman tonight.

I decide to go for a nice relaxing bath to soothe my aching muscles from a busy day at work and lots of sex with Evan last night.

Pouring some bubble bath into the jet of water it starts to foam as the bath fills with water and white soapy bubbles and the smell of caramel, vanilla and white musk fills my nostrils.

I get undressed and step into the hot bubbly water, lay down and close my eyes hoping it will take away the stress of my predicament on whether I should continue seeing Evan or not.

Who knows Sally could be right he might feel the same way about me and he's just not admitting it. But if he doesn't and I carry on seeing him knowing how I feel about him I'm just going to end up getting hurt.

After laying in the bath for a while until my fingers are starting to turn wrinkly, I wash my hair and shave my legs then grab a towel and wrap myself in it.

Looking into the steamed mirror I wipe it with the back of my hand so I can see myself and stare at my tired face. How can I stop seeing Evan he is the best thing that has ever happened to me and what else have I got going on in my life? Nothing! If I keep seeing him he might realise he has feelings for me and I still might get my happy ending after all. It's like Sally said 'You often have to take a risk in life and sometimes it pays off but you will never know unless you do.'

Feeling more positive I dry myself and get dressed then go back to my bedroom to dry my hair. I'm drying my hair thinking about Evan when I remember I didn't text him back when he text me this morning. I bet he thinks I'm ignoring him especially after being quiet this morning when he dropped me off at work and thinking he has done something to upset me. I find my phone and type out a text.

Hi Mr Hamilton, sorry I haven't text you back before now, you haven't upset me and I'm sorry for making you think that you had. I've been busy and I was quiet this morning because I was tired. I hope you don't enjoy your dinner date too much this evening like when you have dinner with me. K xx

I wonder if he'll text back? Don't expect anything he's probably off enjoying himself already with that woman.

I sigh and throw my phone on the bed but to my surprise my phone beeps almost instantly and Evan's name flashes up on the screen, he's sent me a reply.

My heart skips a beat.

Why Miss Davis, I thought you had forgotten me or fallen out with me as I haven't heard from you all day. I'm pleased you are ok. I am meeting Miss Radley at 8pm in the hotel restaurant so I'm just making myself presentable and don't worry Kara I only order room service when I am with you. You're not jealous are you? E xx

Mr Hamilton, I have not forgotten you in fact you are all I think about these days and for the record I am not jealous, why should I be? K xx

I am so jealous. Beep, another text.

You don't need to be jealous. I am a one woman guy and frankly I don't have the energy because you are enough for any man. I however would be jealous if it were you going to dinner with another man. E xx

I smile thinking I can use this piece of information to my advantage.

How do you know I am not going for dinner with another man? I like that you feel jealous. K xx

After pressing send I suddenly regret what I put remembering the argument we had about me mentioning being with other men, 'Shit what did I have to put that for.' I wait anxiously for his reply, it comes instantly.

Don't say things like that Kara you know I don't like it, the thoughts of you having dinner or even being with another man makes me mad.

I am only having a business dinner that is all. Don't worry beautiful, the only woman I will be thinking of is you. E xx

I can't help but feel the relief from reading Evan's text thinking Sally could be right, he is kidding himself and has feelings for me. He is definitely acting like I am more to him than fun, you don't say things like that to someone you are supposedly just fucking. I smile and send my final text feeling happier because it's nearly 8pm and Evan will be going for his meal soon.

Ok Mr H, I feel a lot better now knowing that and I'm sorry for making you mad. I wish I could make it up to you. Have a nice meal and I look forward to seeing you soon. K xx

Feeling thirsty and fancying a cup of tea I go to the kitchen and see Jodie washing up at the sink.

"Hi, where's Matt?"

"Oh he left about 10 minutes ago, he has a darts match on tonight so has gone home to get ready."

"Oh right, I heard him getting some practice in hitting the bullseye earlier so I'm sure he will be on form later."

"Sorry," Jodie grins flicking some water at me from her washing up gloves, "we were trying to be quiet. Anyway I'm dying to know, how did it go last night staying with Evan?"

I fill Jodie in on what's been happening and how confused I am about everything and she thinks the same as Sally. This makes me feel much happier knowing it's not just me getting mixed signals from him thinking it's more.

After having a good chat about our day and what Jodie has been up to it's getting late and time for bed so we say good night to each other and take ourselves off to our bedrooms.

After getting ready for bed I check my phone before turning off the light to see if Evan has sent any more messages but there isn't any which reignites my jealousy again. I can't help but allow my mind to wonder if he's in his hotel room with her. I bet she's gorgeous and he couldn't resist her. No please don't let that be true. I think about the texts he sent me earlier and decide I have to trust him.

Don't read too much into it Kara. I turn off my bedside light and forgetting my worries I make myself comfortable and go to sleep.

Fourteen

It is Thursday morning and I open my eyes to a sunny bedroom as light pours in through the curtains.

Sitting up in bed and turning off the alarm I think about the first time I met Evan and our time together, making me smile.

Since having a chat with Sally and Jodie yesterday I'm feeling a lot more positive this morning and also the reassurance of Evan's text last night before he went to his business dinner has made me feel more settled about things.

I turn on my phone but I'm disappointed when there are no messages from Evan this morning. Deciding not to dwell on it and that I need to be more relaxed about things, I get up out of bed and get dressed. Putting on a knee length red skirt and a navy round necked blue top with white silky underwear underneath I go to the kitchen to get some breakfast.

"Morning Jode." I say in a chirpy voice seeing her sat at the kitchen table eating a bowl of cereal.

"Morning Kar, you seem happier are you feeling better today after our chat last night?"

"Yeah much better, thank you for listening to my moans."

"That's okay, I think you just need to take each day as it comes and go with the flow."

"Yeah you're right."

I put my phone on the table and get a bowl from the cupboard then help myself to some muesli and join Jodie at the table. *PING!*

While I'm tucking into some muesli my phone signals a text and feeling excited I pick it up with a smile on my face hoping to see Evan's name flash up on the screen. I open the messages and my smile drops, it's a text from my mum.

"Is that Evan?" Jodie enquires.

"No it's my mum she's inviting me around for dinner tonight."

"Oh right, have you not heard from him since he went for a meal with that woman then?"

"No not a thing since he text me last night just before he went to dinner with her, hopefully he will contact me later. I'm going to go and have food with my mum because I can't hang around waiting for Evan all the time, I've already told him I'm not here for his beck and call. Anyway, he cancelled me last night to go out for dinner with some woman, he hasn't text me this morning so he will have to be the one sat home alone being bored."

"I like this side of you Kara, what do I always say to you? 'Make them work for it,' if he likes you he will put the effort in so making yourself unavailable for a night will do him some good. Say hi to your mum for me won't you."

"Yeah will do."

"Matts coming around later after work I think he wants to go out for dinner somewhere. Anyway, I'd better go as I have some marking I need to finish before the kids arrive. I can't wait until tomorrow when we break up from school," she squeals.

"Oh yes you break up tomorrow for the summer holidays don't you, you lucky thing."

"I know anyway I'll just finish getting ready and then head off, I'll see you later then before you go to your mums."

"Ok Jode, see you later." I smile.

After finishing texting my mum and eating my breakfast I wash up the pots then go to clean my teeth and apply make-up. Once I'm ready I lock up the flat and set off for work in the sunshine.

Arriving at work I walk into the coffee shop and Sally is sat at one of the tables in the shop doing some paperwork.

"Morning Sal so did Tim offer you his banana last night then?" I smirk.

"Oh well good morning to you too, no but he had better tomorrow night because I missed out on our actual anniversary because I was ill with a migraine so we need to make up for it. I'd better not get a bloody migraine this week because I've bought new sexy underwear especially and not had chance to wear it yet."

"Oh yes, poor Tim is not going to know what's hit him when you get your hands on him."

"Too right, we haven't had it for a week because he's been really tired from a busy week at work; when he gets home he just has his dinner and then falls asleep on the settee. It's alright but a woman has needs sometimes."

I laugh. "I know what you mean."

"Anyway I thought I'd let him get as much rest as he can this week and then by tomorrow night he will have plenty of energy so we can relive our wedding night. I was thinking we might start trying for a baby."

"Oh my god Sal, really, wow, does Tim know this?" I ask excited for my friend. I feel guilty, I have been so absorbed in my own feelings and drama, I haven't even considered what is happening in Sally's life.

"Yes and no, I thought we could discuss it over dinner. If he agrees, we can start practising tomorrow after our romantic meal. It won't be a complete shock when I bring the subject up though because we've had a brief discussion about it before and I have been dropping hints just lately and he did seem up for the idea but nothing has been confirmed."

"How exciting, I'm really pleased for you Sal, you will make a fantastic mum."

"Thanks Kara, if I end up having a daughter like you I will be the happiest mum in the world."

"Oh Sal, you are so sweet. I can imagine you having a little boy or girl with bright ginger hair."

"Oh I know it would be so cute wouldn't it."

"Yeah it would, I hope everything goes okay at your talk then."

"I'm sure it will."

"I received a text from my mum this morning while I was getting ready for work inviting me around for dinner, she probably hasn't got any of her clubs on tonight so I'm going there straight from work."

"That will be nice to catch up, I wish my mum was still alive I'd love to go and have food with her. Anyway say hi to your mum for me. Right I'll just put this paperwork away in the office and then we had better open up as it's nearly that time of day."

"Okay."

The morning goes quick because we are getting busier with holidaymakers visiting the area as it's the middle of July.

While I'm serving a gentleman a latte I notice something out the corner of my eye and looking up I see the biggest bouquet of pink and white roses. Seeing the man carrying them my heart skips a beat because Evan is behind them.

"Hey you," he says giving me one of his sexy smiles.

"Hi," I blush taking the roses from him as all eyes are on us from the people in the shop.

The public display of affection is attracting quite an audience and Sally notices.

"Do you both want to pop out back for 5 minutes?" she smiles.

"Yes thanks Sally," I smile feeling a little embarrassed because I can hear people commenting in the background.

Evan follows me through the door to get to the office and once we are in I shut the door and turn to look at him and he is staring at me.

"These are gorgeous and unexpected, thank you," I say looking for a space on the desk to put the flowers on.

"You are very welcome, beautiful flowers for a beautiful lady, how are you today?" he says not taking his eyes off me.

"I'm good thanks and you?"

"I'm good, I was just wondering if you are free later?" continuing to stare at me but not making any attempt to touch me.

"I'm actually going to my mums later she invited me for dinner this morning I think one of her clubs got cancelled so I said I would go."

"Oh that's a shame I really wanted to see you because I didn't get to see you last night."

"Well I've said I would go now."

"I've really missed you," he says walking over to where I am stood at the side of the desk.

He bites his lip, giving me that dashing smile, his gaze wonders down to my breasts.

"I didn't get to have you last night or these," he says putting his hands on me and massaging my breasts through my top as I stare back at him enjoying his touch but not touching him.

"Sorry but that wasn't my fault was it." I glance at him.

"I want to spend some time with you," he says moving closer and kissing my neck, running his tongue up towards my ear.

Closing my eyes and feeling his tongue licking around my ear I let out a small moan, "Sorry but I've said yes now I can't let her down she'll be looking forward to it," knowing what I would rather be doing instead.

"Do you think I can come for dinner as well?" he asks planting soft kisses on my cheek and then back onto my neck again.

"Oh god Evan." I pant, "my mum doesn't even know you and I think meeting the parents does not feature in the love them and leave them rule book either."

Evan stops kissing me and stands back to look at me with a serious face clearly not impressed by my comment.

"Don't say that, I've told you I don't like it."

"Sorry."

"I just want you as many nights as I can before I leave town, please change your mind?" he pleads moving towards me and pushing his erect cock into my front to try and persuade me. Evan then brings his lips to mine and kisses me holding my face in his hands, our tongues mingling together as I cup his erection through his trousers.

"I'm sorry I can't," I pull away breathless.

Evan is not happy with my decision and pulls away from me sulking.

"Okay, I'll just have to find something else to entertain myself with tonight then," he huffs.

There's an awkward silence, his comment upsets me. 'What? Is this why he's chasing me? I'm just someone to entertain him so he doesn't get bored?'

"Something or someone, maybe you should I'm sure there are plenty of girls who would love to entertain you." I snap.

"Hey what's made you all prickly today?"

"You have, I can't just drop everything because you want to have sex with me Evan. When you have moved on to your next conquest I will still be here with my friends and family and I'm not dropping them for you."

Evan just stands there taken aback. He needs to know that this is not okay.

I should not have to explain this to him.

"I appreciate the flowers, I truly do, but it's not fair to expect me to be at your beck and call whenever you want, I do have a life other than you."

Evan moves closer to me and takes hold of my shoulders, I look away from him. "Look at me."

I turn my head to look at him, "I'm sorry I shouldn't have made the comment about entertaining myself with something else, I'm just frustrated because I didn't get to see you last night and now I'm not seeing you tonight either."

"I know I am disappointed too. I can see you tomorrow night?" I suggest as he leans towards me and kisses me making everything better with just the touch of his lips on mine.

Thinking for a moment he looks at me and grins, "I can do better than that, come away with me for the weekend? We can spend the whole weekend together, I haven't got any business concerns that need addressing, what do you think?"

"Evan, I'm not sure, is going away what people do when it's a casual thing? Can I think about it?"

"No because if you think about it you are going to come up with excuses as to why you can't go so I'm taking charge.

I'm picking you up tomorrow after work, no questions asked."

I go to speak and Evan crashes his lips onto mine kissing me fiercely like he's been starved of me for a long time and needs to get his fix.

My legs feel like jelly.

"But what will people think, this is crazy I've only known you for a short time, we can't just go away together we hardly know each other."

"Yes we can and we do know each other Kara, plus it will be a good chance to get to know each other a lot more and I don't care what people think. Please let me whisk you away somewhere nice," he says with a boyish grin.

"But I do care and why do we need to get to know each other more anyway when you are only here for a short time."

"I'm not promising anything, but I just want to spend some time with you, you are a welcome distraction in my busy life and I like being with you so what's wrong with that?"

I think for a moment and then decide why the hell not.

"Okay I'll come."

"Really?"

"Yes really."

He picks me up making me squeal and swings me around in the tiny space of the office.

"Evan put me down you idiot. Where are we going anyway?"

"Let me worry about that it's a surprise and I have the perfect place in mind."

"Okay but what should I bring to wear then?" I ask as he lowers me slowly down his body smiling.

"It doesn't really matter what you bring to wear because you won't be wearing any of it," he says staring at me with lust in his eyes as I feel his erection pressing up against me.

"Oh okay then, I like the sound of that." I smile.

"I wish I could fuck you right now," grinding his hips and pushing his erect cock into me while kissing me passionately.

Consumed in the moment I kiss him back feeling sensations between my legs as I become turned on by him. His lips move from my mouth to my neck and he cups my breasts with his hand as I enjoy being devoured by him until I hear Sally calling me from the shop sounding flustered.

"Hey you finished Kara, I could do with your help out here?"

"Oh god," I panic. "Yes I'm coming," I shout.

"You will be, you will be shouting those words over and over again this weekend Kara I guarantee it, I can't wait I'm so hard thinking about it and I need to stop thinking about it and get rid of this hard on before I walk out into the shop again full of all those people." He grins. "We had an audience before when I gave you those flowers but I would definitely give your customers something to look at with this jutting from my trousers." he laughs as I stand back to look at him laughing.

"Oh yes I think you had better wait in here until it's gone down," I giggle.

"It's alright for you when you're turned on you can hide it but us men can't, can I just pop to your loo."

"Yes, it's through there, what are you going to do get yourself off?"

"Kara I am not going to 'get myself off' in your work toilets thank you. I will hide in there for a few moments until it's fully gone down in case Sally comes in the office, I don't want to give her an eyeful do I." he laughs.

"No, I'd best go and help her," I laugh opening the door and walking out of the office.

As I walk through the door I turn back and smile, "I'm looking forward to going away with you Mr H thank you for asking me and thanks again for the lovely flowers."

"Your welcome baby," he says following me out of the office to the toilets checking that the coast is clear.

"Sorry for taking so long Sally I'm here now, Evan is just using the toilet before he goes."

"No problem love, sorry to interrupt you both. Your flowers are beautiful, he has good taste," she teases.

"Yes the flowers are gorgeous aren't they and thank you for allowing us to have some privacy, " I smile.

"No problem" she smiles.

I greet a customer, "Yes sir what can I get you?"

A few minutes later while I'm getting a slice of chocolate cake from the glass cabinet on the counter Evan appears from the back looking more presentable than a few moments ago, he grins walking over to me I grin back both of us knowing what the other one is thinking about.

"Enjoy dinner at your mum's, I'll text you later."

"Okay, will do."

I watch him walk out the door thinking how gorgeous he is and also about our weekend away together, a whole weekend spent with Evan, I can't wait. I'm not going to be able to walk on Monday.

After an hour of serving coffee and sandwiches it has started to quieten down so Sally and I can have a break and a chat.

"So can you please tell me what your secret is Kara because this guy you are seeing has only known you for a short while and has brought you the biggest bouquet of pink roses and I have known Tim for eight years and he has never bought me flowers like that?" Sally says feeling envious.

"Well I wish I knew Sal I wake up every morning thinking how the hell did I get this lucky to be with someone like Evan, I mean he could have the pick of any girls and for some reason he seems to have taken a fancy to me."

"Kara you really don't know how gorgeous you are do you girl?"

"I'm no supermodel Sally, yes I'm curvy and have big tits but I would say he is definitely out of my league so I feel like I've won the lottery. Anyway, I must tell you he's just invited me away with him for the weekend."

"Oh my god Kara, he definitely has it bad for you, are you going?"

"I've said I would but what do you think? Do you think I'm making a big mistake after our chat the other day?"

"I'd say go for it, a weekend away with a hot guy who just bought you roses, you can't possibly turn him down. Where is he taking you?"

"I don't know, he said it's a surprise."

"I'm so happy for you I want to hear all about it on Monday okay?" Sally smiles.

"It's a deal and you can tell me all about your anniversary dinner at that new place and how the baby thing went." I say, nudging her cheekily.

"Oh yes but my dinner doesn't sound very exciting compared to your weekend activities."

"Sally, you're celebrating your wedding anniversary and also maybe the chance to try for a little Sal or Tim so you can't get any more exciting than that." Sally would make such a wonderful mother.

"Aw thanks Kara, you're right I'm looking forward to it and lots of trying, poor Tim is going to be worn out."

I laugh. "Sally I don't want that image in my head thank you, it's bad enough when I look at Tim now after you told me the banana story. Anyway I hope it all works out for you both. Shall we get these mugs cleared up and then have a cuppa because I don't know about you but I'm ready for one after that busy hour."

"Good idea," she smiles scooping up some mugs ready for washing up.

Fifteen

After a busy day at work I arrive home and briefly see Jodie before going to my mum and dads for dinner. I tell her Evan has invited me away for the weekend and she thinks I should go and enjoy myself because I never go anywhere.

I arrive at my parent's bungalow and walk up the path to the front door thinking how pleased I am to be having one of my mum's home cooked meals.

I open the front door to the smell of sausages cooking in the oven, "Hi Mum, something smells good." I call walking in and through to the kitchen to find my mum standing at the sink washing up.

"Hi darling," she smiles drying her hands on a towel and then walking over to me and giving me a hug. "I've made your favourite sausages, mash, veg and gravy tonight, have a seat at the table it won't be long. Have you had a busy day at work love?" she asks continuing to wash up.

"Yes it's been really busy today there has been lots of tourists walking about, our town seems to becoming more and more popular with visitors, there is even a new hotel opening up on the outskirts of town at the Manor on Danes Avenue."

"Oh I heard that someone has bought the Manor so it's going to be a hotel is it how do you know that?"

"Umm…just heard someone say something in the coffee shop that's all."

Thinking a change of subject would be good because I can't stop thinking about Evan as it is and now I'm thinking about the Manor and what happened in the games room and I'm suddenly feeling a bit flushed.

"So how's dad, is he okay?" I ask taking a seat at the kitchen table and putting my bag on the floor at the side of me.

"Yes he's fine love, he's busy as usual but he will be home over the weekend if you want to pop and see him then."

"Umm … I can't, I'm away this weekend." I say feeling awkward.

"Sorry did you just say you are going away? Where are you going, you never go anywhere Kara?"

"I know I'm just going to visit an old school friend, can you remember Jess from school, her parents moved to that big house in the country she has invited me to come and stay with her this weekend, its only for a couple of nights. It's only just been arranged."

"Ok dear, it's no problem I was just curious that's all, it's good for you to get out of town. How are you getting there, do you need to borrow my car?"

"I'm going to get the train after work tomorrow night and then Jess' dad will pick me up at the station the other end."

I hate lying to my mum about what I'm really doing this weekend but I can hardly say that I'm going away with a gorgeous man that I've only known for a short while and that I'm having a weekend of hot, raunchy sex.

Snapping me out of my thoughts my mum declares that food is ready.

I pour us both a glass of chilled water with slices of lemon floating in it from the jug on the table while my mum serves.

Mum joins me at the table and smiles, "This is nice having you here for dinner, I thought I would do your favourite because I know how much you love sausages and mash."

"Yes when I was about ten." I giggle with her, I know she loves cooking for when I am home.

"So what have you been up to then?" mum asks picking up her knife and fork and looking at me as I put a forkful of food in my mouth.

Almost choking I reply, "Umm nothing much just the usual, working hard … wow this is good, thanks Mum."

"That's okay love. Is Jodie alright, is she still loved up with Matt?"

"Yes and Jodie is fine, she said to say hello and so does Sally by the way."

"Oh that's nice and how about you Kara, is there a young man in your life? You deserve someone nice to look after you."

I feel awkward at the mention of a man in my life. I really want to tell her and to scream it from the rooftops that I've met the most perfect man but I know there is no future, so I say nothing.

"I've had a few dates but nothing that's going to go anywhere. Besides I need to start thinking about my career before any man because I don't want to work in the coffee shop all my life."

"Good for you, I'm sure whatever you decide to do you will be great at it." She smiles, "now eat up, I have dessert!"

After eating, we move to the lounge to sit down with a cup of tea and a slice of mum's homemade chocolate cake.

A text notification sounds on my phone.

"What was that?" my mum enquires.

"Oh I just received a text, I'd better see who it is in case it's Jess."

I look at my phone and feel excited when I see Evan's name flash up on the screen.

"Is it her?" mum asks looking at me with a curious look on her face.

"Yes its Jess," I lie feeling terrible.

Hi beautiful, hope you are having a nice time at your mum's? I am sat in my suite all alone, bored and thinking of you. E xx

"What did she say? Is there a problem?"

"No she's just confirming details for the weekend I'll just send her a quick reply." I can't help smiling knowing that he's bored and thinking about me.

Hi, I'm having a lovely time thanks. I've just had sausages, mash and veg with gravy followed by chocolate cake. I would love to come and relieve you of your boredom but it's my parents turn tonight to have my company K xx

My mum is sat on the other settee and is busy chatting away to me about the classes she has been to this week; cake making, origami, Zumba and I occasionally drop in a 'uh huh' because I'm not really listening and distracted waiting for a reply from Evan.

Sausage eh? I wish it was my sausage in your mouth ... please come and see me later, I'm lonely and frustrated because I want you NOW! E xx

Mr H, you are making me blush and horny and my mum is sat near me so behave you will have to sort yourself out tonight. K xx

"Mum, I'm sorry but would you mind if I left now? I have loads of packing to do and as much as I would love to stay and chat I need to get sorted because I'm leaving straight after work tomorrow night."

"Of course love, I don't mind at all I know you have a busy life. Do you want me to run you home?"

"No it's okay, I'll walk, it's not far and it's such a nice evening I could do with a walk after that big dinner anyway."

It always takes half an hour to get out the door and she always tries to pack me up some dinners in takeaway boxes.

"Okay sweetheart, I'll see you out. I hope you have a lovely time at your friend's and I'll tell dad you will see him next weekend when it's your birthday," she smiles.

"Thanks mum and thanks for my food and the cake it was delicious."

"You're welcome darling, it was lovely to see you," mum sees me to the front door and I give her a kiss on the cheek and a quick hug.

"See you next weekend then, have a lovely weekend, I look forward to hearing all about it, love you."

I wave goodbye to her as I walk down the path and my mum stands and watches me waving until I'm out of sight. Walking down the road towards home I pull my phone out of my bag and see that I've received another text from Evan.

I don't want to sort myself out, I want you to do that, what are you doing now? Still bored and lonely. E xx'

I have just left my mum's house and now walking home to go and do some packing as I am going away this weekend to who knows where with an insatiable gorgeous, sexy man. If you fancy COMING to mine I can help you with your problem that needs sorting ... K xx

I'm leaving now. E xx

As I reach the front door, I hear Evan's car engine purring behind me and coming to a stop. Turning around he waves and smiles at me through the car window then opens the door and gets out. My heart starts racing as I take in the sight of him wearing a tight white t-shirt that shows off his pecs and muscly arms, some dark blue stonewashed jeans that show off his toned legs, some casual lace up brown boots with aviator sunglasses, he looks so good I'm salivating.

"Hi beautiful, thanks for inviting me around," he says walking up to me as I stare at him in some sort of trance. He plants a quick kiss on my lips before taking off his sunglasses.

"Hi, well you did sound quite lonely and bored on your text so I'm sure I can remedy that for you," I smile.

"Oh yes baby I'm sure you can and I'm looking forward to it, it's been too long," he says excitedly.

"Well I have lots of packing that I need help with so that will relieve your boredom won't it?" I grin.

"You little tease, I was hoping for a bit more than that," he says as I turn to unlock the front door and he smacks me on my bum.

"Ouch." I look at him and grin, "well, if you tell me where we are going I will oblige."

"Oh no it's a surprise," he says turning me around after I've unlocked the door and kissing me passionately on the front door step.

I can feel his excitement growing and pulling away breathless I think we need to go in.

"Come on we best get inside because the neighbours curtains will be twitching and I can feel something else twitching too."

"It's your fault, you are so god damn sexy every time I see you my cock just comes alive," he grins as I turn and walk through the door into my flat followed by Evan.

"Jodie are you home?" I shout walking into the kitchen followed closely by Evan. There is no answer and walking over to the fridge I see Jodie has left me a note pinned on the outside saying she won't be home.

'Oh yes she said Matt was taking her out for dinner somewhere tonight.'

"Well it appears I am home alone tonight because Jodie is staying at Matts," looking at him with a sultry look on my face.

"Matt's her boyfriend right?"

"Yes." I say looking at Evan and biting my lip.

"Well I am more than happy to stay and keep you company," he says looking me up and down with greedy eyes like he's imagining me naked.

"Yes I can see you are more than happy," looking at Evan's erection that's straining in his jeans.

"Do you want to make me extremely happy now?" he asks walking slowly over to where I'm stood by the fridge.

"I would love to." I breathe welcoming Evan into my arms.

He puts his hands in my soft blonde hair and pulls me closer to him for a hot, sensual, lingering kiss our tongues entwined as we devour each other against the fridge. "Oh god Evan I love kissing you," I whisper my body tingling all over and becoming wet in readiness for him.

He pulls away and rests his forehead on mine, "And I love kissing you." Noticing the pink roses that he bought me on the windowsill behind me he smiles, "the roses look good in the window."

"Yes they were a lovely surprise from this man I know, he is gorgeous, sexy and great in bed." I whisper biting my bottom lip staring back at him.

With that we can't hold back any longer and we both lunge at each other our mouths crashing fiercely together. Evan grabs the hem of my t-shirt lifting it up as our mouths part briefly for him to lift it over my head as I help him before kissing each other wildly again.

Evan pulls away breathless to look at my breasts and gasps at my erect nipples showing through the white silky material of my bra.

"I could come just by looking at your gorgeous tits," he pants cupping them in his hands and massaging them stroking his thumbs over my nipples that are longing for his mouth.

"Oh god that's good," I moan arching my back as he pulls the cups down and sucks one of my nipples into his mouth, moaning as he moves over to the other nipple. Reaching around my back while teasing my nipples with his tongue he unclasps my bra letting it fall to the floor.

"I can't get enough of you and you're incredible body, you have the most perfect tits."

"Oh god Evan, you are so good at that." I breathe his tongue driving me wild as the sensation travels downwards to my core.

Evan moves down my body and pushes up my red skirt then moving my knickers to the side he circles his tongue over my pulsating clit causing me to cry out and hold his head in my hands while I watch him leaning against the kitchen worktop with my back to the window.

"Evan, I need to shut the blind or people will see." Evan stops immediately obviously not liking the idea of people seeing me and stands up, he then picks me up and carries me to my bedroom. Placing me on the floor next to my bed he shuts my bedroom door and quickly draws the curtains.

"I've been thinking about fucking you all day," he says moving towards me and kissing me fiercely. Putting his fingers in the elasticated waistband of my red skirt he pulls it down my body until it's at my feet and I step out of it leaving me standing in a pair of white silk knickers as he relishes the sight of me.

"I love your knickers you look so virginal in them but I want what's underneath," he says pulling my knickers down my smooth, long, silky legs until my knickers are off and on the floor. He then grabs hold of my shapely hips and carries on what he started in the kitchen tasting how turned on I am.

"Evan I need you naked." I moan.

After a few more licks with his tongue he stands up and starts to undress himself with me helping to rip his clothes off desperate to see his toned naked body. Moving closer to each other so our naked bodies are skin to skin, his erection jutting into my stomach he looks at me then places one hand behind my head and brings his mouth to mine. He then plunges two fingers inside me and I moan into his mouth enjoying the feeling and our passionate kiss. He can feel how turned on and wet I am and I can't hold back the loud moan when he touches my clit with his thumb causing me to fling my head back from the intensity of it all.

"You are always so ready for me baby, you like that don't you?" he says moving his fingers in and out of me and rubbing me. Evan then pulls his fingers out and kneels down on the floor moving straight in quickly with his mouth and tongue to my clit as I hold onto his head while he performs slow circles with his tongue, my breathing becoming quicker, my legs shaky.

"Oh God, oh GOD." I breathe my whole body experiencing such a rush and I don't think I can hold on much longer as the urge to come is becoming stronger and stronger with every stroke of his tongue. Evan knows I'm on the brink of an orgasm and so gently encourages me to sit on the edge of the bed and to lie back.

"You taste so good," he says continuing to circle my clit with his tongue and just the erotic sight of Evan pleasuring me with his mouth and the feel of his expert strokes has me coming in seconds.

"I'm coming … OHHHH …" my whole body bucks and shakes as my orgasm tears through me like a tidal wave crashing onto rocks. My brain feels fuzzy and the feeling is exhilarating. Sitting up and looking into those gorgeous brown eyes of his I pull his mouth to mine tasting myself on his lips as we kiss with so much passion I almost tell him I love him.

"Are you okay, was that good?" he asks smiling at me as I look at him with glazed eyes and an overwhelming feeling of contentment.

"That was just, there isn't even a word to describe how intense and amazing that was but I want to give you pleasure too." I answer stroking his face.

"Just knowing that it's me making you feel that way and me giving you an orgasm gives me pleasure … if you would like to pleasure me my cock is so hard I would like to fuck you now, I need to be inside you," he says standing up his erection pointing upwards in all its glory the tip glistening showing his excitement. I move back onto the bed and Evan climbs on top of me, "are you ready for me baby?"

"Oh I am so ready for you." I reply as he positions his cock in between my legs and then slowly pushes it inside. We both feel the intense connection instantly, the spark that drew us together as he moves into its rightful place easing in and out of me.

"You fit me so perfect Kara, you are so tight I think we'll start off nice and slow."

"Oh god your cock feels amazing, oh yes like that, yes that's so good …"

Evan moves in and out holding himself over my naked body with his powerful arms and his hands either side of my head as he thrusts slowly in and out and in and out. I move slightly so he's hitting the right spot and it makes me moan as we look into each other's eyes maintaining eye contact the whole time.

"Oh god it feels so good Evan."

"Feel it baby," he pants gyrating his hips around in circles filling every part of me, "feel how good it fits you, it was made for you."

"Oh god yes …" I mumble as Evan moves in and out around and around making me moan louder and louder as the intensity of the feelings increase.

"Fuck …" Evan swears as I squeeze his cock and he lets out a guttural moan, "that's it baby."

"I missed this last night, I can't get enough of you."

"Me too, feels good doesn't it."

"Yes … god yes… OHHHHH… "

"FUCK you're so wet, I'm sliding in and out with ease."

"You make me so wet."

Evan thrusts inside me filling me deep and brushing my insides with his solid form giving me just what I need, what he needs.

"I'm going to fuck you harder now so hold onto me okay."

"Okay, give it me."

I hold on to his broad shoulders, this pleasure is like a drug we can't get enough of.

"Like this baby?" Evan replies thrusting into me with force.

"Oh yes ... like that."

"Fucking hell ..." Evan moans.

"Yes. ... harder, give it to me."

"Fucking hell woman..."

"Evan."

"FUUCCK ..."

"I'm going to come ..." I pant holding onto him as he thrusts deep inside me. It feels so good, as the tingles get stronger feeling my release.

"I'm with you baby," my insides squeezing his length bringing him closer and closer and bang, one strong powerful thrust and I scream crying out with elation as I orgasm followed by Evan, his cock pulsing and twitching as he spills his come inside me.

"OHH … wow."

"You okay?"

"Yes …yes… god that was unbelievable."

Collapsing, out of breath and wet with sweat Evan rolls off me and lays down at the side of me breathing hard as the best feeling floods our brains with utmost intensity.

"You really are amazing," Evan smiles turning to me and seeing me grinning at him from the pleasure we have both just received.

"You are and that was amazing as always." I grin snuggling into his arms.

I feel so happy being with Evan and I'm wondering if this is the right time to tell him that I'm falling in love with him as we lay contented in each other's arms, but not wanting to spoil the moment I keep quiet suddenly remembering that I'm supposed to be packing some clothes for the weekend.

"I really need to do some packing and have a shower." I sigh not wanting to move because I would prefer to stay in the warm, safe arms of Evan who is starting to drift off to sleep.

"Okay baby just a few more minutes."

"Okay." I reply happy to just lay and snuggle with him. After a few minutes Evan falls asleep.

"Evan … Evan …" I call nudging him.

"Hey … what, what's wrong?"

"Nothing you fell asleep."

"Did I?"

"Yes you did." I giggle.

"Well I apologise but you having such a high sex drive has zapped all my energy I just needed a power nap to recharge."

"My high sex drive eh?" I laugh.

"Anyway I thought you wanted a shower and to do some packing."

"I did."

"Well you'd better get up then." he smirks grabbing hold of me and tickling me making me squeal as I try to get away from him.

"Aargh … stop … aargh …"

"Okay come on then," he says letting go of me as I playfully hit him and sit up on the bed. "Let's go and get a shower and then I'll help you with your packing but like I told you before you don't need many clothes because you won't be wearing them."

"I'm a girl Evan all girls need plenty of clothes with them. Please tell me where we are going because I don't know what to pack, warm clothes or dresses and bikinis?" I pout.

"No it's a surprise but I will tell you this, pack dresses and bikinis because it will be hot and you will also need a passport, I hope you have one?" he smiles getting up off the bed and stretching.

Sixteen

I wake up and see Evan is fast asleep at the side of me. It's 1.00am and I feel wide awake. I can't wait to go away with him this weekend, I have the same feeling of excitement you do as a child on Christmas Eve. This sexy man laid next to me with his hair all ruffled and stubble on his face is so gorgeous, he looks striking with his chiselled features and his beautiful long eyelashes that touch his face while he's sleeping. I can't take my eyes off him.

Feeling thirsty I creep out of bed quietly so not to disturb him and go to the kitchen to get a drink of water. Finding a glass I turn on the cold tap to fill it up and then sit at the table to drink it thinking about Evan.

Meeting Evan is turning out to be the best time of my life, getting to know him, spending time with him … not least the great sex that we are having and now going away with him for the weekend, it has all been such a whirlwind but I've never felt so happy and alive.

"Can't you sleep?" Evan says making me jump. I nearly spit the water out all over the kitchen table.

He walks into the kitchen naked. He must have sensed me not being next to him and woken up.

"No, I'm excited about the weekend, I was just thinking about what a crazy time it has been from meeting you, having the best sex of my life to now going away with you for the weekend."

Evan beckons me up off the chair to sit on his lap.

He strokes my back lightly with his fingers, "It has been crazy hasn't it, who would have thought when I bought the Manor that I would end up meeting an incredible girl who has the most amazing body and tits," nuzzling his face in between my naked breasts and shaking his head from side to side making me laugh.

"Hmm …" I can feel Evan's cock twitching beneath me.

"Just think this time tomorrow, we will be in, in …"

"… I'm not telling you Kara," he laughs.

"Please tell me," I plead looking at him.

"No," he says and he gives me a peck on the nose, "come on, let's go back to bed and get some more sleep it's going to be a busy day tomorrow and you are going to need plenty of energy for what I have planned for the weekend."

"Okay." I yawn as I place my glass on the table.

Evan picks me up in his arms and carries me back to the bedroom. We get into bed and then cuddle each other until eventually we fall asleep again.

Beep … Beep … Beep …

I stretch and turn off the alarm at the side of the bed and Evan grabs my boob and squeezes it making me squeal. Turning around I see his face grinning at me.

"Morning beautiful."

"Morning." I yawn getting comfortable again under the duvet as Evan moves nearer for a cuddle. I can feel his morning erection pushing into my side.

"Someone's pleased to see me this morning," I say giving his cock a rub under the covers.

"I'm always pleased to see you and so is my friend," he replies pushing his length into my hand.

"I wish we could stay in bed and not go to work." I sigh.

"So do I but we can stay in bed all weekend if you like."

"Oh yes we're going away aren't we." I squeal suddenly sitting up in bed.

"What are you doing?" he laughs.

"Getting up."

"Hey I thought we were going to say good morning properly," he says stroking my back.

"Sorry, but I need to check I have everything seeing as you are picking me up straight after work tonight and we're going from there."

"I thought you checked and packed everything last night?"

"Yes but I never go away so I want to make sure I haven't forgotten anything and have everything I need. Oh and I need to take my pill and pack them seeing as we are not using condoms anymore." I grin leaning over and taking the packet out of my bedside drawer and swallowing one without water.

"Yes don't forget them." Evan says looking serious.

"I won't don't worry," I smile getting out of bed. Bending over looking in the open suitcase I give Evan the perfect view of my naked bum, he's sat up in bed watching me.

"If you keep doing that we won't be going anywhere."

I turn to look at him and grin. "Are you getting up?" I smile loving the fact that he can't seem to stop looking at me.

"I'm already up," he teases pulling back the covers to reveal his erection.

"Evan you are insatiable, does it ever go down?" I laugh, shaking my head.

"Not when you're around and especially looking like that."

I choose some underwear opting for a black lace bra with a matching thong and Evan wolf whistles approvingly. I put them on, then finish getting dressed and find something to change into after work for the journey. Evan gets out of bed and comes up behind me putting his arms around my waist and hugging me from behind.

"It's going to be great spending the whole weekend together," he says moving my hair to the side and kissing my neck.

"Yeah it is, now get ready because we need to go to work soon," turning around to face him loving how happy and excited he is to be going away with me.

I smile cupping my hand against his jawline, feeling his perfection.

"Okay beautiful." He puts on his boxers then gives me a quick kiss before going to the bathroom.

"I've checked the weather forecast of our destination and it's currently 25 degrees so it's going to be nice and warm …" Evan says walking back into the room and getting dressed.

"Oh great so I might get a tan then." I close my eyes with my arms out, imagining the sun radiating down on me.

"Maybe," he smiles.

After having a quick breakfast, Evan puts my suitcase in the boot of his car then drives me to work and I flamboyantly waltz into the coffee shop to begin my shift.

"Good morning sunshine," Sally says looking up and seeing me walk through the door. "I bet you're excited, have you found out where you're going yet?"

"I'm so excited Sal and no he won't tell me. I have been trying to get him to but no such luck, he did say I would need a passport and to pack dresses and bikinis though, oh and the weather is 25 degrees at the moment."

Sally squeals "Ooh I wonder where he's taking you?"

"I know it's frustrating not knowing but also kind of fun."

"It can't be anywhere too far then because you are only going for the weekend so I'm guessing Europe."

"It could be, he has a hotel in Spain so maybe we are going there. If you google Hamilton Hotels you can see the hotels he owns. I suppose I'll just have to wait and find out where we are going when we get to the airport."

"I wish I was going away for the weekend somewhere hot," Sally says daydreaming.

"Yes, but you are going out for your belated anniversary meal with your lovely hubby tonight and from what you've been saying it sounds like it's going to be hot."

"Yeah I know." She giggles, "and I can't wait."

The day drags and I look at the clock every hour feeling like it's the longest day of my life and when closing time finally comes around I'm so excited because it's time for the weekend of fun and frivolity to start.

After turning the sign on the door to close I quickly go to the toilets to get changed out of my work clothes, whilst Sally finishes wiping down the surfaces ready for the next day.

I appear back in the shop wearing a low-cut red, polka dot tea dress with black block heeled shoes and some lip gloss.

Sally looks at me and smiles. "Wow you look lovely Kara, I'm sure Evan is going to be very impressed when he sees you."

"Thanks." I blush, "is there anything else we need to do before we go?" I smile.

"No, we're all done so grab your bag and let's get out of here." Sally squeals walking over to the door and opening it for me to walk through. Sally locks the door of Walt's Coffee Shop and notices Evan sat across the road waiting for me in his car.

Evan gives her a wave and one of his knockout smiles and she gives him a shy wave back.

"Have a lovely meal Sal and enjoy your night with Tim." I say giving her a quick hug.

"Yes and you have a great weekend too, see you Monday I shall look forward to hearing all about it," she grins and heads off to meet Tim.

I cross the road to where Evan is sat waiting in his car and he watches me the whole time as I walk towards him and jump into the passenger seat.

"Hi beautiful, I like your dress," he says eyeing me up and down, then looking at my cleavage which the dress accentuates.

"What this old thing?" I grin at him.

"Are you ready for lots of fun and even more sex?" he asks giving me a lovely tongue mingling hello kiss followed by a cheeky grin.

"I am more than ready," feeling tingles build between my legs at the mention of the word.

"I'm taking you out for dinner first before we board the plane at 8.45pm."

"Sounds lovely, where are we going for dinner?"

"Just some place I know in central London, are you ready?"

I strap myself in the seatbelt. "I'm ready let's go." I'm excited but also a little nervous.

I notice the road signs as we head into London's Royal Borough of Kensington and Chelsea with its stunning white stucco-fronted facade and neatly trimmed rows of box trees.

"This is my neck of the woods but I'm not taking you home because I have somewhere else in mind to have dinner," Evan says proudly showing me the neighbourhood where he lives as we approach Knightsbridge.

"It's just up here," he says squeezing my knee.

As we drive a bit further I can see an impressive tall majestic building coming towards us on the right and as we get a bit closer I can see it is a hotel called 'Hamilton Tower." It displays a logo next to the name of the hotel with HH on it. 'Hamilton's Hotels.'

"This is one of your hotels?" I state, recognising the look of the building from my late night google search results of the Hamilton empire.

"Yes it is babe, I thought we could eat here as the airport is only a 45-minute drive from here. The food is excellent, I recommend it and the chips are to die for," he winks smiling.

"Well that's just sold it to me." I grin, feeling butterflies in my stomach, I feel so lucky.

Evan pulls off the side street into a car park filled with expensive cars at the back of the hotel and pulls into a reserved parking space with a sign saying 'Mr Hamilton' on it.

"You have your own parking space?" I smile.

"Well I do own the hotel so I think I'm entitled," he laughs.

Evan parks the car and then opens the passenger door for me to get out. I'm so happy.

"I could quite easily take you up to one of the rooms right now, seeing you in that dress has made me all excited but we are pushed for time so come on let's go and get some food," he says looking at his watch then taking my hand and leading me to the back door of the hotel.

I look up at the tall, impressive building with its tower standing over us in complete awe.

Evan explains the hotel is a contemporary luxury hotel with a tower of rooms providing majestic views over Knightsbridge and Hyde Park, the suites offering breath-taking views over London's skyline. He walks with me through the back door into a high-ceilinged hallway and a gentleman greets us.

"Good evening Mr Hamilton your table is ready for you." The concierge ushers us further into the grand reception.

"Thanks Tony." Evan places a hand on the small of my back and we follow the man.

I take in the plush décor and the splendid modern paintings decorating the walls of the long corridor as I walk towards a private room with a table in it set for two. It's dimly lit with candles burning and very romantic.

"Here we are, may I?" Tony says pulling out a chair for me to sit down on while Evan takes a seat opposite me.

Evan is wearing some dark blue jeans, a white designer T-shirt which complements his tanned muscly body and some dark brown leather boots. He looks gorgeous as ever.

"Thanks Tony, this is Kara," Evan says as he gestures his hand towards me.

"Nice to meet you Kara," Tony says shaking my hand.

"You too," I smile.

"Tony I would like a bottle of champagne when you are ready please along with some sparkling water for the table," Evan says.

"Certainly sir," Tony offers us the menus to look at and leaves to get the drinks.

I take my jacket off now that I am feeling a little more relaxed.

"I really love your dress Kara it makes your tits look even bigger.

I can't stop looking at your cleavage I wish I could just bury my face in those beauties right now but Tony will be back in a minute and I wouldn't want to embarrass him." he smiles licking his lips looking at my impressive chest.

"Then you will just have to wait until later then won't you." I tease pushing my breasts together and staring straight into Evan's eyes with a lustful look on my face.

Evan coughs and shifts in his seat.

I can tell he's excited by the expression on his face and so to tease him some more I lift my foot under the table and gently stroke his leg up towards his crotch feeling his hard on with my foot.

Evan takes a deep breath and grabs my foot just as Tony comes back into the room with the bottle of champagne.

"Umm thanks Tony just give us a minute we haven't decided what we want to eat so come back in five minutes thanks," Evan says trying to get his words out but distracted by my foot on his crotch as Tony pours two glasses of champagne and then leaves the room again.

I continue to touch Evan playfully under the table and he laughs. "Thank god for tablecloths eh? You little minx just you wait," he says making me giggle.

I drop my foot so I can concentrate on the food menu and Evan tries to distract his thoughts of what he would like to do to me at this moment in time by looking at the food menu too.

"What would you like to eat then babe?"

"I'm not sure, I'm not used to having fancy food."

"I'll order for the both of us then if you don't mind, you are going to enjoy eating some of the best food that you have ever tasted," Evan smiles touching my hand resting on the table.

"Great and I love all food so whatever you choose will be lovely thank you."

Evan takes the menu from me just as Tony comes back into the room to take our orders. He orders a herb crusted fillet of salmon served with creamed mushroom confit and tomato salsa for us both and a bowl of chips to share. He knows how I love chips.

"I know I haven't seen the hotel properly but from what I have seen of it so far it's gorgeous Evan; will the Manor be like this when it's finished having the renovations done?"

"Yes the finish of the interior will be similar. I tend to have the same style and décor in all my hotels so it's consistent and people recognise my hotels. I like them to look stylish, elegant and modern with clean lines."

"Oh that reminds me, how did you get on with the interior designer the other night?" I ask.

Evan smiles. "I'm surprised it's taken you this long to ask seeing as how jealous you were that I was having dinner with another woman."

I roll my eyes at him smiling.

"It went very well actually she's meeting me at the Manor next week."

"Why don't you have the people who did your other hotels do the interior design for you?"

"Well I like to use people from the local area where my new hotel is located and also different people have different ideas so although I stick to the same décor, this hotel is very different to the Manor so there will be some new designs I need like the spa and the garden room."

"Oh I see. What did you do after your meal then?"

Evan raises his eyebrows at me and smiles. "Once we had finished our meal she invited me to have drinks with her in the bar."

"Oh right."

'What else did she invite you to do, have sex? Because I didn't hear from you all night.'

"You will be pleased to know that I declined her offer and I went back to my room and fell asleep on the couch. I woke up early hours of the morning and then took myself off to bed," giving me a sweet smile.

"So that's why I didn't get a text from you after your meal then, I thought you might have been too busy having fun with her that you forgot about me."

"You didn't think I was with her did you?" he smirks.

"I know you said that you wouldn't, but well because we're not dating I wasn't sure."

"Kara I wouldn't do that to you, I've never cheated in my life. I have been on the receiving end of it once as you know and it's not nice and besides I couldn't get any better than you babe."

Evan looks lost in thought as though he's thinking about something that happened in his past and his face is serious and his jaw is clenched.

"Evan, are you okay?"

"Yes sorry, lost in thought." He smiles.

'I wonder what he was thinking about?'

He picks up his glass of champagne and letting his thoughts go he raises his glass, "A toast to being faithful, to a great weekend, lots of fun in the sun, to you for agreeing to come away with me and most of all the fantastic sex we are going to be having," he grins.

"Sounds perfect and thanks for inviting me." I pick up my glass and we chink glasses. I take a sip of the ice cold, fizzy champagne and it tastes divine.

While we're drinking our champagne waiting for the food to arrive Evan's mobile phone starts ringing in his jeans pocket. He takes it out to see who is calling him, he frowns and presses the reject call button.

"Everything okay, did you need to take that?" I ask noticing Evan looks uneasy.

"No it's fine," he says just as his phone starts ringing again, "for fuck's sake I'm so sorry I'd better answer or it will just keep ringing, I won't be a moment." He stands up from the table and walks over to the corner of the room for some privacy.

"It's okay," I look around the candle lit room to look as though I'm not interested in who he's calling but try to listen because I'm desperate to know who it is.

Evan

I wonder what she wants this time. I dial the number and wait for her to answer.

"Hi son."

"Mother, I'm busy, what is it?" I pace the room.

"You're always busy I want to talk to you."

"Look it's difficult right now."

"I need to tell you something. Have you seen him?"

"Who?"

"Sebastian."

"No I haven't heard from him why?"

"He's back in London."

"Like I told you the other day I'm not interested."

"Here you go again burying your head in the sand, you can't ignore this Evan."

"For fuck's sake why can't you just drop it?"

"You need to pay him the money Evan, I'm scared of what he might do he's so angry."

I laugh. "You know how I feel about this and I wish you would stop bringing it up all the time. Do you think if you keep mentioning it enough times I will cave and give in?"

"Well that's what I'm hoping for son, I can't believe how stubborn you are, you're just like your father."

"You need to understand I will never change my mind on this and you can't ask me to feel differently either this is beyond repairable so if that's all you are ringing me for then you're wasting your breath."

"Evan please, do it for me, I can't stop worrying about it."

"I have to go. Goodbye Mother."

I shift in my seat a little uncomfortable after what I've just overheard. Although Evan was speaking quietly in the corner of the room his voice had become raised and I could hear bits of an awkward conversation and that it was obviously something that involves his mother.

"Is everything okay?" I ask as Evan joins me back at the table.

"Nothing for you to worry about," he smiles trying not to look affected by the phone call but clearly struggling to hide his feelings because his face looks a picture of anger and pain.

I want to ask him why he's upset but he obviously didn't want me to hear the conversation. I try to take his mind off it and back to our weekend away.

"So how long is the flight to wherever we are going?"

Evan still a little distant replies, "It's not long, as soon as we've eaten we will leave for the airport and our plane should be about ready."

"I'm so excited, I can't wait." I smile.

"Yeah me too."

As soon as we have finished our meals I put my jacket back on and grab my bag. Evan talks work to Tony for a few minutes and then tells him that we are ready to leave. Tony walks off with the plates in his hands saying goodbye to us and Evan takes my hand and leads us out of the hotel back to the car. Opening the boot he gets our cases out.

'I wonder why he's doing that?'

"Are we getting a taxi to the airport because you've been drinking?" I ask.

"No, my manager Curtis will be taking us and here he is now." Evan says looking over his shoulder to a 6 foot 2 inches tall blonde-haired pure muscle of a man who obviously works out regularly walking towards us.

"Hey my man," Curtis says slapping Evan on the back gently and shaking his hand.

"Hi big guy, how are you?"

"I'm good thanks and who is this lovely young lady?" he asks holding out his hand to shake mine.

"This is Kara and hands off she's with me."

"I can see that Ev," he smiles taking hold of my hand and instead of kissing me on the hand he pulls me closer and kisses me on both cheeks.

"Hi I'm Curtis, it's a pleasure to meet you," smiling at me showing his brilliant white teeth.

"Back off Curtis," Evan scowls looking at his friend.

"If you're ever interested in ditching this guy and going out for a drink with me some time I'm available," he winks purposely trying to wind Evan up.

"Curtis would you like to keep those perfect white teeth of yours?" Evan says glaring at him with a stern look on his face.

"Hey chill out, I'm only joking, it's nice to meet you Kara," he laughs giving my hand a rub that's still in his then letting it go. I smile. They have clearly been friends a long time.

Evan explains that he has known Curtis for ten years and they met each other whilst surfing on holiday at Manly Beach in Australia. He tells me they were chatting and found out that they were from the same area of London and after they got back Evan was opening up his new hotel in Knightsbridge and Curtis being a Hotel Manager already was offered a job to manage Evan's new hotel. Evan says he trusts Curtis with his life and that he's like a brother to him.

"Anyway as much as I'd love to stand around and chat we have a plane to catch so we'd best go." Evan says grabbing the suitcases.

"Ok mate, the car's over here." Curtis says pointing to a red Audi TT and pressing his key fob to open the car before grabbing the cases off Evan to put in his boot.

The car only has two doors so Curtis opens the door for me and pulls the seat back and I climb into the back seat.

Evan

"Nice ass," Curtis whispers looking at Kara's bum as she climbs into the back seat of his car.

"Behave, I'm serious, I like her."

"Okay dude relax, I was only looking she's stunning, wherever did you meet her?" he asks.

"I met her in a coffee shop where she works near where I've bought my new hotel, I stopped by to ask for directions because my Satnav wasn't working and there she was."

"Are you keeping this one then? She's special, it's about time you started dating seriously again, you're not getting any younger mate." Curtis says slapping me on the back.

"It's complicated."

"You can't let what happened to you in the past ruin your future mate, you need to let it go man, does she know?"

"No, she doesn't know. Anywhere are you driving us to the airport or what?" I smile.

"Yes boss." Curtis laughs.

Curtis backs out of the car park space and turns onto the side road before turning onto the main road heading for London City Airport putting his foot down. He tells me he's doesn't want us to be late because his boss won't be happy and I laugh.

Once we arrive, I catch sight of the plane sat on the tarmac in front of us. Surely that's not our plane? I look at the private jet stood on the runway looking superior and tap Evan on the shoulder sat in the front passenger seat, "Oh my god Evan is that our plane?"

"It certainly is baby," Evan turns around flashing a smile at me.

As it starts to sink in that we'll be getting on it soon I suddenly feel sick with nerves, "Evan I'm so nervous I've only ever flown once before."

He laughs. "You'll be fine babe, I'll look after you, come on they're waiting for us," he says reassuring me before getting out of the car. "Thanks for the lift Curtis, I'll be in touch soon okay."

"No problem, enjoy your weekend, later dude." Curtis shakes his hand then looks at me, "Don't forget if you ever fancy going out for a drink just let me know?" he winks giving me a kiss on both cheeks before jumping in his car laughing at Evan's face of thunder.

I wave at Curtis and watch him speed off out of the airport smiling.

"He's nice, I like him, I take it you are good friends?"

"Yes he's my best mate but he won't be my friend for much longer if he can't keep his eyes off you asking you out like that in front of me," he says grinding his teeth.

I touch his arm, "Hey he was only joking and besides I'm happy being with you to even want to look at anyone else." caressing his face with my hand.

Evan leans into my hand and kisses my palm snapping out of his jealousy, "Are you ready to join the mile high club?" he grins.

I blush and follow Evan to the private jet. "Have you got your passport ready because you will need it to board the plane with?"

"Yes it's in my bag. Wait I need to take a photo, Jodie is never going to believe this otherwise." I say grabbing my mobile and taking a selfie of us both stood outside the plane.

"Ready?"

"Yes I'm ready." I take a deep breath to try and calm my nerves.

"Great then let's go."

Seventeen

Evan hands over our luggage to a steward and then we board the jet giving the air hostess our passports. There are no check-in queues or duty free as we step onto the private jet and I marvel at the stylish luxurious interior as Evan shows me to a grey leather reclining seat.

"This is amazing Evan thank you so much." Evan helps me to strap myself in the seat before taking his own.

"Happy?" he asks giving me one of his knockout smiles.

"So happy," I smile grabbing hold of his hand, "although I'm really nervous."

"Hey once we've taken off I'll take your mind off things." he says with a glint in his eye.

"What if I need the toilet or something can I move or do I have to hold it? I knew I shouldn't have had two glasses of champagne at dinner."

Evan laughs, "Hey relax, as soon as we are in the air you can unbuckle your seat and move around."

"Really? I thought you could only do that on big planes, I thought it was like when you are in a car or a bus you have to stay seated. It's such a long time since I've flown I can't remember what you do."

"No babe, being a passenger on an aircraft is different to a car or a bus, for one we are in the air and you don't have things like traffic lights and zebra crossings to contend with."

I hit him playfully, "It's alright for you Mr 'I've flown lots of times'."

"Sorry babe, I'm sorry," he laughs squeezing my leg and giving it a rub.

The pilot announces we are ready for take-off and within a few minutes we are taxiing down the runway. I close my eyes and squeeze Evan's hand tightly. "Oh my god are we in the air now?"

"Almost," he says loosening my grip on his hand as my fingernails dig into his skin leaving a slight mark.

Forced back into our seats as the pilot puts the plane into full throttle we power down the runway at lightning speed before cruising off into the air and flying through the skies bound for foreign shores.

Opening my eyes and casting an anxious glance at Evan I ask, "Are we flying now?"

"Yes we are flying now, it's only a short flight so it won't be long before we are landing in a warmer climate," he says unbuckling his seatbelt.

"This is fantastic I never knew flying could be so exhilarating." I feel less nervous now looking out the window of the plane.

"Welcome to my world baby," he says leaning over and unbuckling my seatbelt, "come I want to show you something," He stands up and takes my hand.

"Excuse me can I get either of you anything to drink or something to eat?" a voice from behind us asks making us turn around.

Stood behind us is a glamorous air hostess who must be in her mid-forties and dressed in a navy suit with a red cravat, her dark hair is tied up in a bun on the top of her head and her bright red lipstick stands out on her perfectly made up face.

She smiles at us showing perfect white teeth.

"No we are fine thank you, Kara's not used to flying and is feeling a bit sick so we are going to have a rest for a while until she is feeling better," Evan replies. 'I am? I feel fine … I thought he said he was going to show me something?'

"Oh I am sorry to hear that Madam. Let me know if I can get you anything," she says looking concerned.

"Thank you." I reply feeling guilty because the lady is being caring and nice as I rub my stomach for effect.

The air hostess then turns and walks away back to the cabin at the front of the plane.

"What was that all about, I feel perfectly fine Evan and what was it that you wanted to show me?" I whisper looking puzzled.

"Well I wanted to show you this," he says grabbing hold of my hand and putting it on his erection straining his jeans. "I couldn't really tell her that could I so I had to make up something quick. Come on," he smiles grabbing my hand and pulling me towards a door at the back of the plane.

"Where are we going the toilets?" I ask shocked.

"No I think we can do better than the toilets Kara, this way," he smiles stopping outside a door at the back of the plane.

"What's in here?" I laugh. "Is it a cupboard?"

"Well open the door and find out," he smirks.

"Are we allowed in there?"

"Listen, we are allowed anywhere when I have paid a large sum of money to hire the whole plane for us."

"What, really?"

"Yes really, you are endearing." Evan chuckles.

"Don't laugh at me or I might just go and sit down again."

"The only place you will be sitting is on my cock so you'd better get your ass in there before I take you here because I've been looking at your great tits and your gorgeous cleavage for most of the night and thinking about fucking you. I can't wait much longer Kara, it's been too long already," he says smacking me on the bum as I open the door.

"Ouch." I squeal walking through the door into a luxurious cabin with a double bed, a small bar area and a small bathroom.

"Wow this is some cupboard." I laugh Evan following me inside and shutting the door behind us and locking it.

I turn around and can see the hunger in Evan's eyes as he stalks towards me backing me up towards the bed and I'm tingling all over.

"What do you want Evan ... these?" I tease pushing my breasts together emphasizing my cleavage even more.

Evan surges forward taking me in his arms and holding my head in his hands as he kisses me passionately delving his tongue into my mouth.

He then lifts my dress up my body slowly and over my head revealing the black lace bra and black lace thong that he enjoyed a preview of this morning.

"I really like this underwear you look hot." He says running his hands all over my lace covered breasts.

I fumble with the button on Evan's jeans but he stops me.

"Not yet, I want to savour you first before I take you." He then pulls the front of my lace bra cups down to reveal my erect nipples and rolls his fingers around the tips as I close my eyes enjoying the sensation.

"Evan what if the air hostess comes in?" I breathe.

"That won't happen the door's locked, you just have to be quiet okay."

"Okay I'll try but it's not easy, oh god." I pant as he fondles my breasts and tweaks my nipples sending a tingling sensation to my core. Reaching around my back to undo my black lace bra because he wants better access to my breasts he drops it onto the floor and takes a nipple in his mouth and sucks hard "Oh god Evan."

Easing me down onto the bed gently he crouches over me and continues to suck my nipples causing me to throw my head back and cry out.

"Shh ... baby you have to be quiet or the air hostess will hear you and she will be coming to see if you are alright," he smiles.

"Oh god I am more than alright Evan," I say breathless.

The double bed is dressed in expensive cotton white sheets with a white and plum duvet cover that could be in any interior design magazine and the mattress feels soft and deluxe as I lay on it being pleasured by Evan.

"You look so hot Kara," he says trailing his tongue down my body all the way down to my left ankle and back up the other leg up my smooth inner thigh. I gasp feeling Evan's tongue gliding over me.

"God you turn me on so much."

"I love this lace thong," he says tracing a light finger over the lacy material, "but it's in my way." Reaching his fingers in the sides and pulling them down my legs slowly as I lift my hips to help him.

Evan's erection is straining through his jeans and I try again to undo them desperate for him to be inside me but again Evan stops me.

"All in good time beautiful," he says pushing my legs apart with his hands and then lowering his mouth onto my throbbing clit making me cry out "OHH SHIT …" and then remembering I need to be quiet trying to stifle my moans.

Evan laughs, he loves how he affects me and the tiny noises I'm making and he knows I'm finding it hard to be quiet as he circles my clitoris with his tongue.

"Evan I need you." I beg sounding desperate.

"Not yet beautiful, I haven't finished devouring you yet."

He trails his tongue up to my navel and pushes two fingers inside of me.

"You're soaked and always so ready for me aren't you?" he smiles as he continues to move his fingers in and out of me while I thrash my head from side to side moaning.

Evan continues to trail his tongue over my soft skin moving slowly back up over my breasts skimming my nipples and then up to my mouth delving his tongue inside kissing me.

While he kisses me he rubs my clit with his thumb and fucks me with his fingers and I can feel my body getting ready and he knows I'm getting close to having an orgasm. I pull away from kissing him and moan.

"I'm going to come …" and I grab a pillow burying my face in it making Evan smile as my orgasm rips through my body, "Oh YES …" my cries muffled by the pillow while I experience the most incredible orgasm at 41,000 feet.

After coming down from such a rush, Evan removes the pillow from my face. "Was that good baby?" he grins before kissing me gently my hands in his hair as I kiss him back.

"Hmm … the best." I resume the kiss as my tongue entwines with Evan's while he fumbles with the button and zip on his jeans.

Standing up to take off his t-shirt, jeans and boxers releasing his bulge my eyes light up at his impressive manhood as he climbs back onto the bed. Evan kisses me again passionately and then looks into my piercing blue eyes, "I want you to ride me baby. I want to see your beautiful face and breasts as you take my cock inside you."

Evan lays on his back and I climb on top of him. Straddling his powerful thighs, I tease him by rubbing myself up and down his length before positioning the tip at my entrance. "Slow to start with," he says.

I lower myself carefully onto his awaiting erection, the wetness making it easy for me to accommodate him. He fills me completely and we both feel the powerful connection making us both moan.

"You feel so good," he says massaging the fullness of my breasts.

"Yes so good." I moan moving up and down on top of him.

Gradually increasing the speed, I ride Evan giving us both the best experience of our lives. Moving up and down with precision the intensity and intimacy of our eye contact looking at each other intensely is beyond anything I've ever felt before.

"That's it baby, aargh that's good," he says grabbing hold of my legs panting. "Oh Jesus baby I'm getting close." He moans and I continue moving up and down over and over again pleasuring us both, his cock filling me deeply.

Every thrust brings us closer and closer both of us enjoying fantastic sex thousands of feet in the air.

"Fuck I'm there baby, are you?" he says through gritted teeth.

Before I can answer I stifle a scream and orgasm.

"Yes, yes, yes."

I cry out triggering Evan's release, "Aargh fuck ..." and we both enjoy the sensational feeling of our mind blowing orgasms together.

Feeling out of breath I roll off Evan exhausted and shaky legged and he engulfs me in his arms. We are both satisfied and happy and we can't stop smiling.

"Welcome to the mile-high club," he laughs stroking my arm caressing me.

"I would like a permanent membership please, this club is definitely one I'd like to be in." I laugh.

"We had better get cleaned up because we shall be landing soon," he says looking at his watch.

"I have already landed on cloud nine." I smile stroking his semi erect cock.

"Don't or I will have to tell the pilot to circle a few times before we land while I take you again," he says jabbing his fingers lightly in my side making me flinch.

"Hey." I giggle, "okay, I'll behave for now." Smiling getting up off the bed and going into the small bathroom to clean up and use the toilet.

After cleaning ourselves and finding our clothes we get dressed and just as we have finished putting our clothes back on there is a knock on the door. Evan opens it to be greeted by the air hostess.

"I'm sorry to bother you I hope that the young lady is feeling better but we are due to land in 10 minutes so the captain has asked if you can return to your seats and put your seatbelts back on please."

"Yeah sure she is feeling much better thank you, we were just coming," he replies hearing me giggling in the background.

Evan tries to keep a straight face. "We will be there in a minute, thank you."

"Okay sir," the air hostess smiles knowing full well what we've been up to behind closed doors and walks off back towards the front of the plane.

Evan quickly closes the door and laughs, "That was close."

"Just coming …" I giggle.

"Well we were," he laughs. "Come on we had better do as we are told and get buckled in ready for landing."

"Okay," I smirk. Evan opens the door for me and smacks my bum as I walk through making me giggle as I return to the grey leather recliner seat.

The pilot announces that we're ready to land being given the green light from the control tower at the airport and says he hopes that we enjoyed our flight. I look at Evan and we can't help smirking because we have definitely enjoyed the flight.

"Are you okay beautiful?" he asks squeezing my hand as the pilot circles in readiness for landing.

"Perfect."

"Welcome to Italy," Evan smiles leaning over and giving me a kiss on the lips.

"Oh my god with all the excitement of flying on a jet plane for the first time and the excellent inflight entertainment I actually forgot that we were going somewhere." I'm really excited.

"I told the hire company when I hired the jet to tell the pilot not to announce where we were going so it would be a surprise for you and I could tell you before we landed."

"It's a lovely surprise thank you so much and Italy; I've always wanted to go to Italy I love pizza and pasta."

Evan laughs, "There is much more to Italy than pizza and pasta Kara."

"Are we staying at a hotel?"

"No we will be staying at my villa."

"Really you've got a villa, oh my god can this get any better?"

"It certainly can and will," he smirks.

Eighteen

On arriving, Evan steers us towards a single storey building which has a sign on it saying private hire vehicles.

"What about our luggage?" I ask looking back at the plane wanting my things.

"Don't worry it's all taken care of."

We walk up to a building hand in hand and Evan opens the door and ushers me inside. We enter into a minimal reception area consisting of a seating area with some grey cloth covered chairs and there is a round faced gentleman sat drinking a cup of coffee at a desk.

The man looks up from behind his coffee cup, puts his coffee down and says "Buonasera."

"Err hi?" I smile and then Evan starts speaking to the man in Italian.

"Great, grazie e arrivederci," Evan replies. Not that I understood the conversation but I think we are hiring a car.

The man hands Evan some keys and a bag and he takes them off him then looks at me and says, "Come on baby."

When we get outside I smile at him. "I didn't know you can speak Italian? You sound so sexy."

"Yes there are lots of things you don't know about me Kara. I thought if I'm going to buy a home here I had better speak the language, so I took a course a few years back."

We approach a sign saying 'Bay 3' and I think the guy at the hire company must have made a mistake because there is no hire car parked there but some flashy motorbike and I wonder what's in the bag he gave him?

"Now let me introduce you to another passion of mine ... are you ready for the next ride of your life baby?"

"Oh ... my ... god, seriously?" I'm shocked.

"Yes it's the best way to get around and I know how you enjoy having something powerful between your legs so you are going to love this."

I blush. "I've already had something powerful between my legs earlier Evan, you're joking aren't you?"

"Just trust me," he says handing me some leathers. Evan can't stop smiling at my shocked face.

"Evan I've never ridden on a motorbike before I'm scared, I'll just get a taxi and meet you there."

Evan smiles and puts a reassuring arm around me.

"Don't worry you will be perfectly safe with me, I've been riding motorbikes for years, you'll be fine honestly, you trust me don't you?"

"Yes but …"

"Good so put them on and then we can get out of here and I can get you home and in my bed," acknowledging the bike leathers with a smile.

"Evan I'm wearing a dress."

"Yes and a lovely dress it is too but you need to take it off or the all in one leathers are not going to fit properly."

"But someone might see. Did you buy these for me?"

"Yes why?"

"How did you know what size I needed?"

"I have ways and means of finding out, here let me help you," he says holding one of the legs of the leathers for me to step into.

I put my bag down on the floor and begrudgingly slip off the strappy shoes I'm wearing gather up my dress and put one foot into the leather trousers, then the other and Evan pulls them up to my waist. Looking around to see if anyone is looking I pull my dress off quickly and stand there half-naked in just biker leathers up to my waist and a black lacy bra.

"God you look fucking sexy as a biker chick look what you do to me," he says taking hold of my hand and placing it on his crotch so I can feel the solid muscle in his jeans.

"I prefer this helmet to that one." I say rubbing it with my palm looking at the bike helmet that I have to put on.

Evan runs his fingers through his hair. "Come on we need to go," he says. Letting go of his crotch I squeeze the top half of my body into the leathers zipping up the front and squashing my breasts into the tight leather all in one suit.

"Fucking hell you look hot baby, this is fucking torture I have a raging hard on that I can't do anything about which is really frustrating," he says pacing up and down on the tarmac.

"Here put the helmet on because the sooner we get out of here the sooner I can get you home and start fucking you." Evan rambles clearly affected by me in my bike attire.

I put my strappy black shoes back on which really doesn't go with my outfit but Evan had forgotten about footwear so it will have to do. I put my bag over my shoulder and then put the helmet on.

Evan puts on a leather jacket to go with his dark blue jeans and white t-shirt, looking pretty hot and then checks to see if my helmet is strapped on properly.

Giving me a reassuring hug and a squeeze of my leather clad bum, he then straddles the 600cc motorbike and holds out his hand for me to get on.

Evan starts the motorbike revving the engine a few times and I can feel the power of the bike as the vibrations on the seat catch my attention. 'I think I might enjoy this after all.'

"If you want to stop just tap me on the shoulder and I'll pull over okay?"

I nod too afraid to speak and then putting on his bike helmet Evan revs the engine a few more times, puts the bike into gear and pulls off out of the car park.

'Oh my god … I can't believe I'm actually riding on the back of a motorbike.'

Evan is probably thinking I'm enjoying the ride because I've not tapped him on the shoulder yet, but to be honest I'm too scared to let go of his waist.

The power of the bike is thrilling and Evan moves up the gears and speeds down the clear open road. After a while I begin to relax and enjoy myself.

I'm beginning to feel more confident and being on the back of Evan's bike is just the best feeling, I feel free and I would never have thought I would ever be doing this and it's awesome.

The journey from the airport to the villa goes quickly. Evan pulls off the main road onto a side street and steers the motorbike down a long drive towards a gated property.

As he pulls up at the gates he takes his keys out from his jean pocket and presses a button on his key fob which opens the gates. I can see the villa ahead of us. Evan clicks the button to shut the gates then pulls up outside the magnificent property turning off the engine as we come to a stop. He puts the stand down and then holds out his hand for me and helps me dismount from the bike then gets off afterwards. My legs feel like jelly because I've done two very different kinds of riding tonight and both made me go weak at the knees.

"So what did you think?" Evan asks grinning at me as I pass him my helmet. He hangs them on the handle of the motorbike and I smile then tip my head upside down. I shake my hair and then flip my head back running my fingers through my long blonde hair flattening it down. I look at him seriously.

"That was just … the best feeling in the world, I can't believe how I managed to stay on but it was bloody brilliant, I loved every minute of it, thank you, thank you." I grin lunging myself at him almost knocking him off his feet and giving him a hug.

I smile glancing around at the impressive building and grounds lit up with the glow of warm white lights, "this must be your villa then?" I smirk.

"Yes, I bought it five years ago, I came to this part of Italy a long time ago with my parents and I remember loving it so much that when I had made quite a bit of money from my first two hotels I chose to buy this. I like to come here any chance I get, it's more of a holiday home as my main residence is in London."

I look at the exterior of the villa consisting of terracotta walls and white windows. "If you're ready let's go inside and I'll show you around."

I follow him to the front door and he unlocks it and ushers me inside. The interior of the villa is a prime example of luxury and grandeur, boasting a combination of elegant architecture and distinguished furnishings. Evan shows me around. The open plan living area is filled with elegance and marble, all overlooking the private lakefront terrace and balcony.

Evan points out a door off the entrance hall that leads to a private self-contained apartment where his housekeepers, Mary and her husband George, live. He explains they reside here permanently so they can look after the place while he is away.

Stairs off the sitting room lead to the first floor accommodating a grand suite with double aspect, dressing room and marble bathroom with shower and sunken Jacuzzi as well as three bedrooms with exclusive marble en suite bathrooms.

Evan tells me the outside space features an infinity swimming pool located in the well-maintained gardens within the gated property, a large garage housing four motorbikes and his sports cars and several uncovered parking spaces. It really is an Italian paradise.

"Wow this place is exquisite, so where are we exactly?"

"We are on Lake Como."

"Wow, I've only ever read about Lake Como in magazines."

"It's beautiful here and the scenery is spectacular as you will see tomorrow in daylight, anyway I'm sure you must be tired it's been a long day. Would you like a nightcap before we go to bed?"

"Sounds good but I'm not tired I'm actually buzzing from the adrenalin rush of that ride on the motorbike," I smile.

Evan leads me to a stylish kitchen and looks in the large well-stocked fridge for a bottle of wine. A short man in his early fifties with short grey hair, a golden tan, a pot belly and a really friendly face appears and walks into the kitchen greeting us.

"Good evening Mr Hamilton, madam, did you have a good trip?"

"Hi George, it's good to see you again, we did thanks." Evan says shaking George's hand, "this is my friend Kara."

"It's a pleasure to meet you Kara," George says shaking my hand.

George has a soft charming voice, the sort of voice that you would hear on television adverts advertising some delicious food. He has a southern accent like Evan's and is well spoken so I'm guessing he's from the same area of London.

"Your luggage has arrived and I have put it in your suite for you sir."

"Thanks George I was just getting a bottle of white wine to relax with after a long day."

"Very good sir, what time can I tell Mary that you would like your breakfast tomorrow?"

"9.00am would be great and thank Mary for me; the place looks wonderful as always."

"Will do, goodnight to you both." George smiles.

"Goodnight."

"He's seems lovely." I mention.

"George and Mary are just the loveliest couple and I trust them implicitly to look after the place, they have lived here since I purchased it."

"Oh I see how do you know them?"

"They actually worked for me at one of my first hotel's I owned, they happened to mention one day about their son living here, on Lake Como and that they didn't get to see him too often and when I bought this place I offered them both a job to look after the place and they gladly accepted."

"I bet they are really grateful to you."

"Yes they are but it suits me as well because I know this place is in good hands when I'm not here."

Evan takes two wine glasses out of one of the kitchen cupboards and picks up the bottle of white wine.

"Come on we'll drink this upstairs."

He walks out of the kitchen and I follow him down a hallway through a sitting area to some stairs leading to the first floor then along another long hallway leading to a door at the end of the hall which leads to the master suite.

Evan walks into the bedroom and puts the wine and two glasses on a dressing table at the side of the room.

"Your villa really is lovely Evan, this is a gorgeous room."

I look around taking in the size of the room and flop onto the huge bed that's dressed in sumptuous bedding of silver and purple luxurious fabric with scatter cushions and crisp white expensive sheets. Evan's bedroom is decorated in soft and soothing greys and silvers to create a luxurious feel. With an ultramodern chandelier hanging over the bed to the cool marble floor, I imagine waking up in this room will be heavenly.

"Thank you," he says closing the door. I get up off the bed and start to unzip the leathers. Evan looks at me, "Stop, don't take them off yet." I look at him and frown. He pours two glasses of wine and then walks over to where I'm stood and hands one to me.

"Thanks I'm so hot," I reply fanning my face with my hands taking the glass from him and taking a sip of the cool liquid. "Hmm this is nice."

"Hmm you do look hot and that's why I want you to leave your leathers on for a bit longer, here's to us and as they say in Italy 'Salute'."

"Salute." I smile.

Evan finishes his wine quickly and puts his empty glass down on the dressing table then slowly stalks over to me with lust in his eyes. He takes the glass out of my hand and puts it on the bedside table.

"Oh I was enjoying that," I protest but smile as he takes me in his arms and kisses me long and slow our tongues mingling together in our joined mouths. Evan breaks away and walks over to a tub chair next to a table in the corner of the room and sits down in it leaving me stood alone next to the bed wondering why he's left me after sharing a passionate kiss.

"Now you can take your leathers off I want you to do a striptease for me and take them off while I watch you," he smiles sitting with a prominent bulge in his jeans.

I blush. "Okay."

Evan takes off his jacket and hangs it on the back of the chair then makes himself comfortable and puts on some slow love songs.

I've never done a striptease for anyone before, no one has ever asked but the sound of the music playing is making me feel sexy, so I start to sway my hips to the music taking hold of the zip at the top of the leathers. I keep my eyes fixed on his the whole time as I slowly lower the zip until the front of the bike leathers are fully open exposing my cleavage covered in a black lace bra.

"God you look sexy as fuck," Evan growls watching me closely.

He takes a deep breath and lets it out slowly pinning me with his eyes as I trace light fingers over my lace covered cleavage.

"You like my tits don't you?" I say placing one hand on my shoulder to ease my arm out of the sleeve of the leathers on one side and then repeating the motion the other side until my top half is free.

"I do I love them … god you are so sexy," he says his chest moving up and down rapidly his breathing becoming faster the more turned on he becomes.

Swaying in time to the music I sway my hips slowly pushing the leathers down my long, silky legs leaning forward to give Evan a good view of my breasts until the leathers are down to my ankles.

I then turn around so my back is facing him and bend over slowly giving him the perfect view of my bum covered in the black lace thong. "Fucking hell…you drive me crazy."

I take the leathers off and fling them to the side of the room turning to look at him feeling excited because he's unbuttoned his jeans letting his solid erection spring free. Taking all of his clothes off, I watch him excitedly anticipating his hands being all over me at any moment but I'm disappointed when he sits down on the chair again.

"Don't stop I'm just getting ready," he says looking serious and hot.

I'm turned on and desperate for his touch.

I carry on with the striptease, unclasping the back of my bra and letting it fall to the floor showing Evan my naked breasts.

Evan's hungry eyes grow wide at the sight of me and I massage them whilst looking at him and he strokes his cock watching me.

"Do you like watching me Evan does it turn you on?" I ask sitting on the edge of the bed facing him.

"I do … I'm so fucking hard, look what you do to me," he says moving his hands up and down his length stroking himself.

I can see the tip glistening with excitement.

I slide a single finger into my mouth and suck on it keeping my eyes firmly fixed on Evan's while I do, "I'm imagining my finger is your cock." I tease sucking on it and pushing it in and out of my mouth slowly moaning and staring into his wide eyes.

"Fucking hell," he says drawing a breath and fidgeting on the chair.

"Hmm …" I moan taking my wet finger from my mouth and circling my right nipple with it looking at him.

"Jesus Kara." I trail my finger down my breasts and slip my hand into my black lace panties and in between my legs feeling the wetness.

I touch myself rubbing my clit and moaning closing my eyes and throwing my head back pushing out my breasts. The erotic display is making Evan wild with desire. I stand up and turn around so I'm facing away from him and putting my fingers either side of my thong I slowly slide them over my hips and down my legs until they hit the floor, I kick them to the side.

"Oh wow," he says breathless.

"Thanks," I smile climbing onto the bed on all fours facing away from him so he has a full view of my peachy bum and my wet sex. I throw my hair over one shoulder and turn my head to look at him, "I'd like you to fuck me now."

Evan can't resist me any longer, "Fuck yes" he rushes to his feet and comes up behind me. Expecting him to enter me straight away I'm surprised when he lowers his head and plunges his tongue inside me causing me to cry out.

"Oh my fucking god." He circles his tongue around and around and I moan loudly while he tastes me, the feeling is exhilarating. "Evan." I pant.

"You like that do you?" he asks continuing to turn me on in this way.

"Shit … yes …" The intense feeling and aching from my insides is making me desperate for him and for my release.

"Fuck me Evan please I'm so ready, fuck me." I'm turned on to the max waiting for him to enter me.

Evan moves onto the bed behind me and rubs his cock up and down in between my legs gathering some of my wetness.

"You are ready aren't you, you're soaked, hold onto the bed sheets." I do as I'm told and Evan grabs hold of my hips as he positions at my entrance and slams into me hard making me scream.

"OHHH ..." He claims my body with his, driving into me with such expertise each thrust hitting the spot every time; he fucks me hard over and over again sending me closer and closer to the edge, his powerful cock giving me phenomenal feelings throughout my body and to my brain.

"Oh yes ... yes ... that is so fucking good."

"Fucking hell, Jesus that's good...."

"OHH ... you turn me on so much."

"FUUUCCCKKK ... I need to see you," he says pulling out of me and flipping me over onto my back quickly and then ramming into me again looking at me intensely with a look of adoration on his face.

I hold onto his back clawing at his skin and he's panting out of breath using all the energy he can muster into making us both come. The incredible feeling of him filling my insides and Evan ramming into me, in and out in and out soon has my body shaking and bringing my orgasm to the surface.

"Yes … Evan… I'm coming …" I cry and my orgasm rushes through me like a wild tornado. Evan finds his own release too filling me with his warm seed, jerking and bucking inside me and we both moan as the incredible feeling fills our brains.

"Oh wow …"

"That was unbelievable."

He kisses me slowly and passionately, then eases out of me and flops exhausted on the bed sweating and breathing hard.

"Yes it was."

"I loved your striptease," he smiles turning to look at me.

"I've never stripped for anyone before but seeing how much it turned you on and me for that matter I want to do it again sometime." I grin.

"You would never have known you were incredible and I will definitely be asking you to do it again for me," he grins taking me in his arms for a cuddle and kissing me softly.

"So what's the plan for tomorrow then?" I snuggle closer.

"Well I have lots of surprises planned for you, so you will just have to wait and see," he smiles stroking my back.

"Okay, well I love your surprises," I smile. "I can't wait."

Nineteen

We arrive in the dining room just off the kitchen and Mary is setting the table, she looks up and sees us walking towards her. She puts down the cutlery and smiles walking over to Evan giving him a big hug and a kiss on the cheek.

"Now then my boy, it's great to see you and who is this lovely young lady?" she asks giving me a warm welcoming smile.

Mary is a petite lady in her early fifties with dyed blonde hair, a golden tan and she has lovely blue eyes.

"This is my friend Kara."

"Hello Kara, it's lovely to meet you dear," she says giving me a hug and kiss on the cheek too.

"Kara's looking forward to trying one of your fry ups Mary after I told her how great they are."

"Yes I am." I smile.

"Oh good well it's almost ready, if you want to take a seat I'll bring them straight out to you once I've plated up," she says going back into the kitchen.

Evan pulls out a chair for me to sit down and then sits opposite me, the morning sun is glistening over the lake.

"Would you like some orange juice?" he asks picking up a jug of freshly squeezed orange juice that's in the centre of the table and pouring some into a glass.

"Yes please."

Evan passes me the one he's already poured and I take a sip of the delicious juice and then Evan pours another for himself.

Mary walks back into the dining room carrying two hot plates of food and places them in front of us. "Enjoy your breakfast I'll be in the kitchen if you need anything," she says then leaves the room so we can enjoy our breakfast together alone.

After we have eaten the delicious fry up, we head out onto the private terrace to enjoy a cup of tea.

"Oh wow the view is just simply breath-taking Evan." I stand on the balcony in awe looking across at the blue rippling waters of the lake in the distance.

"Yes the view from here is one of the things I loved about this property when I bought it, it really is breath-taking isn't it," he says placing an arm around my waist as we stand drinking our cups of tea in the sunshine.

"I don't think I've ever been anywhere so beautiful in all my life, thank you so much for bringing me here." I lean my head back against his shoulder.

"And I've never had the pleasure of being with such a beautiful person in my life so we are both thankful," he smiles kissing me on the top of my head.

We sit down onto the sun loungers to finish our tea and I send my mum a quick text to tell her I'm having a good time with my 'old school friend Jess'.

Of course this is a total lie and I feel bad for lying but it's easier this way than telling her about Evan and our complicated arrangement of fun.

I also text Jodie to tell her where I am and that I'm having an amazing time.

"Are you ready to go babe? I have a full day planned."

"Yes," I put my phone away in my bag, "we're not going on that motorbike again are we?"

"No, first we are going to take a stroll in the gardens and then you will be pleasantly surprised at our mode of transport for today," he says giving me a quick kiss on the lips.

"Okay, I'm intrigued, lead the way Mr H."

On the way out, Evan pops his head into the kitchen and is handed a picnic hamper by Mary. He then escorts me down a corridor to a door at the back of the villa. On opening the door, I can feel the summer heat from outside and a warm breeze wafts in through the door.

"First thing's first, we will need protection." Evan says putting the basket down.

I give him a smile, "What do you mean protection?"

"Protection from the sun, duh?" he jokes getting a bottle of sun cream out of the basket.

"I'll put some on you then you can put some on me," he moves my hair out of the way and squirts some in his hand then massages the cream into my soft skin on all the areas he can see needs it. Then returning the favour I put some lotion on him.

Once we are both lathered in sun cream, Evan picks up the basket again and then linking hands we walk out the back door into the hot sunshine and down a pathway which leads us through the well-maintained gardens surrounding the villa. The scent of Lavender and flowers including Orchids, Roses, Calla Lilies and Dahlias fill the air as we walk through the gardens filled with beautiful flowers.

"This garden is just beautiful Evan."

"Thanks, I have a gardener come once a week to maintain it."

The path takes us past an infinity pool. I get my phone out of my bag and take some quick photos of the colourful garden and the infinity pool so I can show Jodie.

"Come on you," he smirks. I put my phone back in my bag and he takes hold of my hand and leads me further down the path through some shrubbery to reveal the crystal waters of Lake Como.

"Oh my god I can't believe I'm actually here." I smile taking in the breath-taking view.

"Believe it baby."

We walk further and a boat mooring comes into view with the most magnificent yacht moored up called 'Spirito Libero'.

"That's not yours is it?" I ask, clapping my hands with excitement.

"Certainly is."

"Is that our mode of transport today?" I squeal, jumping up and down like an excited child.

"No, I just wanted to show it to you, I've booked for us to go on one of those tourist boats to tour the lake." My face drops. I look at him and he's grinning at me. "I'm joking," he laughs.

"Evan you are asking for it." I laugh shaking my head.

"Hmm and I really hope you are going to give it to me," he winks grabbing hold of me for a quick kiss.

I peruse Evan's yacht stood on the jetty looking out towards the lake and think for a moment.

'I can't believe how my life has changed over the last few weeks. I've gone from being single wiping tables and making coffee to meeting the man of my dreams and being whisked away by a millionaire to a private villa in Lake Como, Italy. This does not happen to people like me. Somebody pinch me.'

"Care to step aboard madam?" he says holding out his hand snapping me out of my thoughts.

"Certainly Captain." I take his hand and he helps me on board the expensive yacht. He then passes me the picnic hamper while he unties the mooring ropes on shore so we can set sail.

Evan then jumps on board and takes charge at the wheel.

He starts up the engine and does some checks before steering his boat out towards the vast lake.

"I noticed the name on your boat, what does 'Sprite Liberty' mean?" I innocently ask standing at the side of him.

"No idea." Evan chuckles, "but if you mean the name

'Spirito Libero' it means Free Spirit in Italian, I thought it was quite an apt name."

"Oh," I laugh, feeling silly.

Evan's mood today is different.

He seems loved-up and his jovial nature puts such a smile on my face. I would like to think it is me making him this happy, or it is because we are sailing? I am happy to ignore that we have an expiry date for now and just enjoy being with him.

Delving into my bag I take out my mobile phone and open up the camera.

"Selfie time." I say taking a picture of us, Evan leans in and kisses me on the cheek.

After taking a few shots of Evan steering his yacht and a few of us together in the sunshine I put my phone away and take a seat on his lap, "Can I drive?" I ask with a pleading look on my face.

"I'm not sure this yacht cost me a lot of money, it's my pride and joy and I don't want it turning into driftwood." he smirks.

"Hey." I smack him playfully on the leg, "I promise I would be really careful."

"No I think I'll be in charge of the boat today, you just relax and enjoy the ride."

"Ok well if you won't let me steer your precious boat I think I'll do a bit of sunbathing then." I pout climbing off his lap and moving towards the sun loungers opposite the driving seat.

Evan presses a button on the steering column and it opens the retractable sun roof.

I can feel the heat instantly as the sun rays beat down on us, 'could life get any better right now?'.

Looking him in the eyes as he turns and watches me put my bag down on the floor I grab the hem of my sundress and pull it slowly up over my body. Evan tries to keep an eye on where he's steering but can't help looking at me while I undress in front of him.

"Jesus," he mumbles as I pull the dress off my body revealing my flat stomach and a skimpy red bikini with high leg bottoms and a plunging balconette top underneath which shows off my assets perfectly.

Evan distracted by me swerves the boat slightly making me stumble, "Watch what you're doing Captain you wouldn't want to crash your precious boat." I laugh.

"Kara, I know what you are doing," he says adjusting himself in his shorts.

"I'm not doing anything Evan, I am merely getting undressed to do some sunbathing I think I will lie down on this lounger over here so I can watch you steer your pride and joy."

I turn away from him and walk over to the lounger knowing full well that Evan will be watching me. I sit on the lounger noticing he keeps glancing my way so I lean forward to take my shoes off giving him a view of my cleavage as I bend down. I then lie down on the cream and wood sun lounger, look at him and smile, "Oh this is so nice lying here in the sun, it's a shame you can't join me."

He looks at me and I tease him some more pretending to stretch pushing my breasts out and arching my back. Evan draws in a deep breath as he desperately tries to steer his boat while regularly glancing at his other passion that is laid on the sun lounger teasing him … ME!

"Kara you are not playing fair, you're turning me on and I can't do anything about it until I find a safe spot to moor up." he smirks.

"It's a shame I couldn't come and relieve you of your sexual frustration but I wouldn't want to distract you in case you crash." I smile licking my lips.

"You're wicked," he grins adjusting his cock in his shorts.

"Oh I'm so hot I could do with a drink to cool down." I bend my knee bringing my long smooth leg up resting my foot on the lounger and turn to look at him.

"Uh huh, you certainly look hot from where I'm sitting,'" he says with hungry eyes, "there are some bottles of water in the picnic basket over there if you want to get one, we'll have the champagne later when I can enjoy it with you."

"Okay would you like one?"

"Yes please I would love for you to give me one but I'll just have to settle for the water for now," he grins. "I'm feeling hot myself and need to cool down," he says adjusting his groin.

I smirk and get up off the sun lounger to get two bottles of water out of the picnic basket. I pass one to Evan and he grabs hold of me pulling me onto his lap. He then kisses me fiercely while keeping one eye on where he's steering his boat.

"I love your bikini," he says licking his lips and massaging my breast with his free hand.

"Thanks, but you need to steer and I need to sunbathe," I smile peeling myself away from him. He smacks me on my bum as I walk away.

I sit down on the sun lounger and pick up the bottle of water and take a big drink. "Oh that is so good." I moan drinking more of the cool refreshing water.

I notice Evan can't keep his eyes off me, so I pour some of the water over my body and rub it into my stomach and over my breasts making them all wet.

"What are you doing to me?" he says fidgeting in his seat making me giggle.

"I'm merely trying to cool down, Oh yes that feels so good." I tease.

"You just wait until this boat is anchored Kara," he says breathing deeply and shaking his head, trying his best to navigate the yacht through the rich blue waters.

"How much longer Evan, it's kind of lonely over here?" I pout running my hands over my wet breasts and stomach.

"We're almost there, there is a private cove around this corner, we'll moor up there for a little while and then you are getting it lady."

"Oh good because I'm all wet and it's not just from the bottle of water Evan," I touch myself over my bikini bottoms.

"Fuck Kara."

"Oh no I almost forgot," I look at Evan as I sit up on the lounger to face him.

"What baby?" he says looking puzzled and turned on.

"I don't want to get any bikini tan lines, so this is going to have to go," I unhook my bikini top and fling it to one side. I feel so liberated by knowing nobody will see, but Evan. I feel so naughty.

"Jeez, this spot will have to do," he says cutting the engine and then dropping anchor. Scurrying over to me with his erection jutting from his white shorts he scoops me up in his arms, "That felt like the longest time of my life finding somewhere to drop anchor you little tease. Finally I get to have you and these babies," he says lifting me higher shoving his face in my breasts making me giggle.

He walks with me in his arms. "I haven't given you a tour of the boat yet have I? I think we'll start with the master bedroom." Evan puts me down briefly so I can climb down the steps to below deck and then he picks me up again and walks us down a corridor to the front of the boat. Carrying me through the door to the master suite he gently puts me down on the large double bed.

"I love the bedroom." I smile.

"Hmm and I love these," he says lowering his mouth onto one of my erect nipples and sucking it making me moan and arch my back. He raises his head to look at my half naked body, "we definitely need to get rid of these," he smiles taking hold of my red bikini bottoms and rolling them down my legs.

I lift my hips to help him and he throws them to one side.

"Are we feeling sexually frustrated Mr H?" I ask grinning at him looking at his huge erection.

"You could say that after the show you were putting on out there." He removes his shorts quickly followed by his t-shirt until he is also naked.

"I was merely sunbathing that's all and I needed to cool down with the water." I smirk.

"Well you looked hot splashing water over your breasts and you look even hotter right now laid there naked waiting for me to fuck you," he says grabbing his cock and stroking it up and down while looking at me.

I bite my lip, "I want to taste you."

Evan climbs onto the bed at the side of me. He lays down with his length in line with my mouth and his mouth in line with my sex.

Moving closer I take hold of his hard length and circle the tip with my tongue, licking up and down as Evan grabs hold of my bum and pulls me forward onto his mouth sucking and licking my clit, both of us turning each other on.

"Aargh fuck …" he moans hitting the back of my throat as I suck him hard.

"Hmm …" I moan as he pleasures my sensitive spot with his tongue, both of us enjoying giving and receiving as we lay opposite ways on the bed. I gorge on him sucking and tasting while Evan pleasures me at the same time.

"My cock feels so good inside your greedy mouth," he pants as I continue over and over again sucking, the sensations making his legs shake as his release comes further to the surface.

The sensations between my legs are increasing too, I moan as his tongue circles around and around my swollen clit and it's giving me so much pleasure.

Evan is just too good, I can feel my insides pulsating and aching getting ready to give me the rush I desperately long for but I don't want to come yet so I release Evan from my mouth.

"Oh god Evan stop, or I'll come. I want you to fuck me."

Evan stops and sits up.

He then turns around to face me and he's grinning at me, his mouth wet and glistening from my excitement. "You want me to fuck you do you?" he pants with a desperate look on his face as he climbs on top of me.

"Yes, fuck me." I'm desperate, so I open my legs wider for him to enter me. He kisses me fiercely then plunges his hard length deep inside me and holds it there for a few seconds, "OHHHHH …" I grab his cock with my insides.

"Oh Jesus baby … you're just perfect." I pull my legs up around Evan's back and then he powers into me again, his back is sweaty from the humidity of the air and the hard drives as he fucks my curvy body. I cling onto his muscly back digging my nails in slightly, the boat gently rocking on the blue crystal waters of Lake Como while we both enjoy each other's bodies on Evan's yacht.

Evan thrusts in and out, in and out, "God that's good," his breathing erratic and his face full of ecstasy moaning loudly, I'm moaning too.

"Oh god yes."

"You are so beautiful Kara."

"Oh god, oh god, oh god …"

"Does that feel good baby?"

"Yes … yes… so good." I answer breathless.

"You make me so hard with your incredible body and the sounds you make when I'm inside you."

"Evan … I'm nearly there … oh god … I can't hold it much longer." We are both so turned on we are almost at the point of letting go, our orgasms are getting closer and closer.

"Yes baby … I can feel you … I'm with you Kara."

"Evan I'm going to come …" I scream.

"I'm with you baby let it go," he groans.

I've reached the point of no return and turned on by the sounds of me having a sensational orgasm and the feeling of my insides pulsating around his cock Evan follows with his own, "FUUUUCCCKKK …" his body stills and his cock jerks as he comes inside me moaning loudly.

Evan's hot sweaty, contented body is laid on top of mine and he's looking into my blue eyes, a big grin is on his face.

"That was awesome," he says kissing me softly and giving soft licks with his tongue as I happily kiss him back.

"You're awesome," I smile before kissing him passionately again. "Are you okay?" I ask.

"Yes but I'm bloody knackered now though," he laughs.

"Me too, I've never had so many amazing orgasms, I'm so glad I met you or I would never have known just how amazing sex can be."

"Well it's a good job I stopped by the coffee shop that day then isn't it because you would have missed out on all this," he says moving his semi-erect cock around that's still inside me.

"Do you feel better now after relieving some of your sexual tension, you were getting impatient on deck when you couldn't find somewhere to drop anchor?" I laugh.

"Yes much better thank you and I'm not surprised I was getting impatient the way you were teasing me, I loved it!" he smiles bringing his face to mine again for another slow, soft kiss.

"I love having sex with you."

"Me too. I think we could both do with a shower now because we're all hot and sticky then shall we have our picnic?" he says pulling out of me and rolling over onto his back.

"Sounds good." I smile.

"You go and shower first I just need to check my phone in case I've missed any important calls with any problems at the hotels."

"Okay." I give him a quick peck on the lips then walk into the en suite bathroom. I turn the shower on and the water descends like a gentle rainforest mist.

After Evan has made a few calls he joins me in the bathroom as I'm getting out.

"I'm all done so you can jump in now," I smile tying a towel around my body.

"Great and there were no problems to deal with so all's good," he says stepping into the shower and turning on the water spray. I dry off and retrieve my bikini bottoms from the bedroom floor then remember my bikini top is still on deck that I had flung off earlier so I grab Evan's t-shirt and put it on so I can go and retrieve it.

Taking in the scent of his top, I bring the t-shirt up to my nose and inhale. I love the smell of him. After going on deck and getting my bikini top I return to the bedroom and whilst I'm taking Evan's t-shirt off his mobile phone rings from the bedside table where he left it earlier after making his calls.

I pick it up and see a ladies name flashing up on the screen called Julia, 'who is Julia?' I wonder if I should answer it or not?

Deciding not to, I put the phone back on the side put on my bikini top and go into the bathroom to see Evan who is just getting out of the shower.

"Who is Julia?" I ask making Evan spin around quickly and look at me in shock.

"Why, where did that come from?"

"Oh she tried ringing you a minute ago when you were in the shower. I wasn't sure whether I should have answered it on your behalf."

"You didn't answer it did you?" Evan says looking a bit nervous.

"No, I didn't but you didn't answer my question?"

"She's no-one," he answers trying to sound casual.

"Well you're acting awfully uncomfortable considering she is no-one?" I glare at him.

"She is of no concern to you and I don't like your tone, you are acting like I am guilty of something."

"Well are you?" I snap, "for all I know she could be your girlfriend sat at home waiting for you to return and you are just shagging me to pass a bit of time until you are back with her? I know how much you like having sex and it must be hard not getting any when you are away on business working."

"Don't be stupid, I told you I am not in a relationship and stop acting jealous because you are not my girlfriend and I don't have to justify myself to you."

"Don't you dare call me stupid and well that just clarifies it there doesn't it I am just a shag to you. Do you know what Evan, quite frankly you can just go and fuck yourself because I am not doing this anymore."

I storm out of the bathroom leaving Evan stood in his towel looking shocked and angry. How dare he treat me like that.

I go and sit on the main deck on one of the sun loungers and my emotions get the better of me, I put my head in my hands and cry. Why did we have to be on a boat at this precise moment in time so I can't escape?

A few moments later I sense him, I quickly look up and see Evan emerging from below deck with wet hair and his white shorts on walking over to me.

He sits next to me on the other lounger and looks at me warily, "I'm sorry."

"Sorry for what, me finding out about Julia?" I snap wiping the tears from my eyes.

"Please don't cry, I'm sorry for what I just said and I should have just been honest with you."

"Yes you should have."

"Julia was my girlfriend a long time ago and when you said her name it shocked me because I've not heard from her in a while."

"Is she the reason you don't do relationships?" I turn to him.

"Yes she is, I just don't like to talk about it. And you are not just a fuck so please don't degrade yourself."

"Yes but that's what I am Evan whichever way you put it."

"I think we both know that if you were just a fuck then I'd have ditched you by now and certainly not have invited you to come away with me for the weekend."

"So what are you saying you have feelings for me?"

He takes my hand in his, trying to calm me down.

"I think you are amazing Kara, you are beautiful, funny, kind and I really enjoy being with you but saying that does not mean I want a relationship. Like I told you in the beginning I don't do relationships and I have my reasons which I don't want to get into but I know that I love spending time with you and want to carry on seeing you when we get back to England. If you are starting to have feelings for me then maybe we need to stop this now because I don't want to hurt you."

"This is all so confusing, I don't know how I feel, I don't know what to think, I just know that I love being with you too and when I'm not with you I feel lost."

Evan kneels in front of me and puts his hands on either side of my legs.

"Look don't cry I hate that I've upset you, please let's just forget about it and enjoy every moment we spend together and our weekend here in Italy. When we get back to England if you decide that you don't want to carry on seeing me then I will completely understand. As for Julia, well she is irrelevant."

"Why was it a shock when you heard her name do you not see or speak with her anymore?"

"No."

"Is she the one who betrayed you?"

"Yes she was my girlfriend and we finished a year ago, I've not heard from her since. We were together for a year and a half and I thought she was the one; I was planning on proposing to her until I found out something and then my whole world came crashing down."

"Why what happened?"

"I'd rather not talk about it."

"Do you still love her?"

"No not anymore and I really don't know why she is ringing me because I've not spoken to her since we split up. I'm surprised she still has my number."

"But you still have her number because it came up on your phone."

"I didn't realise that I had, I thought I had deleted it."

I am struggling to know what to believe. Is this an easy way for Evan to not admit something or am I just overreacting?

I know I have willingly allowed myself to get whisked away knowing Evan is not prepared for a relationship. This is so hard, I'm not sure how much longer I can convince myself that this is okay.

"Okay fine, look I'm sorry too, I don't want us to fight." I cup his face.

"So does that mean we're friends again?" He pouts at me.

Looking at me with his big brown eyes and giving me a sweet smile, how can I not be?

"Friends." I smile.

Evan pulls me onto his lap and kisses me with so much passion I don't want him to stop.

"Do you want to go and make friends properly, I can give you plenty more of this to cheer you up?" Evan says pushing his cock into me and grinning.

"Evan." I roll my eyes at him and laugh.

"I'm only joking come on babe let's go get some lunch.

"Are you not going to phone her back then and find out what she wants?"

"I'll phone her later anyway she's not a priority whereas food is right now because I'm famished."

Evan reaches into the picnic basket and takes out a bottle of champagne, some strawberries and some chopped up pieces of melon, cucumber sandwiches and a selection of crisps.

We eat and drink the champagne and things are better between us. Evan tells me about his yacht and that he had it built to his specification and how much he loves Italy. I listen to him but I can't help feeling a bit sad inside.

I was hoping that this weekend away would be the time that Evan admits his true feelings for me but after the argument that has just taken place it's obvious that he isn't going to. He doesn't want a relationship.

The call from Julia is a sharp reminder that I don't really know much about Evan's life at all. The easiest thing would be to walk away knowing this relationship is not going to go anywhere but I'm not ready to give up yet, I know there is definitely something between us and I know he feels it too.

Twenty

The crystal blue water is twinkling with the sun reflecting off it. We cruise around the lake in the afternoon sun, celebrity property spotting and taking in the magical surroundings. Looking at the time and seeing it's almost 4.00pm Evan manoeuvres the boat and heads back towards the villa.

"It really is beautiful here." I say admiring the view as the warm breeze wafts through my blonde hair.

"Sei bellissima potrei guardarti tutto il giorno." Evan replies.

"Oh my god, you sound so sexy when you speak Italian, what did you say?"

"You're beautiful I could look at you all day," he smiles.

I take a seat on Evan's lap while he steers the boat and snuggle into him, "Thank you, I think you are beautiful too." I blush, "say something else to me."

"Like what?"

"I don't know something nice like you did just then."

"Hai un bel seno e ti amo baciarti."

"God just the sound of your voice turns me on but when you speak Italian that's another level of sexy I love it so what did you say?"

"I said you have lovely breasts and I love kissing you."

I playfully smack him on the arm and then lean in and give him a soft, slow sensual kiss. Evan kisses me back while trying to keep an eye on steering his boat in the right direction.

As the jetty comes into view at Evan's villa he slows down and expertly manoeuvres his boat into its mooring space with precision. Jumping off to tie the mooring ropes to secure her in place, I watch while he does all the checks.

"All done, are you ready to go?" he calls.

"Yes and thank you for an amazing day I've really enjoyed it." I smile looking at him feeling a little flushed and sunburnt from all the sun.

"You are very welcome but the day is not over yet, I would like to take you out tonight if you are not too tired?"

"No that sounds lovely, where are you taking me? Don't tell me it's a surprise."

"You got it babe but first I need to take you shopping."

"Shopping, why?"

"Because I'm guessing you have only bought summer clothes with you in your suitcase and you are going to need an evening gown for what I have in mind."

"Oh right, yes I definitely don't have anything like that in my case."

"I thought as much so we'll drop the picnic basket off at the villa then go and get you a dress, it won't take long and then we can have a rest before I take you out later."

"Okay, but I don't have much money with me so I will have to owe you if I don't have enough."

"I tell you what I'll treat you to a new dress if you treat me later?" he says with a twinkle in his eye.

"It's a deal." I blush because I know exactly what his treat will be.

We walk up the path through the fragrant gardens hand in hand back towards the villa. Evan puts the picnic basket inside the back door and then we walk around to the front of the villa. As we approach the garage, Evan presses a button on his key and the garage door begins to unfold revealing an array of vehicles, I can't believe what I am seeing.

There are the four motorbikes that Evan mentioned when we first arrived at the villa and three sports cars lined up all looking shiny and new.

"How many vehicles do you need, I don't even own one?" I smirk.

"I love cars and motorbikes what can I say."

Walking into the garage I admire the motorbikes that Evan is so passionate about and Evan tells me about them, how long he has had them and how fast they go then moving towards the shiny, polished cars he says, "Today I fancy taking one of Italy's finest sports cars the Ferrari 458 for a spin." He runs his fingers along the bonnet admiring its workmanship.

"Oh wow, it's gorgeous Evan, I love red cars."

"Jump in." He clicks the remote to open the door and I get in and Evan gets into the driver's seat.

"This car must have cost a fortune." I say looking at the plush black and cream leather interior.

"Enough," he replies squeezing my leg and grinning.

Evan starts the engine and revs it a few times then pulls out of the garage towards the security gates opening them as he drives up to them.

Then putting his foot down throwing me back into the seat he speeds off down the open road towards Lake Como town.

Evan laughs looking at me clinging on to the sides of my seat. "I fucking love this car."

Driving along the coast road of Lake Como I enjoy the stunning views, an area of Italy that I never knew I would ever get to see.

Arriving in the elegant and bustling town Evan pulls into a car park not far from a street lined with expensive boutique shops.

Evan opens my car door for me and points out the shop that he's taking me to. "Come on let's go and get you a nice dress to wear," he says with a smile. Clicking the remote to lock the car we cross the road and enter one of the well-presented designer shops. We are greeted by a lady dressed in a chic black suit paired with some stunning Louboutin shoes.

"Buon pomeriggio," Evan says.

I'm learning this means 'Good afternoon'.

He speaks to the lady and I wonder what he's saying to her because he seems to be saying a lot. After they have finished their conversation the lady smiles at him flirtatiously looking him up and down, she obviously fancies him as she fiddles with her hair.

I roll my eyes, I don't like the way she is looking at him so I take hold of Evan's hand to say 'eyes off he's mine'. The lady then goes away and Evan tells me she is going to get some dresses for me to try on.

After gathering up handfuls of dresses the lady beckons me over to a fitting area at the back of the shop. I feel out of my comfort zone, Evan noticing me holding back ushers me forward, "Go on you'll be fine, I'll be out here waiting for you."

I take a deep breath "Okay."

Just as I'm about to walk off he grabs my arm, "I would offer to come and help but if I come in there when you are taking your clothes off there will be no trying on clothes," he whispers. I blush.

I make my way into a changing room behind a velvet navy curtain. With that the lady appears and comes into the changing room to assist me with trying on the dresses.

"You have a well-defined waist, and your shapely top and bottom are about equal in size these dresses will look gorgeous on you." she says in English with an Italian accent.

I smile and undress out of my red sundress down to my bikini and then take off my shoes putting them to one side. The lady picks up my shoes and seems to look at them for a few moments before moving them further into the corner of the changing room. I wonder what she's thinking? Most probably that my shoes look cheap compared to the shoes she is wearing.

'We can't all afford designer you know …'

Once changed I appear in the first dress which is a deep red with thin straps, fitted at the waist and flares out at the skirt and Evan shakes his head "No."

I stick my tongue out at him playfully and go to try on another dress. After Evan has discounted about five dresses I'm getting fed up and hoping he loves this next dress because it is my absolute favourite I come out of the changing room in the sixth dress and Evan's eyes nearly pop out of his head.

The dress is long and classically beautiful. I feel elegant, and sexy in it and I've never felt so beautiful in a dress in all my life.

The off-the-shoulder dark navy dress has a fold-over sweetheart neckline with thin spaghetti straps for added support.

The long skirt stretches over my curves before flaring out in an elegant mermaid style to brush the floor.

Evan coughs slightly to clear his throat, "Sbalorditivo."

"What does that mean, yes, no, what?"

"It means stunning, you look absolutely stunning Kara."

He shifts in his seat and I can tell he likes what he sees from the bulge in his trousers.

I laugh, "Evan," I point to his crotch with my eyes.

"What can I say baby you have this effect on me."

"Shush." I giggle looking to see where the lady is and seeing she has gone off to serve a customer.

"Do you need a hand getting that dress off?" he teases.

"No I can manage thank you and you wouldn't just be helping me get the dress off would you, you would be getting off in other ways as well."

"Okay then, you will have to make my treat extra special later if I can't have you now," he grins.

"Behave." I giggle, "will you unzip me please?"

Evan unzips the dress then kisses my bare neck trailing soft kisses all the way up my neck to my ear making me tingle with excitement.

"Is everything okay?" the lady asks walking back into the changing area catching Evan kissing me.

"Yes we will have this dress thanks," Evan replies, clearly unaffected by her intrusion while I scurry off into the changing room to take the dress off, feeling embarrassed.

"Certainly sir" she replies then goes to prepare the payment for the four-figure price dress.

While Evan waits for me to change I can hear him speaking to the lady some more in Italian.

'I wonder what they are talking about?'

Having changed back into my sundress I carry my new

dress and hand it over to the lady who packages it up in some tissue paper and puts it in a box.

"I'll take care of this have a look around," Evan smiles.

I look around at the other clothes in the shop noticing the price tags.

'Jeez it's expensive in here, that's like a month's salary for me just for one of those dresses.'

Once Evan has paid for the dress, he passes me the box it's packaged in and I waltz out of the shop with my new ball gown. Evan is carrying a smaller box too.

'I wonder what he's bought?'

"What's in that box?" I enquire.

"Oh it's just something for my mother, she loves this shop and I sometimes treat her to a new designer handbag when the new range comes out," he smiles.

'Aww that's sweet of him, what a lucky lady.' We head back to car and to the villa. I feel amazing. Evan really is spoiling me!

'I wonder where he is taking me to require such an expensive dress?'

Evan

We arrive back at the villa and take a short nap to recharge. It's now time to get ready so while Kara is in the shower freshening up I decide this is the perfect opportunity to ring Julia back.

'I wonder what she wants?'

"Hello, it's Evan."

"Evan, hi, how are you?"

"I'm good thanks but I'm a little confused as to why you called me earlier today, especially after all this time? We have nothing left to talk about."

"I know it's been a long time hasn't it and after everything that happened in the past, I'm surprised you called me back at all." Julia responded.

"I admit the last time I saw you it wasn't the best."

"I know and like I told you then I'm sorry, if I could turn the clock back I would but I can't." Julia sighs.

"Look I don't want to drag all that up again. Why the call out of the blue? What do you want Julia?"

"Evan please don't be like that towards me, we were in love once and we were great together can't you find some way of forgiving me. Please? It was a mistake."

I laugh. "I can't believe this, you just don't get it do you? Is that all you rang me for to apologise again, it's been a year Julia, save it I've heard all this before."

"Evan wait, please listen to me."

"No you listen, what did you think give him some time and he'll come around?."

"You know how charming he can be, how he manipulates people, I didn't know what I was doing."

"How can you say that? You knew exactly what you were doing when he was fucking you in your bed."

There is a long silence neither one of us speaks ...

"... Anyway, if that's all you wanted to say Julia I ... ?"

"... No it isn't wait I need to tell you something."

"What, look I'm busy, so just say what you have to say."

"He's back in London and I've heard he has been asking about you."

"I've already heard, Mother told me and like I told her I'm not interested."

"Everyone deserves a second chance Evan, you seriously need to listen to me you need to make it up with him and pay him his money."

"What are you kidding me, I need to listen to you?" I laugh, "like you listened to me when I told you to stay away from him but no you just fell for his charm. The lies you both told and then finding you both that day."

"I'm sorry."

"It killed me Julia I was going to ask you to marry me for fuck's sake."

"No," Julia replies sounding shocked and tearful.

"Yes … I was."

"I didn't know Evan we never spoke about getting married. I'm sorry." she sobs.

"You had an affair Julia and managed to get yourself pregnant with him, of all people, how could you do that to me? No one made you have an affair behind my back for months, no one made you lie to me and to be honest the thoughts of what you both did to me makes me feel sick even now."

"It was mistake, please forgive me." She begs.

"Yes it was a BIG mistake and now you are paying for it by raising his kid alone."

"I lost the baby."

"What do mean you lost the baby?" I'm shocked.

"I had a miscarriage at 13 weeks. I guess that was my punishment for all the wrongs I did."

"I didn't know I'm sorry," Julia sobs uncontrollably. "please don't cry, look you hurt me and you've apologised so let's just leave it at that okay."

"I wish you could forgive me and I could make it up to you, I still love you Evan."

"Julia don't."

There's a long pause and Julia sounds calmer now.

"Have you not heard from him then, I thought now he's back in London he would have been in contact?"

"No I've not heard from him, not yet anyway, why have you?"

"No not for a while."

"Does he know you lost the baby?"

"Yes."

"Well if it's any consolation he wouldn't have been a very good father so it's probably a blessing."

Julia remains quiet.

"I'm sorry I shouldn't have said that. Look thanks for the warning but I can look after myself. Anyway I need to go."

I look up and see Kara stood in the doorway of the bathroom staring at me with a towel wrapped around her body. "Goodbye Julia."

Twenty One

Evan looks at me. I'm guessing he's wondering how long I've been stood here for.

"Who was that?" I ask knowing it was Julia.

"I think you know who it was," he says walking towards me.

"What did she want then?"

"Nothing much, she just wanted to catch up," he says pushing a strand of wet hair behind my ear.

"Evan don't lie to me, you don't just ring someone up after a year of not seeing them who you used to be romantically involved with to just catch up." I walk around him and pace the bedroom floor.

"Look stop reading into this when it really is nothing, she didn't want anything."

"Then why say thanks for the warning and you can look after yourself?"

"Oh you heard that did you." He looks serious.

"Yes I did." I snap.

Evan closes his eyes, sighs and shakes his head, "Come here sit down with me for a minute."

He walks over to the bed and sits down on the edge patting the space at the side of him for me to sit.

I sit down and look at him, "So what's it all about then?" I ask feeling anxious.

"Julia was warning me of some guy who has returned to London that I have been avoiding."

"Who is it and why are you avoiding him?"

"Look it's all in the past and I don't want to talk about him, but if I see him then I will deal with him okay."

"Is he dangerous?"

"No he isn't dangerous he is just pent up on jealousy and revenge for something he thinks is owed to him."

"But who is he Evan?" I'm now feeling slightly annoyed.

"It's just someone from my past and that's all you need to know."

"How does your mother know them? I heard you talking on the phone at Hamilton Tower,"

"I don't want us to be late and I haven't had my shower yet," he says getting up off the bed and walking into the bathroom ignoring any more questions. "I am done talking about this Kara, please just drop it."

I know something isn't right and he's holding back and really it's none of my business but I hate secrets.

I don't want to spoil our evening by having another argument so choosing to drop it, I get up off the bed pick up the hairdryer and sit down at the dressing table to dry my hair.

I feel better after a nap earlier and after drying my hair I wonder where Evan is taking me. Feeling excited I go to my suitcase and search for some nice underwear to wear under my new dress.

I pick out a black silky bra with matching knickers and put them on.

All of a sudden it dawns on me that I have no shoes to wear with my dress, I can't wear sandals or canvas shoes and now I'm panicking.

"Oh god what a disaster," I mutter sat next to my case with my head in my hands.

"What's the matter babe?" Evan says walking into the bedroom naked, I look up and stare straight at his groin.

"Nothing now." I giggle looking him up and down admiring his toned abs and muscly body from where I'm sat.

"I thought I heard you say something about a disaster?" he says getting a pair of boxers out of a chest of drawers and putting them on.

"Yes I suddenly realised that I don't have any shoes to wear with my dress, I can't wear these," I say pointing to my casual shoes and sandals.

"Then it's a good job I think of everything isn't it," he smiles walking into the dressing room and returning with the box he carried out of the clothes shop earlier. "Happy Birthday beautiful."

I stand up, he comes over to me and passes me the box.

"What? I thought this was for your Mother?" I ask surprised.

"No I lied, it's for you, surprise," he grins.

"You remembered me telling you it was my birthday soon?"

"Yes, you told me on our first night together at The Kingsman that it was soon so I thought I would buy you a birthday present. What date is your birthday anyway?"

"It's the 28th July." I reply, slightly shocked he took any notice.

Evan comes and sits next to me on the bed as I untie the white silk ribbon from around the silver patterned box, peeking inside.

Taking off the box lid I place it at the side of me on the bed and pull back the tissue paper to reveal a gorgeous pair of silver, strappy Louboutin shoes.

"Oh … wow, Evan these are gorgeous." I say giving him a kiss, "this is too much, first the dress and now these."

"I wanted to buy you them because you have brought nothing but sunshine into my life since I met you."

"Thank you so much Evan, this is just the best birthday present I have ever had, I have seen these shoes in magazines but never once thought I would actually own a pair. Thank you, thank you, thank you."

I put them down on the bed then launch myself at him pushing him backwards and kissing him all over his face laid on top of him.

Evan can't stop laughing as I smother him in kisses. I roll off him and we both sit up and I look at the shoes again properly.

"You're welcome, I hope they fit okay, I asked the lady in the dress shop in on the secret too, so I could buy them for you," he smiles.

"I wondered why she was looking at my shoes closely, I thought she was thinking they looked cheap or something," I confess making Evan laugh. "Wait until Jodie sees these she is just going to die with jealousy, I love them." I squeal taking hold of them and slipping them on my feet. I stand up still only dressed in my black matching silky underwear and prance around the bedroom in my new shoes.

Evan can't take his eyes off me. Standing up and walking over to me, he places his hands either side of my face and kisses me gently.

"You look hot, I feel like cancelling tonight now and having a night in because I'm desperate to be inside you," he says with lust in his eyes.

"But I have a nice new dress and new shoes to wear now and it would be a shame not to wear them after all the money you have spent."

"Okay." He sighs looking at his watch, "I really wish I could fuck you right now." He takes some deep breaths, "Let's finish getting ready then because we have a reservation for dinner and we don't want to be late," he says begrudgingly feeling horny and frustrated.

"Don't worry I'll make it up to you later when I give you your treat," I smile sitting back down at the dressing table crossing my legs and starting to apply my makeup.

"I need to move away from you because this is torture," he says looking at me sat in my underwear at the dressing table with a reflection of my cleavage in silky underwear looking back at him. "I can't wait for my treat, I'm already excited," he says adjusting himself in his boxers and walking off into the dressing room to find some clothes willing his erection to go down.

"I can see you're excited," I shout giggling knowing that my teasing has him out of control.

"It's you in that underwear and those strappy shoes, it does things to me I can't help it," he shouts back, as I can hear him fumbling for clothes.

It turns me on knowing I have this effect on him.

I decide to tease him some more, so I walk to the dressing room and lean in the doorway rubbing my leg up and down the doorframe watching him putting on a pair of smart trousers.

Evan looks at me out the corner of his eye.

"Kara I know what you are doing can you please put your dress on because I'm really struggling here. I am so hard right now and it's not going down." He grins at me and I giggle.

"Go … go and put your dress on so we can get out of this bedroom," he says with a serious face but trying to hide a smile.

"Okay but you will have to help me zip up the back," I turn around to walk off and I know he is looking at my barely covered bum because I can hear him gasp.

I slip into my new dress and put on my new shoes and call Evan to say I'm ready for him to zip up my dress.

A few minutes later he reappears out of the dressing room.

"Wow you look absolutely stunning," he says giving me a quick kiss and zipping up the dress.

"Are you okay now?" I grin looking at his crotch.

"Yes thank you for the concern," he smirks.

Once we are both ready, Evan escorts me downstairs and George is hovering about in the lounge area.

"You make a gorgeous couple, you look stunning Kara and Evan you scrub up well too lad," he says smiling at us both.

"Thanks George," Evan nods at him.

"George, would you mind taking a photo of us on my phone please?" I ask.

"Of course I wouldn't mind."

"Thank you."

George takes some photos of the two of us and then passes the phone back to me. I look at the photo with a big smile on my face.

'He's right we do make a gorgeous couple.'

"We're heading off now, so we'll see you in the morning George. Please can you tell Mary that we will not require breakfast in the morning because we will be out late tonight so we can all have a lie in tomorrow as it's Sunday," Evan says shaking George's hand.

"Yes sir, thank you sir, have a great evening both of you." He smiles and we both walk out the front door of the villa to Evan's Ferrari that he left parked out front earlier.

Evan opens the car door for me and I gather up my dress to step in to the passenger seat. I blush, "Thank you, I feel like a princess." I get in and he shuts the car door.

Evan starts up the engine of the Ferrari and pulls away from the villa opening the security gates and powering out of the driveaway.

"So, will you tell me where you are taking me tonight now?" I ask feeling apprehensive but excited.

"First of all I'm taking you for dinner to a favourite restaurant of mine in Como which does exquisite food and then afterwards I'm taking you to see an opera at Teatro Sociale Opera House. I've reserved a private box."

"Oh my god, really," tears well in my eyes. "What's the opera house like?"

"It's beautiful, it was built upon the ruins of a medieval castle, I think you'll like it."

"Will you pinch me please? Am I dreaming? It sounds so romantic."

"Are you okay babe?" he asks looking at me noticing my watery eyes and placing a hand on my knee.

"Yes I'm just so happy, I have never been to an opera before and have always wanted to experience one and you are making my dreams come true Evan, I can't thank you enough."

"You can thank me properly later," he winks.

On arriving at the restaurant Evan speaks to the Maître d' in Italian and gives his name then a hostess shows us to our table.

It's a warm amorous evening and as we walk through the room I can't help but notice people's heads are turning. I start to feel self-conscious.

"Evan why are these people looking at me, do I look okay?" I whisper.

"They are looking at you because you look stunning I feel proud to have you on my arm," he says giving me a warm, sexy smile.

I blush. We follow the female hostess to our table and take a seat. The whole place is modern and elegant in style. White tablecloths floating over the tables. A delicate candle is flickering in the middle of each table, garnished with a flower arrangement centre piece.

It's so romantic.

"This is lovely, you are spoiling me today," I smile as the lady passes us both a menu each and then leaves to return to front of house.

"You deserve to be spoilt Kara because you are a very special lady."

"Evan." I whisper looking at the menu, "I don't understand what any of this means, it's all in Italian, do they have one in English?" looking confused.

"Don't worry I will order for the both of us" he smiles.

Evan peruses the menu for a few moments and I smile at the waiter as he comes over to our table to take our order.

Evan orders for the two of us and from what I can gather they appear to be acquaintances.

I don't mind not being able to understand what they are saying I'm just happy listening to Evan speaking Italian, he is just mesmerizing.

He could be talking about steak and chips for all I know and it would still make my heart skip a beat listening to the sound of his voice and looking at his gorgeous mouth.

"What are we having then?" I ask wondering what he ordered.

"We are having grilled beef fillet, soft potato purée with Lariano black truffle and Barolo reduction, accompanied with a bottle of their finest wine."

"Hmm sounds lovely, thank you." I smile.

Evan hands the menus to the waiter.

"Grazie," the waiter smiles and winks at me flirtatiously and Evan catches a glimpse.

"I'm so excited about the opera, what are we watching?"

"It's called 'La Traviata by Giuseppe Verdi' and it's a tragic love story of Violetta and Alfredo. This opera is one of the most famous operas in the world; it's one of my all-time favourites."

"Have you seen it before then?"

"Yes, once but it was a very long time ago, my mother wanted to see it and I begrudgingly said I would take her after my father died."

The waiter returns with the bottle of wine and both him and Evan converse in Italian while glancing at me.

Evan nods and smiles at the man while he pours us both a glass of wine. Turning to look at me again the waiter winks at me again before walking off.

"What did he say to you?" I ask puzzled.

"He said you look beautiful tonight and I'm a lucky man."

"What did you say?"

"I said I know I am a lucky man and that you're mine. I didn't want him getting any ideas. Then he said if you were his he definitely would keep you and never let you go."

"No, he didn't say that." I shake my head.

"He did."

"So what did you reply then?" I pick up my wine and take a sip waiting for his answer curious to know what he said.

"I didn't because he poured the wine and then left, what does it taste like anyway?" he asks picking up his own wine to taste it. It doesn't go unnoticed that Evan changed the subject about his feelings for me.

"The wine is delicious, thank you." I've already drank nearly a full glass; it's superb.

"I'm pleased you like it because I'm only having the one glass, seeing as I'm driving, so the rest is yours," he says sipping his wine.

"If I drink all that I'll be drunk." I stifle a giggle.

While we are waiting for the food to arrive Evan tells me about the places he has visited in Italy and other places he has been to around the world with his family and best friend, Curtis. The waiter returns to our table with the food and it smells delectable.

I struggle to look the waiter in the eye now that I know what him and Evan were talking about.

Our meal is divine and I want to savour every moment of being spoiled by Evan.

Another glass of wine later it has definitely gone to my head. I'm feeling quite tipsy by the end of the meal.

"If you are ready to go Kara, I will ask for the bill?"

"Who is bill and why do you want to ask him something?" I giggle, "and where's the lovely waiter gone I want to thank him for our nice meal and the lovely wine?"

"Okay lady I think you have had enough wine now and behave, he fancies you so don't encourage him." Evan flashes an unimpressed glance at me.

"Okay 'Mr Jealous', I only wanted to say thanks,"

I smile seeing the waiter walking towards us.

"Kara …" Evan warns.

"Thank you for a lovely meal and the wine," I say and the waiter takes hold of my hand and kisses the back of it.

Evan glares at him.

"Can we have the bill please?" the waiter looks at Evan and can see he doesn't appreciate the attention he's giving me so backs away.

"He's friendly, I like him," I say looking at Evan who has jealousy written all over his face.

"I don't, he can't take his eyes off you and I don't like it."

"Relax, he's only doing his job and besides it will be your cock inside me later not him."

A lady who has obviously just heard the work 'cock' looks over in disgust, the alcohol has raised my voice level.

"Kara." Evan smirks rolling his eyes, shaking his head and smiling.

I giggle as the waiter returns with the bill.

Evan swipes his credit card and then stands up when the waiter leaves.

"I think you could do with some fresh air," he helps me up from the table and puts his arm around me to escort me out of the restaurant. "Come on let's have a steady walk back to the Opera House and see if we can sober you up a bit. I fancy a nice walk after that lovely meal." Evan says as we gingerly walk out of the restaurant.

"I fancy you," I smile as we step outside. I look at him and pull his mouth to mine for a drunken kiss.

"Okay, come on beautiful." Evan says taking hold of my hand and guiding me along the streets of Lake Como both of us enjoying the warm night and the ambience, Evan points out the Cathedral which is situated near to the theatre.

"Thank you for taking me to dinner I had a lovely time, I'm sorry I'm a bit drunk but the wine was so nice."

"It's okay, you're cute when you are drunk," he smiles.

"… And horny," I give him a sultry look.

I put my arms around his waist, as he puts his arms around me. "Evan I'm really turned on right now and I don't think I can wait until later to have you." I put one hand around his neck and pull him to me for another drunken kiss and cup his crotch with my other hand.

"Kara," he laughs shocked but amused while I cup him through his trousers in the middle of the street feeling him coming to life.

"I want you." I breathe rubbing his semi-erect cock feeling it grow underneath my palm while plunging my tongue into his mouth.

"Kara we are in the middle of a busy street and there are people around and I know that if you were completely sober right now you wouldn't be doing this," he laughs.

"Please Evan, I need you, you look so gorgeous tonight, we don't have to necessarily need a bed to have sex?" I tease him biting my lip.

Evan peers at his watch while kissing me and calculates that we have 20 minutes until we need to be seated for curtains up. "Come on we need to be quick."

We arrive at Evan's Ferrari.

Evan opens the car door quickly for me to get in then runs around to the other side to get into the driver's seat. As soon as he is sat in the car, Evan pushes the seat back as far as it will go and I pull up my dress around my waist and climb onto his lap facing forwards grabbing hold of the leather steering wheel.

"I want you to take me this way." I say excitedly turning my head to face him.

"Your insatiable," he smiles undoing his trousers letting his hardness spring free.

Evan grabs hold of his length while I pull the thin piece of material of my thong to one side making it easy for him to enter me and then helping to guide his cock inside I sit on him taking him fully.

Up and down I ride him over and over again turning us both on by the naughtiness of having sex in Evan's sports car.

"Jesus Kara, you need to be quiet baby because we'll be attracting attention and then we'll be arrested for public indecency." He laughs.

"I can't help it Evan you feel so good." I cry breathing heavily and moaning loudly.

"I know babe ... fuck ...you're a sexy minx."

I am so turned on my orgasm comes quickly. "Oh god I'm going to come ... OHHHHHH ... " and I orgasm moaning and panting as it gives me such a rush.

Evan laughs happily stroking my back with his hands.

"Are you okay beautiful, that didn't take long?" he laughs.

"Oh yes that was so good I'm sorry I came quickly, I couldn't hold it."

"Hey don't apologise," he smiles.

"But you didn't come." I suddenly feel guilty.

"It doesn't matter you can make me come later when you give me my treat."

"Oh yes I definitely will and I'll look forward to giving it to you as well."

"So will I, anyway we really need to get going because the opera will be starting soon." he says pulling out of me and zipping himself back into his trousers.

"Okay." Evan opens the car door for me to climb off his lap and out of the car.

As I'm getting out and pulling my dress down I accidently catch my elbow on the car horn, it sounds loudly making me giggle and Evan laughs as people passing in the street glance over. We must look like school children.

"Oops." I giggle looking at Evan following me out of the car with a big grin on his face.

"What are you like?" he laughs as he takes my hand and we cross the street.

" I can't believe we just did that." I whisper giggling.

"No-one saw us my little exhibitionist, at least we made it to the car because the way you were acting earlier I thought you were going to take my cock out in the street."

"Oh god I'm so embarrassed, it's that wine it was so strong." I hold my head in my hands.

"Don't be, I wish I had taken a note of the name of it."

Arriving at the front of the Opera House, I take a quick photo then taking hold of my hand Evan says, "Come on," and leads me through the door.

The exterior of the theatre is an impressive monumental structure with six columns supporting the middle section of the pointed roof. Outside lights shine to light up the front of the building and the architecture is astounding.

Once we are inside we head straight for the private box that Evan has hired for the night and we take our seats.

The décor of red plush seats with a gold trim makes the place feel palatial; the atmosphere in the theatre is magical.

"This place is magnificent." I smile settling down into my seat.

Evan squeezes my hand and leans into me to give me a kiss. "It should be starting any minute. I hope you enjoy it, feel the music and the emotions as they sing and get your tissues ready."

My eyes are sparkling at the joy I'm feeling sitting in this magical Opera House.

We sit back as the lights dim and the show begins to start.

Twenty Two

As the performance finishes the theatre erupts with applauding and loud cheers and Evan looks at me and smiles.

"I thought you would enjoy it and there is nobody I would rather be here with," he says passing me a clean tissue from his trouser pocket so I can wipe the tears from my eyes. "Are you ready to go? It's late and I'm ready for my treat you promised me?" he says grinning at me.

"Yes I'm ready to go and more than ready to give you your treat after bringing me here, I loved it, thank you." I smile taking hold of his hand as we get up from our seats.

"Jesus I'm getting hard already just thinking about it, come on." He says almost dragging me out of the private box in a hurry to get back to the car.

On the drive back Evan is putting his foot down in a rush to get back to the villa as thoughts of my treat are on his mind making him excited and impatient.

"Evan is there anywhere private you could pull over as I really want to give you your treat now?" I ask putting my hand on his leg and licking my lips as he glances at me.

"We're nearly home baby, it's not far."

"Please Evan, I want to give it to you now, can you find somewhere where we won't be seen? This is my treat and so I decide when and where." I say assertively.

"Well if you put it like that then your wish is my command and I know just the place," he says driving a bit further before turning off a side road down to a wooded area off the beaten track.

"Would this be suitable for what you have in mind?" he asks grinning at me loving my sass.

"Perfect."

Evan pulls up and cuts the engine. I get out of the car and walk around to the driver's seat to where Evan is sat watching me. I open the car door and grab hold of Evan's hand and pull him out of the car.

Evan laughs. "I like this dominant side to you Kara it's sexy as fuck."

I pull him around to the front of the car so his back is against the bonnet and he's facing me and then turning my back to him I say, "Please can you unzip me?"

"With pleasure" he whispers into my ear.

He moves my hair away from my shoulders, kissing my neck giving me goose bumps all over my body. Sliding the thin straps off my shoulders I pull the dress down my shapely hips until it falls onto the floor. Stepping out of it I turn around to face Evan in my racy black silky underwear and high heeled shoes, feeling sexy and confident.

"You look hot" Evan says looking me up and down.

The moon is bright tonight providing enough light to see what we're doing and adding to the ambience being outside in the open air making it all the more exciting for the fear of being seen.

Evan goes to put his hands on my silky covered breasts but I stop him, "No, not yet babe, take off your shirt." Evan unbuttons every one of the buttons on his white shirt to reveal his tanned hairy chest and toned abs. He then begins to undo the button on his trousers but I stop him again.

"That's my job." I smile looking him straight in the eyes and pushing him gently so he's leaning on the bonnet of his car for support. Standing in front of him I kiss him deeply while undoing his trousers and he moans into my mouth.

Breaking the tongue mingling kiss to pull his trousers down to his ankles I do the same with his boxers leaving him stood with a massive erection feeling turned on at the thought of what I'm going to do to him and what's coming next.

"You are so hard." I smile.

I grab him and feel the solid length sliding it up and down in my palm making him moan.

"You make me hard, your hands feel so good around my cock baby," he says his hands splayed out at the side of him supporting him as he leans on the red bonnet of his Ferrari.

"Now for the first part of your treat." I grin sounding confident as I lower my mouth onto his awaiting erection sucking him hard in my mouth.

"Oh fuck, you are so good at that," he moans bringing his hands to my head and holding it while I devour him with my mouth, the sexual act feeling so erotic in the moonlight.

Evan is so turned on and so am I as I pleasure him circling my tongue over the glistening tip teasing him before taking him fully in my mouth again.

"Oh yes baby, keep going, just like that." His legs are shaking slightly as he moans loudly, I can tell he is losing control as he grabs my head more fiercely helping me to move up and down the length of him.

"Hmm ... tell me when you're going to come." I whisper.

Sucking, licking and tasting Evan's manhood I love how I affect him, "Shit … yes baby keep going."

Reaching my hands behind my back I unclasp my bra and let it fall to the floor as I continue working him with my mouth while he supports himself on the bonnet of his car.

"Jesus …"

"Hmm …" I moan around his tip so he can feel the vibrations of my mouth.

A few more sucks and licks and I can feel his cock pulsating, Evan moans. "Aargh fuck I'm nearly there baby."

I can tell he is really close now I can feel him swelling in my mouth and the veins pulsing as I slide it in and out sucking and tasting him.

"Shit … I'm going to come …" I quickly pull him out of my mouth and push his pulsating cock between my large breasts and he cries out "FUUUUCCCKKK …" he orgasms spilling his seed all over me. "I've always wanted to come all over your gorgeous tits ever since I saw them for the first time," he pants stroking my blonde hair, I look up at him smiling.

With Evan's come all over my breasts I reach for his shirt on the floor and grin at him while I use it to clean myself then I throw the shirt back down on the floor.

"Hey that's an expensive shirt," he laughs pulling me to stand up then kissing me fiercely.

After a few moments I pull away from him. "I'm not done giving you your treat yet," smiling as Evan's face lights up.

"Well if that's only part of my treat, bring on the rest." He grins still hard and turned on.

I roll my black silky knickers down my legs and Evan watches me with hungry eyes.

"Your body looks incredible in the moonlight," he says looking at my tits and running his hands all over my voluptuous curves.

Looking at him with a lustful look I smile, "For the next part of your treat I would like you to fuck me against the bonnet of your Ferrari." I swap places with him and lean on the bonnet of his car.

Evan grins. "I would love to." His trousers and boxers still around his ankles. He kisses me first plunging his tongue into my mouth and then coming up for air Evan turns me around and I lay naked across the bonnet of his car looking back at him over my shoulder.

He smiles feeling my naked bum with his warm, soft hands and I part my legs for him making an easy access for his hard length.

Grabbing hold of my hip with one hand he takes hold of his length with the other and guides it to my wet, greedy entrance then slams into me making us both cry out from the strong physical connection and the thrilling pleasure.

"This is going to be hard and fast baby, are you ready?" he says taking hold of both hips.

"Oh god, yes, yes I'm ready," and he rams into me again fucking me hard over and over again. I stare at my hands splayed out on the shiny red bonnet of his Ferrari steadying myself while his powerful thrusts take me to a place of pure ecstasy, the feeling is incredible. Evan claims my body with his turning us both on to the extreme both of us moaning loudly. "God you look so hot laid across my car while I fuck you," he pants.

"Oh god Evan you feel amazing … give it to me … yes … yes." It doesn't take long for the incredible rush to reach our brains. "OHHHHHH yes I'm coming …" I cry and Evan holds my hips firmly giving one last sharp thrust.

"FUUUUCCCKKK …" he stills as his cock pumps into me, both our bodies shaking and tensing as we orgasm together. The mind-blowing orgasm rips through my body like waves crashing onto the shore making me see stars and Evan is moaning loudly after being taken on a sexual high feeling satisfied and out of breath.

"Jesus that has to be the best treat I've ever had," he laughs leaning over my body his cock still inside me and kissing the soft skin on my back. Both totally out of breath and exhausted we stay stuck to each other for a few moments bent over the car bonnet in the warm air and the moonlight.

"Fucking hell there are no words to describe how amazing that was," he says trying to get his breath back.

"You're welcome and thank you I've had the most amazing night and day." I smile as he pulls out of me and pulls up his boxers and trousers.

"It's been great hasn't it," he smiles turning me around to face him. He's looking at me like I'm the most precious thing in the world to him as he pushes my hair away out of my face and holds my face in his hands before kissing me gently.

"Come on let's get you home," he says picking up my dress and underwear off the floor.

'I love it when he says that.'

"Yeah I'm starting to feel cold now." I shiver.

"Oh yes I can see that," he says touching my erect nipples and smiling as I shudder from the cold.

Evan helps me back into my now slightly dishevelled dress and zips up the back for me.

"Please can you put my thong in your pocket until we get back to the villa because its dirty now it's been on the floor?" I ask.

"Yeah sure I think I'll leave my shirt off now because it's dirty too," he grins.

'Oh yes I used it to wipe his come off my boobs … oops.'

I throw my thong underwear at him and Evan catches it in his hands.

"I might just keep this as a reminder of this incredible night," he says with a boyish grin. "I'm never going to be able to look at this car again without an image of you spread naked across the bonnet of my Ferrari and me fucking you."

"Good, I like that," I reply playfully.

"Come on baby, let's go home."

Twenty Three

I open my heavy eye lids and turn to see Evan isn't in bed, glancing over to the clock I see it's 9.00am.

Wondering where he is, I stretch and sit up pulling the sheet around me so I'm covered. I can hear a rattling sound coming from down the corridor towards the bedroom.

The bedroom door swings open and Evan walks into the room with a tray in his hands containing a delicious array of food and drink for our breakfast in bed.

"Good morning beautiful I thought I would surprise you with breakfast in bed," he grins obviously feeling pleased with himself for making it.

"It looks lovely thank you." I smile warmly towards him. He puts the tray down then sits on the bed at the side of me and gives me a good morning kiss.

"What time is our flight later?" I ask, remembering we have to return to our lives in the UK, unfortunately.

"We need to be at the airport at 1.00pm." Evan says as he takes a sip of tea.

"I wish we could stay here a bit longer I've loved being here with you in this beautiful place, it's going to be hard to leave." I sigh grabbing a croissant.

"I know baby, I've loved spending the weekend here with you too but sadly we have to return to work."

After we have finished eating breakfast, Evan suggests we sit out on the terrace overlooking the view of Lake Como until it's time to leave.

George and Mary join us and we tell them about our amazing night at the Opera. They tell us about their son moving to Italy for work and how they have moved out here from England to be Evan's Housekeepers so they can be near their son and his family.

"I can see why you love living here, it's beautiful." I smile.

"Just like you," Evan says making me blush in front of George and Mary. "George I've organised for the motorbike I hired to be picked up, they should be collecting it this afternoon. I thought we would get a taxi to the airport so you didn't have to ride pillion again." Evan says looking at me smiling.

"Oh I wouldn't have minded going on the bike Evan."

"I know but I didn't want you to feel hot and bothered

with your hair all messy before you boarded the plane to go home."

I smile. "That's sweet of you thank you."

George looks at his watch, "It's almost midday, I'll go and see if the taxi is here."

"Okay thanks George." Evan replies.

Once the taxi arrives, Evan gives Mary a hug and says he will be in touch and then goes to find George to help load the suitcases.

Mary turns to me and gives me a hug too and whispers in my ear, "You make Mr Hamilton very happy you know I can tell, I do hope I see you again soon," and gives me a peck on the cheek.

"Thank you Mary, he makes me happy too but he's a hard nut to crack, he says he doesn't want a relationship so I have my work cut out ... but I'm working on him."

"You'll get there girl, sometimes what men say isn't always what they mean. You just have to show them what they would be missing out on. Anyway it was lovely meeting you and have a safe journey home."

"Thanks Mary, it was lovely meeting you too." I smile and give her one last hug. Before getting into the taxi I take some last-minute photos of the villa wondering whether I will ever get the opportunity to return.

Looking out of the car window admiring the scenery on the way to the airport I suddenly feel sad that our weekend has come to an end and I'm heading home back to reality.

"Hey babe you're quiet, are you okay?"

"Yes I'm fine, just sad to leave that's all, I've had such an amazing weekend, thank you."

"You're welcome it's been great hasn't it." Evan replies giving my leg a squeeze.

The private jet is sat waiting for us on the tarmacked runway when we arrive at the airport. Climbing the steps to board the plane we hand in our passports to the same air hostess on the flight here.

"Welcome on board," she flashes a smile at me.

After a few checks, the pilot announces we are clear for take-off and I look out of the window deep in thought as we lift away from the ground into the skies.

'I wonder what is next for Evan and I? Is this all coming to an end soon? Can he really just walk away from what we have together? I want him to want to be with me just as much as I want to be with him.'

"Hey beautiful what are you thinking about?" Evan asks seeing the distant look on my face.

I turn to look at him and smile, "Just that I'm not really looking forward to going back to work tomorrow."

Evan doesn't say anything, he just smiles. I turn back to look out of the window and sigh. He obviously doesn't realise the real reason I'm sad.

It's not just the thoughts of going back to work can't you see I'm falling in love with you?

I can feel tears welling in my eyes, I shut them and take some deep breaths trying to calm myself so I don't cry in front of him.

The air hostess comes by my seat and offers us refreshments. I need a drink to numb my pain, I've a feeling this bubble we are in is going to burst soon and the thoughts of losing Evan is becoming unbearable.

"I would love a large glass of white wine please." I smile.

"Bring a bottle of Prosecco and I'll have a whisky thanks." Evan says watching me closely.

We sit in silence until the air hostess brings our drinks over. She pours me a large glass of wine and placing the rest of the bottle on the table, she hands Evan his glass of whisky.

He watches me drink half the glass of wine. Hopefully this will help me to forget my thoughts for a while. I finish the glass and start on the bottle of Prosecco.

"Talk to me." Evan says looking concerned.

"There's nothing to say."

Evan frowns and drinks some of his whisky, "Hey I've just had a thought … we should do something for your actual birthday next weekend?"

"Yeah okay." I sigh, "I always go to my parents for a birthday lunch but I'm free afterwards," continuing to sip the Prosecco. Evan looks concerned that I'm drinking excessively.

"Kara what's wrong? You are knocking that drink back like it's going out of fashion and don't tell me it's going back to work that's upsetting you."

"Nothing is wrong." I say slurring my words.

"Don't give me that, you've changed ever since we boarded this plane. You have drunk half a bottle of Prosecco in no time at all and now you're drunk."

"I'm not drunk I'm pissed … pissed at you."

"Why, what have I done?" he asks shrugging his shoulders and holding out his hands puzzled.

"Oh you, no you haven't done anything … no … apart from treat me like a princess, give me the best sex of my life and for what, you are going to leave and go and find yourself a new bit of fun instead of facing what is really going on here." I scoff raising my voice.

"I think we should have this conversation in private."

Evan says unbuckling our seatbelts and escorting me by
the arm into the bedroom.

"What do you want Evan a bit more fun is that it? Do
you want to fuck me again? Is that all I'm good for?" I say
flopping onto the bed.

"Kara please don't say things like that."

"What's going on here, this … us because I'm confused
and I don't know what the hell to think anymore." I sit up
on the bed and he comes to sit next to me.

"Kara you're drunk you don't know what you are saying."

"I may be a little drunk, but I know exactly what I'm
saying and how I feel. Can you not see it Evan? I'm
completely falling in love with you. But I need to know
how you really feel about me, am I wasting my time here?"

"I like you and I love spending time with you Kara, but
that's all I can give you. I don't want a relationship."

I stand up and pace the floor. "Oh yes, you've been put
off relationships for life because of one bad experience.
Why can't you see I am not like her Evan? I've been hurt
too but you get over it and move on. You clearly haven't
got over it which says to me you are still in love with her."

Evan shifts uncomfortably, he's running his fingers
through his hair looking stressed.

"I'm NOT in love with her Kara."

"Okay, then explain it to me please because that's all I have." I snap flinging my arms about in frustration.

"I don't want to …"

"Oh that's right you don't want to talk about it. Well don't then, maybe you should just go and talk to Julia, maybe it would do you some good, let you move on from whatever it is that is holding you back from having a relationship."

My stomach is starting to feel queasy and saliva is pooling in my mouth. I feel so emotional right now and drinking the Prosecco too quick has certainly not done me any favours, I feel sick. 'Oh god I'm going to be sick.'

I run into the small bathroom, shut the door behind me and throw up in the toilet. Evan can hear me and he knocks on the door. "Are you okay, can I come in?"

"Go away." I shout crying and washing my mouth out with water at the sink before sinking down onto the floor of the tiny bathroom and leaning against a cupboard.

Evan ignores me and opens the door slowly peering inside to see I'm sat on the floor hugging my knees. He sits down next to me and tries to pull me into his arms.

"Don't touch me." I sob pushing him away.

"Okay, but I'm worried about you."

"Why won't you talk to me about how you feel and why are you so adamant on not having a relationship, why can't you let me in?" I sob between breaths.

Evan takes a deep breath and blows it out slowly. "Julia and I had been dating for a year and a half and things were great, I loved her deeply and like I told you I thought she was the one.

I was thinking of proposing but then she changed and started acting differently towards me.

I could sense something was wrong so I confronted her about it and she said I was imagining things and everything was great. Then I used to call her and she wouldn't answer her phone which was out of character and she started to go out with her friends more or so she said. I had a spare key for her house and one day she had bailed on our plans because she was unwell, so I wanted to check she was okay. I let myself into the house and that's when I found them."

I listen feeling shocked at what I'm hearing.

"The person who she was trying to warn me about yesterday on the phone, was the guy she was fucking in her bed. I felt my heart break in two that day and I have never felt pain like it. I found out it wasn't the first time either and to top it all off she was 11 weeks pregnant with his child. I couldn't believe it, this woman who I was thinking of marrying was fucking my…" Evan stops to take in a deep breath.

Looking into his watery eyes I bring my hand up to cup his face. "I'm sorry, I know it must have been hard dragging that all up again and it is obviously still painful for you to talk about, thank you for telling me. I understand how you feel about wanting to keep detached from people and relationships because you have been terribly hurt in the past and it has made you wary but I'm not her Evan. I'm not Julia and if you just let me in here." I say putting my hand over his heart, "I think we could be really happy together?"

"I can't do it Kara, I'm sorry I can't take the risk of getting hurt again, it broke me," he says getting up off the floor.

Holding his hand out to me he helps me up and then leads me into the bedroom to sit on the bed.

"I've built a very high wall to protect myself and I don't think it's coming down anytime soon, I'm a stronger person now and when it happened it crushed me Kara. I'm so sorry I just can't," he says lowering his head and breaking our eye contact.

"I understand." My lips begin to tremble and tears well in my eyes again, I look down at my hands.

"I'm sorry I never meant to …"

A knock at the door interrupts us and Evan gets up off the bed and opens the door slightly to the air hostess asking if we can return to our seats because we will be landing soon.

"Yes we will, thank you, we will be right there," he says closing the door, "we need to go back to our seats."

I can feel my heart pulsing in my chest.

"Okay." I wipe my eyes with the backs of my hands and get up off the bed, walking slowly past Evan towards the door. He grabs my arm making me turn to look at him.

"Are we okay?" He looks into my blue clouded eyes.

I smile a painful smile, "Yes we're okay."

We touch down in England and you can cut the tension with a knife, neither one of us speaking, we don't really know what to say to each other. A steward is waiting for us and hands Evan some car keys for his Aston Martin which is parked on the tarmac.

"Oh I thought Curtis would be picking us up." I say quietly looking at him.

"No I arranged for Curtis to deliver my car so we could drive straight back from here."

"Oh okay."

The car journey home is not the same as it had been going, there is no excitement about our weekend away, only thoughts of work tomorrow and the awkward atmosphere after what we have just spoken about on the plane.

We arrive back at my flat and we get out of the car. Evan takes my case and the gift boxes out of the boot and carries them for me to the front door.

I take out my keys and stand for a moment with my back to him breathing deeply, tears are beginning to bubble under my eye lids again.

"I'll call you then about doing something for your birthday?" he smiles.

"Okay."

"Can I have a goodbye kiss?"

All I can think is this might be a final goodbye kiss. I turn around to put my arms around his neck and look into his chocolate brown eyes for a moment, then pull him in close to my body.

Putting my hands at the back of his head and in his hair I give him the most sensual, passionate kiss, the type of kiss that makes you go weak at the knees, the type of kiss that says I love you without saying the words and that I don't ever want you to let me go.

As we break away breathless, I smile at him. "Thanks for a great weekend. Goodbye Evan." I then walk through the front door, not looking back.

I dump my suitcase and the gift boxes in the hallway and walk into the kitchen, Jodie is stood at the sink washing up .

"Hi Jode, did you miss me?" I smile.

"Hey Kar, I did actually, wow you've caught the sun, so how was it?" she smiles.

"It was wonderful, it was very hot. Italy is such a beautiful place and going abroad was amazing, it's made me want to visit other places now so I've decided I'm going to start a holiday fund."

"Sounds good, so tell me all about your weekend then, what did you do? Where did you go? I'm dying to know."

"I have loads to tell you. How about we have a cuppa and sit in the lounge and then I'll tell you all about it." I smile.

"Great, I'll put the kettle on."

I put my suitcase and the gift boxes in my bedroom while Jodie makes the drinks then join Jodie in the lounge to tell her all about my weekend with Evan.

I tell her about Evan's villa, his fancy yacht, the night at the opera and I also tell her in confidence about the surprise phone call from Julia. I explain what had happened in Evan's past relationship and the conversation we had on the plane.

After telling my best friend I feel like a weight has been lifted from my shoulders. I couldn't carry the emotional baggage alone any longer.

"The thing is I'm not sure if he's moved on from everything that happened and I think that's what's stopping us from being together. What would you think and do if you were in my shoes?" I ask wanting Jodie's advice.

"Oh god Kara I really don't know and I'm pleased that I'm not in your shoes I can tell you."

"Oh god speaking of shoes I forgot." I jump off the couch with excitement and run down the hallway to my bedroom.

"Forgot what?" Jodie calls after me.

I walk back into the lounge grinning holding two gift boxes in my arms sitting down on the couch next to her again.

"Well before he took me to the opera I forgot to tell you he took me shopping, you never guess what he bought me?"

"What?" Jodie replies sounding excited and curious to see what's in the boxes.

"Well first of all he bought me this."

I show Jodie the beautiful navy dress, twirling it around the room with me as I dance.

"Oh wow that's gorgeous and looks very expensive," she says standing up and putting it against her body imagining herself in it.

"It is expensive and he also bought me these to go with it Jode." I open the box and hold up the pair of Louboutin shoes.

Jodie squeals her eyes nearly pop out of her head.

"Shit Kar." Jodie never usually swears and it makes me giggle because it's such a rare word to come out of her mouth.

"I know right."

"Oh my god he actually bought you Louboutin shoes, are you kidding me these must have cost him a fortune Kara. I'm sorry babe but honestly this man is seriously into you, he just can't see it yet or admit it to himself but he is."

"I hope you're right because I'm seriously into him and I can't stand the thought of losing him." I smile.

"Oh hun, I know. Love you Kar."

"Love ya Jode."

"Seeing as you love me can I borrow these sometime?" Jodie grins gesturing her hands to the dress and shoes.

"I don't love you that much." And we both laugh.

Twenty Four

It's only five days until my birthday and as I walk to work on the Monday morning, I remember my birthday last year. Jodie arranged a night out at the Italian restaurant in the town followed by a pub crawl. I remember it was a great night and we had stuffed our faces with pepperoni pizza and then danced it off at the end of the night in the local night-club.

I smile as an image of myself attempting to pole dance comes to mind and Jodie trying to hold me up, but we ended up falling into a heap on the dance floor.

As I pass the pub which is on my way to work I see Evan's car driving towards me, he slows down pulls up alongside me and opens the car window.

"Good morning you look beautiful today," he grins acting like normal as he gives me one of his knock out smiles and looks me up and down cheekily.

I'm wearing a knee length yellow tea dress which nips in at the waist showing off my hourglass figure and it matches my blonde hair which is tied up in a high ponytail.

I feel like a ray of sunshine with my sun-kissed tan from the Italian sunshine over the weekend.

Still feeling slightly awkward after our conversation on the plane I had wondered how it would be when we saw each other again. I thought he might be running for the hills now I've told him I'm falling in love with him but he's just acting like normal? Aargh ... MEN!

"Thank you and you look gorgeous as always, are you just heading to the Manor?" I ask with a smile.

"Yes, I have the builders starting work today."

"Sounds like you are busy then, so I best not keep you."

"Yes I am but I have always got time to speak to you," he smiles, "did you sleep well last night?"

"Yes I was so tired I fell asleep as soon as my head hit the pillow how about you?"

"It was strange not having you in my bed I missed giving you a cuddle and especially waking up to you this morning." He glances at me.

"I know after spending all weekend together it did feel strange."

"I wish I could take you to bed now."

"Me too." I blush, "anyway you'd better go I don't want you to be late meeting your builders and I need to get to work too so …"

"I'll text you later okay" he calls.

I start to walk off but Evan calls me back. "Hey I need one of your kisses to last me through until I see you again." I smile feeling pleased, he just can't resist me, how is this man going to manage without me when he has to leave?

I turn and walk back and bend down putting my head through the driver's window giving him an eyeful of my cleavage. I can't resist him either.

I smile resting one hand on the side of his cheek and bringing my lips to his I kiss him slowly plunging my wet tongue into his mouth. I move my hand from his face to stroke his already erect cock feeling his arousal under my hand.

"I've missed you." He moans.

"And I've missed having you inside me so don't make me wait too long." I tease backing my head out of the car window and leaving him with his erection jutting from his trousers. "Have a good day," I call and I walk off feeling pleased with myself.

I arrive at the coffee shop and sigh as I think it was only a few days ago that I was walking out of the shop on my way to Italy for the weekend and here I am again starting another week at work. Sally is stood at the counter and as soon as she sees me she squeals. "Kara oh I haven't stopped thinking about you all weekend, I can't wait to hear all about your trip!"

"Morning Sal, I have loads to tell you," I smile.

After telling Sally all about my weekend away I'm dying to know how the baby talk went.

"So how was your meal and the baby chat with Tim?"

"Well the meal was lovely, we had the chat and we both agreed it was the right time so we went home and started trying for a baby, well actually we tried quite a few times that night" she laughs.

"Oh Sally that's brilliant news," I grab hold of her for a hug. "does that mean I'll be an auntie then?"

Sally's eyes fills with tears. "Yes I would love for you to be an Auntie Kara."

"This is so exciting" I grin.

"Yeah it is, I can't wait until I'm pregnant."

"I'm so pleased for you Sal, you'll make a brilliant mum, anyway do you think we should open up today, have you seen the time?"

"Oh my god all this talk of sex and babies has sent me doolally, bloody hell I think we better had." she laughs.

After a busy day at work I arrive home and Jodie is in the kitchen looking in the fridge for something for dinner.

"Hi Kar, busy day?"

"Yeah what's for dinner?"

"How about Spaghetti Bolognese?"

"Sounds good."

Jodie insists on making dinner so I check my phone to see if Evan has messaged me, there are no messages so I go for a shower while it's cooking.

Feeling refreshed from my shower the smell of Spaghetti Bolognese fills my nostrils as I open my bedroom door, it smells so good.

I can hear voices coming from down the hallway. 'I wonder who that is?'

As I approach the kitchen Jodie is talking to a man and thinking it's Matt I suddenly stop in my tracks when I recognise the alluring sexy voice and who it belongs to, it's not Matt it's Evan and he is sat in my kitchen.

"Hi." I say surprised to see him sat there casually at the kitchen table talking to Jodie like he's known her for ages.

"Hi, nice shower?" Evan smiles looking at me with an amused look on his face.

"Yes thanks, what are you doing here?" I awkwardly smile in his direction, whilst glancing at Jodie,

"I wanted to see you and the lovely Jodie here has just kindly asked me to join you for some Spaghetti Bolognese because I haven't eaten yet, I hope you don't mind?"

"No not at all."

"I thought it would be nice to get to know Evan a bit more, you are always talking about him, so I thought we could all have dinner together." Jodie grins.

I smile at Jodie who is smirking behind Evan's back.

"No of course I don't mind, I'm just surprised I wasn't expecting to see you."

"Change of plan." He smiles getting up from the table and taking me in his arms giving me a lingering kiss.

"Matt is joining us too, I text him earlier, he'll be here in a minute." Jodie grins at me then looks out of the kitchen window to see if he is here yet.

I sit down at the kitchen table next to Evan and while Jodie is busy concentrating on cooking the meal at the stove, Evan puts his hand on my leg under the table and whispers in my ear, "You told me not to keep you waiting too long so here I am," he smiles.

"Here he is." Jodie says clapping her hands together in excitement and going to the front door to meet Matt. While she's out of the kitchen Evan trails his hand up and down my leg under my dress and leans towards me.

"I wish I could fuck you right now on this table."

"Oh god." I whisper, feeling turned on.

He's making me breathless and I can feel my cheeks becoming more and more flushed by the second.

"Evan." I whisper closing my eyes at the thought, just as Jodie and Matt walk in hand in hand.

Evan pulls his hand out from under the table and smiles at Matt.

"Matt, this is Kara's boyfriend Evan, umm friend whose a boy …" Jodie says feeling a little awkward after the reference to who Evan is.

"Hi Matt." Evan says standing up offering his hand to shake.

"Hi I'm Jodie's boyfriend it's nice to meet you mate."

Evan shakes Matt's hand and says, "Likewise" and then sits down again at the table next to me.

"So I understand you are opening up a hotel at the Manor?" Matt says sounding interested. "I'm a builder by trade if you ever need anything."

"Yes I am and I'll bear that in mind thank you."

Jodie dishes up four plates of Spaghetti Bolognese.

"This is lovely thank you." Evan says appreciating the home cooked meal.

"Does everyone fancy a glass of wine?" Matt asks.

"Yes please" we all reply so he gets up from the table to get some white wine out of the fridge.

After pouring everyone a glass Matt raises his glass in the air and says, "Cheers to a splendid meal cooked by the love of my life Jodie and to meeting Evan, the love of your life Kara." I almost choke on a piece of food that I'm chewing in my mouth, what the hell, my cheeks turn a deeper shade of red and I kick Matt under the table.

"Ouch." He lowers his head to rub his shin where I kicked him and laughs as I glare at him feeling uncomfortable. I look at Evan to see he's smirking which makes me feel better.

The meal is a hit and the conversation is flowing as much as the wine.

"That was lovely thanks Jodie." I say and everyone agrees.

"Your welcome." Jodie replies taking the plates away from the table.

"Shall we take another bottle of wine into the lounge with us Kar and leave the boys talking about boy stuff?" Jodie says getting another bottle out of the fridge.

"Yes good idea."

Matt gets up from the table, "I'm just popping to the toilet mate be back in a minute." He follows Jodie out of the room.

"Are you coming Kar?" Jodie shouts from the lounge.

"Yes, I'm coming."

I stand up from the table and Evan pulls me onto his lap, "I will look forward to hearing you scream those words later," he grins giving me a long lingering kiss.

"Me too." I whisper grinning at him then picking up my empty wine glass and walking out the room to find Jodie. I take a seat next to her.

"Hey, you haven't told Matt what I told you last night about Evan's relationship troubles have you?"

"Relax, no I haven't don't worry and I really like him Kar, he's really nice and you make a great couple. Looking at the way you are with each other I would say you have been together for months, years even, you just jell together so well like me and Matt."

"I know that's why it's such a shame that …"

"… What's such a shame?" Evan asks walking into the room Matt following behind him.

"I was just saying it's such a shame that it's a work night because we could have gone clubbing." I look to Jodie for some back up, trying to change the conversation to lessen any suspicion.

"Well I'm game if you are?" Matt says and Evan agrees with him.

"No let's stay in now we're comfortable sat here drinking our wine aren't we Jode?" I turn to look at her, hoping she isn't going to agree to going out.

"Yes we are, but speaking of games, why don't we play one?" Jodie suggests grinning at me.

"What sort of a game, not strip poker?" I reply pulling a face then taking a sip of my drink.

"How about a game of truth or dare, are you game for that both of you?" Jodie asks looking at Evan and Matt smiling.

They both look at each other. "Bring it on." Jodie moves to sit on the two-seater couch next to Matt and Evan sits down on the couch next to me.

"Oh god I've a feeling we might need more wine after this bottle," I say feeling and sounding nervous.

"Fancy a beer?" Matt asks Evan.

"I can't really I've already had a glass of wine and I'm driving, but thanks anyway."

"Why don't you stay over, I'm sure Kara won't mind ..." Jodie suggests grinning at me.

"Yeah sure, if he wants to," I blush.

"Okay thanks I will," Evan smiles squeezing my leg.

"Then that's settled." Jodie says, "get him a beer Matt you know where they are."

When Matt returns he gives one to Evan and then sits down again next to Jodie.

"Right are we all ready to start?" Jodie asks.

"Yes!" we all reply.

"Okay, we will take it in turns to answer truth or dare questions and we will do it in alphabetical order of names so its Evan's turn first then me then Kara then Matt okay?" Jodie says in her 'teacher voice'.

I pour Jodie and I another glass of wine.

"What if I don't want to answer the truth question?" Evan asks sounding a little nervous.

"No that's not allowed you just have to or there is no point in playing." Jodie replies assertively.

"Okay, then I'll have a truth question and get it out the way first," Evan says.

Matt and Jodie whisper among themselves and decide what question they want to ask. "Right Evan we want to know what did you think of Kara the first time you saw her?" Jodie asks with a glint in her eye.

Sighing in relief Evan replies. "That's easy I thought she is the most beautiful girl I have ever laid eyes on, she has a beautiful smile, a fantastic body not to mention great tits and I love the way she blushes when she's embarrassed or shy."

I blush at Evan's words and everyone looks at me and laughs. "Aww that's so sweet," Jodie says as Evan kisses me on the cheek.

"Oh god it's my turn now, I might regret this but I'll have a dare," Jodie laughs nervously taking a big gulp of her wine.

Evan and I whisper to each other and I start giggling. "Jodie we dare you to go outside and shout at the top of your voice to all our lovely neighbours, "I love Matt Cornell because he's a great kisser."

"Really Kara …" she scowls making us laugh.

"Well we were going to say because he's good in bed or because he has a big cock but we wouldn't want you to tell a lie being a respectable teacher and all."

"Hey, I am good in bed and have a big cock." Matt says making us all laugh.

"Yes Dear, but I can't shout that in the street can I, what if one of my pupils is walking past. I'll stick to being a great kisser thanks, oh god, where's my shoes, just you wait you two," Jodie laughs getting up off the couch to go and look for some slip on shoes.

After putting them on Jodie opens the front door, it's still light outside but the air is cool and standing on the front step with her arms cuddling her body we all gather around behind her while she prepares herself to shout to all the neighbours.

"Go out a bit further." We all snigger.

Jodie scowls at us and walks down the path towards the road. Taking a deep breath she shouts at the top of her lungs, "I love Matt Cornell because he's a great kisser!" We all start laughing except for Jodie because a man rides past on a bike and shouts "He's good with his hands too."

"Oh god how embarrassing" she says running back into the flat as we all fall about laughing on the doorstep.

"Don't worry babe I know him, he's a mate of mine and a builder too." Matt says trying to make her feel better.

After each taking a turn and a few more bottles of wine down we've all had a great laugh playing 'Truth or Dare' but it's getting late so we all decide we've had enough and take our drunken selves off to bed.

Twenty Five

I close my bedroom door and Evan stalks over to me taking off his tie and throwing it on the floor.

"Have you enjoyed yourself tonight?" I ask with a smile.

"Yes it's been a good laugh but I'm so ready for bed and now I'm going to enjoy myself even more." He smiles as I find the buttons on his shirt and start undoing them while he kisses me.

"Hmm ... me too."

Once all the buttons are undone I push back the shirt over his shoulders and look at his toned abs.

'I'm such a lucky girl.'

I'm becoming more aroused by the minute at the sight of Evan's gorgeous body. I undo his belt, button and zip on his trousers then pull them down his muscly legs for him to step out of.

I roll down his boxer shorts and they join the other items of clothing on the floor. He is now naked with the most impressive erection waiting for my next move.

"What do you want?" I ask taking my clothes off and licking my lips, my eyes roaming up and down his naked body looking at his solid length in front of me and seeing the tip glistening as his excitement shows.

"First I want to fuck your mouth then I want to come all over your gorgeous tits again like I did in Italy and then I want to fuck you until you can't stand up."

'Oh my god, yes please.'

I guide him to my mouth and take the full length of him.

Evan's head flies back. "Fuck ..." and he moans low in his throat while my soft lips and wet mouth tease his cock up and down, sliding my tongue over the tip and circling before taking him fully in my mouth again.

I cup his balls gently; they are full and warm. In and out, my tongue and mouth devour him as he grabs the back of my head and helps me with the rhythm moaning and breathing deeply. Up and down, in and out his moans get louder and I can sense his orgasm is getting closer and closer.

"Oh fuck, you're so good at that." I love turning him on giving him pleasure. I want to please him and from the sounds he's making I am doing just that. After a few more sucks he moans, "Kara I'm going to come …" so I take him out of my mouth flick my hair out of the way quickly and push his cock in between my naked breasts. He cries out as he comes spilling his seed all over them panting and swearing as he orgasms.

"That brings back memories," he smiles stroking my hair.

"Hmm … it does." I stay still letting him come down from his orgasm for a moment then I reach for my pyjama t-shirt that's under my pillow and mop up Evan's come off my breasts with it making Evan laugh.

"Have you not got a tissue?"

"This was easier to reach." I grin looking up at him. Once I'm clean he lowers his head and kisses me deeply.

I break away breathless, "I'll just get rid of this I'll be back in a minute."

I leave the room for two minutes and when I re-enter Evan is sitting on my bed, smirking at me.

"Look what I found, I think we can have a bit of fun with this," he grins, a devilish look on his face.

"OH … Have you been routing through my drawers?" I blush.

"Yes I was looking for a tissue, I wasn't expecting to find a vibrator though," he laughs.

"Well girls have needs as well as men you know but I much prefer the real thing so let me put it back."

I walk over to him and hold my hand out for him to pass it to me.

"Oh no I want to play" he says, "I think we can have some fun with this, lay on the bed and don't move I just need to get something."

'Oh god okay.'

Evan puts the vibrator on the bed at the side of me and finding his clothes he picks up his tie off the floor "Perfect," He says walking over to me, "sit up, I'm going to blindfold you, is that okay?"

"Yes." I breathe squeezing my thighs together feeling wet and turned on.

"Can you see anything?" he asks tying the silk tie around my head.

"No I can't see a thing."

"Good, just lie back and relax, you are going to love it."

I can hear Evan moving about and the first thing I feel is his mouth on mine giving me a lovely slow kiss, I take his face in my hands as our tongues dance together.

Then his lips leave mine and he moves lower making me gasp when I feel his mouth on one of my erect nipples.

He sucks it gently making me moan and I arch my back

as he teases the peak with his wet soft tongue. I feel light fingers trail down my body giving me goose bumps and stopping in between my legs he gathers up my wetness and plunges two fingers inside me, the feeling is intensified because I'm blind-folded and my body feels on fire with his expert touch.

Evan moves his fingers in and out of me while continuing to tease my nipple with his tongue and rubs my swollen clit with his thumb. "Oh god Evan."

I love how he always takes charge and knows exactly what I want and need, my body is responding to his every touch as he pleasures me with his tongue and fingers.

"Does that feel good baby?" he asks working me up into a frenzy.

"Yes ... oh god ... so good ..." I pant.

I feel the bed move and Evan stops what he's doing while I lay there turned on and desperate for his touch again.

Then I hear a buzzing sound, Evan has switched the vibrator on. I grab the sheets either side of me waiting and wondering what he's going to do with it. I'm breathing faster in anticipation as the buzzing sound is getting closer to my naked body.

"Are you ready?" he whispers.

"Yes I'm ready."

'Oh my god.'

I feel the vibrator across the top of my breasts and moving it slowly around over my erect nipples it causes them to stiffen more. "OHH …" Repeating this motion a few times I enjoy the feeling as I writhe around on the bed moaning. Evan trails the vibrator further down my body and I can feel the buzzing sensations on my stomach and then down one of my legs.

"Oh god, oh god …"

I moan as he trails it back up the other side of my body and back to my breasts again.

"Feels good doesn't it baby, hmm … where should I put it next?"

I open my legs giving him a hint and I can tell he's smiling even though I can't see him. He skims the vibrator up and down my inner thigh and opening my legs even wider, Evan gives me just what I'm craving. He positions the tip of the vibrator at my entrance then pushes it slowly inside me. "OHHHH …shit. " The vibrations are incredible and it's sending me crazy with desire and just when I think it can't feel any better Evan lowers his mouth onto my throbbing clit making me cry out even more when he sucks it gently. "Evan … OHHHHHH …" My body tenses as the rush of my orgasm pushes forward. I'm soaked and as Evan eases the head of the vibrator in and out of me slowly increasing my arousal even more the most explosive orgasm rips through my body and my body convulses violently.

'The man is a sex god, wow... just wow.'

Evan removes the vibrator and I know he's watching me enjoy the most powerful orgasm just like he did when we first met. He removes the blindfold and smiles then once my breathing has slowed down he kisses me passionately.

"That was incredible it's so much better when you use it on me than when I use it myself not that I've used it much lately." I smirk feeling so happy and contented after being given such a rush.

"I told you that you would love it" he smiles moving onto the bed at the side of me, taking me in his arms and spooning me from behind.

"You certainly know how to please a lady," I smile.

"You are the only woman I aim to please," he says snuggling into me and kissing my neck.

I can feel Evan's erection pushing into my back, he's clearly not finished with me.

I rub up against him. Evan pulls me back against his chest and hugs me tightly I can feel his cock at my entrance so I help him to slide into me from behind.

I arch my back pushing my bottom into Evan's front feeling all of him inside me. "Oh …" I'm still sensitive from the orgasm I've just enjoyed and still wet so Evan's slides in and out of me easily.

I moan softly enjoying the sensation of Evan filling me deeply over and over again. Evan's soft hands feel my breasts and he plays with my nipples as he thrusts in and out.

"I need to see your beautiful face," he whispers pulling out of me and moving his body on top of mine then pushing into me again slowly, "that's better I want to look at you" he smiles.

I bring my legs up and wrap them around his waist and he kisses me softly, our tongues melding into one. The closeness of our naked bodies caressing each other is total bliss and both our needs become more urgent by the second as our slow love making takes on a different form.

Our kiss becomes fiercer and Evan picks up the pace supporting his body with his arms and looking into my eyes.

He starts to drive into me with force working towards us reaching the end goal of our release. We can't get enough of each other and each powerful thrust makes me cry out loudly and Evan moan low in his throat, in and out, in and out, he powers on. He decides he wants to change position again so he pulls out of me.

"I want you to ride me," he says rolling onto his back breathless. I climb on top of him quickly straddling his thighs and dropping down onto his awaiting hard cock.

"Fucking Hell …" Evan feels my breasts and tweaks my nipples with his fingers while he watches me intimately as I move up and down riding him, my hands on his chest. He moves his hands to my hips and I give it to him hard, my breasts bouncing up and down, my hair swishing around my shoulders with every move.

After so long my legs are shaking and I'm getting out of breath, so Evan says, "Get on all fours." I kneel before him, my bum in the air waiting for him to enter me. Evan grabs hold of my hips and slams into me with force.

I grab hold of the bed sheets to steady myself before he thrusts into me again. Evan fucks me hard from behind and we are both panting and moaning loudly. It's so good.

The feelings are building and Evan recognising the signs that we are close to orgasm, he slows down and plunges deeply into me once, twice, four or five times more until his whole body stills as he cries out in euphoria.

"Oh FFUUCCKK …" his cock jerks inside me and I orgasm too.

"OHHHHHHHHH …" Evan clings to me from behind totally out of breath as we enjoy another mind-blowing orgasm as it races through our bodies and minds.

"Jesus that was intense," he says pulling out of me and we both collapse on the bed.

"It bloody was … that was unbelievable." I feel on such a high from the amazing sex we've just had, "I wish you could stay here forever."

"Me too which reminds me I need to tell you something," he says with a serious tone.

"What?" I don't like the sound of this. I turn on the bedside lamp and I sit up to look at him because I want to see his face when he tells me what's on his mind.

"I'm heading back to London on Sunday because after this week there is no reason for me to be here."

'No, I've dreaded this day when Evan tells me he's leaving.'

"What about me, am I not a reason for you to be here?"

"Kara we've spoken about this."

I remain silent.

"I will be coming back at some point. I just can't tell you when it will be so it's not like we won't see each other again," he smiles.

I'm lost for words and after being on such a high I now feel like the wind has been knocked out of me.

"I know it's not what you wanted to hear but if it's any consolation I would like to stay in contact with you so we can meet up again when I come back."

He's trying to make things better but it still doesn't change the fact he's leaving.

My eyes well up and I feel a tear roll down my cheek. I brush it away and Evan notices I'm crying, he takes me in his arms and holds me.

"I'm sorry babe but you knew this was coming one day."

"I know, I just thought it might have been in a few weeks' time, I don't want you to go, I like having you around." I sob.

"Listen like I said I will come back one day and then we can catch up again, I will be spending quite a bit of time here in the future when the hotel is ready for opening but in the meantime I can't hang around and I have to go home at some point. I'll still be here for the rest of the week though so we will just have to make the most of it."

"I can't believe you are being so unaffected by this, I honestly don't know what I'm going to do without you when you've gone?" I sob into his chest.

"Hey you will be fine, just remember I'm coming back so you are not getting rid of me altogether."

"I won't be fine Evan, I know I won't."

"Baby you will be fine. Look let's not dwell on me leaving now and make the most of the time we have left together. I had to tell you and I thought it was better to tell you now. Please don't cry, I hate seeing you cry," he says placing his finger on my chin and bringing my head up to look at him.

"I can't help it," I sob.

Evan passes me a tissue from my bedside drawer to wipe my eyes with.

"Let's not think about it, let's think of something special to do for your birthday. What would you like to do, anything you want?"

"I don't know, I can't think about that now." I wipe my tears as more continue to fall.

"I have something in mind, what time will you be free on Saturday after you have been to lunch at your mum and dads?"

"I don't know, probably about 2.00pm why?"

"Well I remember you telling me when you first met me that you have always wanted to go see a show in the West End so I could take you for dinner somewhere, we could go and see a show, stay the night at my house in London and then I could drive you home on Sunday morning how does that sound?"

I smile. "That's sounds lovely, it will be the best birthday present ever."

"Plus it will be our last night together for a while so let's make it one to remember."

Evan drifts off to sleep. Only I can't sleep. All I can think about is Evan leaving and that I only have six days left to work my magic on him. I want him to realise he has feelings for me so we can be together and have a relationship.

My mind is whirring with all kinds of thoughts as I stare into the darkness of my bedroom looking at the shadows on the wall made by the street light shining through the curtains. Eventually with tired eyes I fall asleep.

Twenty Six

It's Tuesday morning and the sunshine is beating through the curtains, pounding my already aching head from the wine. I roll over to see Evan is still sleeping.

I stare at him thinking I need to try and melt away some of the coldness and pain that is stopping him from being with me before it's too late, to reignite the passion within him and let the love in his heart come forward so he can forget his past and we can be together now and for always.

I decide to put the conversation we had last night about him leaving at the back of my mind for now and to just try and be happy and enjoy the time we have left together. I can't force him to be with me but I can try and show him it will be a mistake to let me go.

Evan stretches and rolls over putting his arm around me, he just looks so damn cute in the mornings.

"Good morning beautiful."

"Good morning yourself," I smile feeling his morning erection brush against my front. "I would love to sort that out for you but I really need to get in the shower and so do you," giving him a quick peck then getting out of bed.

"Spoilt sport." He pouts.

His hungry eyes follow my naked body around the room but I ignore the look he's giving me and gather up some fresh clothes to wear.

"I'll have a shower when I get back to the hotel, I have no clean clothes or undies with me."

"Oh okay, if you're sure."

"Yeah I'll just wait here in your comfortable bed until you're done" he says snuggling under the duvet making himself comfortable.

"Okay."

I give him a quick kiss put on my dressing gown and go take a shower.

Evan

I could stay here all day, for the rest of my life even.

What is wrong with me? Why can't I commit to this girl? She is the best thing that has ever happened to me yet I am just going to walk away from her because I am weak.

I hate what they did to me, the cheating, the lies and I am still letting it affect the way I live my life now. I don't care for Julia anymore but I hate him, I hate that he was ever born, I hate that he just takes what he wants from people and doesn't care if he hurts them in the process. How could he do that to me? Of all people. I can't do it to Kara, how can I be in a relationship with her while he is still trying to hurt me at every given opportunity. I know we would have a great relationship for sure but I just can't take the risk. No I need to protect her from him and the only way to do that is to walk away however much I don't want to, I have to.

Evan is still lying in my bed when I am finished in the bathroom.

"Are you getting up?" I pull back the duvet and get a surprise, "oh I see something is already up," I smirk.

"I was just lying here thinking of you," he smiles getting out of bed, taking me in his arms and kissing me passionately.

"Come on you need to get dressed because you know I can't resist you standing there naked with this pointing at me." I grin grabbing hold of his hard length.

"He can't resist you either and he wants to play."

"Evan behave you need to get some clothes on because we need to go to work." I laugh. His hands are everywhere and his mouth fiercely kisses mine.

"Just a quickie?" he pleads taking hold of my hand and placing it on his cock and helping me to stroke him.

"No we haven't got time." I laugh moving my hand away from him smiling, "anyway I was thinking when I was in the shower and as much as it kills me to say this I've decided I'm not having any more sex with you until Saturday night."

"What?" he says sounding shocked.

"Well I need to start weaning myself off you slowly and if Saturday night is going to be our last time together then I need to start getting used to the idea of no more incredible sex.

Also I thought if we abstain from having it for the next few days then Saturday night is going to be so intense, we are both going to be gagging for it so when it happens it will add to the intensity of it all, like you said a night to remember, our last night."

"No, no, no, I don't like the sound of that we need to be having sex as much as possible before I leave," he says putting his boxers on and genuinely looking gutted at my proposal.

"But then it will be harder to just stop and I need to start withdrawing from you slightly for my own sake Evan, you may be able to just walk away and that's that but it's not like that for me."

"Please don't say this Kara."

"It's how I feel."

I'm hoping this will help him to realise how he feels about me because if he can't have sex with me anymore and he misses being with me then maybe he will decide not to walk away.

I pick Evan's clothes up off the floor where he left them last night during our moment of passion and throw them at him.

"Get dressed big boy." I smile taking one last look at him and walk out the room leaving him with a hard on and a frustrated look on his face, being a tease makes me feel so sexy.

I walk into the kitchen to find Jodie and Matt sat at the kitchen table eating breakfast together.

"Morning you two." I say getting two mugs out of the cupboard to make Evan and I a cup of tea.

"Morning Kar, what have you done with Evan have you worn him out that much he can't get up or is he chained to the bed?" Jodie grins.

"I've left him chained to the bed, he is now officially my sex slave," We all laugh. "No he's just getting dressed he'll be here in a minute. Are you two okay for a hot drink?"

"Yes we are fine thanks, so did you have a good night then?" Jodie asks grinning at me.

"Yes we did thanks and did you two have a good one?"

"Well it was more than once," Matt laughs. Jodie rolls her eyes and smiles.

We are having a catch up on the previous night's antics when Evan joins us in the kitchen. "Hi babe, I'm just making us a cup of tea." I smile.

"Thanks baby," Evan replies taking a seat at the table.

"Have you got a busy day ahead then mate?" Matt asks Evan.

"Well I have a meeting with my hotel manager today, he's coming to look around the Manor for the first time and we need to discuss a few things."

"Oh are you talking about Curtis?" I say joining them at the table with two mugs of hot tea.

"Yes, Kara met him when I took her away for the weekend and he gave us a lift to the airport." Evan says accepting the drink off me, "thanks."

"He's really nice, I like Curtis."

"He's not as nice as me though right?" Evan asks frowning at me.

"I don't mean nice as in I fancy him." I laugh.

"Good because I don't want you going out for a drink with him if he asks you again."

"He was only joking Evan. Curtis asked me out for a drink in front of Evan when I first met him, he was doing it to wind Evan up."

"Oh right." Jodie and Matt smile, sensing the tension.

"That may be so but don't give him any ideas he obviously fancies you by the way he couldn't stop looking at you when you first met."

"Evan he was winding you up which clearly worked by the looks of it."

There's an awkward silence in the room. Evan stares at me and I stare back as we drink our tea.

'What is his problem? Curtis shouldn't be a threat, he is one of his closest friends.'

"Anyway mate it was good to meet you but I need to make tracks, hopefully I'll see you again sometime." Matt says getting up from the table.

Evan stands up and they both shake hands. "Yes it was good meeting you too but I'm actually going back to London on Sunday so I may not see you for a while."

"Oh right." He replies, just as Jodie flashes a knowing glance at me, realising I am not okay.

"Well see you around then mate and I'll catch you later Kara." Matt walks out the kitchen and Jodie follows him to the front door to say goodbye leaving Evan and I sat at the kitchen table finishing our tea.

"Hey do you fancy going bowling tonight after work, I remember you telling me you like bowling and we did say we would try and make it a fun week before I have to leave," Evan asks with a smile.

"Yeah sure, I haven't been bowling for a while." I half-heartedly smile.

"Great." Evan replies, "thanks for the tea it was delicious, you make a good cuppa."

"You are welcome." I smile, "I'm just going to finish getting ready for work and then we had better go, I won't be long."

I get up, collect the empty mugs from the table and put them in the sink to be washed later. I then walk out the kitchen leaving Evan alone sat at the table.

I pass Jodie in the hallway and she catches my arm "Kara" I know she wants to talk about Evan leaving but now is not the right time.

"Later" I smile and I head off to my bedroom.

Evan

Jodie walks back into the kitchen and sits down at the table opposite me. She doesn't look very happy.

"You do realise when you leave on Sunday, Kara is going to be in bits, she has developed strong feelings for you and looking at the way you are with her I would say you feel the same. I don't want to interfere because it's none of my business but she is my best friend and I will be the one picking up the pieces. Kara is one in a million and you should think very carefully about giving her up because you won't find anyone better than her," she says warning me.

I look at Jodie and give her a sad smile. "I know she's one in a million and deserves the best but it's not me, I can't give her what she wants. I don't want to hurt her so it's best for everyone this way. I was going to stay in contact with her but knowing how she feels about me I've decided when I leave on Sunday I'm not going to contact her again."

"Does she know this?"

"No she doesn't but she needs to get over me, this, whatever this is we have going on, I want her to be happy and I'm not the one to do that, so I'm going to walk away, I'm sorry but it's for the best."

On the drive back to the Kingsman Hotel after dropping Kara off at work, my mobile phone starts ringing.

I pull over at the side of the road thinking it's Kara or someone from work but I'm disappointed when I see Julia's name on the phone. What does she want?

Taking a deep breath I sigh and accept the call.

"Hello Julia."

"Hi Evan, sorry to bother you I just wanted to let you know I found out from my friend Jackie that Sebastian approached her in a bar the other night. He must have recognised her being a friend of mine and he was asking questions about you and I. He was apparently using me to get to you and didn't seem concerned that I lost the baby. Anyway he said he wants to catch up with you for old time sake and that you owe him for taking me off your hands, she said he seemed drunk."

"Ok nothing I've not heard before anything else?" I reply.

"Oh and if she saw you to pass on a message from him to say he is looking for you and he wants the money that you owe him."

I laugh. "Well that's nothing new, thanks for letting me know. Like I always told you, he is bad news so if you do see him I would stay away from him if I were you. But hey, why would you ever listen to me?"

"I will, I do wish I had listened to you before when we were together and then things would be different. You were the best thing that ever happened to me Evan, we were so good together, I miss you. Do you ever think about us?"

I sigh. "Julia there is no us."

"But there could be if you wanted there to be, if you could just forgive me, I've changed Evan I'm not that person anymore and nothing like that would ever happen again."

"Julia I'm sorry but what we had it was over a long time ago and it will never be that way again."

"Please Evan just one more chance?"

"I'm sorry Julia but I feel nothing for you. A lot has happened and I will never forget what you both did to me. Anyway if there is nothing else I need to go."

"Please just think about it, please Evan. If I hear anymore I'll let you know."

"Goodbye Julia."

I cut the call and hit the steering wheel in frustration. Why can't they both just get on with their lives and leave me alone. There is no fucking way he is getting a penny out of me and Julia declaring her love for me? What the fuck!

The Stranger

It's the end of July and the warm rays of the summer sun are shining down over the city of London as tourists fill the streets on their travels to visit popular destinations that the city has to offer.

After working up quite a sweat on my early morning run I walk into a nearby newsagents desperate for a cold drink to quench my thirst.

"Good morning, it's a lovely day" the man behind the counter says as I walk past him to the chilled drinks cabinet in the corner of the shop.

I select a bottle of mineral water and make my way to the counter. At the side of the counter there is a newspaper stand and a headline catches my eye.

'New Hotel for Hamilton Hotel Group.'

Opening the newspaper, there on the front page of the well-known tabloid is a photograph of a man I know very well with a familiar face. I read the strapline under the photo.

'Business Tycoon Evan Hamilton of Hamilton's Hotels outside his new hotel in the Surrey Hills due to open in the new year.'

I pass the paper and the bottle of mineral water to the newsagent and pay him. I walk out of the newsagents and stand under the canopy of the shop shielding me from the sun and drink some of the cold water.

Opening up the paper I read the article. "Interesting, I've never been to the Surrey Hills before, I think I might have to pay a visit."

Twenty Seven

I don't have to wait long before Evan pulls up outside the flat for our bowling date. I grab my bag, lock the front door and saunter down the path in my black strappy block heeled sandals, black skinny jeans and cute red top.

"Hi beautiful," he says as I jump in the passenger seat to be greeted by his gorgeous smile.

"Hey you."

He places his hand around the back of my neck and pulls me towards him crashing his lips onto mine for a tongue mingling kiss.

"You look gorgeous as always."

"Thanks, you look pretty hot yourself," I smile looking at him wearing a pair of dark blue stonewash jeans, a white t-shirt and his dark brown hair is styled to perfection.

"Are you ready to go?" he asks not taking his eyes off me.

"Yes do you know the way?"

"No not really I was hoping you would direct me."

Evan pulls away from the kerb and I give him directions on what roads to take.

"You need to turn down here into Cook Street and then the bowling alley is on the left."

"Okay beautiful."

The Stranger

I recognise that Aston Martin, let's see where he is heading.

I hold off on the accelerator and watch them take a sharp turn into a car park. I need to keep a safe distance so they don't see me. I have followed Evan and his passenger to a bowling alley. It would seem he has lowered his standards from his usual lifestyle.

Now I can see his passenger clearly, his companion is an attractive blonde, very nice. I wonder who she is?

I wait some time to allow them to get into the building, and then I make my move to follow them inside.

I take a seat by the bar on the upper level of the fast-food restaurant. I'll just sit here and watch them secretly for a while over at the bowling lanes and then I'll head back to my car and wait for them to return.

Watching them interact with each other it's clear to see they are close.

We walk over to lane four and change into the red and blue bowling shoes putting our shoes under the seats of the lane we are occupying. I program in our names onto the computer ready for the game to start and Evan is up first.

He picks a ball carefully and takes his first bowl while I watch him loving how strong he is and how well he handles the bowling ball with precision and speed.

The bowling ball speeds down the shiny wooden floor knocking over all the skittles in one go.

"Strike," he shouts grinning at me walking back to the seating area and giving me a kiss.

"Beginners luck," I smile walking past him.

I give a little run and bend over rolling the ball down the alley towards the skittles standing tall at the end of the lane.

All the pins go down except one and turning around smiling I pick up another ball catching Evan smirking sat in the seat watching me.

"It's my first go I'm only warming up," I say looking at him as I take my second go.

Walking back to Evan feeling happy that I've managed to knock down the last one, I give him a sexy smile. "Those balls are heavy, I bet you will know what heavy balls feel like after a few days of no sex with me." I grin.

"Oh you think so do you, we'll see and I know what you are doing Kara trying to distract me bending over sexily like you did," he laughs walking over to pick his next ball.

I blush feeling relieved that the bowling lanes next to ours are not occupied.

"First of all you are not going to beat me at bowling Evan and secondly I'm not giving in on the no sex rule so don't get your hopes up as it's not happening."

Evan grins. "We'll see, but it won't be my hopes I'm getting up Kara," he smiles going to take his turn and delivering yet another strike.

As the game is coming to an end I'm winning by ten points but Evan is yet to take his last go and with a cocky grin and a wink he chooses his ball. Is losing at something even in his vocabulary?

"I'm looking forward to celebrating my win Kara, you are going to be bowled over later when you are shouting my name when I fuck you."

I blush and feel tingles in between my legs; this no sex rule is not going to be easy if he keeps saying things like that and now I'm regretting saying it in the first place because I'm becoming aroused at the thought of Evan fucking me.

Evan takes his final bowl and wins the game. I roll my eyes at his victory dance and he takes me in his arms and kisses me passionately whilst whispering, "better luck next time babe." After handing back the bowling shoes Evan takes hold of my hand and we walk outside to the car.

The Stranger

My trip to Surrey has been a success so far.

By looking at the way he acts around this girl tells me all I need to know, he is obviously taken with her. I've never seen him be so affectionate, I haven't seen him like this with anybody, not even Julia. It's a shame it might have to end.

Evan has ruined my life and so I will continue to ruin his. If he's not going to pay me my money then he will have to pay in other ways. He has certainly found himself a beauty and I think she could be the perfect solution into getting the money Evan owes me. I think I can use this to my advantage. I'm going to enjoy hurting him to the point he will be paying me my money sooner rather than later.

"What are we doing now then?" I ask as Evan starts the car knowing what he is going to say before he's even answered.

"We are going to celebrate my win naked," he grins backing out of the car park space.

"I'm not having sex with you Evan not until Saturday so you can think of something else to do."

"You can tell yourself that all evening Kara, but we will be having sex later I guarantee it."

"Oh will we Mr Hamilton you think so do you, you may have won at bowling but you are not winning on this."

"Okay, how about we go for a drink then, I saw a lovely little pub down the road on the way here we could stop there on the way back."

"So the plan is to get me drunk and then seduce me?" I smile thinking how hot Evan looks tonight. How on earth am I going to turn down his advances towards me when I'm struggling to control my own urges?

"I don't know what you mean?" he smiles.

The Stranger

They set off from the bowling alley car park and I follow them. Evan puts his foot down. He is such a show off, I hate him.

I follow them to a pub car park. Again, I try to keep my distance so they don't see me and suspect anything.

I watch the two of them get out the car, fondling, kissing, pretty much wanting to rip each other's clothes off, you can see the obsession all over their faces.

I wonder if it's lust or love? They walk inside the quaint pub. I think I have seen enough. It's time for me to head back to London, I know what I need to do.

We walk inside the old English pub with wooden beams on the ceiling and Evan points to a booth seating area, "Shall we sit over there?"

The booth is in a secluded corner and the seats are covered in a crimson velvet material.

"Okay." I edge over to the other side of the cosy nook.

"What would you like to drink?" Evan asks.

"I'll have a white wine please."

Evan gives me a quick kiss and then walks over to the grey-haired gentleman behind the bar. The man is friendly and I can see them chatting away while he serves Evan our drinks.

Evan returns with a tray and on it there is a bottle of wine, a wine glass and a glass of coke for him.

"Evan I only wanted a glass of wine not a bottle."

"Well I thought you might need to drown your sorrows seeing as you lost at the game of bowling," he smiles.

Evan sits down next to me and fills my glass.

He is really happy tonight probably because he won at bowling but I like to think it's because he's with me. I love that he's relaxed as we enjoy being in each other's company.

"So it's Wednesday tomorrow, what are you doing any exciting plans?" Evan asks before taking a sip of his coke.

Before I have a chance to answer Evan's mobile rings from his pocket. He takes it out and looks at the screen.

"Damn it, I don't hear from her for weeks then all of a sudden she won't leave me alone," he mumbles. "Sorry, it's my Mother, I had better call her back because she will just keep ringing otherwise, I won't be long."

Evan

I step outside the pub and call my mother, it's not long before she answers.

"Evan, hi."

"Hi Mother, what can I do for you?"

"I've just seen a photo of you on the front of a London newspaper advertising your new hotel."

"Oh you've seen the article, yes it came out today, what do you think?"

"I think it sounds wonderful, I will have to come and have a look when it's finished."

"Yes it's going to be amazing when it's had the renovations done. How did you get a copy of the newspaper being on a yacht in Monaco?"

"My friend Cynthia took a photo on her phone and messaged it to me. It would have been nice if my own son had sent it to me though."

"I'm too busy to think about sending you newspaper articles."

"I know. Listen son, I'm sorry for upsetting you the other day talking about …"

"Hey it's fine don't worry about it, I'm sorry but I haven't really got much time for a chat because I have a young lady waiting for me." 'What did I say that for?'

"Really who is she, is it serious? It's about time you move on from the whole Julia thing."

'Great now she wants details.'

"She's just a friend."

"What's her name?"

"Kara."

"What a lovely name I do hope you find love again it will make me so happy to see you settled with someone."

"Yes, but like I said she's a friend so don't go getting your hopes up, anyway I really need to go."

"Okay I love you son."

"You too, speak to you soon, goodbye Mother."

Feeling rosy cheeked and slightly tipsy I look at the door as it opens and Evan walks back over to me smiling.

Evan sits down to finish his drink and after having most of this wine to myself, I'm feeling horny. I place my hand on Evan's crotch and stroke it on the outside of his jeans under the table.

"Do you fancy getting out of here?" Evan says smiling, his cock twitching in excitement under my palm.

Lisa Jane Lordan

I slide out of the seat and holding Evan's hand gingerly walk out of the pub. As the warm fresh evening air hits my face the effects of the alcohol are really starting to kick in.

Evan guides me to the car opening the passenger door for me to get in then gets into the driver's seat.

I reach across and put my hand on his crotch again and look at him, "I love your cock." I smile.

He laughs. "Well it loves you so would you like to have some fun or are you still denying yourself of a mind-blowing orgasm later?" he says giving me a cheeky smile and starting the car.

"I may be drunk and feeling horny but I'm not having sex with you until my birthday."

"Okay beautiful, I'll just take you home then."

"Oh ... I don't want to go home I want to stay with you." I pout.

"Okay then would you like to come back to the hotel for a night cap?" he smiles.

"Yes as long as you behave." I tease.

"Okay but you're the one caressing my dick," he laughs.

"Okay, I was just checking you knew the rules." I tease.

We reach the Kingsman Hotel and the valet takes Evan's keys off him to park the car and seeing that I'm swaying a little he picks me up and carries me into the hotel.

Guests are staring at us as he carries me through reception to the lift.

"Good Evening." Evan grins.

We enter the lift and Evan places me on my feet and props me up against the wall while he presses the button for the Penthouse Suite. Then he stands back and looks at me with hungry eyes as the lift ascends. This no sex rule is definitely going to be broken. He is just so gorgeous and I want him desperately, it was a stupid idea anyway.

We walk out of the lift and Evan opens the door with his key card. We walk into the suite and Evan kicks the door shut behind him.

We look at each other intensely and then not being able to help it because the urge is too strong I lunge at him kissing him passionately.

Evan pushes me up against the nearest wall neither one of us wanting to break the contact. I pull at the bottom of Evan's white t-shirt and briefly breaking the kiss he helps me slip it off over his head revealing his naked torso before finding my lips again.

Evan finds the zip on my cropped jeans and pulls it down while he kisses my neck, he nibbles my ear gently and runs his tongue along the soft flesh on my neck making me moan.

I pull my jeans and knickers down my legs throwing them on the floor and then sit on the couch with hungry eyes as I watch Evan take off his own jeans and boxers, his erection springing free.

Evan helps me to take my top and bra off and we are both desperate to feel each other's bodies skin to skin, we can't get enough of each other.

The sexual desire to be joined as one is so strong, the urge to have him inside me is extreme and there is no way I can stop this now and I don't want to.

Evan lowers his body over mine on the couch our mouths crashing together again.

Evan slides into my wetness and holds himself still for a few moments. I know he's majorly turned on just as much as I am and he looks like he is ready to explode.

"Jesus Kara …" he says breathless.

After a few moments he's ready and he thrusts deep inside me in and out, in and out slowly making me cry out.

"Oh god Evan your cock feels so good." I moan. "Oh yes, so good."

Evan's drives hit the spot every time.

After a few more thrusts he pulls out of me and pulls me up off the couch, he then carries me over to the study area placing my bare bum on the coldness of the wooden oak desk making me flinch as I feel goose bumps all over my body not only from the cold of the wood but also from the heat of how turned on I am.

"I want to fuck you on this desk, in fact I want to fuck you everywhere I can't get enough of you."

I rest my bum on the edge of the desk and he guides his cock into me once again holding onto my hips and thrusting inside with force.

"Oh god … yes … Evan … fuck me …" Hearing those words and feeling wild with desire he gives it to me hard.

I cry out from the contact of our bodies slapping together "Yes like that, OHHH …"

"Oh fuck …" he moans breathlessly as I dig my fingernails into his tanned back.

"Yes give it to me baby, harder."

He slams into me over and over again and I'm struggling to hold onto him so I grab hold of the sides of the desk for a better grip.

I throw my head back moaning as the feel of Evan sliding in and out of me is bringing me closer and closer to orgasm, sweat is forming on Evan's forehead as he powers on and on.

I'm panting my chest is going up and down faster and faster the more turned on I become and the sounds of Evan groaning low in his throat and the feel of him deep inside me adds to the intensity of it all.

"Oh yes, fuck me, yes …" I cry.

"Fucking hell …"

Evan thrusts his greedy cock into me moaning with every stroke. "You … are … so …fucking … amazing …" he says powering into me over and over again. "OHHHHHH …"

With every drive he brings us closer to the end goal. "Evan … I'm going to come …" and with a few more expert thrusts I orgasm followed by Evan

"FUUCCCKKKK …" And his warm seed fills my insides as he comes too.

The mind-blowing rush of pleasure sweeps through our brains. We are totally out of breath and we feel amazing at how we have made each other feel.

Evan looks into my eyes and smiles. "You are so perfect Kara, I'm so glad I met you, you've made my time here phenomenal."

He takes my flushed face into his hands and kisses me intensely and passionately.

Tears spring in my eyes "I'm so glad I met you too, the time we have spent together has been the best time of my life."

I stroke his face lightly with my fingers feeling emotional. Evan knows how I'm feeling because I think he feels it too but he just won't acknowledge it.

He looks thoughtful for a moment then trying to lighten the mood he laughs. "Well I can honestly say that was the best no sex I've ever had."

"Yeah okay it was a stupid rule wasn't it, I can't help it if you are impossible to resist," I grin pulling him to me for another kiss.

After getting dressed again we are relaxing on the sofa waiting for some food to be delivered from room service when a text message pings. I check my phone.

It's not mine.

Evan opens up his phone.

"Who's that?" I ask curious to know.

"I'm not sure, it's a number I don't recognise" he frowns.

Evan looks troubled and deep in thought.

"Are you okay Evan, who is it?" I ask not caring that I'm prying. 'I bet it's Julia.'

"It's no one of any importance," he replies looking agitated. He seems stressed running his hands through his hair.

"Then why the strange look on your face?"

"I don't have a strange look on my face."

"Well if you could see what I'm looking at it's a strange look and not a happy face either."

"For fuck's sake Kara, why do you have to ask questions all the time why can't you just leave it. I'm trying to prot ... I'm trying to ..."

"What Evan you are trying to what?"

"I'm trying not to hurt you."

"Why is it Julia, is that who it is, is she missing you?"

"No and I've told you I'm not interested in her and I told her that too."

"What so she has been messaging you?" I can feel the heat prickling up by arms and the back of my neck.

'How are we still having this same conversation?'

"No we haven't been messaging, she called me and she mentioned she still has feelings for me. I promise you they are not reciprocated."

"So if it's not from Julia who is the text from then? and why are you acting like you are? Just be honest with me Evan?"

"I just need you to not ask questions okay, we need to keep this casual. If I start talking to you about stuff that's what you do in a relationship and then feelings come into it. Can we please just have fun for these last few days and then everything can go back to normal."

"What do you mean everything can go back to normal? Why can you not see that this has never been casual for me Evan, feelings are already involved, I'm in love you Evan, I love you." I sob into my hands.

I want him to say he loves me too but he just sits next to me in silence. 'Say something, anything.' The silence is interrupted by a knock at the door. Evan gets up to answer it and I run off into the bedroom sobbing throwing myself onto the bed.

Evan

After taking delivery of the food I put it down on the coffee table and pick up my mobile phone feeling angry. With shaky hands I read the text again that was sent from the unknown number.

I see your taste has improved my dear friend, she is world class compared to Julia. I was passing through the area and saw you two looking cosy, you had the look of love my friend, sorry I couldn't stop to say hello. We must catch up soon. Be in touch.

I know exactly who it's from and who is trying to get under my skin. I type out a reply.

I don't know how you found my number and I am no friend of yours and never will be again. The woman I was looking cosy with is no-one, she is just someone who works in a coffee shop I picked up for a bit of fun so if you want to get your kicks out of hurting me again with her you are wasting your time. She is nothing to me and I won't be going there again. Don't bother getting in touch again you are wasting your time.

"Shit." I pace the floor running sweaty hands through my hair. I need to end this now, it's the only way I can protect Kara from him. I refuse to have Kara dragged into his games, like a cat teasing its prey. He won't stop until he gets what he wants, I can't have her involved, it's the only way.

I make my way down the hallway to the master suite. Opening the bedroom door I slowly peer inside and see Kara lying on the bed crying.

There is nothing more I want to do than cuddle her and tell her it is all going to be okay. I have been nothing but a headfuck since we met and I can't cause her anymore pain. I know what I need to do.

"Kara I'm sorry I never meant to hurt you I only ever wanted a bit of fun and you knew that" I say awkwardly.

I sit up and look at Evan with my tear stained face, "I know but I've fallen in with love you and I think you love me too but you won't let yourself be happy because you are too hung up on the past to have a future."

Evan takes a deep breath. "Kara I'm sorry but I don't love you and how can you say you love me? You hardly know me." He hangs his head in shame.

"I do know you, I know that you are a beautiful person inside and out, I know that you are kind and considerate. I know how incredible we are together in and out of the bedroom, you like the same things I do, going to the theatre, the same foods particularly strawberries and cream …" Evan smiles. "I know that you make me happy and no one has ever made me feel this way before. I know that you are hurting over what has happened in the past and I wish I could make the pain go away so you can be with me." I cry.

"Kara please don't cry, what we have has obviously gone beyond friendship and I can only apologise for that because I didn't mean for it to and I shouldn't have let it happen. I did tell you I would leave and the last thing I want to do is hurt you but this has to stop. We can't be together and I'm not going to change my mind on this, I wish I could but it's for the best."

"For the best, for the fucking best?" I scream.

"Kara ... I ..."

"You're a coward Evan that's what you are. I hope one day you realise that letting me go was the worst decision you have ever made and when you do realise it will be too late."

"I'm sorry." He can barely look me in the eye.

"I'm sorry too, I'm sorry for ever laying eyes on you." I pick up my bag and walk out of the door for the last time sobbing.

"Please, don't go, not like this," he pleads standing in the doorway guilt written all over his face.

The lift arrives and I step inside, I can't even look at him. The lift door closes and descends down to the lobby. My heart is breaking.

"Goodbye Evan."

The taxi journey home feels like forever. I can hear the driver talking to me but nothing is registering. All I can think about is Evan and the words.

'I don't love you.'

It's past midnight, I fumble for my flat keys in my bag as I wipe away the tears rolling down my cheeks and hurry inside.

Trying to be quiet so I don't wake Jodie I take off my shoes in the hallway and lock the door. Walking quietly into the kitchen I turn on the light and jump when I'm met with a shocked face with wild brown hair and sleepy brown eyes looking back at me.

"Jodie what the hell are you doing you scared the shit out of me standing there in the dark?" I clutch my thumping heart in my chest.

"What am I doing? I could say the same to you; I just woke up to get a glass of water, I heard a noise and thought you were someone trying to break in so I was hiding in the dark."

"Sorry no it's only me, sorry if I scared you." I laugh.

"I thought you were staying with Evan tonight?" she says yawning.

"I was but …" I burst into tears clutching my face in my hands.

"Oh god Kar what's happened, here sit down," Jodie guides me to a chair at the kitchen table.

"It's over." I sob uncontrollably trying to get a breath to talk to explain.

"Oh no honey, come here." She puts her arms around me and hugs me for some much-needed comfort knowing I'm heartbroken.

"Sit there and I'll get you a drink you look like you need one," she says getting a bottle of vodka and a glass from a cupboard pouring some and passing it to me.

"Drink this it'll help." she says as I down the neat vodka in one go coughing as the strong liquor burns the back of my throat. "Thanks Jode."

"Talk to me Kar, what's happened?" she refills my glass, encouraging me to drown my sorrows.

"Everything was good, we had been bowling and had a lovely time then we went back to his hotel suite and he got a text on his phone."

"Okay, so who was the text from?"

"I don't know I asked him and he just said it was of no importance."

"What does that mean?"

"He said he needed me to not ask questions, that we're not in a relationship and he was trying not to hurt me. He just wants us to have fun for our last few days together and then he said everything can go back to normal."

Jodie looks worried. "Okay so you don't know who the text was from then?"

"No he wouldn't tell me. I think it was from Julia and he was lying. For all I know he could have been lying to me all along."

"So you think he's still hung up on his ex?"

"Yes, no, oh I don't know he said he's not interested in her but if he won't tell me who is texting him it says to me that he's hiding something or someone. He said she's been calling him."

"It does seem weird, why doesn't he just be honest?"

"He said we were only supposed to be a casual thing and when he starts telling me stuff that's when feelings are involved. I told him feelings are already involved, I told him that I love him," Jodie looks shocked.

"I thought he was my happy ending Jode. I don't know how I'm going to cope without him, I do I love him and I know it's crazy after only knowing him a short time but I honestly and truly have never felt like this about anyone in my life." Tears flood my eyes and I need another tissue, Jodie hands me the whole box. "He says he doesn't love me, why can't he just love me back? I sob.

"Oh Kar … I need to tell you something." Jodie says looking awkward.

"What?" I can feel a hot rush of prickles creeping up my back, suddenly filling me with a nervous energy.

"Evan told me he wasn't going to contact you anymore when he left on Sunday."

"Really, what? When did he say that?"

"It was the morning after he stayed over."

"Oh, why haven't you told me this before now?"

"I haven't told you because I said to him that it would be a mistake to walk away and I guess I thought he would think about what I said and change his mind. Sorry I didn't tell you."

"Oh, no it's fine Jode."

"I'm sorry babe, if Evan can't see what is right in front of him then he's a fool."

"I'm the fool for loving him" I sigh.

"Listen I will help you get through this okay and you will have your happy ending one day Kara. And don't worry you are still going to have an amazing birthday because I will make sure of it, I think we should go out and get really drunk, have a good dance and then stagger home eating a greasy kebab, what do you reckon?"

"Maybe … I don't know, I can't think about my birthday right now."

"There is no maybe about it you are going to enjoy your 25th birthday and it is my personal mission to make sure it happens."

"Thanks Jodie I don't know what I'd do without you as my friend." I give her a kiss on the cheek.

"No worries babe, we're besties for life and I'll always be here for you." She nudges me.

"I know you're a great friend to me, the best."

Feeling much calmer now Jodie leaves me to go to bed and I pour myself another drink. I sit at the table feeling subdued and emotionally drained from the night's events and the excessive crying. All I keep hearing in my head is 'I don't love you, I don't love you.' I wish things were different.

I put the empty glass in the sink, turn off the kitchen light and go to the bathroom to clean my teeth, I'm exhausted.

Staring into the mirror on the bathroom cabinet door, all I can see is a tear stained face staring back at me, a different face to the one I've been looking at recently. I have been so happy and at this moment in time I would give anything to roll the clock back to feel that way again.

To be in Evan's arms, to kiss his gorgeous mouth, to hear his sexy voice, to be close to his body and to feel his heart beating as I lay my head on his chest.

I put on my pyjamas, find my phone then get into bed. I check my phone to find Evan has messaged twice.

I'm so sorry beautiful, I hope you are okay? I really didn't mean to hurt you. E xx

Hi, it's me again please just let me know you're okay, I feel terrible, I can't sleep! E xx

I start to type out a reply then delete it. I don't really know what to say, no I'm not okay, yes you did hurt me and good you can't sleep because I'm not going to be able to sleep either.

Twenty Eight

It is only a few days until my 25th birthday and while I should be feeling happy and excited, I feel like my whole world has fallen apart.

The pain is unbearable and lying in my bed thinking about the previous day all I want to do is to stay in the comfort of my bed, lock myself away and forget but I can't I have to get up and go to work.

I roll over to turn my alarm clock off to see Jode has brought me a cup of tea, I smile as I sit up to begin to wake myself up.

I turn on my phone to see further text messages from Evan, further desperation as to why he made the decision he did. He's also left me a voice mail, he sounded drunk.

I send him a reply.

You hurt me Evan. And I am so confused. I know you said you wanted us to be casual in the beginning but after the amazing times we have shared together I thought we truly had something but obviously not. I understand you just wanted to have fun well so do I, so I'm going out Saturday night for my birthday and that's exactly what I'm going to do. I wish you all the best with your hotel and future. But most of all, good luck with your lack of commitment and new conquest. Have a nice life. K

I feel proud with that response, I am so done. I throw my phone on the bed, drink the tea then get up and have a shower hoping the water will wash away some of the hurt I'm feeling.

I then make my way to work on this beautiful summer morning. As I turn the corner on the last stretch of my journey to work I hear the rumble of a car engine. I glance out of the corner of my eye, I recognise that sound all too much.

It's Evan in his Aston Martin. Normally when I see him I get butterflies and feel excited but the way I'm feeling today I really just want him to piss off and leave me alone.

Great timing Evan. I carry on walking but he follows me slowly in his car. He opens the car window, "Kara please wait." He calls in a pleading voice.

I stop and glare at him.

"What do you want Evan?" not giving him eye contact.

"How are you?"

"Oh I'm great thanks, how do you think I am?"

"I got your text, it wasn't very friendly" he sighs.

"Are you just going to work?" he asks.

'He knows exactly where I'm going.'

"Well that's where I normally go at this time of day isn't it." I reply sarcastically.

"I'm just heading to the Manor; I'm meeting Curtis, we have a business meeting."

"Oh that's nice; say hi to him for me, you'd better go then. Bye."

"Kara wait don't be like that, it doesn't have to be like this, can't we just go back to how it was before?" I turn to look at him bitterly.

"Are you kidding me? No Evan we can't, too much has been said and like you pointed out it's for the best."

I feel tears welling in my eyes and I don't want him to see I'm upset so I turn and walk off, "Goodbye Evan."

I hear him punch the steering wheel and then the car wheel spins and he speeds off down the road.

I stop walking and take a few deep breaths to try and stop myself from crying before I carry on my way to work.

I hate this.

I arrive home from work and can hear Jodie in the kitchen. The smell of homemade lasagne hits me as I take off my shoes and walk into the kitchen to say hi.

"Hi Kara, are you ok?" Jodie asks looking concerned.

"Yeah I'm ok I'm pleased to be home though. It's been hard putting on a fake smile to customers when you're feeling like shit."

"Yes I can imagine. Glass of wine?" Jodie asks holding up a chilled bottle out of the fridge.

"Sounds good."

Jodie gets two wine glasses out of the kitchen cupboard and pours us both a glass.

"I think we should have a toast," she smiles.

"Oh what are we toasting to?" I frown.

"To independent women who don't need men because that's why vibrators were invented."

Her words make me laugh. "Cheers," and we chink glasses.

"Like I've said to you before Kar you sometimes have to kiss a lot of frogs before you find your prince and your happy ending will come one day babe."

"I know you're right," I smile taking a big gulp of wine.

I just wish my prince was Evan.

Twenty Nine

There is a gentle knock at my door and I am awoken by Jodie swinging the door open singing.

"Happy birthday to you, happy birthday to you, happy birthday dear Kara, happy birthday to you …"

"Thanks Jode." I stretch and open my heavy eye lids as she opens the curtains slightly to let in some natural light making me squint. Jodie is holding two gift bags and a purple and silver balloon with birthday girl printed on it.

I sit up in bed trying to wake up as Jodie passes me the balloon and sits on the edge of the bed.

"Thanks Jode" I smile. I glance at my alarm clock wondering what the time is, I pull a face at the fact it is 8am on a Saturday.

"Jodie it's only 8 o'clock why are you up so early?"

"Well it's your birthday and our big night out tonight and I'm really excited. You should count yourself lucky I was going to come in at 7.00am but thought better of it," she laughs giving me a hug and handing me one of the gift bags filled with presents.

"Aww thanks Jode," I take the bag off her feeling excited to see what she has bought me.

"Open them then," Jodie says impatiently with a big grin on her face.

"Okay okay," I laugh loving how excited Jodie is that it's my birthday.

I unwrap the presents from the first gift bag one at a time. Jodie has bought me some fluffy socks, perfume, a gift voucher for the local beauty salon, a sparkly keyring of the letter K and other gifts for me to pamper myself with.

I take out the last present from the bag and it's in a box, it makes a noise, I give it a shake and something rattles inside.

"What on earth is this?" I smile tearing off the paper.

Opening the box, I pull out a money box in the shape of a suitcase which has the words holiday fund on it.

"Aww thanks Jodie, that's great just what I wanted, I'm definitely going to start saving for a holiday in the sun."

"I know you said when you came back from Italy that you wanted to start saving for a holiday so you can visit other places. I thought this would be ideal to store those pennies in and just so you know I'm coming with you," she laughs.

"Of course."

"Thanks Jode, I love them." I smile.

She hands me the next bag, I give her a funny look.

"More presents, you're spoiling me."

"Oh this isn't from me."

"Oh who is it from?" I ask puzzled.

"It's from Evan."

'What?'

"I heard a light knock on the door early this morning when I was in bed so I got up to see who it was thinking it might be Matt and found this on the doorstep."

My stomach churns. It is a tiny, matte black giftbag with a slick, white velvet bow to tie it together. It looks expensive.

'He already gave me a birthday present? He bought me the Louboutin shoes?'

I read the label 'Happy Birthday Beautiful E xx.' I gently untie the bow on the small box and open it.

Inside is a delicate silver Tennis bracelet featuring a heart with a tiny diamond in the centre.

"Oh my god Kar that's gorgeous, it looks expensive."

"I know." Tears fill my eyes, it really is gorgeous.

I hold the heart in between my index and middle finger and turn it over to find an engraving on the back saying 'With Me Always.'

"Can I take a look?" Jodie says holding her hand out for me to pass it to her.

I pass it to her. "It's beautiful," she smiles at me.

"I know, I think it's his way of telling me he does care."

"Yeah I think so too." She smiles.

Jodie looks in the velvet gift bag and sees he has bought me another gift.

She wolf whistles as she takes out some sexy lingerie. I am so taken aback by the bracelet I didn't think there would be anything else.

I recognise the label from one of the Italian boutiques we visited in Lake Como.

I roll my eyes and smile thinking he did owe me some underwear after tearing my knickers off me in the games room at the Manor. Why does he still have to have such an effect on me? After everything, I still get those butterflies in my stomach.

"Wow Kara they are so nice," Jodie says as I look at the sexy lingerie thinking the same thing.

"What is he doing to me Jode?, I feel so hurt and pissed off at him one minute and now he's bought me these lovely gifts for my birthday and I just want to see him, tell him I love him and give him a kiss."

"You don't have to feel guilty for loving somebody Kar, love is not planned, it certainly can't be hidden and the journey of falling in love in not always a smooth ride as you know, if you really want him and love him like you say you do then just go for it, fight for him Kar," she smiles.

"Hmm … I want him to fight for me though Jode."

"Yeah I know. Anyway, more importantly, have you decided what you're wearing tonight? Because we need to go out looking fierce."

"God no, I need to try on at least ten different outfits first before I can make a decision like that, I'll have a look later."

"Well whatever you decide you always look lovely. Right I'll go and make us a cuppa and some croissants for your birthday breakfast, see you in a bit," Jodie says getting up off the bed.

"Thanks Jode and thanks again for my presents."

"You are welcome," she smiles walking out of my bedroom.

With all the excitement of my morning opening presents and enjoying a birthday breakfast, I forgot to turn on my phone.

I scroll through the happy birthday posts from family and friends. Sally text to say she will drop my present off later. There is no message from Evan, I'm guessing he is waiting for a text from me after giving me these gorgeous gifts and not being on great terms. I pluck up the courage and text him.

Hey Evan, it's me. I just wanted to say thank you for my bracelet, it is the most precious, beautiful gift, I love the engraving. I didn't expect it at all especially since you bought me that beautiful dress and the shoes. The underwear was a nice touch too, you did say you owed me some I suppose, you know how to make me smile. I am still mad at you for making me believe we had something special, but thank you for my birthday gifts, it was very kind of you. K xx

I am just getting myself ready to walk to mum and dad's for a birthday lunch when I receive a text. Evan has sent a reply.

Happy Birthday Kara. I'm glad you like the presents and I can still put a smile on your face. I wish I could see you in the lingerie, I can imagine what it looks like on your sexy body. I hope you don't stay mad at me for too long. I miss you. E xx

I can't help the smile on my face reading his text, he misses me.

It is scorching hot today and it reminds me of the heat in Italy as I reminisce of my time spent there with Evan and it makes me smile as I remember our day on the yacht.

I reach my parents' bungalow and I can see my mum looking out the kitchen window waving at me.

I walk up the pathway to the house and my mum opens the door and runs to greet me giving me a big hug.

"Happy Birthday my gorgeous girl, I can't believe you're 25!" she says with tears in her eyes.

"Thanks Mum," I smile hugging her back. I see my dad standing in the doorway over my mum's shoulder and he is grinning at me. I let go of her and walk over, "Hi Dad, it's good to see you."

"Hi love, happy birthday," he says taking me in his big strong arms and cuddling me.

It feels good to be home. As we let go of our embrace, my mum squeals and makes me jump, I wasn't expecting this much of a fuss for my 25th.

"Just before you go inside Kara we have a little surprise for you, don't we Dad." My mum looks at my dad with a grin from ear to ear.

"Yes love we do," my dad replies. "Just a minute," and he disappears into the hallway. "Close your eyes and hold your hands out."

"Open your eyes, happy birthday!" I open my eyes to see a set of keys with a heart keyring holding them together.

"What are these for?" I ask puzzled.

"Well if you turn around and walk back down the path you will see your birthday present out the front gate in white."

I walk down the path with a smile on my face feeling excited and intrigued as my parents follow behind me. Parked outside the bungalow is a white Fiat 500 with the Italian stripes on the roof.

"Wait, what, this is mine?" I grin pointing to the car looking at my parents.

"It certainly is my darling." My mum answers then squeals again.

I laugh and can't believe what's happening, my parents have bought me a car.

"Oh my god. Thank you so much." I look at the car detailed with coloured stripes of the Italian flag on the roof

Two Risky to Love

and bonnet and I immediately think of Evan and my time in Italy.

I turn to look at my parents who are stood proud watching me at the side of the road and I run up to them and hug them both. "Seriously, I'm shocked, thank you so much I absolutely love it. But are you sure you can afford this?"

I step back and look at them concerned because I don't want them spending their savings on me. My mum smiles.

"Yes of course we can afford it and let us worry about things like that. We are so proud of the woman you have become and thought it was time you had your own set of wheels."

I let it sink in for a moment that I now have my very own car and then hug them both again. "Thank you, thank you."

"I'm sorry it's not a brand new one out the showroom but…"

"No don't be silly I don't care how old it is I'm just pleased to have my own car, I love it."

'I love my parents so much, they are the best and I'm so lucky to have them. I hate that I have had to keep such a huge secret from them being with Evan.'

Watching my dad while he's pointing out the various things in my car reminds me of when I was little.

He would bring his lorry home and we would spend hours together in the cab pretending to be a trucker.

After spending time checking out all the gadgets on my new car we head inside and have lunch.

My mum has made my favourite chocolate cake with a whipped cream filling and has put candles on the cake like she does every birthday, although now I'm getting older she has opted for two candles with the numbers 2 and 5 instead of 25 candles.

My love life may be a shambles but seeing my parents has certainly cheered me up.

They always make me smile and the way they act and love each other reminds me of the way I am with Evan when we're together.

Love is electric when it is there. I just wish I knew why Evan is holding back, is it because of Julia or is it something else? Or is it because he truly doesn't love me, but it sure feels like he does from the way he acts when we're together and like Jodie told me, you can't hide it when you love someone and he is definitely acting like someone in love?

I stay with my parents for a few hours and then it's time to head home, I need to get ready for my night out. I am feeling much more in the mood for a celebration now.

It's great because I don't have to walk home this time, I have a car to drive.

"See you both soon, and thanks again for my car, I absolutely love it, love you both."

"You're welcome darling, love you, see you soon."

Arriving home and walking into the flat Jodie and Matt are sat in the lounge drinking a cuppa, I am so excited to tell them about my present from my parents.

"Hi guys."

"Happy birthday Kara!" Matt says.

"Thanks. You'll never guess what my parents have bought me for my birthday."

"What did you get?" Jodie asks looking at me.

"They've only gone and bought me a car."

"You're kidding?" They both get up off the couch as quick as anything and I take them outside to give them a guided tour of my new motor.

After a thorough inspection Jodie kisses Matt goodbye and says she'll see him later in the club, he's going out with some of his friends tonight and they have agreed to meet up at the end of the night. As Matt is leaving, Sally drops my birthday present off which is a designer handbag and I quickly show her my new car.

Jodie and I then have some food to line our stomachs with before starting on the bottle of wine that is chilling in the fridge waiting for us. As I am grabbing a couple of wine glasses my phone pings.

Evan has messaged me.

I hope you are having the best day, you deserve it. Have a great night out tonight but don't have too much fun eh! E. xx

"I take it that's a text from Evan?" Jodie says looking at the smile on my face.

"Yes he is just saying have a good night tonight."

"Oh we will definitely be having a good night don't worry about that." Jodie says taking a sip of wine.

She can tell that I feel conflicted, but she is adamant to take my mind off things and not to let it ruin my night.

I choose to respond.

Thanks and you can never have enough fun Evan. K xx

I press send.

I wonder if he thinks I'm going to have fun with someone else tonight? It doesn't hurt to keep him on his toes, I mean I'm a great catch, he just needs to realise it.

Jodie is always the best at getting the party vibes going. The wine is flowing and I am genuinely enjoying myself.

Dancing around the living room to a dance playlist, taking pictures and having no cares in the world we are having so much fun.

Chinking glasses Jodie says, "Happy Birthday to my best mate, here's to a good night and maybe a birthday kiss with a stranger or some break up sex, who cares!"

"Cheers I'll drink to that," and we down our drinks.

We begin to get ready and my phone goes off again with another text from Evan.

I hesitate at opening the message, I don't want to spend my evening thinking about someone who broke my heart but my heart still belongs to him so I open it.

I can't help myself.

I hope the fun you are talking about is not the type of fun we enjoy doing together because I don't like the thought of you having fun with anyone else. E xx

'So he doesn't want me but no-one else can have me? Hmm …'

It does make me feel slightly better knowing he is jealous, my text clearly worked!

Putting my phone down on the bed I decide not to respond and to leave Evan hanging, he isn't a priority tonight. I want to enjoy my birthday and to have fun with my best friend Jodie. I finish the wine and go to get a refill from the bottle we left in the lounge.

An hour later we are all refreshed, we have put our make up on, changed into our party dresses and we are feeling excited looking forward to having a good night.

I'm thankful for the expensive lingerie Evan bought for me. I feel sexy and confident wearing it under my little black strappy dress that clings to my curves and shows off my impressive cleavage. My hair is tied up with tussles of it spiralling down either side of my face and I feel good.

I also have my Louboutin shoes on to compliment my smooth legs and the bracelet that Evan gave me with the diamond heart is sparkling on my wrist.

Jodie is wearing a royal blue short skater dress with her legs on display and her hair is all sleek and straightened.

"Ready to go Kar?" Jodie says all excited.

"Certainly am, let's go."

Thirty

The pubs along the high street are all in a row on the same street and the club that we always end up at the end of the night is at the end of the main high street. This makes the pub crawl straightforward because the pubs are in one long line down the long high street. The atmosphere in the town is buzzing and there are lots of people walking about enjoying the golden summer evening and the pubs are starting to get busy.

Jodie orders two white wines and we take a seat at a table over near the window looking out onto the high street in the first pub. While we are sat down chatting two guys wander over to us and ask if they can join us.

"Sorry but my girlfriend gets jealous when I talk to boys." I smile grabbing hold of Jodie's hand that's resting on the table. The guys look awkward and soon turn on their heels walking away quickly as we both burst out laughing.

"Kara you're terrible." Jodie laughs taking a sip of her drink.

"Well they interrupted our conversation and they looked boring anyway." I giggle.

We only stay for a couple of drinks in the first bar and I'm already beginning to feel slightly tipsy.

The next pub we end up in is a cocktail bar where we bump into one of Jodie's work colleagues Rob who is out with his friends.

Jodie tells me Rob is single and around the same age as me, but he's not my type. He smiles and waves when he sees us and comes over to say hi.

Jodie introduces me and then Rob buys us both a drink, we stand chatting for a while and having finished my drink and needing a wee I excuse myself to go to the toilets leaving the two of them to talk about work. On my way back from the toilets feeling rather drunk, I recognise Greg who took me on a lousy cinema date the other week.

'Oh no I really don't want to talk to him.'

"Hi Kara, how are you?" he smiles looking pleased to see me.

"Oh hi Greg, I'm alright thanks and you?"

"I'm great and I'm even better now, you're looking lovely tonight" he says looking me up and down pausing far too long on my boobs before looking at my face again and smiling.

"Err thanks I'm just heading back to my friend, I'd better not keep her as she will be wondering where I am."

"Oh okay, I really enjoyed our date the other week I'm sorry I haven't text you but I've been really busy. If you fancy going out again I could take you out sometime next week?"

"Oh right well … um … thanks I'll be in touch, see ya."

"I'll maybe see you in the club later then?" he calls.

"Okay bye." I nervously laugh trying to get away as fast as my 3 inch heels will take me.

'Why did I say I'll be in touch? I definitely won't be.'

I get back to Jodie as soon as I can who is stood on her own by the bar waiting for me, Rob has gone.

"Oh god you'll never guess who I just bumped into when I was coming out of the toilets Jode."

"Who?"

"Greg from the newsagents, he was looking me up and down undressing me with his eyes and said we should go out again next week."

"Oh no what did you say?" she laughs.

"Well I was a bit shocked and didn't like the way he was looking at me, so in a hurry to get away I stupidly said I would be in touch."

Jodie is still laughing. "What are you like? Maybe he will be your birthday kiss," she giggles.

"Urgh I don't think so." I laugh.

We arrive at the next pub and order two soft drinks. We are both feeling the effects of the wine and cocktails due to starting early at home with pre-drinks and in need of something non-alcoholic. Looking around Jodie sees Matt sat in the corner at some tables with his builder friends Luke and Connor so we make our way over to them to say hello. When Matt and his friends see us they all cheer and Jodie walks over to Matt for a snog while I sit down at the table with his friends.

"So you must be Kara? I'm Luke and this is Connor." We all shake hands.

"Hi nice to meet you both."

Luke is blonde with short hair spiked up at the front with blue eyes and Connor has dark brown hair which is long on the top, short at the sides with hazel eyes, both of them look like they could be in a boy band.

I blush for a split second looking at them both and think about a possible birthday snog with one of them later but then Evan always pops back into my mind and I feel guilty for thinking it.

'I wonder what he's doing tonight and if he's thinking about me on my night out?'

"So are you single Kara?" Luke asks who is sat to the left of me leaning in close to talk so I can hear him over the loud music. Being so close I can smell his aftershave and all I can think is 'that it's not as nice as Evan's scent'.

"Err yes I suppose you could say that yes."

"Why what do you mean?"

"It's complicated."

"It always is, well he's a fool if he doesn't want you," he says getting rather close to my face, I can feel his breath on my cheek.

'Why do I feel like I am cheating on Evan? I feel like I am betraying him giving another guy attention.'

Connor who is sat to the right of me begins competing with his friend for my attention and starts talking to me.

"Are you going to the club later?" Connor asks.

"Yes we are."

"Great," he smiles.

If I had never met Evan then this would be a great opportunity to get to know the guys and to see who I hit it off with better but Evan is all I want and can't stop thinking about. While we chat I can tell there is some rivalry between the two friends as they both ask me questions, each of them wanting me to talk them and not the other.

I can tell they are both interested from the way they are flirting with me and I can handle their flirty drunkenness until Luke leans in to whisper in my ear and puts his hand on my leg.

"I really like your dress you look hot," he says with a drunken slur.

"Thanks." I reply feeling uncomfortable and removing his hand off my leg. Although the man is attractive and I'm flattered that he likes me, I'm not having some stranger putting his hand on my leg unless it's Evan's.

"Jodie are you ready to move on yet?" I shout to her over the loud music. Jodie is sat on Matt's knee snogging his face off which she has done ever since we arrived at the pub.

Coming up for air she replies, "Yeah sure." Her lipstick smeared on her face.

"If we leave now we won't have to queue for ages to get in the club."

'Yes that's a good excuse so we can leave.'

"Okay I'm coming," she says giving Matt another kiss to say goodbye and he helps to sort her face out from the smeared lipstick before she walks away.

"See you later, nice to meet you both." I say looking at Matt's friends. I can't get away from these two guys fast enough. Two men come along at once wanting my attention which rarely happens and I don't want them because I only want one man, Evan, but I can't have him, aargh, why is my love life so complicated.

I feel happier to be away from them as I link arms with my best friend walking to the next destination, Pulse Night Club.

"Sorry you had to leave Matt, but his friends were coming on to me and Luke was getting a bit hands on and I felt awkward." I say sounding apologetic.

"Hey no worries Luke can be a bit flirtatious, he is really nice but when he has had a few drinks he gets a bit touchy feely."

"Yes I noticed anyway I'm ready for dancing now are you?"

"Definitely." Jodie says as we join a small queue outside the club at the top of the high street.

While we are waiting in the queue I get my phone out of my purse and decide to send Evan a drunk text.

I can't stop thinking about him so I decide to stop being mad at him, like Jodie said 'if you love him fight for him' so that's exactly what I'm going to do.

Having a good night, been to lots of pubs now I'm stood in a queue waiting to get into Pulse Nightclub. What are you doing? Miss you and your sexy body, wish you were here. I'm wearing the sexy lingerie you bought me. K xx

I wait for a reply and after a few minutes has passed I begin to panic thinking I made a mistake in sending it, maybe he is bored and is entertaining someone else?

'Why did I have to text him that?, nice one Kara.'

We arrive at the kiosk ready to pay, so I put my phone back in my purse and get my money ready for the admission fee.

After we've paid we enter the loud, pulsing club as the dance music fills our ears and the beat of the music thumps loudly in our chests.

We cut our way through the sea of young people in groups dancing away to make our way to the bar.

"What are you having?" I shout over the music.

"I'll have a Jaeger Bomb please."

"Ok me too." I reply as a young bar man with a clean-shaven face and a big smile greets me and asks me what I would like to drink.

After I've been served we lean against a pillar in the club while we down our drinks. I feel drunk, but I'm a happy drunk. The rhythm of the music gets my feet moving and I start dancing on the spot shaking my hips and bottom to the music while talking to Jodie.

"Are you having a good night?" Jodie asks.

"The best, I'm so pleased we decided to come out, what a great way to celebrate turning 25 having a few drinks and a good dance with my best friend."

"Aww thanks Kara, love you babe."

"Love you too," I give Jodie a drunken hug.

The music is thumping and I feel great soaking up the tunes as I dance around on the spot in the club. Swaying my hips and dancing to the music I suddenly feel a pair of hands on my hips and I can feel a man gyrating against my body from behind.

I feel excited hoping it's Evan but I'm disappointed when I turn around and it is Greg from the Newsagents.

"Greg get off me what are you doing?" I stop dancing trying to get out of his hold.

"I'm dancing," he replies, he is clearly drunk as he flings his arms around me holding me close to him.

"Get off me you idiot."

I try to prise his arms off me but he is clinging to me laughing, so Jodie tries to help. He's much bigger than what I am and it is becoming uncomfortable.

Then a six-foot, tanned muscly man strides over to us and gets Greg into a headlock from behind.

"The woman said get off so take a hike dude," he says pushing him away. Greg looks up at the man who is bigger built and taller than he is and staggers off like a scared rabbit.

When I turn to say thanks to the guy who helped me I realise it's Curtis standing in front of me.

"Oh my god Curtis, hello and thank you," I give him a hug, feeling relieved and he gives me a kiss on each cheek. "Hi Kara, happy birthday" he smiles.

"Do that again and we will not be friends," says a familiar voice. Evan walks over to us shocking me and stands in front of me wearing a pair of black jeans, a white short sleeved shirt and a pair of brown boots looking totally gorgeous. His hair is styled and he's clean shaven. I can feel my heart beating fast in my chest when he leans towards me and kisses me on the cheek to say hi. I hold my cheek where he pecked, I don't know whether to laugh or cry.

"Chill out man I was only wishing her happy birthday, I'm getting the drinks in do you want another beer mate?"

"Go on then, if you are." Evan replies not taking his eyes off me and looking me up and down in my black strappy dress and Louboutin heels.

"You look gorgeous, I like your dress and your hair like that, happy birthday." He holds his gaze at the bracelet he bought me that is around my wrist.

"What are you doing here?" I ask surprised to see him.

"Having a few drinks with Curtis hoping I might bump into you."

"Oh." I smile, "I sent you a text, have you seen it?"

"Yes so are you still mad at me then or am I forgiven now?" Evan asks with a smile.

Now I'm here stood with him again I can't be angry, it just feels natural like it always does, talking to him and enjoying being around him. Also knowing it's Evan's last night here in my hometown I don't want him to leave tomorrow and we are still on bad terms.

"I guess you're forgiven," I smile.

"Good," he says pulling me to him and putting his arm around my waist. "I've missed you and you're sexy body and I'm imagining you in your new sexy lingerie under that dress and I'm getting hard just thinking about it" he smiles.

I blush.

Curtis returns with two bottles of beer passing one to Evan he takes it off him and swigs a mouthful.

"Cheers bud."

Curtis gets acquainted with Jodie and while they are chatting Evan and I catch up too. I'm telling him about my day when I suddenly remember something, I grab his arm as I squeal telling him about the Fiat 500 my parents bought me for my birthday.

"Hey I could come and visit you in London now that I have my own wheels?" I suggest.

"Kara we've spoken about this."

"What as a friend? I meant I could visit you as a friend."

"What friends with benefits?" he grins.

I smirk as I nudge him with my elbow, he still makes me feel so nervous.

Before Evan has a chance to say any more Jodie interrupts us. "Hey are we going to have a dance then or what?"

I want to carry on the conversation I'm having with Evan. I want to know what he was going to say about being friends with benefits.

"Yeah go and enjoy yourself, I'll see you in a bit," Evan smiles.

"Okay come on then." I reluctantly go as Jodie grabs my arm and pulls me towards the dance floor. Evan is watching me, with a hunger in his eyes. I'm going to shake my booty and show him what he is missing.

I feel deliriously happy, the wine is giving me confidence and I keep glancing over at Evan while I dance. I think he is enjoying the show because his eyes haven't left me for a second and I know he'll be hard.

I'm just about to leave the dancefloor to go and see him when someone picks me up from behind and swings me around making me squeal. The man then lowers me down to the floor grabs my hips and starts gyrating behind me. I turn to see who it is and see Luke's drunken face looking back at me.

"Hello again gorgeous, dance with me!" he says slurring his words and grabbing hold of me pushing his body up against mine and rubbing his cock against my bum.

'What is it with these men grabbing hold of me tonight?'

"I've been looking forward to seeing you again, dance with me," he says holding onto me and turning me around so I'm facing him and then going in for a kiss.

"Luke get off me." I hiss turning my head away from.

Before I know what is happening, Evan has seen what's going on and is on the dancefloor closely followed by Curtis. Evan pushes Luke off me then grabs hold of him by the throat looking fiercely at him.

"Get your fucking hands off her." Evan shouts his voice full of anger.

"Leave it mate." Curtis says grabbing hold of Evan's arm while he looks at Luke with a deathly stare. I stand back watching the scene in front of me with caution in case it all kicks off.

Curtis calmly puts his hand on Evan's shoulder. "Come on dude be cool, he didn't mean any harm he's just had a bit too much to drink and was being a bit over the top that's all."

Evan continues to stare at Luke. "You should show women a bit more respect if they say get off they mean get off, don't fucking touch her again you piece of shit because if you do I'll break your fucking legs."

Luke looks shocked and holds his hands up in defeat as Evan eases off his throat. "I'm sorry mate I was just dancing with her I didn't mean to upset anyone."

Matt sees what's going on and wanting to diffuse the situation approaches Evan cautiously, "Evan let him go he really is harmless, he's a mate of mine. He doesn't mean anything by it he's just had a few too many beers."

Evan turns to Matt. "Okay but warn your friend if he goes anywhere near Kara like that again in the future I won't be so lenient next time."

"Okay, everything's cool." Matt says holding his hands up and Evan backs off just as two burly bouncers approach.

"There's nothing here fellas, it's all good," Curtis says to the bouncers not wanting them to be thrown out of the club.

Evan holds his hand out to shake Luke's hand who is now rubbing at his neck. "Sorry pal."

Matt pats Luke on the back. "This is Evan, Kara's other half." Luke nods.

The bouncers warn everyone if they start anything again then everyone will be out and the men part ways. Jodie goes to stand with Matt and his friends and Evan and Curtis walk over to where I'm stood at the edge of the dancefloor.

I suddenly feel really angry with him for overreacting in that way, I could have handled the situation a lot better than he has just done.

"Are you okay?" Evan smiles.

"What the hell do you think you're doing?" I reply giving him a dirty look and his smile turns into a frown.

"I was saving you from that prick; his hands were all over you, what did you think I was doing?"

"Yes but you didn't have to grab him by the throat like that, its Matt's friend; I can't believe you just did that. Also, that line about treating women with respect was rich coming from you."

"Look he had his hands on you and he was persistently grabbing you and trying to kiss you. I didn't like the way he was helping himself to you so I dealt with it."

"You can't act like that Evan, I could have handled it. What are you going to do when you leave, you're not going to be around to save me then are you?" I start to walk away, but he grabs my arm.

"I know," he says lowering his head then looking at me with a sorrowful look, "I'm sorry I overreacted I shouldn't have grabbed him around the throat it's just …"

"It's just what, you need to sort your shit out Evan, every man you see is not a threat, it doesn't mean every man is trying to get with me, he's drunk and he just lifted me up and was trying to dance with me that's all. This guy whoever he is who did the dirty on you with Julia has got a lot to fucking answer for. I don't know why you are acting jealous anyway because it's not like you want me anymore is it." I yell before storming off.

"Where are you going?" Evan says trying to keep up with me as I push my way through groups of partygoers.

"The toilets, if I'm allowed?" I snap.

Evan remains quiet and follows me until I barge through the toilet door of the ladies in a mood.

'Who the hell does he think he is?'

Taking a few deep breaths I try to calm down. I understand he was protecting me but it doesn't give him the right to throttle someone on my behalf. Poor Luke I bet he was shocked when Evan grabbed hold of him by the throat like that.

I use the toilets then leave to find Evan is still waiting for me.

"Are you okay?" he asks warily.

"Yes I'm fine. I know you were trying to protect me but I don't need a bodyguard Evan I can look after myself and not every man wants to have sex with me you know, not even you anymore." I snap.

I'm angry because he's leaving me and there is nothing I can do about it. Evan grabs hold of my arm as I go to walk past him and pulls me into the disabled toilet next door to the ladies and locks it behind him.

"What are you doing let me out please, I don't want to talk to you at the moment, you've really pissed me off." I look at him with my arms folded defensively across my chest and Evan is stood staring at me.

"No you are staying here while I apologise and you are going to listen and we are going to make friends. I'm not leaving tomorrow with things like this and besides it's your birthday and I don't want your night to end badly."

"Well say what you need to say and hurry up so I can get out of here." I reply nastily.

"Look I apologise for reacting the way I did and I'm sorry for upsetting you but I can't help how I feel when some bloke has his hands on you. It sparks something in me that I find hard to control. Yes I feel threatened by every man that shows an interest in you and yes it's because of what happened with Julia and this is what I need to work on. I know I have a lot of issues, commitment, jealousy and yes after tomorrow you can do whatever the hell you like but while I'm here I will do whatever it takes to keep you safe and to keep you away from men like that."

I look at his gorgeous face while he tries to apologise for his actions and seeing him like this and knowing that he cares so much sparks something in me and I can't hold back, my anger has turned to lust and I want him desperately. I walk over to him and crash my mouth onto his.

My tongue fiercely fights with his as he accepts the passionate kiss. His hands are moving up and down my back then he grabs my bum and pushes his erection into my front. He reaches for the hem of my dress.

"Evan we can't not in here." I say breathless while he kisses my neck and nibbles my ear turning me on.

"Kara please I need you." he growls.

I need him too, badly. "Okay," and he carries on, he undoes the fly on his jeans then pushes me up against the wall next to the hand dryer kissing me passionately.

"Oh god Evan." His erection springs free and he reaches for my knickers moving the barely existing material of my new black lace thong to the side to make way for his hard cock. I part my legs for him and he encourages me to lift one of my legs up his thigh and he holds it there with his strong arms.

"I've missed you, I want you so much," he whispers and I hold his head in my hands while kissing him and he guides his cock to my wet entrance with his hand and slams into me with a loud moan claiming me.

I cry out. "Evan,"

He's forceful as he pounds into me hard, "You are always with me Kara, do you hear me, always, you're mine," he says fucking me over and over again.

"I'm yours," I moan feeling him pressing and rubbing against my clit with each powerful thrust. "I love you Evan."

"Fuck baby, you feel good," he pants.

"OHHHHHHH …"

"Jesus, you're so wet and greedy for me."

"Yes …"

"Fucking hell Kara …"

Evan fucks me hard against the toilet wall and I cling onto him feeling elated but also emotional because time is running out for us and soon he will be gone.

"Yes … feel how hard you make me … fuck it feels good."

"Oh god Evan … yes … I'm going to come …" and my body shakes and I stifle a scream as my orgasm rips through my body making me see stars. Evan can feel me pulsating around him and after a few more hard thrusts his orgasm rushes forward and he moans loudly as he comes too.

"Oh Jesus, I … I've tried to stop wanting you but I just can't."

"I love you so much." Tears are rolling down my cheeks as he kisses me softly holding my face in his hands while I kiss him back.

"Can I stay with you tonight?" he asks kissing me all over my face, kissing my tears and looking at me with pleading eyes.

"Yes I'd love that," I smile. Evan pulls out of me and tucks himself away doing up his jeans. He then passes me some paper towel to clean myself with. Once I'm finished he takes me in his arms and kisses me again deeply.

"I really am sorry for upsetting you please don't cry baby," he says as tears continue to fall down my cheeks and I wipe them from my eyes with the back of my hand. Evan rests his forehead on mine.

"I know you're sorry and I'm fine, I just miss you, I don't want you to go, every time I think about you leaving it makes me upset."

"I know baby, I know. Come on let's get out of this toilet and go and find the others."

After checking my face in the mirror and sorting out my hair Evan opens the door for me and we walk out hand in hand like nothing has happened.

Returning to the noise of the club we spot Jodie and Matt stood with Curtis chatting and laughing. As we get nearer Jodie sees us. "Here they are, we wasn't sure if you had gone."

"No, we were just having a chat near the toilets." I reply smiling at Evan.

"Is everything okay mate?" Curtis asks looking at Evan.

"Yes all good." Evan replies smiling at me.

Evan turns to Matt, "I'm sorry if I hurt your friend and I apologise for reacting the way I did."

"Hey he's a big boy, he's had worse than that, unfortunately when he's drunk he can't keep his hands to himself and has found himself into a few scrapes with jealous boyfriends in the past so don't worry about it mate."

"Thanks pal." They both shake hands.

"I don't know about anyone else but I'm starving, how about we head off and get a kebab?" Curtis says rubbing his rumbling toned abs.

"Great idea." Everyone agrees.

After we have all finished eating a weary Jodie says, "Is everyone ready for home, I'm ready for my bed?"

"I'm ready for your bed too," Matt grins as Jodie rolls her eyes at him.

We all say goodbye to Curtis as he is staying at the Kingsman in Evan's suite tonight and then we set off walking back to the flat.

"My feet are killing me," Jodie says.

"Yeah mine are too," I reply after dancing in our 3 inch heels and walking from pub to pub all night.

Being the perfect gentlemen Evan and Matt offer to give us a piggyback and we gladly accept.

"Let's have a race," I giggle holding on to Evan's neck while he walks with me on his back with no effort.

"I think I'll pass," Matt says who is clearly struggling to carry Jodie after all the beer he has drank tonight.

"Come on Matt," Jodie laughs squeezing him with her legs like she's sat on a horse trying to make him go faster.

"Bloody hell Jode I can't go any faster your heavy," he says out of breath.

"What do you mean I'm heavy? are you saying I'm fat?" Jodie huffs.

"Don't be stupid," Matt says.

"Oh so I'm fat and stupid am I, thanks babe?" Jodie snaps.

Listening to them argue is amusing and Evan walks alongside them with me hanging off his back, we are both sniggering at the pointless argument.

We arrive back at the flat and I point out my new car to Evan before going inside. I've had the best night celebrating my birthday and I'm so glad Evan has come home with me. We are going to be having more incredible sex and knowing it is our last night together, I'm going to make every second count.

Thirty One

It is the early hours of Sunday morning, Evan leaves today to go back to London and my life is going to change again. This is my last chance to convince him that we are meant to be together.

"What are you thinking about?" Evan asks seeing me deep in thought while I fill a glass with water from the tap.

"Just about you leaving." I sigh.

"Don't let's just enjoy our last night together okay."

"Okay, would you like a glass of water?"

"Yes please." I fill another glass.

"I see you wore the bracelet I bought you, I wanted to say something to you earlier when I noticed it in the club." Evan smiles.

"Yes it reminds me of you. I didn't think I was going to be seeing you tonight so wearing the bracelet makes me feel like you are with me." I blush. Evan smiles.

We take our water to the bedroom and I turn on the bedroom lamp.

"I like your birthday balloon." Evan says noticing it in my room.

"Thanks Jodie bought it for me," I smile taking off my dress while Evan watches me and his eyes nearly pop out of his head and I realise it's because I'm wearing the sexy lingerie he bought me for my birthday.

"Jesus Kara, I must say this lingerie was a bloody good choice, you look sexy … come here," he says grabbing hold of me and kissing me passionately.

Evan stands back to admire my curvy body dressed in black lace, "Wow."

He then moves to behind me and I'm aware I'm holding my breath waiting for his hands on me.

"Relax baby," he says in his sexy voice and I relax as he rests his hands lightly on my shoulders and gently massages them. He moves my hair away from my neck and plants soft kisses from my shoulder up to my ear.

'Oh my god, his touch turns me on so much.'

"It feels so good to be able to touch you again" he says running his hands all over my curves while kissing my neck. I lean my head back against him.

"Hmm…" I moan enjoying his touch once again.

"Do you know how gorgeous your bum looks dressed in this black lace thong." I can hear him licking his lips as he crouches down behind me and trails his tongue around my bare bum cheeks in circles making me moan.

"Hold onto the bed and bend over slightly for me."

I move nearer to the bed and bend my body forwards like he wants me to holding the bed for support giving Evan a glorious sight of my barely covered bum.

"Fucking hell I could come just by looking at you," he says kneeling down on the floor and trailing his tongue up the back of my legs making me squirm because it tickles slightly and up over my bum cheeks.

He then moves the thin material of the lace thong to one side and slides two fingers inside me. He pushes them in and out turning me on more and more then after a short while he pulls them out and rolls the thong down my legs exposing me. I step out of them.

Evan draws in a deep breath and I clench my aching, wet core as he runs his hands up and down my soft legs which encourages me to open my legs wider.

I want him to stand up and claim my body with his hard cock but he doesn't he stays kneeling on the floor and surprises me by sliding his tongue inside my wetness, holding onto my hips.

"OHHHH …" I cry out moaning loudly feeling his tongue devouring me, licking and tasting me from behind, I grab a handful of the duvet as he slips his tongue inside pleasuring me.

"You're so wet, hmm you taste good. You're so ready for me aren't you?"

"Yes … Evan please."

Evan pulls away from me and stands up to turn off the bedside lamp the room now dimly lit by the streetlight outside my bedroom window providing enough light for us to see each other's faces and naked bodies. He comes up behind me and grabs hold of my hips teasing me with his cock. He holds it in his hand and rubs against my bum cheeks then teases my entrance.

"Oh god, I need you Evan, please fuck me, I want you so bad." I arch my back and push my bottom out wanting him to push his cock inside me.

"Soon baby" he says undoing my bra strap with one hand. I pull it off and throw it on the floor. He continues rubbing against my wetness and cups both breasts tweaking my nipples teasing me and just when I think he's ready to fuck me senseless he says, "Lie down on the bed and close your eyes," tormenting me some more.

I'm desperate.

I do as he asks thinking he is definitely making the most of every minute we have left together as I plan to because he's not rushing to be inside me. I wait for his next move loving how he makes me feel and how much he turns me on. I sense Evan lean over me and he lowers his lips to mine kissing me softly, I wrap my arms around his neck bringing him closer. The kiss is so tender and sweet our tongues are exploring each other's mouths delicately, this kiss is the type of kiss that will stay in our minds forever and an overwhelming feeling of togetherness shows through our joined mouths.

Evan caresses my naked breasts gently with his hands tweaking my nipple in his fingers while continuing with our tongue mingling kiss. I moan finding his cock and stroking it up and down gently, he moans into my mouth too.

Taking my arms from around him and removing my hand from his hard length he says, "Put your arms at the side of you, keep your eyes closed and don't touch me until I say so okay?"

"Oh god, okay." I'm panting with excitement as I wait for him to pleasure me some more.

I hear Evan walk over to the chest of drawers and pick up one of the glasses of water, he takes a sip of the cold liquid and swills it around in his mouth before swallowing it. I then hear him put the glass down on the bedside drawers. It's so intense hearing him moving about with my eyes closed not being able to see and to know what he's doing. I'm not waiting long to find out his next move.

I feel a cold finger swirling around the tip of one of my nipples, hmm that feels so good, I moan from the sensation of the coldness of the water on my skin making my nipple erect.

"Hmm …" Evan repeats the same action on my other nipple I wriggle and moan loving how it feels.

'Oh … that feels so good.'

Evan takes a small sip of the cold water and lowers his mouth onto my nipple letting the water trickle down the side of my breast as he sucks it in his mouth.

He then does the same with the other nipple, sucking and trailing his tongue around over and over again turning me on to the extreme.

"Evan please I'm aching for you, I need you to fuck me now," I'm desperate and needy for him to take me.

I open my eyes and look at him.

"Soon baby," he smiles ignoring my plea. Moving slowly up the bed he looks at me and then says in a husky, erotic whisper. "Will you suck me?"

'Oh god yes please I'm so turned on.'

I smile at him as he lays back on the bed and then taking hold of his length I lick around the tip before taking him fully into my mouth tasting how excited he is. "Oh yes, fuck …" he moans as I suck slowly in and out of my mouth moaning, licking and sliding my tongue around the head.

Holding the back of my head gently he fucks my mouth slowly in and out, in and out, he's moaning and panting.

After turning him on in this way for a while I release him from my mouth, crawl up his body and kiss him.

"I want to drive you crazy and turn you on so much so you'll never forget me."

He kisses me while manoeuvring my body so our mouths are still joined and he climbs on top of me.

"Kara I'll never forget you and you do drive me crazy and turn me on, no-one has ever turned me on like you do," he says looking into my eyes and stroking the side of my cheek softly.

I hesitate before I say my next words to him but then feeling like I have nothing to lose. "I don't want you to fuck me tonight Evan I want you to make love to me slowly and softly."

I stroke his back and he nods then kisses me again delving his tongue into my mouth.

I can feel the steady beat of Evan's heart as his naked body presses up against mine and I can feel tears in my eyes when he positions his cock at my entrance.

Pushing his hard length inside me on a low guttural moan we feel the strong physical connection that's been there since the beginning, that's always been there between us and won't ever go away, I cling to him as he makes love to me slowly and sweetly in my bed.

"I love you Evan." I whisper kissing him softly savouring the moment feeling tears roll down my cheeks.

I can feel the tingling sensations in between my legs getting stronger as he thrusts inside me.

"I'm going to miss you Kara," he smiles looking like he wants to say more but doesn't.

"I need you." I cry his hips circling around and around rubbing me in the right spot while my tears continue to fall.

"Don't cry baby please," he says looking at me while he drives into me slowly, "god you feel so good."

Slowly Evan's cock rub my insides, the friction causing me to moan over and over as his body rubs against my clit.

The feeling of love and togetherness is so obvious, even though we are both struggling with our feelings.

"Evan I'm going to come."

Pleasure takes over the upset and my body begins to tremble in readiness for the explosion of my orgasm. Evan continues to drive into me and I can tell he's getting close too.

"I want to hear you baby, I want those sounds in my head so I can remember this night," he pants loving the sounds I'm making as he brings me closer and closer wanting more.

"OH God ... yes ... yes I'm coming ... EVAN ..." Once, twice a few more times and I'm crying out and moaning from the intense feelings my orgasm gives me, my body is jerking as the sensation makes me see stars.

Evan's cock is still thrusting inside of me and then he comes too, he comes inside me, his own orgasm filling his brain with ecstasy, both of us clinging to each other feeling all kinds of emotions, happiness, contentment, pleasure, satisfaction but the most strongest emotion of all that I'm feeling is love.

We lay in each other's arms cuddling after having the most amazing, earth shattering sex of my life. We didn't have sex tonight, this was something different.

Evan

Making love to Kara is the most incredible feeling in the world, an earth shattering feeling I've never felt before.

As we lay in each other's arms I desperately want to tell her how much she means to me. It's killing me having to walk away but I have to do this.

My past is catching up with me again and if she gets hurt because of him then I will never forgive myself.

I'm weary and heavy eyed after not having much sleep. I watch him get half-dressed and creep out the bedroom to go to the bathroom.

I lay in bed thinking and hoping that there is still a chance for us that he'll have a change of heart and declare his love for me but knowing that's unlikely to happen I feel desperate and decide I have to do something before it's too late.

I get up and find his phone that he left in my bedroom last night.

Luckily it's not password protected so I have a snoop to see if I can find out his address or something, anything that will help me to find him in the future.

I have to be quick because he will be back any minute. I feel like some kind of stalker.

I know where his hotel is where he took me for dinner but if I go there he can get his staff to say he's not in or shield my calls.

I'm so desperate, I open up his messages and pause for a moment.

I really shouldn't be invading his privacy like this but curiosity gets the better of me because I want to know if Julia has been in contact. I scroll through the messages and notice an unknown number, I wonder if that's her?

I open the message thinking it could be her or maybe even a secret girlfriend.

I see your taste has improved my dear friend, she is world class compared to Julia. I was passing through the area and saw you two looking cosy, you had the look of love my friend, sorry I couldn't stop to say hello. We must catch up soon and talk about the money you owe me. Be in touch.

Oh my god. I read further Evan has sent a reply.

I don't know how you found my number and I am no friend of yours and never will be again. The woman I was looking cosy with is no-one, she is just someone who works in a coffee shop I picked up for a bit of fun so if you want to get your kicks out of hurting me again with her you are wasting your time. She is nothing to me, I've had my fun and I won't be going there again. Don't bother getting in touch again because you are wasting your time. You will never get a penny out of me.

What? I'm in shock, I can't believe what I have just read, I feel the colour drain from my face, I feel sick to the stomach, how can he say those things? How can he say I'm no-one, just some girl?

I read it again with tears streaming down my face, I'm so hurt and god I am such a fool, I should never have trusted him, all this time he has been using me.

I am just someone he has used for sex, the way he has treated me the lovely things he has said to me was all just a ploy to get me into bed.

My upset quickly turns to anger, I wipe away my tears, I'm breathing fast and my heart is beating hard in my chest.

'The bastard.'

Evan walks back into the bedroom, takes one look at my face and sees his phone in my hand, his face drops.

"What is wrong Kara, why are you crying you look as white as a sheet?" he asks concerned walking over to me. I am so angry.

I am seriously about to lose it right now.

"What are you doing with my phone?" he frowns looking confused.

I answer him calmly. "Why something to hide Evan?" I stare at him with hatred in my eyes.

"No why do you say that? Can you give me my phone please?" he asks holding his hand out nervously.

"Why are you afraid I might see something on here?"

"No just give me my phone," he says sounding more urgent.

I continue to stare at him. "Sorry but it's too late I've already seen it and it has definitely made things a lot clearer for me I can tell you." I'm trying to hold back from completely losing it altogether.

I throw the phone towards Evan on the bed and he picks it up and looks at the screen. He looks at me as I get out of bed and swiftly put on a pair of grey joggers and a black t-shirt out of my drawer.

He thinks for a moment looking like he's trying to find the right words to say.

"Kara this is not what it looks like," he says walking over to me to try and explain.

"It looks pretty fucking clear to me you, how could you, you're a fucking asshole."

My anger gets the better of me and I slap him hard across the face catching him unaware.

Evan holds his face feeling the sting and glares at me.

"Kara listen if you'll just let me explain then ..."

"How could you?" I scream as he tries to comfort me.

The tears and anger I've been trying to hold back now come pouring out of me.

"Get your fucking hands off me," I scream in his face.

"Get out of my flat I never want to see you again." I shout.

I sit down on my bed and sob with my face in my hands.

"Kara please, I can explain it's not what you think honestly."

"No?" I laugh sarcastically. "It was there in black and white Evan, she is no-one, she is nothing to me I've had my fun and I won't be going there again, you've been using me and stringing me along the whole time. What are you some sort of sicko who gets a kick out of making girls fall in love with you and then you just discard them after you have had enough, you can't treat people like that."

My heart is breaking and I'm sobbing uncontrollably.

"Kara please baby." He approaches me with caution and sits next to me, I can tell he wants to touch me to make things better but he doesn't probably in fear of getting another slap to the face.

I just want him to leave.

I lift my head to look at him. "I'm not your baby and you never get to call me that again, this sham is over."

I feel emotionally drained. "Please I want you to go." I glance towards my bedroom door.

"Kara I just … I didn't mean … Fuuuuccckkkk." He stands up and picks up his white shirt off the floor and puts it on, "that text is not how it is, it's complete bullshit and you should never have seen it," he says angrily.

"Yes but I have seen it and you're just sorry because I've found out about your little game of seduction. Well congratulations you have lead me on, made me fall in love with you and now you have completely ruined my life."

My anger is building again and I sarcastically give him a round of applause.

"That's bullshit," he says running his hands through his hair looking stressed.

I stand up and start pacing the floor, I don't know what to do with myself I feel like I'm in a nightmare. I just want to wake up and for all the bad stuff to have gone away.

"So why say it then if it's not true? Just go, I want you to go."

Evan moves closer to me, "Kara please just sit down and I'll explain."

"Just GO!" I scream at the top of my lungs, I can't handle this situation any more I feel like I'm having a breakdown, my palms are sweaty, I'm shaking, my head is saying one thing, my heart is saying another, I want to listen to him but then after reading the words on that text I just don't

know what to believe anymore.

Jodie comes running down the hallway in her dressing gown closely followed by Matt, they must have heard the screaming and shouting and come to see what all the noise is about.

"What the hell is going on?" Jodie says bursting into my bedroom. I take one look at my best friend and run to her sobbing uncontrollably. "What's happened, what's all the screaming about?" Jodie says looking at Evan because I'm too distraught to answer.

I try to speak but my words are coming out jumbled as I try to catch a breath from crying so much.

Evan looks at Jodie and takes a deep breath.

"Kara read a text on my phone which she should never have read because the meaning behind it is not what I really meant."

He runs his hands through his hair looking at me in a distressed state.

"I don't understand." Jodie replies looking confused.

"Please Jodie please, I want him to go, please get him out of here." I manage to say through my sobs.

Matt is stood in the doorway. "I think it's probably best you leave mate," looking at Evan who is utterly deflated. Evan picks up his shoes and takes one last look at me, "I'm sorry …" then he walks out the door.

Evan

"FUUUCCCKKKK!" I hit my forehead with my hand walking down the path away from Kara feeling upset and angry, what the fuck just happened?

What was Kara doing snooping on my phone anyway? I should have deleted that bloody text because now he has ruined everything and this is what I was trying to avoid, hurting Kara because of me. Now she thinks she's nothing to me and it's all because of him.

"FUUUUCCCCKKKK …"

I put my shoes on and start walking down the road. It's a long walk back to the Kingsman Hotel so I take my phone out of my pocket and dial Curtis's number, he stayed in the Penthouse Suite last night, so he can come and pick me up in my car.

After making the call I sit on a nearby wall to wait for him. I have never felt so upset and angry in my life, I've known hurt before this is on a whole different level, it's colossal in comparison. All I can picture is Kara's face, the total look of devastation and hatred as I walked away from her.

I can't control my emotions any longer and tears start to fall down my cheeks as I think I've just walked away and ruined the best thing that has ever happened to me.

I wipe away the tears with the back of my hand and look down at the pavement.

A few weeks ago a beautiful girl came into my life and they have been the best few weeks of my life. I've made her trust me, I've made her feel special, I've treated her like a princess and then I've ruined her life and all because of him.

"Fucking bastard … no more Sebastian enough is enough." Why can't he just leave me alone? A man who is set on hurting me until his last breath, who is so pent up on revenge and money and if he knew what he has caused right now he would be laughing in my face.

I need to talk to Curtis and tell him what's happened, maybe he can help me figure out this fucking mess. I feel numb as I stare down at the floor waiting for him.

It doesn't take long before I hear the engine of my car speeding down the road.

Curtis sees me sat on the wall and pulls up alongside the curb, then gets out the car.

"You alright mate?" he asks looking concerned.

"It's Kara, she …"

I can't speak, I can't believe it has come to this. I had planned to leave Kara's house today on a positive note, I wanted to leave her knowing that we are okay.

We have shared such happy times together and I will always remember those times for as long as I live but now she hates me, the look on her face when I walked into her bedroom and saw my phone in her hand. I knew she had read the text message.

I need to make things right… no I need to leave her alone, she's better off without me in her life.

I've fucked everything up I should never have gone beyond a one night stand with her but I couldn't help myself, she's so beautiful, she...

"Come on mate let's get in the car."

"What's happened?" Curtis asks looking at me.

"I fell in love mate that's what's happened." Tears roll down my face.

"And does she not feel the same way?"

"Yes she does, she says she's in love with me but now everything is ruined and it's all because of him."

"It's all because of who mate?"

"Sebastian."

"Shit Evan how come?"

"Because he will not stop interfering in my life and trying to hurt me. I made the decision to walk away from Kara to protect her from him and for what, for nothing that's what because he's found out about us. I received a text message from him goading me, about the money, about Kara and instead of ignoring him I stupidly sent a reply. Kara has just read the text message I sent to him basically saying she is nothing to me so he would leave her alone and now she wants nothing more to do with me so he ends up winning again."

"Evan, you can't keep doing this, you can't keep letting him ruin your life, you need to sort him out once and for all and then you can be happy."

"I know but I won't let him hurt Kara to get to me, so I have to let her go, this is the only way, I had to tell him that she is nothing to me so he wouldn't go after her and then she went through my phone and read the fucking message I sent to him and now she hates me."

"Does she know that you are in love with her, have you told her?"

"No how can I?"

"What a fucking mess."

"You could say that." I take a few deep breaths, wipe my face and try to calm down. "I'm sorry for acting like an idiot, I've not cried over a woman since Julia."

"Hey, it doesn't make you any less of a man. So what now bud?"

"I need to go home and work out what I'm going to do."

"Don't worry I'll help you pack your stuff up at the hotel and then we can head back to London, a bit of breathing space might do you both some good and it will give you time to work this shit out and what we are going to do about Sebastian."

"We?"

"Yes, he can't keep doing this and I don't like seeing my best mate hurting over some revengeful, jealous prick so we are going to sort him out once and for all. I'm with you brother."

"Cheers mate that means a lot."

The whole of Sunday is extremely painful, the first day without Evan in my life, a day full of tears and analysing everything in my head followed by anger.

It's early evening and I'm lying on my bed with my phone in my hand looking at photos of the two of us. I read the text messages Evan sent to me previously and I feel sick to the stomach because it's all lies.

My phone rings for the tenth time today Evan is trying to get through to me, I ignore it again, what can he possibly say to me that will make things any better? With thoughts of how he's treated me, the photos and texts and seeing his name constantly flashing on my mobile phone as he tries to call me I see red and lose it, I throw my phone at the wall screaming in anger and it smashes to pieces on the floor.

'I hate him. I wish I'd never met him.'

I flop onto my pillow sobbing, my whole life is in turmoil because of Evan Hamilton, I love him yet hate him so much, it's not going to be easy getting over him. With no more tears left in me, my face red and puffy eyes, I decide to have a relaxing bath to try and destress.

I've lost the man I love and there is nothing I can do about it.

Thirty Two

The following weeks at work are hard. Every time the door opens my stomach churns because I think Evan is walking through it and I'm always disappointed when it's just some customers. The days are long and not because we're not busy but because work is all I have now.

When Evan was around everything seemed bearable, he brought so much happiness into my life.

'I miss him terribly.'

The nights are even longer and I try to keep myself busy by watching films, cleaning something that doesn't really need cleaning or reading a magazine, anything to distract my thoughts of what my life has become, a life without Evan in it.

Every day that passes hurts more and more and each day that goes by is another day of not seeing Evan's face and eventually he will become a distant memory.

I would give anything to hear his voice or to see his gorgeous face again but I know that him and I were not supposed to be.

It has been a month since I last saw him when my whole world fell apart and I wish more than anything that I could turn back the clock to the day he walked into the coffee shop for the first time and to relive the last few weeks we had together. Those weeks were the best times of my life, I was seeing Evan and everything was wonderful and now I'm on my own again wondering what's going to happen next in my life. A new man? No, I'm done with men for a while. A new job? Maybe, I seriously need to think about what career would make me happy.

"Excuse me love can I have a cup of coffee please?"

I look up and snap out of my daydream to see an old gentleman smiling at me, "Hi, yes sorry sir coming right up." I enthusiastically respond.

It's Friday and it will be closing time soon.

"What will you be up to this weekend then hun?" Sally asks as she collects the last of the empty cups and saucers sprawled over the tables.

"I'm really looking forward to this weekend Sal. Jodie and I are going clothes shopping tomorrow followed by a trip to the beauty salon to spend my birthday voucher, it's just what I need to take my mind off my hopeless love life after feeling miserable these past few weeks."

"I agree, I think it will do you the world of good treating yourself to some new clothes and a trip to the beauty salon it always puts a smile on my face," she says.

"What are you doing this weekend anything exciting?" I ask wiping down the counter while Sally tidies up the menus on the tables.

"Well we are going to see Tim's parents for lunch if you can call that exciting, I would call it more challenging," she laughs. "As you know Tim's mother and I don't actually get along great, she's okay but I think if she had to choose a daughter-in-law she wouldn't have chosen me."

"Why what's her problem she couldn't have found anyone better for her son than you Sal?"

"The problem is she doesn't have a sense of humour and I do but as long as Tim loves me then that's all I care about, Tim even admits she is a bit of a battle-axe, I feel sorry for his dad because he's lovely."

"There is no question that Tim loves you Sal, you only have to see the way he looks at you." I wish Evan loved me and then we could have been happy together like they are.

"I know I love him so much and I can't wait to make him a father of our child."

"How is the baby making going?"

"Well we are practising loads but I suppose it just takes time, I'm keeping everything crossed that I fall quickly."

"As long as you don't keep your legs crossed Sal because it will take a hell of a long time if you do," I laugh.

"Hey it's almost 5.00pm shall we shut up shop and get out of here?"

"Yes let's do that," Sally says wiping the last table. The elderly gentleman is the last customer to leave, Sally then goes to turn the sign on the door to 'closed.' Just as she goes to turn away, another man stands at the doorway and startles her.

"Oh god you made me jump sorry we're closed," she says pointing to the sign smiling and looking at the man's face stood before her then frowning.

"Sorry for making you jump but is Kara here please?" he asks.

I hear my name being mentioned and turn around as Sally says, "Kara you have a visitor."

I look at Sally then look at the man, his face is familiar. He is tall, looks to be in his early thirties with a few days worth of stubble on his face, has dark brown hair slightly long but styled. He's wearing a pair of dark blue jeans with black boots, a black sweatshirt and he looks quite muscly.

I study him carefully then the man speaks "Hi Kara."

His voice, oh my god, the cloth in my hand falls to the floor as I stare at his features.

He's familiar to me in every way, his looks, the sound of his voice, the build of his body but he looks so different.

He's not shaved, his hair is longer and he's far from the man that I remember.

Standing staring into his chocolate brown eyes, my heart is thumping fast in my chest as he stares back. His eyes are locked on mine as I feel my face pale in shock. "Evan?"

I often wondered what I would do if Evan was to come walking through the door of the coffee shop. Would I duck under the counter, smile, cry? I just didn't know how I would react. Now he is here stood before me again I know exactly how I feel, I feel numb.

"Hi Kara."

"Evan … you look so different I almost didn't recognise you, what are you doing here?"

Author's Note

Hi, thank you for reading the first book in the 'Two Series,' I hope you enjoyed reading it as much as I did writing it.

I would love it if you could leave me a review and if you have any friends or family members that you think would enjoy reading 'Two Risky to Love' please feel free to spread the word.

As a new Author I completely rely on people like you to help get my book noticed so thank you for choosing my book to read and keep an eye out for the second part of the 'Two Series' continuing Kara and Evan's love story.

Lisa Jane Lordan

x

www.lisajanelordan.com

Acknowledgements

To my wonderful Husband and our two beautiful Daughters … thank you for believing in me and encouraging me even when I have doubted myself.

To my lovely family and friends, thank you for the support I have received on my journey of becoming an Author.

I would like to say a huge thank you to Partnership Publishing, an amazing team of people who have guided, advised and supported me along the way to produce my first debut novel. It has been an absolute pleasure working with you all.

To my late Father, I miss you and love you always.

To my late Grandmother, thank you for helping me to achieve my dreams.

And finally thank you to you, my readers.